*She was looking for a poor husband,
not to fall in love…*

"*I do not suppose you know any lovely young ladies with bags of coin and a desire to marry a fellow down on his luck?*"

"Me!"

Daniel's jaw dropped. She was looking as excited as a child at Christmas. This was not the response he'd expected.

"But this is perfect," Suzette said happily. "I need a poor husband and you need a rich wife. It's as if it were meant to be."

"I highly doubt—" Daniel swallowed the rest of what he'd been about to say and nearly swallowed his tongue along with the words as she suddenly grasped one of his hands in both of hers and raised it to squeeze excitedly. It wasn't the fact that she was squeezing his hand in hers that startled him so much as the fact that, in her excitement, she was also pressing it against her chest. He didn't think she even realized what she was doing. Truly, the woman was beyond excited.

Frowning, he asked, "You're rich?"

"Oh, goodness yes. Isn't it wonderful?"

By Lynsay Sands

Lynsay Sands

The Heiress

AVON

An Imprint of HarperCollinsPublishers

This is a work of fiction. Names, characters, places, and incidents are products of the author's imagination or are used fictitiously and are not to be construed as real. Any resemblance to actual events, locales, organizations, or persons, living or dead, is entirely coincidental.

AVON BOOKS
An Imprint of HarperCollins*Publishers*
10 East 53rd Street
New York, New York 10022–5299

First Avon Books paperback printing: March 2011

The
Heiress

Prologue

"𝒥t's barely dawn and yet already so busy."

Suzette nodded silently at her sister's comment as she peered out the carriage window at the bustling activity on the streets they were passing through. London was fascinating and exciting in comparison to the sleepy village outside the estate where they had been born and had grown up. Or it would have been if Suzette's thoughts weren't preoccupied with worry for her father.

"Do you think we will find Father at the town-house?" Lisa asked as if reading her mind.

Suzette sighed and sank back in her seat, her gaze skipping over the other two women in the carriage. Suzette's maid, Georgina, was older by a decade, which was reflected in her silent composure as she peered out the opposite window at the passing buildings. Lisa's maid, Bet, was as young as Lisa herself and in comparison the girl was practically vibrating in her seat with excitement. Her freckled face reflected animated awe as she too looked out the window.

"I hope so," Suzette said finally, her gaze sliding back to her sister.

Lisa sank wearily back in her own seat and Suzette frowned as she noted the small dark smudges around the girl's eyes and the pallor of her skin. Lisa had been favored with their mother's pale hair and coloring, her skin always a fine porcelain that Suzette had often envied, but she didn't envy the way the skin around her eyes would darken, making them appear sunken when she hadn't had enough sleep. And between their worries and the discomfort of travel, neither of them had had enough sleep of late.

"What if he isn't there?" Lisa asked, her gaze moving dully out the window on their side of the carriage.

Suzette felt her mouth tighten at the thought. They hadn't heard from their father since he'd left for London more than a month ago. Lord Cedrick Madison had headed to town to sign some business papers, and had assured them he would return by week's end. He could have returned sooner, but intended to check on their sister Christiana as well while there. The oldest of the three, Christiana had married Richard Fairgrave, the Earl of Radnor nearly a year ago and the pair had moved to his townhouse in London.

Suzette missed her older sister. She was also a touch worried because, while she and Lisa had been writing Chrissy regularly, they hadn't received responses. That hadn't concerned them too much at first. They understood that Chrissy would have many changes to adjust to and no doubt had a busy, exciting life in London now with little time for correspondence. But as the time had lengthened with still no response, they'd begun to fret, so it had been a relief that their father would have this opportunity to check on her.

However, their father hadn't returned at week's end with tales of Christiana's well-being and happiness. He hadn't returned at all. Neither had there been a message from him. After two such weeks, Suzette had sent a letter inquiring after his well-being and asking what word he had of Christiana. At the three-week point without an answer, she'd sent another message, along with one from Lisa. When they'd reached the month point with still no word, Suzette hadn't been able to stand the worry and strain of wondering anymore. It was starting to seem like London was swallowing up her family members one at a time. She'd decided she would follow their father to town and find out what was happening. It hadn't been very surprising when Lisa had insisted on accompanying her.

The two had set out, taking along their maids and four footmen to ward off any highwaymen who might see them as easy pickings. It appeared to have worked; they'd arrived in London unaccosted and would soon arrive at the family townhouse. Hopefully, they would also soon learn what was going on.

"If he is not there, we shall find out where he is," Suzette finally answered, and was glad Lisa didn't then question her as to how they would manage that because she really had no idea. This was the first time either of them had visited London and she hadn't a clue what to expect. So far it wasn't very impressive. It seemed a world of endless buildings all crowding together under a thickening cloud of sea-coal smoke which she assumed was from so many hearths being lit this cold morning. Suzette preferred the quiet, tranquil life in the country where she was able to at least see the sky.

The only way Suzette knew they had finally arrived at the Madison townhouse was that the carriage stopped. While it had been in the family for generations, she'd never actually seen the Madison London residence before and found herself peering curiously over it as she stepped out of the carriage. It was rather large and grand looking, but then it had belonged to their mother's family, the Seftons, and they had been notoriously wealthy. Her grandfather had actually been called "Old moneybags Sefton" due to the wealth he had both inherited and increased. The man had left that wealth to his granddaughters on his death, dividing it three ways to give each of them a dower that would surely have the fortune hunters after them when they debuted. Or, it would have had he not insisted it be kept a secret.

"It looks very grand, doesn't it," Lisa murmured as she paused beside her. "Though a little run-down."

Suzette nodded silently, not surprised at the small signs of neglect here and there. There had been little money this last year thanks to her father and she had no doubt he'd cut back on servants and whatever else he'd felt wasn't absolutely necessary in an effort to save money. After a quick word with the maids to ensure they oversaw the unloading of their chests, Suzette led Lisa up the front walk.

One of the heavy double front doors was opened before they'd reached it. A sleepy-eyed butler peered out, his gaze sliding with some irritation over Suzette and Lisa. There was no doubting his annoyance at such an early call, at first, but then his gaze slid to the carriage. Apparently recognizing the family crest of the Madison Barony, he immediately straightened, his expression becoming much more welcoming. Well, as welcoming as a British butler's face got, Suzette supposed as the man allowed just a hint of a curve to touch the corners of his mouth.

"My ladies Madison," the man greeted.

Suzette nodded, forcing a small smile of her own as she led Lisa past the man and into the house. Pausing in the entry, she turned back to him, removing her gloves as she asked, "Where is our father?"

"Er . . ." The man looked nonplussed for a moment, his eyes sliding toward the stairs and then along the hall before he suddenly relaxed and offered, "I believe he is in his office, my lady."

Suzette glanced up the hall in that direction, spotting the crack of light coming from under one door, and knew at once it must be the office. Leading Lisa that way, she said, "Thank you. Our maids shall be following directly. Please have someone show them to rooms we can use while here and have servants help to prepare them."

"Of course, my lady." The man was moving off up the hall, no doubt in search of the requested servants even as Suzette reached the door to the office. Too anxious to bother knocking, she opened it at once and started in, only to pause abruptly at the state of the room. The first thing of note was the smell, the acrid scent of stale pipe smoke and old booze permeated the air and struck her like a fist. Suzette wrinkled her nose with a disgust that only increased as her gaze slid over the empty glasses and plates strewn about the room. Most seemed concentrated around two chairs set by the fire, though there were nearly as many covering the desk's surface around their father's slumped form. While the glasses were all empty of liquid, each plate held a half-eaten or untouched meal left to spoil. It was apparent their father had spent most of this last month in this room. Judging by the smell and state of things, he'd spent most of that time drinking and puffing away on his pipe and very little time or energy eating.

"Oh dear," Lisa breathed. "Something must be terribly wrong."

Suzette grimaced at the vast understatement. This just was not like the Cedrick Madison who had raised them. Obviously, there was something terribly wrong. Their father was without a jacket, his shirtsleeves rolled up, and his hair a ruffled mess. He also lay with his head on his arms on the desktop, obviously asleep, or passed out. She couldn't be sure which.

Swallowing the lump that worry had lodged in her throat, Suzette pushed the door closed and moved toward the desk, saying softly, "Father?"

"He *is* just sleeping, isn't he?" Lisa asked worriedly as they paused at the front of the desk.

Concern growing at the question, Suzette leaned forward to nudge her father's arm and was immediately sorry she had. He did respond to it, rearing upright and then dropping back in his seat, but the man they were now confronted with was even less the Cedrick Madison they knew than they'd first thought. This man had bloodshot eyes, a sallow complexion, and a couple weeks' worth of facial hair that held bits of food caught in it. He also wore a shirt that obviously hadn't been changed in a while, but was a wordless menu of the meals he'd half eaten lately. He smelled atrocious.

Suzette retrieved a hanky from up her sleeve and held it to her nose so as to avoid the smell.

"Papa?" Lisa breathed with disbelief.

Cedrick Madison blinked at them owlishly, confusion on his face. "Damn me, what're ye doin' here?" he asked, his voice faint and bewildered as his bleary gaze slid from Suzette to Lisa, and then he peered around with uncertainty. "Where'm I? Did I come home, then?"

Suzette's mouth tightened grimly. Every word the man spoke was accompanied by the scent of spirits, and he was very unsteady in his seat. It was Lisa who gently said, "You are in your office in the London townhouse."

Cedrick Madison's shoulders slumped slightly with disappointment. "Then 'twasn't a dream? It happened again?"

Suzette felt her heart stutter in her chest and dread begin to gather at the last question. "*What* happened again? What the devil is going on, Father?"

"Oh," he sighed the word on another waft of whiskey-soaked breath and ran one hand wearily through his hair. "I'm afraid I may have got us into another spot of bother."

"Not gambling again, Papa?" Lisa asked with alarm, and he nodded miserably.

"How bad is it?" Suzette asked grimly. The last time, he'd gambled them to the edge of ruin and only Christiana's marriage to Dicky had saved them from falling into that sad pit of shame.

"Bad. As bad as last time or maybe worse," he admitted, shamefaced, and then sounded bewildered as he added, "I dunno how't happened. I didn't mean to. I just—" He shook his head in misery. "But I did, and then I tried to fix it. I've approached everyone I can think of who wouldn't let the secret out. I've begged to borrow. I'd even steal if I could. I just can't seem to fix it."

Suzette stared at him, horror, betrayal and fear rising up in her like a wave, and all churning up a foamy topping of rage that roared through her. Hands clenching, she dug her nails into her palms and growled, "You never had any papers to sign at all, did you? You've never had to come to town to sign papers before. It was all just a ruse to get you to town. The truth is, you came here to gamble. That was why the sudden trip to London. Wasn't it?"

"No," he protested at once, standing on obviously shaky legs. "Langley wrote. He was concerned about your sister. He said he suspected Dicky was mistreating her. He said he had been turned away from the house three times and was worried about her. He knew Dicky couldn't turn me away and wanted me to check on her. I swear."

Suzette merely stared at him with disbelief. Robert Langley was a neighbor and family friend, and usually a trustworthy source of information, but it was hard to believe Christiana's husband, Richard, would treat her poorly. The man had seemed to adore her when they'd married just a year ago.

It was Lisa who made this protest aloud, saying staunchly, "Dicky wouldn't treat Chrissy badly, he loves her."

"He seemed to," their father agreed on a sigh. "But Robert wouldn't lie and if Dicky *is* treating her badly . . ." He shook his head and sank wearily back onto his chair. "Anyway, that was the reason I came to town. I swear I never intended to gamble. I'm not even sure how it happened," he repeated with a frown.

"And how are we supposed to believe that?" Suzette asked, biting out the words in her fury. "How can we believe anything you say? You promised us you would never *ever* gamble again and yet here we stand on the verge of ruin for the second time in little more than a year!"

"I know," Cedrick Madison moaned and covered his face with his hands. His next words were muffled as he said, "I don't understand how it happened. I really don't recall gambling, I must have had too much to drink or something."

"How convenient," she snapped coldly, and then asked, "And how exactly did checking on Chrissy land you drunk in a gaming hell?"

His hands dropped away from his face and he said wearily, "She wasn't in when I arrived at their townhouse, and Dicky took me for a drink at the club. I recall going there and his suggesting a quick stop at the gaming hell. He—"

"*Dicky* took you to the gaming hell?" Lisa asked with a combination of dismay and disbelief.

"I think so." He didn't look at all certain. "I mean, I said no when he suggested it, but I also recall being at the gaming hell, so—"

"Oh, so you do recall that much, do you?" Suzette asked grimly, and then screeched, "You shouldn't even have been there! Obviously you intended to gamble or you wouldn't have gone. How could you do this again?!" She sucked in her breath and then hissed, "Gambling your own daughters to the edge of ruin not once, but twice. I'm glad Mother is not around to see the useless, drunken wastrel you've become."

Suzette didn't wait to see how he reacted to the words, but promptly whirled on her heel and stormed out of the room, too sickened by the sight of him to stay any longer.

Lisa followed quickly, pulling the door closed behind her. She then asked worriedly, "What are we going to do?"

"I don't know," Suzette admitted, coming to a halt. Her throat was tight and she felt light-headed, as if something had been cinched around her chest and was preventing her breathing. She forced herself to take a deep breath in an effort to calm herself, and then began to pace, and muttered, "I need to think."

Lisa nodded and fell silent, simply watching as she strode the length of the hall from the office to the front door and back.

It didn't take much thinking for Suzette to realize what she had to do. They were in the same position they had been in the last time their father gambled, just a year ago. They had only saved themselves then by Chrissy marrying, claiming her dower, and paying off the debt. It seemed obvious that was what had to happen again. Only this time it was Suzette who would have to marry, claim her dower and pay off the debt. The thought had barely struck her when the front door opened and the Madison footmen appeared, carrying their chests.

"Wait," she said, hurrying to block their path. "You need to put those back on the carriage. We are not staying here."

"We aren't?" Lisa asked with surprise, moving to her side as the men began to back out of the door with their burden. "Where are we going?"

"To Christiana and Dicky's," Suzette said firmly, catching Lisa's hand and pulling her along as she followed the men out of the house. "I shall have to marry like Chrissy did to take care of *matters*," she whispered the last word, not wishing to be overheard by the servants. Though they probably already knew, she supposed on a sigh, and continued, "Father spends all his time in the country, but Christiana and Dicky are here in town with invitations to balls and such. They can introduce us to society, which is imperative if I am to find a husband."

"Oh Suzette," Lisa said and sounded almost pitying. She then suggested, "Perhaps Dicky would be willing to pay again."

Suzette smiled wryly at the doubt in Lisa's voice. Apparently she didn't really think it likely, and Suzette understood that fully. Dicky had already paid a huge sum the first time around. Though he'd gained it back via the dower, it wasn't really reasonable to expect him to pay again . . . especially if he was now treating Christiana badly. If that was true, it suggested to her that he hadn't really been in love with their sister at all as he'd claimed, which left only the dower to bring about the proposal. If that was the case, he'd hardly want to give up any more of it, but she merely said, "Nay. Christiana paid for Father's first little adventure in the gaming hells in London. Dicky would be very angry to be expected to pay again and rightly so. Besides, she shouldn't have to pay again. 'Tis my turn."

They had reached the carriage by then and Suzette moved to the driver to tell him where they were going next. She then urged Lisa back into the carriage they had so recently escaped. It was a lot roomier with just the two of them and Suzette wasn't surprised when Lisa said, "What about our maids?"

Suzette sighed and glanced out the window toward the house. No doubt the maids had gone above stairs to help ready their rooms while they waited for the chests to be brought up. She considered going in to fetch them, but then shook her head. "Perhaps it is better to leave them here for now. At least until we are sure we are welcome at Christiana and Dicky's."

"Of course we are welcome. She is our sister," Lisa said at once, seeming startled at the suggestion they might not be.

"Yes, well, but she hasn't written us since leaving, has she?" Suzette pointed out gently.

"I'm sure the letters were just lost," Lisa said at once.

"Or Dicky won't let her write us," Suzette murmured, biting her lip.

Lisa frowned, but then said reluctantly, "I suppose he could have. Father did say Robert claims Dicky treats Chrissy awful."

"Exactly." Suzette frowned and shook her head with bewilderment. "It is so hard to believe. It has only been a year and he was so charming and loving when he courted her." In truth, the man had been the perfect romantic hero, sweeping in to save them from ruin, professing undying love for Christiana and courting her with such verve and charm that all three girls had been half in love with him.

"Robert wouldn't lie," Lisa pointed out unhappily.

"No," she agreed with a sigh. "Which means all that charm and verve he showed in courting Chrissy was probably for show, to bait the trap and get her to fall in love with and marry him."

"Why?" Lisa asked with a frown.

"What else? The dower," Suzette said dryly. "If he didn't truly love her that could be the only reason to want to marry her."

"But no one knows about our dowers," Lisa said at once. "Grandfather insisted on it so we could avoid fortune seekers."

"Well, Dicky must have found out," Suzette said reasonably. "Besides, nothing is ever a secret. You know that. Servants talk and secrets get out."

"I suppose," Lisa said reluctantly. She grimaced. "And it was all rather sudden, a whirlwind really. It was only a couple of weeks between when father came home with the news of our impending ruin and Christiana and Dicky's wedding. I suppose Dicky could have pretended his adoration for a couple of weeks."

"Yes, he could have," Suzette agreed grimly.

"What if you are stuck with a bad husband too?" Lisa asked unhappily.

Suzette felt her lips tighten. There was little chance to meet a man she could love and be sure loved her in two weeks, and she was damned if she was going to spend her life being treated shabbily by her own husband. So she wouldn't look for love, Suzette decided and announced, "I shall look for a husband I can control, or at least one I can insure won't control me."

"How?" Lisa asked uncertainly.

"I shall find a husband who needs coin," Suzette said grimly. "One land rich and desperate enough for money to run that land that he'll agree to a marriage contract that allows me half my dower and the right to live my own life."

"Oh, that's—" Lisa paused and glanced out the window as the carriage jerked forward and they set off. She then glanced back to Suzette and asked uncertainly, "Is that even possible?"

"If we both agree to it," Suzette said, but wasn't as certain as she tried to sound. The only thing she was certain of was that she was going to do her damnedest to achieve that end.

Chapter One

*W*hat is taking so long?"

Daniel Woodrow raised his eyebrows at his friend's impatient words. It was rare to see Richard Fairgrave, the Earl of Radnor, so impatient, but then the situation was a rare one indeed. In fact, he suspected it was a one of a kind situation. Certainly, Daniel had never before heard of a set of events that would lead to a man confronting himself over his own murder.

A wry smile curved Daniel's lips at the thought. It wasn't really an accurate description of what was about to occur, but it was how every single person attending the ball would see it. As far as society knew, a year ago George Fairgrave, the younger twin by a matter of moments to Richard Fairgrave, the Earl of Radnor, had died in a tragic fire. However, George hadn't died. It was Richard who had been meant to die in the fire, one George himself had arranged so that he could take Richard's place in the world and claim his title and wealth. But even Richard hadn't died that night. He had managed to bribe his would-be killers into letting him live and had instead landed in America, penniless, half starved and near death, but alive. Richard had recovered slowly with the aid of kind homesteaders, and then sent a letter to Daniel requesting his help in returning to England and regaining his title and position.

Daniel supposed Richard had sent him the letter because any of their other friends might, understandably, have ignored his warnings not to approach the man parading as Richard Fairgrave to verify the situation. But then most of those men did not have a secret like he had, one that Richard knew and had mentioned in his letter. At least Daniel didn't think they did. Whatever the case, he had known at once that it was Richard's hand writing the letter, and had wasted no time booking a ship to America to find and bring back the man.

"What the devil is the holdup?" Richard fretted again, looking ready to bolt from the carriage and walk the rest of the way to their destination.

"The Landons' ball is the first of the season. Everyone attends it, so the lineup of carriages with passengers waiting to disembark gets long," Daniel pointed out. Hoping to calm him, he leaned out the window to inspect the number of carriages remaining before they would be able to disembark, and sighed his relief as he sat back in his seat again. "There are only two carriages left ahead of us. We shall be able to alight presently."

Richard grunted at this news, but rather than relax, tensed even further and muttered, "I am counting on you to keep me from killing my bastard brother before he confesses all."

"Of course," Daniel said solemnly, not doubting for a moment that Richard was struggling with the desire to pummel the man on sight. Certainly, George deserved it for what he'd done. However, killing him before he confessed all and Richard was assured of regaining his title and position again would not be good. It was why they'd decided to have the confrontation here at possibly the best-attended ball of the season. They needed to startle George into a confession and with as many witnesses as possible. Fortunately, they'd arrived in time to attend it, barely. The ship they'd returned on from America had only set anchor that morning and then they'd had to arrange for the appropriate clothes for both of them to attend.

"Finally."

Richard's heartfelt murmur drew Daniel's attention to the fact that they were now pulling up in front of Landon House. The other man waited just long enough for the carriage to roll to a halt, but could restrain himself no further and immediately opened the carriage door and burst out before it could be opened for them. Daniel followed, offering an apologetic nod to the footman Richard had nearly trampled in his hurry to escape, then rushed after his friend.

Once inside the house, there was a line of people all awaiting their turn to be announced. Daniel wasn't terribly surprised when Richard bypassed the line and walked alongside it to the ballroom entry. Richard had no desire to be announced. They could hardly take George by surprise if the man heard the announcement of the name he'd usurped and been using this last year, and their plan depended on being right in front of the imposter when he realized Richard was not dead and his grand scheme was about to collapse on his head. Bypassing the line, however, stirred a sudden rush of whispers from those waiting. It also caused the servant announcing arrivals to stutter in surprise as Richard and Daniel sailed past. That didn't slow either man, however, and they jogged quickly down the short stairs to the ballroom floor before stopping to survey the crowds in search of one George Cainan Fairgrave, imposter to the Radnor earldom and attempted murderer.

"The Landons always throw a successful ball, and I'd say this is one too, wouldn't you?"

Suzette forced her gaze back to her dance partner and managed a polite smile and nod. She then turned her head away again, unable to bear the man's breath any longer than that. Really, this entire night was turning out to be very disappointing, and she was beginning to think she'd severely misjudged the situation. Suzette supposed she'd allowed her imagination to carry her away. She'd imagined Christiana and

Lisa ferreting out a dozen or so handsome, honorable and charming young men who were perfect in every way except that they were in dire straits financially. She'd imagined each of these men then vying for her hand, eager to woo her and happily accepting both herself and a large dower in exchange for allowing her access to a portion of the dower and the freedom to lead her own life.

She'd been an idiot, obviously, Suzette acknowledged. First of all, women were not allowed to approach the men. The woman was to await the men approaching her. The man would ask to be introduced, request a quadrille or what have you, the lady would then put him down on the dance card and dance each scheduled dance with the man on her card. They had, of course, been forced to work within these strictures, Suzette accepting every invitation, entering the name on her card and then handing it over to Christiana and Lisa while she was dancing so that they could get the gossip on each man on the card. As each man then came to claim her for his allotted dance, Suzette would glance to Lisa and Christiana, who would give her the signals they'd agreed on to let her know if the gentleman in question was an eligible bachelor with a title and/or land, but in need of funds to shore them up.

So far, Suzette had done very well by some standards. Certainly, her dance card was full and she had done little but dance all night. Unfortunately, it seemed that while there were plenty of handsome and charming young men willing to dance with her, few of them filled her requirements of needing a wealthy wife. And those few who did, were not attractive, honorable and charming young men. So far, only one had been anywhere near young.

The first man Lisa had signaled needed a wealthy bride had been older than her father; round and pasty faced. He'd spent their entire dance complaining about his gout while leering at her breasts through her gown. The second prospect had been younger, but he'd been tall, alarmingly thin and had actually asked to check her teeth as if she were a horse at auction, and that without her stating that she was in the market for a husband. The third had been the young one, but he had been far too young. In fact, she suspected he wasn't more than sixteen though he'd claimed to be older. His face had been spotty and he'd had the distressing habit of picking at it as he'd talked to her before and after their dance. Though, he hadn't really talked so much as stuttered out his desire to dance with her.

Now she was dancing with Lord Willthrop, who, while a little younger than her father, also had a hook nose that appeared to cause him some trouble since he was constantly sniffing. He also had terrible breath and a very pompous attitude.

Suzette was beginning to despair that her plan was doomed. For she'd happily embrace scandal and ruination before she'd embrace any of the men she'd so far encountered. Of course, she didn't really have that option, because it wouldn't just be herself cast into scandal if she failed to find a husband and claim her dower. Her father would as well, though it was little more than he deserved for bringing this down upon them all, but so would her little sister Lisa and—married or not—Christiana as well would suffer. Suzette couldn't allow that to happen if she could prevent it.

She grimaced at the thought, and then sighed with relief as the dance finally came to an end. Suzette managed not to rush rudely away from Willthrop to get as far from his bad breath as she could. While she would have liked to, she had been raised better than that and, instead, allowed him to walk her off the dance floor, nodding stiffly as he thanked her for the dance.

"I believe the next dance is mine."

Suzette paused to glance to the man who had appeared at her side as she and Willthrop reached the edge of the dance floor.

"Ah, Danvers," Willthrop said in greeting. He then turned to nod to Suzette before moving off into the crowd.

Suzette watched him go, and then turned to her next partner, vaguely recalling agreeing to dance with him early on in the evening. Her gaze slid over his face, taking note that there didn't appear to be anything wrong with him. He was average in looks, attractive even when he smiled as he was now doing. He was also only five to ten years older than she, and he wasn't sniffling, leering, or picking at spots. In fact, his complexion was spot free. He, of course, would be one of the not-in-need-of-money men, she supposed with a weary cynicism and glanced around in search of her sisters. She spotted Lisa first and raised a querying eyebrow. Her other eyebrow flew up to join it when Lisa gave her first the signal for land, then title, and finally the signal they'd agreed on for no money.

Suzette immediately started to turn back to Danvers, a smile blooming on her lips, but that smile died suddenly and her jaw dropped open as she spotted Dicky making his way quickly through the people on the edges of the dance floor. He was headed straight for Christiana, who stood surrounded by a group of older women, no doubt garnering all the gossip she could on prospective husbands for Suzette.

"It can't be," Suzette breathed with dismay as she stared at the man they'd left for dead when heading for the ball that night.

"Is there something wrong, my lady?" Danvers asked.

Suzette glanced to Danvers with confusion, so overset at the sight of her brother-in-law apparently alive and well that for a moment she couldn't recall why this man was at her side. Recollection struck her a blink later, but she merely shook her head and hurried away, forgetting even to mumble an excuse as she rushed toward Lisa.

"What are you doing?" Lisa asked with amazement as Suzette caught her arm and hustled her through the crowd toward their older sister. "He was a prospect, and much better than the others so far. He—" The younger woman's words died on a strangled gasp as Suzette brought her to a halt next to Christiana and Lisa saw who their older sister was gaping at. When their brother-in-law turned toward them at the sound, Lisa breathed with horror, "But you're dead." Her head swiveled to Christiana. "Wasn't he dead, Chrissy? We packed ice around him and everything."

"The ice must have revived his cold dead heart," Suzette said, anger helping her recover quickly from her shock. Glaring at the man, she added a dry but heartfelt, "More's the pity."

If Dicky looked surprised by her comments, Christiana looked absolutely horrified.

"Suzette!" she gasped, shuffling a little closer as if to physically silence her if Suzette tried to make another such comment. "Perhaps we should go out for some air. Lisa looks ready to faint and you, Suzie, obviously need some time to cool yourself. Perhaps so much dancing has overheated you."

Suzette was about to snort at the suggestion that dancing had brought about her bitter words when her arm was suddenly taken in a firm grip and the words "Allow me" rang in her ears.

Glancing around with a start, she frowned at the man who had suddenly appeared out of seemingly thin air and stepped between her and Lisa, taking both of them in hand like recalcitrant children. He was already turning them firmly away from Christiana and Dicky as he added, "I shall see the ladies outside so the two of you might talk."

Suzette immediately began to tug on her arm, trying to free herself of his hold, but he didn't even seem to notice. Her captor simply held firm and glanced over his shoulder to suggest to the couple he was dragging them away from, "You might consider somewhere more private for this discussion."

As Dicky took Christiana's arm to guide her away in the opposite direction, Suzette scowled at the man dragging her and Lisa through the crowd. She opened her mouth to order him to let them go, but then paused as she took her first good look at the man. He was a good head taller than her, his hair a dark brown, the ends curling a bit as if in need of a cut and his face in profile was quite nice, a strong chin, a straight nose, and eyes— He turned toward her, glancing at her in question, and she decided he had quite the nicest green eyes she'd ever seen, a true green like fresh grass after a rain. He was definitely a good-looking fellow . . . and he was still manhandling her toward the French doors leading to the terrace.

Her scowl returning, she mimicked the tone he'd used with Dicky and Christiana and said, "You might consider letting us go and minding your own business . . . or else I shall be forced to stomp on your foot, sir."

"My lord," he corrected, sounding amused at her threat. "Daniel, Lord Woodrow."

Suzette glowered at the man and was trying to work out how to stomp on his foot while he was forcing them to move so quickly, when he suddenly stopped, drawing her and Lisa to a halt as well. Before she could take advantage and stomp on him as planned, however, someone said, "I believe this is my dance."

Suzette glanced around with surprise, eyes widening further when she saw the handsome, ice-blond man before them. She didn't recall agreeing to dance with him, and was sure she would have definitely remembered him. Besides, she knew she'd already promised the dance to Danvers, but she certainly had no compunction about taking advantage and agreeing to the dance to escape the Woodrow fellow trying to herd her and her sister out of the ballroom. The problem was that it would leave Lisa to Lord Woodrow's tender mercies and she couldn't do that. She was opening her mouth to politely explain to the blond man that he was confused and it wasn't his dance when Lisa blushed prettily and said, "Yes, actually it is. Thank you, my lord. However, I fear I can't leave my sister at the moment and—"

"Don't be silly," Woodrow said easily, releasing Lisa. "I shall look after your sister for you. Go, have your dance."

"Oh but—" Lisa glanced to Suzette with dismay, but the blond had already taken her arm and was leading her toward the dance floor.

Sighing, Suzette waved her on. There was no sense in the two of them being manhandled and dragged about. Besides, she suspected she'd have more luck escaping Woodrow if she wasn't busy worrying about Lisa getting away as well. Still, she watched the couple a little enviously as they moved off. The man was incredibly handsome. Unfortunately, his expensive clothes suggested wealth, which meant he probably wasn't the kind of man she needed were she to save the family from their father's folly; but Lisa was free to marry whom she chose and for no other reason than love . . . and that was what she truly envied, Suzette acknowledged unhappily. It really didn't seem fair that she had to sacrifice herself for the family, but then life rarely was fair, she supposed.

Woodrow urged her forward again and Suzette gave up staring after her sister and turned her attention to her predicament.

"It really isn't proper for a young lady to allow herself to be led outside by a strange man," she pointed out grimly as he ushered her through a set of French doors and out onto a torchlit terrace. "We haven't even been properly introduced."

Daniel glanced down at the woman he held so firmly in hand. The sister to the woman George had married while pretending to be Richard. Truly that news had come as a shock to both him and Richard when they'd heard it from their host. Landon had approached them as they'd still been searching the ball attendees for the apparently not present George. The man had greeted them claiming to be surprised that Richard was attending because his wife had claimed he was too ill to come.

Wife?

That had been a problem neither of them had even imagined and it had sent Richard straight to the woman Landon had pointed out once the man had quit their company to see to his other guests. One of the women around Lady Radnor had addressed the wife as "Christiana," when he and Richard had reached the petite blonde and she in turn had most helpfully named her sisters on their arrival. Lisa was the young blonde one he had released in the ballroom. The little virago who had made such rude comments about Dicky's apparent resurrection, and who now remained in his care, was Suzette.

Daniel's gaze was most thorough as he inspected her. Suzette. The name slid through his thoughts again. A pretty name for a pretty woman. He suspected she might even be beautiful did she not look so vexed. Oddly enough, though, he rather liked the vexed look on her. Most debutantes would have been hiding their anger behind madly fluttering fans and forced smiles. This one had no problem showing her true feelings. It made a refreshing change.

"I did introduce myself," he pointed out mildly as he urged her across the terrace to the steps leading down into the gardens. Daniel had at first only intended on taking the sisters out to the terrace to give Richard some privacy to deal with Christiana and find out what he could about George. However, he now decided he might be able to aid Richard by finding out himself what he could. Certainly, there did seem to be a lot going on that was pertinent to the situation. All three women had seemed equally shocked to see who they thought was Dicky there at the ball, and it had been said more than once that he'd been thought to be dead. If George was dead, then all of Richard's plans could be in jeopardy.

"That wasn't a proper introduction and you know it," she snapped, tugging at her arm again.

"Very true," he agreed easily, holding firm and urging her deeper into the gardens, following a barely discernible path through the trees. "However, I suspect you aren't a proper lady so we should do well enough."

Suzette suddenly came to an abrupt halt and this time even his firm grip couldn't keep her moving, at least not gracefully. If he didn't stop he'd be dragging her along behind him like an old robe.

Pausing, Daniel raised an eyebrow in question.

"Would you care to repeat that?" she asked coldly.

Daniel hesitated and then pointed out mildly, "I simply meant that I suspect you can be a little less than proper at times. Surely a proper young lady wouldn't say what you did back there to Richard?"

Her eyes became daggers, her mouth turning down with dislike. "Dicky deserved it. The man is a bounder. He's a horrible husband and treats Christiana dreadfully." She poked him in the chest with one finger of her free hand and added, "And *you* should be ashamed to be his friend."

Daniel resisted the urge to grab the finger poking him so sharply and said grimly, "I assure you I *have* never and *will* never be friends with your sister's husband." He allowed a moment for that to sink in and then added for good measure, "In fact, I think he's a despicable creature who should be taken out in a field and shot."

"Really?" Suzette asked doubtfully.

"Really," Daniel assured her, thinking George

would have a lot to answer for, when all was said and done. He'd obviously married Suzette's sister, Christiana, in Richard's name, which meant it wasn't a legal marriage at all and the poor woman had been living in sin for however long the marriage had supposedly gone on. Once the truth came out, Christiana, Suzette and their younger sister would be cast into scandal so deep none of them would be free of it.

Neither would Richard of course, he acknowledged. And then there was this business of George possibly being dead. If that was the case, it would make it much harder for Richard to reclaim his name and title. They had been counting on George's confessing to prove Richard's identity. Without that . . . well, Christiana could claim Richard was really George, that he hadn't died in the fire as believed and was just trying to claim everything now that his brother was dead, and many would believe it. Hell, she'd probably believe it. She and everyone else would wonder why he hadn't come forward before "the Earl's" death with these claims, and would doubt every word he said. It was turning out to be one hell of a mess, Daniel thought.

"Then why are you helping Dicky like this?" Suzette asked with open disbelief, drawing his attention back to her.

"I am not doing this to help Geo—Dicky . . ." Daniel corrected himself and then rather than finish his explanation, he paused to consider the situation anew. Everyone so far had just assumed Richard was Dicky, which was obviously what

George had insisted everyone call him. Richard would have never stood for the nickname. In fact, George was the only person who had called him that and had done it precisely because Richard hated it. But the point was, everyone was just accepting Richard was himself, and if George really was dead, surely the simplest way to handle the entire matter was for him to just step back into his life and continue as if he had never left it. Of course, that was, only if George was really dead. And it did mean Richard would have to uphold the marriage to Christiana, but—

"Then why are you doing it?" Suzette asked impatiently, apparently tired of waiting for him to finish the explanation.

Daniel pushed his thoughts aside for the moment and said, "I did this to prevent anyone else overhearing what I did back there. It all sounded just a bit too delightfully scandalous," he said dryly, and then asked carefully, "Did you and your sisters really think Dicky dead and pack him in ice?"

Suzette sighed with disgust at the question. "Yes. Though, obviously it was a bit premature since the man is alive and well after all." She shook her head and added with bewilderment, "Though I'm sure he was dead."

"Perhaps he was just unconscious," Daniel suggested.

"He wasn't breathing," she argued dryly, and then frowned and said, "At least he didn't seem to be. And I could have sworn his body had begun to cool as we packed him in ice, but perhaps my hands were just cold from handling the ice."

Daniel cleared his throat and asked delicately, "Well, what exactly preceded his apparent dying? Did he appear unwell?"

Suzette scowled, her expression turning thoughtful as she set her mind back, and then she said slowly, "He certainly didn't seem ill when he was trying to shoo us away from his door like a pair of matchstick girls. He seemed hale and hearty and pompous as a rooster."

"Shoo you away like a pair of matchstick girls?" Daniel asked curiously.

"Hmm." Suzette scowled. "We went to see Christiana about—well, some family business. But the butler left us waiting at the door while he fetched Dicky and then Dicky wasn't even going to let us see her." She looked amazed as she said that and then added, "Fortunately, Christiana appeared and intervened and managed to convince him to let us in." Her mouth tightened at the memory and she added, "But then the bounder insisted we wait in the parlor while he and Christiana breakfasted first. I gather that was to punish us for showing up uninvited," she added dryly. "And he was pompous as hell about it."

Daniel raised his eyebrows at the curse. Ladies did not generally curse like sailors. At least not the ladies he knew. Suzette was turning out to be a somewhat extraordinary lady, however.

She sighed unhappily, and then continued. "When he finally did let Christiana come to us, he accompanied her at first. Of course, we didn't want to talk about what Father had done again in front of him."

"What your father had done?" Daniel asked gently.

Her expression closed and she ignored the question and went on, "But I managed to bore him to tears with gossip until he went away, and then we told Christiana all."

"All of what?" Daniel asked at once, growing increasingly curious.

Whatever it was appeared to distress her and this time she didn't ignore his question, but gave him a dry look and said, "You do not need to know. No one must know but my prospective husband."

"You are engaged?" he asked sharply. For some reason the idea bothered him.

"No," Suzette said looking as if she thought the very idea ridiculous. "But I have to be and we had gone to Christiana so that she could see that Lisa and I could attend the balls and such and find a prospective husband."

"I see," Daniel said with disappointment. The woman was obviously in trouble and needed a quick marriage to hide that trouble, one that would probably come to fruition in less than nine months was his guess. The thought tarnished some of her beauty in his eyes.

"Anyway, Christiana agreed of course. After all, she had to marry Dicky because of Father's last faux pas, so she understood completely."

That was good, Daniel supposed, but he was now thoroughly confused again, not seeing how a father's faux pas could leave the girl in the kind of trouble where she needed a fast marriage. At

least not the nine months kind. Perhaps he'd misjudged her there, he thought.

"So Christiana went to speak to Dicky about
taking us out and about, but when she found him
in the office, the idiot was dead."

Daniel bit his lip at her vexed tone. There was
absolutely no grief in her voice at all, just irritation
with the inconvenience of it all. But then George
had never been one to inspire the finer feelings
in those he encountered. Clearing his throat, he
asked, "Did he fall and strike his head, or—"

"No. He was simply sitting in his chair dead,"
she said with exasperation, and then added with
disgust, "He was obviously a victim of his own
excess. We suspected his heart gave out. Certainly
the glass and decanter of whiskey next to him
suggested he didn't take the best care of himself. I
ask you, who drinks hard liquor first thing in the
morning?"

Daniel shook his head, finding it difficult to
speak. She was just so annoyed as she spoke of the
man's death, as if he'd deliberately done it to mess
up her plans. After a moment, he asked, "Are you
sure he is dead?"

Suzette gave him another one of those adorable "Don't be ridiculous" looks. "Well, obviously he isn't. He is here now," she pointed out,
and then shook her head and added almost under
her breath, "Though I could have sworn . . . The
man didn't even stir when he fell off the chair
and slammed his head on the floor. Nor when I
dropped him and his head crashed to the hard-
wood floor again, or when we rolled him in the

carpet and dragged him upstairs, or when we dropped him in the hall and he rolled out of the carpet, or—"

"Er," Daniel interrupted, and then coughed into his hand to hide a laugh, before asking, "Why exactly were you carting him about in a carpet?"

"Well, don't be dense," she said with exasperation. "We couldn't let anyone know he was dead, could we?"

"Couldn't you?" he asked uncertainly.

Suzette clucked with irritation. "Of course not. We would have had to go into mourning then. How would I find a husband if we were forced to abstain from polite society to observe mourning?"

"Ah. I see," Daniel said and he did see. Things were becoming much clearer. From her description of the abuse the man had taken without protest, George was most definitely probably dead.

"Of course, Christiana wanted to call in the authorities and report his death. But I reminded her that we only have the two weeks for me to find a husband and claim my dower."

"Hmm," Daniel said dryly, disappointment claiming him again as he realized that Suzette was just another woman in search of a husband with heavy pockets.

"So, she agreed to put Dicky in his bed, pack him in ice, tell the servants he was ill and keep his death a secret for two nights so that I could find a husband." Suzette's mouth twisted and she muttered, "All that trouble and the man wasn't even dead. I just know he shall ruin everything now.

He'll keep us from attending any more balls to find a husband. If he had any sense of honor at all, the man would have stayed dead."

"Unfortunately, it appears he was merely unconscious," Daniel murmured. He was becoming quite certain George was dead. This might greatly simplify matters, or at least it would if Richard was willing to uphold the marriage to Christiana . . . and really, Daniel was beginning to think that would be the most honorable thing to do here. While he didn't think much of their looking to marry a man with money to solve their problems, it did seem a shame to cast the scandal of George's actions on these three women when none of it was their fault at all.

"Unconscious," Suzette spat the word with disgust. "He must have been, and he had obviously been drinking." She tsked with exasperation and stomped her foot, muttering, "Why could the beast not have been dead? I should have smothered him in his bed to be sure he was and stayed that way."

Daniel stared at her with amazement. His first thought was that, really, aside from her fortune hunting and homicidal tendencies, the woman was quite fascinating in her complete and utter lack of artifice. His next thought was that the ton would eat her alive. Artifice and subterfuge were necessary tools to survive society and she was obviously completely lacking in both.

Suzette suddenly heaved out a put upon breath and muttered, "I suppose I had best be sure I find a husband tonight. Otherwise, surely Dicky will find some way to throw a spanner in my plans."

Daniel's eyebrows flew up at her words and then she peered at him with interest.

"You're a handsome enough fellow," she commented thoughtfully.

Daniel blinked, and then muttered, "Oh . . . er . . . thank you. I think."

"You don't seem a dullard either," she added, tilting her head to inspect him consideringly.

"Erm," he said weakly.

"And you aren't old. That's another plus." Daniel was puzzling over that when she asked abruptly, "Are you rich?"

At first, he was just startled by the blunt question. Someone with that artifice and subterfuge she lacked would have gone about finding that out in a much more roundabout way. Actually, most members of the ton wouldn't even have tried to figure it out. They had all assumed for years that Daniel's family was well heeled, and his mother had worked very hard to ensure everyone thought that. However, the truth was that they had been near paupers, selling off old family antiques one at a time to keep the creditors at bay, while trying desperately to uphold the image of wealth everyone expected.

His mother had started pestering Daniel to find a wealthy wife the moment he'd come of age and he'd almost allowed himself to be pressured into it when one night, under the influence of too much alcohol, he'd confessed all to Richard. Richard hadn't been surprised. Much to Daniel's amazement it appeared his mother's efforts hadn't been as successful as she'd thought and his best friend had long suspected their financial state. Or, perhaps being that close he had simply noticed that Daniel wore the same clothes most of the time, treating them gingerly to make them last, or that their parlor was threadbare with wear, and that no one was allowed beyond the parlor, mostly because the rest of the house was nearly empty of furniture.

Whatever the case, Richard hadn't wanted to humiliate him by bringing up the subject, but had waited for Daniel to bring it up, and the moment he did, Richard offered to help. He offered to spot him for an investment he thought a good prospect. He would loan Daniel the money to invest, a loan that would be paid back with interest. It was only the last part that allowed Daniel to swallow his pride and accept the offer and he supposed Richard had known that and it was why he'd added it. So the two men had made the investment, and it had paid off. Even after paying back the loan with interest, Daniel had more than the initial loan, which he then promptly invested in another scheme Richard suggested.

Richard Fairgrave had the Midas touch when it came to investments and was generous in sharing his business acumen with friends. Over the last ten years that feigned wealth his mother had tried so desperately to project throughout his childhood, had become real wealth. That was the secret Richard and he shared, and how Daniel had known it was the true Richard sending the letter.

"Well," Suzette asked. "Are you rich?"

Daniel scowled at the bellicose female. The answer was he was now one of the wealthiest lords in England thanks to Richard. But while that meant his own mother had eased up on pressuring him to find a *rich* wife, she still wanted him to find a wife and give her grandbabies. However, he also found himself constantly stalked by marriage-minded mamas and their braying daughters, and, frankly, while he'd thought it rather amusing in a twisted way when he'd been poor and knew they were getting no bargain, Daniel now found it vastly annoying. He was more than a stallion for stud with a bag of gold between his legs. And as entertaining as Suzette was, he didn't appreciate her interest in him being based only on his wealth. So he did what any reasonable man would do in this situation . . . he lied.

"I am as poor as a church mouse," he announced with feigned regret. "In fact, poorer than a church mouse since just this last year I inherited Woodrow from my uncle and it is a terrible mess in need of a great deal of repair and care that I cannot afford."

The last part wasn't a complete lie. He actually had inherited the family seat from his father's older brother a year ago, and it *was* in horrible repair, nearly falling down really. He did have the money to repair it, however, and had been doing so for the last year. Actually, he'd inherited the estate shortly before George's supposed death which had been meant to be Richard's death, and had been at the estate taking in the poor state of repair and seeing what needed to be done to return it to its earlier glory when he'd received news of George's death in the townhouse fire. By the time he got the news, the man's body, or what everyone had thought was his body, was interred in the Fairgrave family vault and the dust had settled. Daniel had sent a letter of condolence to Richard, or who he'd thought was Richard in London, and offered to come to him if he needed a friend, but had never received a reply.

Still, he'd intended to visit town and seek him out to see how he was handling his twin's death at some point, but there had seemed to be one problem after another with the reparations at the estate, and then his mother had fallen gravely ill and nearly died. She had recovered, fortunately, but it had been a slow recuperation for her and it was nearly six months before he'd felt he could leave and make his way into town. Daniel arrived after midnight, and had considered heading to Richard's townhouse at once to see how he faired, but the late hour and his own exhaustion from the journey had made him decide to go to bed instead and visit the next day. But he'd woken that next morning to Richard's letter coming to him from America of all places.

Once he'd read the contents, Daniel hadn't bothered visiting the townhouse where George was now installed, a pretender to his brother's name and title. Instead, he'd booked a cabin on the first ship heading to America to fetch Richard back.

"Really?" Suzette asked. "You're poor?"

Daniel blinked at her amazed expression, once

again recalled to their talk. He then decided to embellish a bit and said, "Yes, really. In fact I am supposed to be here tonight seeking out a wealthy bride to marry. The money is needed to repair Woodrow as well as to pay what little staff is left." He feigned a sigh. "I do not suppose you know any lovely young ladies with bags of coin and a desire to marry a fellow down on his luck?"

"Me!"

Daniel's jaw dropped. Not only had she squealed the word as if it were quite the most wonderful thing in the world, but she was looking as excited as a child at Christmas. This was not the response he'd expected. He'd truly thought his words would have her stomping off back into the ball, or at least trying to since he hadn't finished seeking to worm information from her yet and would have prevented it. He'd just hoped that as a woman in search of a rich husband, his response would get her thoughts off his being a prospect. Instead, she was now looking at him as if he were the answer to her prayers.

"But this is perfect," she said happily. "I need a poor husband and you need a rich wife. It's as if it was meant to be."

"I highly doubt—" Daniel swallowed the rest of what he'd been about to say and nearly swallowed his tongue along with the words when Suzette suddenly grasped one of his hands in both of hers and raised it to squeeze excitedly between both of hers. It wasn't the fact that she was squeezing his hand in hers that startled him so much as the fact that, in her excitement, she was also pressing

it against her chest. He didn't think she even realized what she was doing. Truly, the woman was
beyond excited and it left him completely bewildered until what she'd said sank in. Frowning, he
asked, "You're rich?"

"Oh, goodness yes. My grandfather Sefton di-
vided his wealth between myself and my sisters
when he died, leaving it to be dowers for each of
us. So you see, I have that fortune you need. Isn't
it wonderful?"

"Sefton you say?" he asked slowly, recognizing the name at once. Everyone knew the name
Sefton. The man had surpassed even Richard for
having the Midas touch and had earned the name
Old Money Bags Sefton decades ago. They said
he'd amassed more wealth than the king himself.
There had been some rumors when he'd died that
he'd left his money to his dead daughter's husband
and his daughters. What was the name? he wondered, but found it hard to think with his hand
nestled in the valley between Suzette's breasts. It
was clasped in her hands and he wasn't actually
touching any flesh, but just the sight was rather
distracting. Fortunately, she eased her hold on
him then and let his hand slip away and he was
able to think again. A name came to him then.
"Madison?"

"Yes, Suzette Madison." She nodded, practically
dancing on the spot with a glee he didn't quite
understand. "And my sisters are Lisa and Christiana."

Daniel frowned, thinking back over what
she'd said. She needed a poor husband? That just

didn't even make sense. A woman only married a poor man for love, and then most noble women wouldn't even allow love to sway them into such a marriage. Wealth was everything in the ton. So why would a rich woman need a poor husband? There was no reason he could think of . . . unless she was in dire straits and needed a man who was poor and desperate enough to marry her at once. Which led him right back to the first reason he'd supposed she needed to marry so quickly.

"You are with child?" he asked uncertainly, his eyes dropping to her petite waistline. She didn't look pregnant, and that wouldn't explain how the father was involved.

"What?" she asked with surprise, but rather than be offended, merely snorted and rolled her eyes. "No, of course I'm not with child. What kind of woman do you take me for?"

A good question, Daniel thought dryly because really, he hadn't a clue what kind of woman she was. He'd never met anyone quite like her and all he really knew so far was that she was in some sort of trouble and full of surprises. "Then why do you need a poor husband? And didn't you say you needed to find one tonight? What other reason is there for such a need than to avoid the scandal of an illegitimate pregnancy?"

Suzette sighed, some of her excitement slipping away as she admitted, "To avoid a different kind of scandal."

When Daniel raised one eyebrow, she hesitated and then said, "I suppose I really should explain if you are going to marry me."

His other eyebrow flew up at that, but Suzette didn't notice. She was looking about, and spotting a bench under a tree a little further into the garden, caught his hand and dragged him that way, saying, "Come, I shall explain all."

Chapter Two

"So you see, I need to marry and claim my dower so I can pay off Father's gambling debts before they become common knowledge and we are all sunk in scandal," Suzette finished in a rush. Truthfully, she had rushed through the entire explanation of the trouble their father had got them into as quickly as she could. Fast as she had been though, she'd included everything, even that Robert Langley's letter had drawn their father to town to check on Christiana. Now she bit her lip and waited, watching as Daniel Woodrow considered all she'd revealed.

Suzette was desperately hoping that he wouldn't be put off by what she'd told him, but had seen no way to avoid explaining it all to him. Besides, he had a right to know, she supposed.

Still, she'd rather not have had to tell him. Daniel was the first man tonight who had matched the imagined suitors she'd dreamed of before the ball. Well, she supposed there was Danvers. He'd been about the same age as Daniel, but while he'd been average in looks, Daniel was . . . well, she supposed he wasn't much more than average in the grand scheme of things, but now that he was no longer dragging her about, there was just something about him that appealed to her for some reason. Perhaps it was his lips, she thought, peering at his full lower lip below the thinner upper one and wondering what it would be like to be kissed by him.

"Why you and not your sister?" he asked. "Lisa was it?"

"Yes, Lisa," Suzette answered and then shrugged. "I am the older of us by a year. It seems more responsible for me to take on the task this time."

"Hmm." He was silent for a moment and then murmured, "So Christiana married Geo—Dicky to claim her dower and pay off your father's first round of gambling debts?"

"Well, Dicky paid them off himself, but got it back through the dower when he and Christiana married," she said slowly.

"And that was the first time your father had ever gambled in his life?" he asked, eyes narrowing.

Suzette sighed and nodded. "Yes, he'd never bothered with things like that before then."

"But now he's gambled again for only the second time, and for the second time lost so much that one of his daughters—you—need to marry to claim your dower and pay off those debts again?" he asked. When Suzette nodded, he frowned and asked, "And you say Geo-Dicky took your father to the gaming hell where he lost the money this last time?"

Suzette nodded again, her mouth twisting bitterly. She really wished the man was dead. It would only be justice considering that what he'd done was forcing her to marry so hurriedly.

"Did he take your father to the gaming hell the first time?"

Suzette blinked with surprise. "No," she said at once and then frowned and said, "Actually, maybe."

Daniel raised his eyebrows. "Which is it?"

Suzette bit her lip. "I'm not sure. I was reading in the attic when Dicky arrived at Madison and I overheard his conversation with Father." She paused to explain, "The attic stretches across the house and for some reason you can hear what's said in Father's office in one spot up there and it just happened to be where I was reading."

"It just happened to be, did it?" he asked with an amused grin.

Suzette blushed, but continued, "Anyway, I heard when Dicky offered to pay Father's debts in exchange for Christiana's hand in marriage and he did say something about feeling responsible for Father's gambling that night." She frowned. "I don't recall him saying why he felt responsible though . . . but it could have been because he took him there that time too, don't you think?"

"It's possible," Daniel agreed quietly, his expression turning thoughtful.

Suzette sat fidgeting for a moment, but finally asked, "So? Will you marry me?"

Daniel seemed startled by the question and suddenly sat up straight. "Oh . . . er . . ."

"It is the perfect solution for both of us," Suzette pointed out anxiously. Truly, she was almost desperate to convince him. She simply abhorred the idea of having to marry Lord Willthrop or any of the others she'd danced with tonight. This man, however . . . Well, she found him attractive at least. And so far he hadn't displayed any unbearable habits like picking at spots, though to be fair, he didn't seem to have any spots to pick at. But he also hadn't leered at her once, there was no incessant sniffling and she hadn't noticed him having bad breath.

Frowning at that last thought, she leaned a little closer to him on the bench seat, put her nose by his mouth and sniffed delicately, but didn't notice any unpleasant smells.

"What are you doing?" he asked with amazement.

"Nothing," she said, straightening quickly. Suzette then continued with her argument, pointing out, "You need a rich wife to gain the money to repair your estate and lands, and I have that money. And I need a husband willing to allow me access to some of my dower to pay off my father's debts and . . ." She hesitated and bit her lip, worried this next part might be an issue, but really she would have to bring it up eventually if she stuck to her plan so plunged on, "And I should like an agreement stating that I may live my own life."

Daniel raised his eyebrows at that. "What exactly does that mean?"

"Well," Suzette said slowly, drawing out the word as she tried to find the words to explain exactly what she did want. The truth was she wasn't sure what she meant by it, except that she didn't want to be stuck having to put up with a nasty, critical husband who would pick at her and make her miserable for the next forty years or so. Sighing, she said, "I suppose it means that I will be free to travel with my maid, or to live in the country while you are in town, or I may live in town while you are in the country if I wish. I mean if I find your company . . . er . . . unpleasant."

"I see," Daniel said dryly. "And if we are always apart, how exactly are we to gain heirs?"

"Oh." Suzette flushed. "Well, I suppose we could arrange for occasional visits for . . . er . . . procreative purposes."

"Occasional visits for procreative purposes?" he echoed with disbelief, and then muttered dryly, "My, how scintillating that sounds."

Suzette frowned, for really it did sound rather cold, nothing like the passionate delirium she had read about in one of Lisa's novels. But then, truthfully, she simply couldn't fathom the ecstasies described in that book. She'd never even been kissed and what if she didn't enjoy his kisses? Just because he didn't have bad breath didn't mean she would enjoy these visits she spoke of so boldly. Coming to a decision, she straightened abruptly, and said, "We must kiss."

That caught his attention and he asked with amazement, "What?"

"Well, we should see if we would deal well together in . . . er . . . that regard," she muttered, blushing hotly. Swallowing, she forced herself to add firmly, "You should kiss me. Then we will know."

"My dear young lady," Daniel began seeming half amused and half horrified, "I really do not think—"

"Oh, for pity's sake," Suzette interrupted impatiently, and then leaned forward again, this time pressing her lips to his. In her rush to get it over with, she lost her balance a bit and had to catch a hold of his jacket to steady herself as she smooshed her mouth against his. She then waited for the warm and wonderful commotion she'd read about to assault her. Unfortunately, there wasn't any commotion. Really this was no more exciting than pressing her mouth to a cup, Suzette thought with dismay, and released him to sit back again with a most disappointed sigh. "Oh dear, I fear you're no good at this."

"Excuse me? *I* am no good at this?" Daniel asked with amazed disbelief. "My dear girl, if you think that was a kiss—"

"Do stop calling me a girl," Suzette snapped a bit impatiently and got to her feet, too agitated now to sit. "You sound like you're old enough to be my father and you aren't quite *that* old."

"Not quite *that* old? For pity's sake! What a charmer you are," he said with irritation, and then stood up as well and informed her with some dignity, "That was *not* a proper kiss."

"Well if you are such an expert, why do you not show me how to do it right?" she suggested, glowering with frustration at this turn of events.

She had started to like the man once she'd realized that he wasn't Dicky's friend and had intervened simply to prevent the encounter from becoming fodder for gossips. And then her hopes had risen as she'd realized he was in need of a rich bride. However, that kiss had been so disappointing, she—

Her thoughts died on a gasp of surprise as Daniel suddenly answered her challenge, pulled her into his arms and lowered his mouth to hers. He certainly did do it differently to how she had. His lips did cover hers, but not quite so firmly. Instead, they moved over hers in a caress as light as a butterfly's wings, just brushing the surface in a sideways motion that stirred her interest. That interest only grew when he then nipped at her lower lip, drawing it between his own and suckling lightly in a way that sent little tingles through the soft flesh. His tongue came into play next, sliding out to run along her lips, and then before she quite knew what was happening, it had slipped past them, pushing its way gently yet firmly into her mouth so that her taste buds were suddenly assaulted by a wholly unfamiliar, yet not unpleasant flavor as he lashed her tongue with his own.

Daniel's hands had been still to this point, but now they suddenly began to move as well, molding her body to his as he invaded her, adding other sensations to the riot of strange feelings he was coaxing from her with his tongue.

Suzette released a little sigh of mingled relief and pleasure into his mouth, her hands creeping up around his neck of their own accord now as the most amazing feelings washed through her. She had the strangest urge to pull him closer and yet she was sure their bodies were already as close as they could possibly get. Suzette also had the strange yet irresistible urge to stretch her body, as if just awaking from a long slumber. Giving in to the temptation, she did so, moaning softly as she found that perhaps they hadn't been as close as she'd thought. The arching and stretching bore her upper body back, forcing him to curve over her to continue the kiss, but it also pressed her hips firmly against him, bringing on a new assault of sensation to join the others.

Now Suzette thought she understood about that warm and wonderful commotion she'd read about. Certainly, she was experiencing a warmth that seemed to be pooling between her legs like liquid heat and spreading outward, and it did feel wonderful as his mouth continued to slant over hers, his tongue lashing her and exploring with a delightful thoroughness.

It was the sound of voices that forced them to end the kiss. Though, truthfully, Suzette was deaf to the voices and even had she heard them would have happily ignored the sound and risked her reputation to continue kissing. However, Daniel appeared to retain more sense than her and broke the kiss to set her firmly away.

"We should return to the ball," he said gruffly, taking her arm to urge her back along the path.

Suzette went docilely at first, still too overset by their kiss to think clearly. She walked silently along, unable to resist running her tongue over her still tingling lips and thinking that those visits for procreation purposes shouldn't be a problem at all. The next thought to strike her, however, was that he hadn't actually agreed to marrying her . . . or anything else.

Frowning, she slowed, and asked, "Are you going to marry me?"

The question brought an immediate frown to his own lips and he muttered, "This is highly irregular, my lady."

"Yes it is," she agreed solemnly. "And if it is too irregular for you, please say so now so that I can move on to finding someone else tonight."

That made him halt abruptly. "Finding someone else? *Tonight?*"

"I did tell you I only had the two nights to find an acceptable and amenable husband," she pointed out quietly. "However, now that Dicky isn't dead, that might change things. He could very well prevent our attending the Hammonds' ball tomorrow night so I really need to sort it all out tonight if I can. So if you are not willing to accept my proposal, I need to approach someone else." Suzette glanced toward the lighted windows ahead and murmured, "I wonder if Danvers would forgive my eschewing our dance and—"

"I shall convince Rich—Dicky to allow you to attend the ball at the Hammonds' tomorrow night," Daniel interrupted grimly.

She glanced to him with surprise. "Do you think you could? I mean, he doesn't appear to listen to anyone, and—"

"He will listen to me," Daniel assured her firmly. "That gives you another night."

"Yes. Thank you." Suzette smiled, her shoulders

relaxing a little, and then she said, "Well, that gives me a little more time I suppose. Still, if you are not interested, then I really should go in and start looking for other prospective—"

"No."

Suzette blinked at him in surprise when he blurted the word. "No?"

"I—" Daniel frowned and glanced away and then shook his head. "Just don't— Give me a night to— This is all so sudden. I— Just wait one night before you make the offer to someone else."

Suzette hesitated, but then shook her head. "My lord, this is—"

Her words died abruptly, smothered by his mouth as he kissed her again. This time it was neither slow nor gentle. There was no butterfly caress, no sweet nipping at her lip. His mouth was firm on hers, and his tongue thrust past her lips, forcing them open with a swiftness that quite left her breathless. That breathlessness merely deepened as he pulled her into his arms.

Daniel's hands played over her body through her gown, one clasping her behind and pressing her firmly against him while the other slid up and around to clasp one breast and squeeze gently. If the first kiss had stirred a commotion of warm and wonderful feelings in her, this one brought an explosion of hot need. Suzette moaned into his mouth, her arms moving up around his neck in a stranglehold and her hips shifting restlessly against him. She had the strangest urge to climb the man like she had the trees at Madison as a child. Only there was nothing childlike in the sensations she was experiencing. Still, she wanted to wrap her legs around him as she was doing with her arms and only her gown stopped her from doing so.

They were both breathing heavily when Daniel broke this kiss, and his voice was again that strange combination of soft and rough as he insisted, "One night. Surely it is not too much to ask. This night is almost over anyway. Just give me until tomorrow."

Suzette would have agreed to almost anything at that point and nodded silently as she tugged at his neck, trying to pull him back for more kissing. Much to her disappointment, Daniel resisted her pull and gently reached around to remove her hands, saying, "We'd best go in."

She opened her mouth to protest, but paused as a tinkle of laughter drifted to her on the night air. They were just on the edge of the trees, but still in their shadow, and she could see a couple talking as they crossed the terrace toward the steps into the garden proper. Sighing, Suzette nodded and allowed him to lead her toward the terrace. She remained silent as he escorted her inside, but her thoughts were anything but. Her mind was a riot of excitement, anticipation and worry. She had found the perfect man for her needs. She merely had to wait until the next day and pray he agreed to her proposal. Suzette sincerely hoped he would. She couldn't imagine marrying anyone else after enjoying his kisses. She simply couldn't imagine Lord Willthrop or any of the others she'd met so far coaxing the heat and passion from her that Daniel had in those few short moments in the garden.

"It's good to see both you and Richard out and about. It's been too long."

Daniel mumbled a polite, but somewhat distracted response to Lord Jamieson's words. Nathaniel, Baron Jamieson had been a comrade in school, one of the group of young men who had kept company with him and Richard in those days. Daniel had been glad to spot the man among the crowd as he'd escorted Suzette back indoors, and once he'd seen her safely to Lisa's side, he'd approached him in the hopes of gaining some gossip on what had been occurring this last year while he and Richard had been absent. It had seemed a good idea to find out all he could. The more they knew, the better prepared Richard would be to make decisions on how to move forward.

Unfortunately, Daniel had barely joined and greeted Jamieson when he'd noted Lord Garrison approaching Suzette to claim her for a dance. The sight hadn't pleased him. Garrison was a bachelor who Daniel happened to know was in dire need of coin if he wished to avoid debtor's prison. He was also handsome, charming and had deflowered more naïve young girls their first year out than most of the other bounders put together. A pure hedonist, the man was known to overindulge in wine, women and gambling in copious amounts. It was what had seen him in the position he was now in.

"In fact, I haven't seen either of you for nearly a year now," Jamieson commented. "Of course, Richard was in mourning and not attending many social functions from what I understand. Word is this is the first ball he's been to since his brother's death."

Daniel grunted in the positive, his gaze following Suzette and Garrison on the dance floor and then—noting that she was peering questioningly back toward her sister— he glanced that way to see the young blonde making several hand signals he didn't understand. Lisa seemed to be telling her something, and also seemed pleased to be able to do so. Judging by Suzette's suddenly happy smile it was obvious she too was pleased. He himself was less pleased when she turned that wide beaming smile on Garrison and began to laugh and chatter with him gaily as they danced.

The little hussy was flirting with the man, Daniel thought with dismay. It seemed that while Suzette had promised not to approach anyone else with her proposal until the next day, she intended to still seek out men who would suit her purpose. While it was probably the sensible thing for her to do, it still annoyed him. Daniel had no intention of marrying her himself. However, he felt sure that Richard would be willing to pay off their father's gambling debts to spare the girl sacrificing herself on the marriage mart to do so. And if he wasn't willing, Daniel had half a mind to do it himself.

Not that he thought much of gambling away a fortune in gaming hells. Having been without for so long, Daniel had a healthy respect for money and didn't think much of people who didn't. But he suspected George, as the much loathed Dicky, had somehow brought that about. It just didn't make sense to him that a man like Lord Madison, who had lived a very respectable and sedate life in the country and never gambled would suddenly do so, possibly at the goading of George as Dicky if what Suzette had overheard could be believed. And then doing so, it was hard to believe Lord Madison would have been so irresponsible as to get himself in so deep that he had been in danger of losing everything if George, again as Dicky, hadn't stepped in to pay the debt and marry his daughter.

On top of that, once a man experienced something like that on his first outing gambling, he was usually more likely to forever after avoid such places, and yet the man had been lured there again, and this time definitely by George as Dicky. Daniel was pretty sure George had instigated both events for some reason known only to him. Though Daniel hadn't a clue why.

Whatever the case, he'd rather pay off Madison's debt himself than see Suzette marrying the first desperate bounder willing to let her pay off the debt. Daniel had no idea why. He'd only met the woman less than an hour ago, but there was just something about her that fascinated him and he found himself reluctant to see her in such a position if he could prevent it.

"Although, if the gossips are to be believed, while he hasn't attended social events, Richard hasn't spent the last year always at home either," Jamieson commented, and then asked, "Is it true he's taken to hanging about with a certain fellow who calls himself Cerberus?"

Daniel stiffened, the last word catching his ear and managing to wrench his attention from Suzette and her dance partner. Cerberus was the three-headed dog who guarded the gates to Hades in Greek mythology. "Who the devil is Cerberus?"

"Ah." Jamieson's lips curved into a satisfied smile at knowing something he didn't. "Of course, I suppose you haven't heard about him, being away from town as long as you have. How go the repairs to the old family estates, by the by?"

"Fine," Daniel said impatiently. "Now who is Cerberus?"

"The owner of a new gaming hell that opened up about a year ago," Jamieson confided. He shook his head. "It's already earned itself the shadiest of reputations and most of the ton steer clear of the place. Rumors abound that the unwary players are drugged and fleeced of as much wealth as can be gained."

Daniel's eyes narrowed. "And you say there are rumors circulating that Geo—Dicky befriended this Cerberus who runs this place?"

Jamieson nodded, but grimaced and said, "I'd heard Richard was having people call him Dicky now. Hard to believe. He always hated it when George called him that."

"Yes, and he still does," Daniel assured him.

"But you just called him that," the man pointed out with a start.

"A slip of the tongue," he assured him grimly, turning back to check on Suzette again and scowling when he saw that Garrison was holding the girl far too close in the turns. Not as close as he had held her in the gardens, but still too damned close for his liking . . . and she wasn't pushing him away either. She obviously considered Garrison a suitable backup if he said no to her proposal. The hell of it was, Garrison would probably jump at the offer to marry her if she made it. He would certainly not find the idea of bedding the woman as any kind of chore. Taking her money would be a pleasure to him, and her request to lead separate lives would probably make him the happiest damned bounder around. Hell, if Garrison had been the one in the garden with her rather than himself, the chit would probably already have been deflowered out in the garden and on her way to Gretna Green even now.

For some reason, that knowledge caused a twisting in his gut that brought a grimace to his face. Daniel could actually see her sprawled amongst the flowers in the garden, her skirts hitched up, moonlight dappling her passion-wreathed face, and Garrison pounding himself into her with happy little grunts. Hell, she would be the perfect prize to the bounder. But Garrison wouldn't treat her right. He'd quickly tire of her, dump her in the country and go off whoring and drinking and gambling away her dower until she found herself on the verge of ruin and scandal again. And then hers would be another life ruined by George's machinations.

Much to his relief the dance ended then and Garrison saw Suzette back to Lisa's side, and then stepped aside as another man, the much older and rotund Lord Alliston, approached to claim her for the next dance. Once again Suzette glanced to Lisa in question as she joined Lord Alliston on the dance floor, and was again given a series of mysterious signals, but seemed more resigned than pleased by them this time, though they appeared similar to those given for Lord Garrison. Knowing that Lord Alliston was in search of a well-heeled bride himself, Daniel guessed the signals were to indicate as much to Suzette but this time she wasn't all that pleased at the knowledge. However, he *was* pleased to see her safely in the old man's arms rather than Garrison's. While Alliston had been a roué when younger, he wasn't known to force himself on a woman and was relatively harmless now.

Daniel's gaze slid to the other couples on the dance floor then. He had noted Christiana dancing with Harburt when he'd brought Suzette back in, and had then spotted Richard standing on the sidelines watching grimly. Now the woman was in another man's arms and he suspected she was happily accepting requests to dance to avoid the man she thought was her husband. Richard was still merely watching grimly from the crowd around the dance floor. It seemed obvious he was in no state of mind to talk to people and find out anything useful. But then, Daniel supposed he wasn't likely to learn much about what George had been up to this last year. People were hardly going to gossip to him about himself. It was obviously up to Daniel to find out what he could.

"So," he said, turning his attention abruptly to Jamieson again. "Tell me everything you've heard this last year regarding Richard."

Jamieson immediately launched into the telling, happy to reveal what he'd heard and Daniel listened silently. He needed to learn all he could. He was really beginning to believe that the smartest thing Richard could do at this point was remove George's body and step back into his life as if he'd never left it. Truly, the more Daniel thought on it, the more he began to think it was the *only* way to guarantee Richard did get his name and title back. It meant remaining married to Christiana though, which didn't seem that bad a deal. She was an attractive enough woman if a little thin, and from his talk with Suzette and the things she'd said, Christiana seemed a nice enough gel. She certainly didn't deserve the scandal that would ensue if George's actions came to light, nor did Suzette and Lisa. And Richard could do worse when it came to wives. Of course, in the end it was Richard's decision . . . and he was going to find out all he could to help him make that decision.

Chapter Three

I swear he was dead, Chrissy. He was growing cold when we left tonight."

Lisa's words made Suzette glance swiftly around the entry of the Fairgrave townhouse as she pulled the door closed. It wouldn't do to be overheard by servants on the subject that had obsessed them all since leaving the Landons' ball They had left the ball earlier than intended. Christiana had suggested perhaps they should stay longer to give her a chance to consider more men, but Suzette hadn't wanted to. She was tired after the long journey to London and the day's many and varied events. Besides, the ball had no longer seemed all that exciting by that point.

While the beginning of the night had been disheartening with all the poor choices she'd been faced with as prospects, the night had seemed to pick up and become much more exciting and hopeful with Daniel's arrival. He had certainly seemed a far more pleasant prospect for a husband. She still tingled in spots when she recalled his kisses.

As if his arrival were some sort of happy harbinger, there had been a couple more pleasant prospects afterward. Lord Garrison had certainly been handsome and charming, but she still found Daniel more attractive, perhaps because of those kisses. There had been at least two more men after him who had been—if not handsome—at least passable and pleasant. Any one of the three would do as a substitute if Daniel chose not to marry her. But they would be second best and Suzette was too anxious about his eventual response to enjoy the chore of weeding out further men.

Besides, the sparkle had seemed to go out of the night after she'd spotted Dicky and Daniel leaving the ball, and Suzette had decided she'd just rather go back to the townhouse and crawl into bed. The sooner she was asleep, the sooner the next day would come with her answer from Daniel. At this time the next night she might even be on her way to Gretna Green with him.

If that wasn't the case, however, Suzette was very aware that she would have to attend the Hammonds' ball to choose her substitute husband, and while Daniel had assured her that he would talk to Dicky and convince him to let the girls attend the Hammonds' ball, she wasn't at all sure he could manage that. Not that she was particularly worried about Dicky. She planned to attend the ball whether he liked it or not and there was little he could do to stop her. He might have full control over Christiana as her husband, but he wasn't hers and she had no intention of bowing to him and his whims. But she suspected if she was forced to do that, Christiana would pay for it in some way and she didn't like the idea of that at all. Perhaps rather than simply walk out and openly going to the ball, she should sneak out to attend it.

Suzette grimaced at the necessity. Truly, Dicky would have been doing them all a favor had he stayed dead, she thought for the umpteenth time that night. It made her cast a pitying glance Christiana's way, for she was the one who would now have to continue to put up with the horrible man's critical and controlling ways, and—from what Christiana had confessed that day as they'd packed Dicky in ice—her marriage thus far had been a nightmare.

Suzette's expression turned to a frown of concern when she noted that her older sister appeared to be a little unsteady on her feet. Christiana had seemed to have a little trouble quitting the carriage when they'd arrived as well and Suzette was beginning to worry that her sister was a bit soused. It wouldn't surprise her. Christiana had accidentally downed Robert Langley's whiskey just before they'd left the ball. Not being a drinker, it was entirely possible the potent drink had gone to her head. That possibility became a certainty in Suzette's mind when Christiana said, "He must have made a deal with the devil to come back."

The words made Suzette's eyes widen incredulously. She was usually the one to make such improper statements. Christiana was more likely to hush her and warn her to be polite and smile and keep such nasty thoughts to herself. It seemed drink had loosened her tongue, however. Worried about what she might say in this state, Suzette found herself in the rare position of cautioning, "Hush, one of the servants will hear."

The words had barely left her lips when Haversham appeared at the end of the hall, hurrying toward them. He paused, however, and turned away when Christiana waved him off. She then staggered a bit to the side.

Catching her arm, Suzette eyed her with concern. "Are you all right, Chrissy? You are not at all steady on your feet."

"I'm fine," Christiana answered gaily.

"I fear those drinks Langley gave her may have affected her after all," Lisa said with concern, taking her other arm as Christiana next weaved in her direction.

"Surely two drinks wouldn't affect her this much," Suzette protested.

"Two drinks on an empty stomach might," Lisa reasoned.

"Three drinks," Christiana muttered.

"Three?" Suzette peered at her with surprise. "When did you have a third one?"

"A firsht one," Christiana corrected and paused to frown at the slur. She spoke with more care as she explained. "I drank Dicky's whiskey earlier. It's okay though, I actually feel good."

"Oh dear," Lisa said.

Suzette merely shook her head. She had no idea when Christiana had consumed the third drink, or the first one as she claimed. However, it seemed she'd had two glasses of whiskey as well as the punch. It was no wonder she was in this state, and it was sure to get worse since the last two drinks had only been downed a matter of ten or fifteen minutes ago and would still be working their way through her system.

"Well, at least she feels good, probably for the first time since marrying that odious man," Suzette said wryly, and then added, "He probably *did* make a deal with the devil to return."

" 'S what I said," Christiana pointed out. Stopping, she flopped her hand vaguely about.

Holding onto the arm attached to that hand, Suzette pursed her lips, not sure what the woman was doing. It was Lisa who sighed pitiably at Christiana's state.

"What are we going to do, Suzie? We can't let her stay married to him."

"Oh," Christiana swung toward Lisa, tugging at the arm Suzette held, but she kept a firm grip on her, afraid she would fall on her face. Christiana stopped trying to get free and simply said, "Don' worry. I'll fixsh it."

"How?" Lisa sounded as dubious as Suzette felt.

"I'll get to the *bottom* of it," Christiana announced, and then burst into a bout of inexplicable laughter.

Suzette watched her uncertainly for a moment, but then shared a worried glance with Lisa who seemed just as confused by this reaction as she was. Neither of them could find anything funny in the situation.

"Perhaps we'd best get her to bed," Lisa murmured. "She appears to be getting worse."

"Aye," Suzette said dryly and they began to urge Christiana up the stairs.

"I think they're gone."

Daniel didn't immediately react to that whisper from Richard. He was considering what he'd heard. It seemed Christiana was a little the worse for drink. He hadn't caught much more than that before the women had moved away up the hall, their voices fading. He and Richard were hiding in one of the guest rooms at the Fairgrave townhouse. Well, he, Richard and George were. Daniel sighed and shook his head at finding himself in this predicament. It was a natural progression of events that had landed him here. He'd garnered all the info he could on what George had been up to this last year as Richard "Dicky" Fairgrave, then gone to Richard with the information as well as the suggestion that the easiest way to handle the situation was for him to simply step back into his life and replace George as if he'd never left it.

Richard hadn't been as resistant to the idea as Daniel had expected once he'd pointed out that it would help him to avoid a lengthy court proceeding to prove he was the Earl of Radnor. Richard had also preferred the idea of evading the scandal revealing George's antics would have brought about, and claimed he'd rather not cast Christiana and her family into scandal and ruin over her not legal marriage. After all, she and her family were innocent victims of George just as he was and really the woman had suffered enough being married to the man this last year. Since revealing all wouldn't punish George, who was beyond punishment now, all going to the authorities at this point would have done was punish everyone else.

In fact, Richard's one protest had been about the marriage itself and the worry that he and Christiana might not suit. After all, the woman did seem to dislike the Dicky she thought she was married to.

Daniel had understood, but pointed out that some time might ease that should Richard treat her well. He'd then suggested that if he wished a little time to decide one way or another they could always remove George's body for now and keep him handy. That would give Richard at least a day or so to get to know Christiana better and decide if he could bear marriage to her. If he did decide they would do well together, they could get rid of the body. If not, they could place George back in his bed and then Richard could go to the authorities as if he had only just now returned to England.

Daniel had barely finished making the suggestion when Richard was striding out of the ballroom, determined to make his way to the townhouse to find said body and move it before the women returned from the ball and realized something was amiss. It wasn't as easy as it sounded. First of all, they could hardly walk in the front door when the dead George hadn't walked out and was thought to be ill in bed by the servants in the house. On top of that, since Richard's townhouse had burnt to the ground, George had purchased a new one, and they hadn't known the layout. They'd had to survey the house, guess at which room might be the master bedroom, and had then climbed a tree to get in the window.

It hadn't taken more than a look to establish that George was definitely dead, but they'd quickly run into the second problem when Richard had noted the scent of bitter almonds by the man's mouth. It seemed the imposter hadn't died of natural causes as the women seemed to think. Poison was the culprit. Deciding that was a worry to consider later, they'd stripped George of his clothes which had been sopping wet from the melting ice, wrapped him in a blanket and started to cart him out, which had led to more problems. The women had apparently locked the door to the hall, no doubt to prevent servants from entering to find their dead lord. Forced to take the body out through the connecting bedroom which happened to be occupied by a sleeping maid, Richard had hefted his brother's stiff body in his arms, leaving Daniel to lead the way and handle the doors.

They'd managed to make it through the room without waking the maid, and all the way to the top of the stairs before the next problem had arisen in the form of the women returning from the ball and entering the foyer below. In a panic,

Daniel and Richard had rushed back along the upper hall, and then ducked into this room to wait for the way to be clear.

"We'd best move while we have the chance," Richard said behind him. "Once they have Christiana in bed, the girls will no doubt seek their own rooms and this could be one of them."

Daniel nodded and eased the door open to check the hall. When a quick glance in both directions showed it to be empty, he pulled the door wide and stepped out of the way for Richard to lead with his burden. He then started to follow, but had barely taken a step when Richard suddenly whirled back toward him. Caught by surprise, Daniel was slow to react. Before he could, Richard cursed, and suddenly thrust George's body on him.

Pure instinct made Daniel grab at the blanket-encased corpse. He then found himself stumbling back under a push from Richard, a very stiff George caught to his chest in some sort of macabre dance as the door closed leaving him alone in the dark room. Regaining his footing, Daniel stood absolutely still in the lightless chamber, simply listening as he tried to figure out why Richard hadn't followed him into the room. He relaxed a little when he heard the other man's voice muffled through the door, saying, "Ladies. Might I convince you both to join me in my office for a drink before you retire?"

Daniel adjusted the hold he had on George, but it helped little. The man was stiff as a board and unbending. He may as well have been a life-sized statue. Shaking his head, Daniel moved closer to the door to listen to what was taking place in the hall as someone said, "No, thank you."

Daniel recognized Lisa's voice and wasn't surprised at the stiffness in it. None of the women liked Dicky and they thought Richard was him right now.

"I need to talk to you!"

Daniel stilled at the panic in Richard's voice, worried about what might have caused it. Dear God, he hoped he wasn't in Lisa's room, he thought, but the desperation in Richard's voice and the fact that he sounded closer to the door wasn't reassuring as he said, "I realize I've been a bit of an ass to your sister—"

"A bit?" That was Suzette and Daniel found himself grinning at her tone of voice. The woman gave no quarter. He liked that.

"All right, a lot of an ass," Richard said sounding pained. "The point is, my brush with death tonight has awakened me to what is important in this life, and I would dearly like to make it up to Christiana and, if possible, mend our relationship. I was hoping you could advise me on how to do that."

Daniel raised an eyebrow at the words, really quite impressed. To his mind it was a stroke of brilliance for Richard to use the whole supposedly almost dying today thing as an impetus for change. It would certainly make it easier to explain away the difference between Dicky and Richard.

"Are you sincere about this?" Lisa asked quietly.

"Of course he isn't," Suzette said with irritation. "A leopard does not change its spots."

"He changed his spots going from nice to nasty after marrying Christiana," Lisa pointed out. "Perhaps he can change again."

"That wasn't changing his spots," Suzette sounded grim. "Those spots were fake ones he'd painted on to get her to marry him so that he could get his hands on her dower. He just washed them off once he'd accomplished that and reverted to his true, nasty nature."

"I'm very wealthy, ladies," Richard said. "I had no need to marry Christiana for money."

"Then why did you marry her?" Suzette demanded.

Daniel grimaced, wondering how Richard was going to answer that one.

"I care about Christiana and her happiness," Richard said finally. Apparently the women weren't buying that, which Daniel supposed wasn't surprising considering they thought Richard was Dicky and had treated his wife horribly this last year. At least that was what Daniel presumed when Richard sighed and added, "My behavior this last year is a direct result of what happened with my brother. I—"

"Oh," Lisa interrupted. "Of course."

"Of course what?" Suzette asked suspiciously.

"Don't you see, Suzette? No doubt in his heart of hearts he has always felt guilty for surviving the fire that killed his brother."

Daniel rolled his eyes at the words. Richard had absolutely nothing to feel guilty about, and he didn't think George had possessed the capacity to feel guilt, but Lisa was not done.

"Meeting and falling in love with Chrissy must

have been a balm to his wounded soul," Lisa continued in earnest tones. "But then they married and moved here, living just up the street from the charred remains of the townhouse where his poor brother died. It must be a daily reminder of his death. His guilt would have returned and trebled, because he was no longer experiencing just the guilt of surviving while his brother didn't, but now also for finding a love and happiness his poor dead brother would never have . . . His soul tortured, his spirit wounded, he lashed out at Chrissy, the woman he loved, destroying her love and their relationship out of the guilt consuming him."

Daniel was so amazed at the dramatic drivel young Lisa had come up with from one simple comment that he almost laughed out loud. The girl might have just a bit too much of a romantic bent for her own good. She needed looking after, that one, and Daniel decided he would point out as much to Richard. If the man stayed married to Christiana, he would really have to look out for the girl.

"Is this true?" Suzette asked, sounding like a suspicious nanny. It was a tone Daniel had heard often as a child, though from his mother, not a nanny. They hadn't been able to afford a nanny. Oddly enough, he suddenly found himself imagining Suzette as that nonexistent nanny, though really the gown he pictured her in as that nanny was nothing a respectable nanny would wear and covered less than it revealed as she approached him in his mind with a naughty smile and a spanking paddle in hand.

"Spank me," he breathed on a sigh, and then muttered, "Better yet, let me spank you." A vision immediately rose in his mind of her turning and slowly pulling up her scandalously short, ankle-revealing skirt to present him with a view of her very fine bottom.

That vision died an abrupt death when Richard's voice intruded, soaked with melodrama as he said, "Guilt can lead a man to act like an ass and do the most foolish of things."

Daniel almost snorted at that. He was standing there in a dark room all but dancing with a dead man while having the most ridiculous sexual fantasies about Suzette. All this while waiting to be able to slip out of the house undiscovered. Oh yes, guilt—and many other emotions—made a man do foolish things.

"Please, Suzette. Can we not at least hear him out?" Lisa pleaded.

There was a moment of silence and then Suzette answered, her voice exasperated, "Very well, but only because Christiana is stuck with him now."

"I know it could not have been all pretense when you were courting Christiana," Lisa said happily, her voice fading as they apparently, finally, moved away from the door.

Daniel pressed his ear to the door to listen as the muffled voices grew fainter. Once he could no longer hear them, he waited another moment to be sure they hadn't just fallen briefly silent, then reached for the doorknob and eased the door open. After sticking his head out to glance both ways to be sure the hallway truly was empty, he finally started out into the hall with his burden, only to stop after one step and back into the room again as a door opened up in the hall.

Grinding his teeth together, Daniel eased the door almost closed and stood peering through the narrow crack until the maid who had been sleeping in the bedroom connected to the master bedroom appeared. Christiana's maid was his guess, and he watched impatiently as she walked by in the direction of the stairs. She moved as silently as a sylph and Daniel frowned to himself as he realized he wouldn't know when she had cleared the stairs and it was safe to exit. Sighing, he leaned his shoulder against the wall beside the door and started to count slowly to one hundred, sure it couldn't take longer than that for her to reach and descend the stairs and then make her way up the hall toward the servant's section of the house.

Daniel grew tired of the exercise by the time he reached fifty, but made himself continue to seventy-five before pulling the door open and easing his head out to peer about again. A gusty sigh of relief slipped from him when he saw the way was clear, and he hurried out into the hall, making for the stairs. He even reached them, but it was as far as he got before the sound of a door opening in the hallway below made him freeze. Adrenaline rushing through his veins, he peered over the railing in time to see Suzette appear below him. She was alone and walking at a quick clip.

Cursing under his breath, Daniel turned and hurried back up the hall wondering why the devil Richard hadn't kept the woman preoccupied longer. He almost went to a different room than

the one he'd just exited, but didn't know which
room would offer a safe haven. Daniel suspected
the room he'd been in was the one Lisa was occupying while here, but that meant Suzette's could
be any of the other rooms and with his luck that
would be whichever one he chose to duck into. In
the end, he decided to return to the original room
as the only relatively safe haven at the moment.
Once Suzette went into her own room, he would
then have to get out of Lisa's quickly though, because with his luck, she would soon follow her
sister upstairs.

Cursing George and even Richard for this ridiculous predicament, Daniel ducked into the room
he thought was Lisa's and eased the door almost
closed so he could watch to see which room Suzette went into. It simply wouldn't do if he started
to leave, needed to find a new hiding spot to avoid
Lisa and ducked into Suzette's room by accident
to escape the girl.

Daniel had the door open a bare sliver, just
enough to see the length of this end of the hall
to the top of the stairs. He found himself smiling
for absolutely no reason he could think of when
Suzette's head came into view as she mounted
the stairs. It was replaced with surprise when
her upper body came into view and he noted the
large damp patch on the front of her pale muslin
gown. But that surprise was replaced with interest as he noted the way the apparently damp cloth
was clinging to the curves of her breasts and her
belly. Dear God, it was indecent . . . in a hell of an
interesting way. The cloth had gone a little trans-

parent with the damping, so that he was sure he could see darker circles where her nipples would be. Damn . . .

Daniel was so taken with the sight that it took him a moment to note that she was coming up the hall, and heading straight for the door he was peering out of. She would walk past, he assured himself, but couldn't help noticing that the angle she was taking was pointing her straight to the door he held cracked open. Daniel stayed put for one more moment, but when she stopped at the table next to the door to pick up the candle holder resting there, and leaned up to the sconce on the wall to light the candle he realized she wasn't going to bypass the door for another after all. It wasn't Lisa's room he was in, but Suzette's.

Sure he couldn't escape before she took the step that would allow her to reach and open the door, Daniel just froze, panic turning his limbs to stone as his mind began scrabbling around trying to come up with explanations as to why he was there in her room, and more importantly, why he had a dead man over his shoulder.

Fortunately, he never had to make those explanations. Suzette was just reaching for the door-knob when Lisa hailed her from the top of the stairs. Much to his relief, Suzette's hand dropped back to her side and she turned toward her sister, and then moved to meet her as the younger girl started up the hall.

Daniel's panic eased enough then to allow him to move and he promptly whirled away from the door and started across the room toward the nearest window. Fortunately, he wasn't in complete darkness. The thin line of light coming from the door as well as the starlight coming through the open drapes of the window allowed him to make out and avoid furniture. Arriving at the window, he wasted no time in opening it, and promptly tossed George out. He felt a twinge of guilt as he heard the solid thud of the man's body hitting the ground below, but only a twinge, he was too busy trying to follow him out to experience much more than that. Daniel had managed to settle on the ledge and lift one leg out the window when the room was suddenly awash with light.

Glancing around with a start, he stared at Suzette who had stopped in the open door, one hand clutching the candle stick with its lit taper. Her mouth was agape with amazement.

"Daniel," she breathed.

"Er . . . yes . . . I . . . er . . . should explain . . ." Unfortunately, no explanations were coming to mind, so instead, he turned to glance down at George's body on the ground a story below and grimaced. The man was sprawled face down in the grass, his head and legs sticking out at odd angles and the blanket now covering his derriere and arms only.

The sound of the door closing caught his ear and he glanced back to the room to see that Suzette had closed it. She had also set down her candle on a table by the door and was now rushing toward him. Daniel immediately drew his leg back into the room and sprang to his feet. Eager to keep her from the view below, he raised his hands to stop her from approaching the window, but she bypassed them easily. Not by feinting one way or the other, but by gliding between them and into his arms. The next thing Daniel knew her mouth was on his.

Suzette had obviously learned a thing or two from their earlier kisses, he noted a bit distractedly. She didn't merely mash her mouth on his as she had the first time, but caressed his mouth with hers as he had done to her earlier. Daniel was so surprised that he simply stood there, his arms automatically closing around her. He had no sooner done that than she pulled back and whispered, "There is no need to explain. You have come to tell me yes."

"I have?" Daniel asked with surprise.

"Of course," she laughed, leaning back to allow her hands to move curiously over his chest. "Why else would you come tonight rather than wait for morning?"

That was a good question, he thought catching her hands with his and bringing their exploration to a halt. It was difficult to concentrate with her fingers playing across his chest, measuring the width and firmness. And Daniel definitely needed to concentrate now. He needed to come up with a reasonable explanation for his presence in her room that didn't include his winding up in Gretna Green getting leg shackled. He definitely needed to make it clear that he wasn't ready to marry.

"Er . . . well, actually, about that," Daniel began finally, but then frowned as his hands holding hers brushed against the front of her damp gown. She was soaked through with something, whiskey from the smell of it, and he asked, "What happened? Why are you drenched in whiskey?"

"Oh." Her smile gave way to annoyance and she glanced down at herself. Daniel followed her gaze, noting that the gown was plastered to her like a second skin, and it was definitely her nipples he was seeing through the now sheer cloth.

"Richard tried to stop me from drinking his whiskey and knocked it all over me," she muttered with disgust. "He claims he's changed and wants to make Christiana happy, but . . ." She shook her head. "I don't think he's changed at all. Chrissy says he won't let anyone drink his whiskey and he was just as selfish about it in his office a moment ago as she claimed. I don't think he's really changed one wit."

"I don't know about that," Daniel murmured, hoping to help Richard in his efforts to convince the women he'd changed so that Christiana would warm to him more quickly. Suzette might be able to influence Christiana if he could convince her that he had truly changed. "Coming as close to death as he apparently did today can make a man reevaluate his life and can be an impetus for change."

"Hmm." Suzette didn't look convinced, but just shrugged, and then smiled and said, "I don't want to discuss Dicky. I want to talk about us."

"Us?" he asked weakly.

"Yes. I'm so glad you've decided to accept my proposal and marry me, my lord," Suzette breathed and then rose up on tiptoe to kiss him again. This time she didn't just caress his mouth with hers, but then she nipped at his lower lip, another trick he'd taught her earlier that night. Damn, she was a fast learner he thought with dismay. And damned good at this kissing business for a beginner, he decided when her tongue slid out to run along his lips. It was a temptation he simply couldn't resist and Daniel allowed his mouth to open to her, his own tongue sliding out to play.

Suzette immediately sighed into his mouth and slid her arms up around his neck, her body arching into his with a rather flattering eagerness. An eagerness borne of the belief that he intended to marry her, Daniel reminded himself grimly and was about to put an end to this when he was distracted by the door opening behind her.

Stilling, he opened his eyes and then almost sighed with relief when he spotted Richard in the open door and not someone else. The other man paused at once on spying them, but then just stood there looking unsure what to do. Deciding it would be better for everyone if Suzette didn't realize they'd been discovered, Daniel waved him away. Richard hesitated another moment, but then apparently decided to trust him and backed silently out of the room, pulling the door closed again.

The moment Daniel heard the soft click indicating it was fully closed he broke their kiss and began trying to disentangle himself. "Suzette, we have to stop now. I should go. It's not proper for me to be in your room like this."

"Oh, but we have to discuss when we should do the deed, my lord," Suzette protested.

Daniel had removed her hands from around his neck and was turning toward the window when she said that, but the words stopped him cold. The term "do the deed" immediately brought to mind a variety of images that he was sure she hadn't meant. All of them included her naked and—

"It does not have to be right away this evening, but it does have to be soon. Father only has two weeks to repay the debt and I think it takes at least two days to get to Gretna Green and then only if you travel day and night. It may even be three days and nights."

Daniel sighed. Of course she wasn't talking about the deed he would prefer. She was talking about leg shackling him. He really needed to clear up this confusion about his presence meaning he intended to marry her. And then he had to get out of the house, find Richard, collect George and— The thought of George made him glance toward the window he'd tossed the man out of and Daniel's eyebrows shot up as he spotted movement on the ground below. Leaning closer to the open window, he squinted into the darkness, just able to make out Richard down below, rolling George back up in his blanket.

"What's that?"

Suzette was suddenly beside rather than behind him and he straightened at once and caught her arm to urge her away from the window, but she tugged at her arm and peered over her shoulder, craning her head to try to see.

"I thought I saw someone down there doing something, Daniel. I—" Her words died abruptly when he did the only thing he could think to do, and pulled her into his arms to kiss her.

It was a desperate attempt to distract her, and it worked. For both of them. At first he was in control, his mouth slanting over hers, his arms holding her firmly in place, his tongue sliding out to enter her mouth and sweep thoughts of what she'd glimpsed from her mind. But when Suzette released a little mewl of pleasure into his mouth and shifted her hips, her body pressing closer and rubbing against his groin, Daniel lost the thread of his plan. In the next moment, instead of a cool controlled kiss, it was a wild demanding one and his hands were moving, searching out the secret delights he was suddenly so eager to touch.

Chapter Four

Suzette gasped as Daniel cupped her behind through her gown and urged her tighter still against his growing hardness. But it was the hand that suddenly slid between them to cup her breast through the damp cloth covering it that made her moan and shudder with delight. His touch and the way he was kneading the tender flesh was sending shock waves of pleasure through her that surpassed anything she'd previously experienced. When he caught her growing nipple through the cloth and pinched lightly, she cried out into his mouth and then tore her lips from his, suddenly afraid that in her excitement she might bite his tongue.

Daniel's mouth immediately slid across her cheek to find her ear. He nibbled there briefly, and then his mouth moved downward, following the line of her throat. The entire time his hand continued to play at her breast, kneading, squeezing, pinching and stirring up such a riot of pleasure in her that she didn't think she could bear it. Suzette honest to goodness feared she was going to swoon from it all. Certainly, she was suddenly finding it hard to breathe, her chest rising and falling in rapid pants, but seeming to take in little air.

Suzette was so consumed by the combination of this worry and the pleasure he was firing to life in her, that she wasn't even aware of him backing her up until she felt the bed behind her legs.

"Daniel," she mewled as he followed the neckline of her gown with his tongue. "I can't brea—"

Her words died on a gasp as her gown suddenly loosened and began to slide off her shoulders. He had managed to undo her stays with the hand previously at her behind, and now removed his other hand from her breast to tug her damp neckline down, baring one breast. In the next moment, Daniel's mouth had swooped to cover the tight, rosy jewel he'd revealed. Suzette sucked air in through her teeth as he drew her nipple between his lips and lashed it with his tongue. She still didn't seem to be taking in the air she was inhaling, but she also no longer cared.

When his teeth grazed lightly across her nipple, Suzette couldn't bear it any longer and curled her fingers into his hair, trying to force him up to kiss her again. Much to her relief, Daniel allowed her nipple to slip from his mouth and straightened at once to reclaim her lips. If she had thought his previous kisses passionate, they were nothing next to this one. His mouth was demanding, his tongue thrusting almost violently between her lips to claim everything it touched. Suzette responded just as passionately, her mouth eager and arms locking around his neck, clasping him so tightly that the buttons of his jacket pressed almost painfully into her naked chest. The discomfort was enough to convince her that if she was to be bare from the waist up, then he should be too, and she eased her chest back enough to find the buttons of his coat. Happily, they were already undone and she promptly began to push the cloth off his shoulders.

When Daniel took over the task, shrugging off the coat and tossing it aside, she blindly undid the buttons of his vest. The moment she finished, he was shrugging out of that as well and her attention turned to his cravat. Suzette managed to undo it and slide the soft cloth from around his neck, letting it slip to the floor as his arms came around her again. She then melted into him, shivering as the coarse hairs on his chest brushed across her sensitive nipples.

Suzette only knew he'd eased her to the bed when she felt it press into her back, but it was a brief awareness before she was distracted by the pressure of his weight settling half on top of her. She felt cool air from the open window kiss her ankles and then her calves and recognized somewhere in her passion-muddled mind that he was dragging her skirt up, but didn't care. Her attention was wholly on where they were joined at the mouth and the excitement and need he was wringing from her with just his kisses. When he broke their kiss to shift his attention to her breasts again, she sighed and then moaned and shifted restlessly beneath him, her hands clasping his shoulders and her head twisting on the bed with mounting need.

Daniel had stopped dragging the skirt up now. Having pulled it up high enough that he could reach beneath it, he now skimmed his fingers up along the bare skin of her upper leg, pushing the light cloth of her gown ahead of it. The sensation caused a confusion of feelings within her. Excitement, anticipation and fear all roiled through her making her moan and squirm a bit, her hips unconsciously rotating on the bed. Suzette froze, however, the breath whooshing out of her when his hand suddenly slipped around to the inside of her leg and began to creep up her thigh, still pushing her gown higher. Those fingers were a bare inch from the core of her when Suzette suddenly snapped her thighs closed. It was an instinctual rather than intentional move, her untried body responding to the situation.

Daniel immediately stopped ministering to her breasts and raised his head to kiss her again. Oddly enough, the fears and tension claiming her miraculously began to slip away then, and after a moment Suzette allowed her legs to ease open with a little moan, but before Daniel could take advantage of what she offered, a knock at the door had them both stilling.

"Suzette?" Lisa's voice came to them through the door followed by another knock. "Suzette, I need to talk to you."

When Daniel broke their frozen kiss and lifted his head, Suzette bit her lip and turned to glance toward the door, wondering if Lisa would go away if she simply remained silent. Her answer came when the doorknob rattled as Lisa announced, "I am coming in."

"No!" Suzette squawked, sitting up abruptly as Daniel leapt off her. Much to her relief the door didn't open. Still she struggled to slip her arms back into the sleeves of her gown and pull it back on as Daniel snatched up his vest and coat and rushed to the window.

"Just a minute," she called, scrambling off the bed now to finish straightening her gown. Her worried gaze was on Daniel as he reached the window and paused to shrug on his vest and jacket. He started to climb out the window then, but suddenly hesitated, glanced back, and then pulled himself back in and rushed back to her side. His kiss was so swift it was done almost before it started. He then whispered, "Tomorrow," and turned to hurry back to the window.

"Suzette?" Lisa called impatiently.

"Just a moment," Suzette snapped and watched worriedly as Daniel climbed out onto her window ledge and then dropped out of sight.

"What are you doing?" Lisa asked.

Suzette rolled her eyes and then hurried to the door. Yanking it open, she scowled at her sister, annoyed that her arrival had brought an end to such a wonderful interlude. She growled, "I was preparing for bed. What are you doing?"

Lisa stared at her, worry creeping across her expression. "Are you all right? You are quite flush."

Suzette held her breath for one moment and then let it out with a sigh before saying more calmly, "I am fine. I just didn't wish to trouble Georgina this late at night, but had a bit of a struggle getting my stays undone by myself." Grimacing to herself over the lie, she shifted where she stood and asked, "What was so important that you just had to speak to me at once?"

"Oh, I . . ." Lisa frowned and glanced along the hall toward Christiana's room. "I just came from Chrissy's room and she was saying the oddest things. She was talking about marrying George and . . ." She shrugged helplessly. "I am just a little worried."

"She is drunk, Lisa," Suzette said patiently. "I wouldn't worry about her saying strange things. Goodness, she was going on about strawberries and seeing Dicky's bottom when we got her to her room earlier. I'm sure she will be fine in the morning."

"I suppose," Lisa said with a little sigh, and grimaced. "I am sorry I disturbed you. I shall go to bed now."

"That is probably a good idea," Suzette said solemnly.

Nodding, Lisa started to turn away and then paused and swung back to say, "Oh, I almost forgot. Dicky had to go through Chrissy's room to get to his just now. We must remember to unlock his bedroom door in the morning."

"I will," Suzette assured her. "Now go on and get some sleep. It has been a long day."

"Yes, it has," Lisa mumbled and stumbled off along the hall.

Suzette watched until she'd slid inside her room before closing her own door. Sighing, she then turned away and walked to the window. A glance outside showed an empty yard. Daniel had already slipped away. He was probably out front, walking to wherever he'd left his carriage . . . If he'd brought his carriage. Suzette had no idea how far away his own townhouse was, if he even had one. He may have walked there for all she knew.

She closed the window and turned back toward the bed, but paused as a bit of snowy white cloth caught her eye. Recognizing it at once as Daniel's cravat, Suzette rushed over to pick it up, and before she'd realized what she planned to do, was rushing out of her room. He was probably gone, of course, but she might still catch him, Suzette thought as she hurried toward the stairs.

Daniel's driver was asleep on his perch when he reached the waiting carriage. He didn't disturb the man yet, instead glancing through the window into the carriage, only to turn back to the house with a frown when he saw no one sitting inside. George's body had been missing from where it had fallen when Daniel had dropped to the ground from Suzette's window. He'd supposed Richard had moved the body to the carriage alone, and had hurried here expecting to find his friend waiting with George. Now he didn't know what to think. Where the hell was Richard and what had he done with George?

The opening of the front door drew his attention and Daniel started to relax, expecting Richard to appear with George's body. However, it wasn't Richard. Instead, Suzette stepped out. A bit of bright ivory cloth fluttered in her hand as she glanced along the road one way and then the other. Before he could decide what to do, she'd spotted him standing beside the carriage and hurried forward.

Daniel frowned and started forward to meet her, but had only taken a single step when his eye was drawn to movement in one of the front upper windows. The sight that befell him brought Daniel to an abrupt halt and had his mouth dropping open with surprise. It also answered the question of where Richard was. The man was framed in the open window of the master bedroom, naked as far as he could tell and suckling at Lady Christiana's bared breasts.

"Oh."

That startled sound from Suzette reminded him of her presence and Daniel glanced down to find that she'd reached him and had apparently followed his own gaze to the window to witness what her sister and the man they all thought was her husband were up to. She was watching the display quite wide-eyed.

Daniel looked back to the window to see that Christiana had wrapped one leg around Richard and he had lifted his head to kiss her. Even as he saw this, Richard picked the woman up by the waist and carried her away from the window. It didn't look to Daniel as if the man planned to join him again that night. However, it didn't explain what Richard had done with George's body, and he briefly debated going back into the house and interrupting the couple to find that out. It seemed to him to be a pretty important matter to resolve.

"You forgot this," Suzette said quietly, drawing his attention from these worries to see that she was holding out the cravat.

Daniel's eyes widened, however, when he also saw that Suzette had rushed out here without even stopping to do up her gown. The neckline was loose and held in place only by her hand splayed across the center of it. He had barely taken that in when the clip clop of horses' hooves drew his attention to a carriage coming up the road toward them.

Realizing that he was standing there, his jacket and vest open to reveal his bare, cravatless chest, and that she was scandalously undone as well, Daniel cursed and quickly opened the carriage door. He bundled Suzette inside and then followed as swiftly as he could, pulling the door closed with one hand even as his other tugged at the drapes at the windows to close them. He closed every last drape, determined that whoever was in the other carriage not see them, and then settled on the edge of the bench seat opposite Suzette and smiled at her wryly.

"Sorry, I just thought . . ." His explanation died as he tried to sit back on the bench and came up against something hard. Frowning, Daniel glanced over his shoulder and felt around to see what was occupying the seat with him. It was only then he noticed the blanket-covered legs hanging off the end of the bench seat next to him. At least he assumed it was George's legs, it was too narrow to be his shoulders and head. Those, presumably were what was taking up most of the bench behind him.

Alarm coursing through him, Daniel swivelled back to face Suzette. He reached for her hand and the door handle at once, intending to hustle her back out of the carriage, but then realized that the clop clop of horses' hooves had reached them and the other carriage was apparently just passing. Cursing, he pulled the door closed again and then turned sharply toward Suzette as she stood and, apparently thinking he'd grabbed her hand to draw her to him, moved to stand crouched before him.

While the carriage was dark, his own eyes had adjusted enough to make out the bulk behind him and he was very aware that Suzette might be able to as well should she look, so promptly pulled her to sit sideways in his lap, hoping to distract her.

Suzette settled there with a little sigh. Her arms then slid around his shoulders and she pressed a kiss to the corner of his mouth, whispering, "There is nothing to be sorry for, my lord. I too am eager and can't wait."

Daniel wasn't sure what she meant by that, but he was more concerned with keeping her distracted from George's presence until the other carriage had passed and moved off far enough that they could disembark without witnesses, so he did the only thing he could think to do and kissed her. Truly, that was the only reason he did it. The fact that he was still at half mast from their earlier activities in her room and that Suzette had settled her bottom directly on top of that growing appendage, and was now wiggling about a little in a quite enervating fashion . . . Well, that had nothing to do with it, Daniel assured himself as he urged her mouth open and deepened the kiss. And when she moaned into his mouth and then shifted delightfully atop him again as she twisted her upper body into him, it was for purely distraction purposes that he allowed his hands to find and cover her breasts through her now dry gown. This of course, made her moan and wiggle delightfully again.

Urged on, Daniel kneaded the soft mounds he held, thrusting his tongue into her mouth in time with each squeeze until Suzette broke their kiss to throw her head back on a long groan. She was grinding her bottom into his lap now, unintentionally rubbing herself against him, and Daniel couldn't resist releasing his hold on her breasts to drag the bodice of her still undone gown off her shoulders. Suzette removed her arms from around his shoulders to help him, and then shivered as the material fell away, baring her chest to his attentions.

Her position made it so that Daniel barely had to lower his head to lave the top curve of her breast above his fingers, but he had to duck it further to find and suck the nipple between his lips. He heard her guttural groan as he flicked it with his tongue, and he continued to do so until it tightened into a small, hard, excited pebble in his mouth. Then he grazed it with his teeth, gratified when that made her wiggle atop him again and cry out.

"Daniel," she gasped, catching his hair in her fingers and urging his head up.

He responded at once, releasing her nipple to raise his head and claim her lips. Suzette kissed him back most passionately, tangling her tongue with his and then sucking on it, her bottom moving on his lap, grinding against him some more.

Growling at the shaft of need her movement sent shooting through him, Daniel nipped at one lip and allowed a hand to find her legs. He rubbed the outside of her far leg briefly and then slid it around to press the heel of his palm between her legs through the skirt of her gown. His touch made her buck almost violently, and he growled again at another shaft of pleasure and then pressed more firmly. Daniel then tried to slip his fingers between her petals to reach her core, but the cloth hampered him. Even so it set Suzette squirming in a most delightful manner, her legs spreading until one slid off his knees, leaving her wide open to him except for the gown.

Daniel promptly began to jerk the material up, determined to get it out of the way. A little sigh of relief slid from his mouth to hers when he finally found the hem and was able to slip his hand beneath it. Suzette shivered at the unimpeded touch, and he smiled against her mouth as he skimmed his hand along the soft skin of her calf, up over her knee, and along her thigh.

He thrust his tongue into her mouth as his fingers finally reached the sweet spot he'd been seeking before Lisa had interrupted them in Suzette's room. Her reaction was most pleasing. She moaned a little wildly and then reached down to cover his hand with her own, urging him on and then went completely still as his fingers found the hot, wet center of her. When he began to run his fingers over and around the excited nub there, she began to move again, her hips shifting in time with his caress, rubbing against his erection with each shift.

"Oh Daniel," she gasped, tearing her mouth from his. "I can't— Please—"

"Shhh," he murmured gently, turning his lips to her ear and sucking the lobe into his mouth as he spread his legs a little. The shift allowed her to slide a little lower between them, making her rub more firmly against his erection as she reacted to his caresses.

"Ohhh," Suzette moaned, using the one foot she had on the floor to push into his touch.

"Yes," he encouraged, releasing her lobe and then shifting the arm at her waist to ease her back enough that he could look upon her bared breasts. It was his first real view of them and he drank them in as his fingers continued to slide over and around her slick center. She was stretched across his lap, arching, twisting and vibrating on top of him in a way that made him ache with need, and he wished like hell that he could mount her right there in the carriage. But Daniel wasn't so far gone that he would deflower an innocent that way, if at all, so he ground his teeth together and ignored that urge.

Suzette took him completely by surprise when she suddenly turned her head toward him and bit his chest. His undone vest and coat were gaping now, leaving most of his chest bare, and her teeth sank into his skin without impediment. It was the only thing she could reach and it wasn't a bad bite, just a frustrated nip as her need built. It startled a breathless laugh from him though, and then she found his nipple and nipped at that and his laughter died on surprise at the pleasure that sent through him. Daniel had been with a lot of women over the years, but not one had ever paid attention to his chest. Not that he'd ever expected them to. He hadn't realized it could be enjoyable, but it appeared it could be. Certainly, she was drawing pleasure from him with her attention, so he was disappointed when she suddenly stopped and shifted violently into his hand as she groaned.

"Daniel, I want you," she complained, squeezing his hand tightly and pressing it more firmly against the swollen flesh he was caressing.

"What do you want?" he asked, sure she would blush and shyly retreat from answering.

Instead, Suzette released his hand to pull his head down for a kiss and then whispered urgently, "I don't care if it hurts the first time. I need you. I want your maypole inside me."

"My what?" he gasped with amused amazement and pulled back to peer at her.

Suzette growled with frustration and suddenly shifted further to the edge of his knees so that she could reach between them and press her hand against his burgeoning erection. "This."

Daniel's amusement died an abrupt death at the bold touch and then he groaned and closed his eyes as she squeezed him. He wasn't aware of her fiddling with his knee breeches, but suddenly the cloth fell open and she was clasping him in her hand. His eyes popped open as she ran her hand the length of the shaft and he growled, "Where the devil did you learn that?"

"I read," she whispered and ran her hand his length again.

Daniel caught her head in his hand and held it in place as he kissed her, unable to resist doing so as she brought him to full, aching attention. Suzette kissed him eagerly back, but continued her clumsy caress, driving every honorable thought he had right out of his poor passion-soaked head. In the next moment, Daniel was shifting them, lifting and turning her so that she now sat on the edge of the bench seat and he knelt on the carriage floor before her, his erection eager to bury itself inside her heat.

"Yes," Suzette breathed, spreading her legs wider for him so that he could move between them. The moment he did, she released her hold on his erection and moved her hands to either side of the bench seat to brace herself.

Daniel kissed her again, a hot, demanding one, and then shifted his hips to rub himself against her heat. Suzette tore her mouth away on a moan, and turned her head away, her hips arching into this new caress. He almost missed her murmured complaint, "So cold."

"I'll warm you," he promised, rubbing himself against her again. He then eased back a bit to reach down and clasp himself, intending that this next time he would enter her.

"No. Not me," she muttered with a small laugh. "Your hand. The one I'm holding."

Daniel paused. She wasn't holding his hand. One of his hands was at her hip, to hold her in place and the other was about to steer his erection into her. What—?

The thought died in his head as Daniel recalled George on the bench.

"What's wrong?" Suzette asked when he froze. Some of the passion left her face, pushed aside by concern as she noted his expression through the gloom in the carriage.

Daniel hesitated and then shifted the hand at her hip to her back and used it to pull her forward and press her head to his chest. Only then did he look at first one of her hands and then the other. Sure enough, apparently all the jostling about had dislodged one of George's arms from the blanket and it was his cold hand she was holding.

"Dear God," he breathed, dismayed that he could forget even for a moment that the man was there.

"What is it?" Suzette asked, releasing the hand and trying to straighten.

Daniel held her in place for a moment, but then allowed her to raise up enough that he could kiss her. This time it really was purely an attempt to keep her distracted. He didn't wish to risk her glancing about to notice they weren't alone, but he needed to tuck himself back into his breeches. Kissing her seemed the best way to accomplish the distracting while his hands took care of the tucking. The moment he had his breeches done up, Daniel broke the kiss and scooped her up off the seat. Fortunately, Suzette instinctively wrapped her arms and legs around him as he launched himself to his feet, else he might have dropped her.

However, he didn't, though the carriage rocked under the abrupt shift of their combined weight, and Daniel was forced to pause for a moment, knees bent and Suzette caught to his chest as he crouched in the center of the carriage. It wasn't necessarily a bad thing, however, since he was unsure about what to do next. She was half naked with her gown around her waist and her skirt up around her thighs as she hugged him with both arms and legs. And he wasn't exactly properly dressed either without his cravat and both his vest and coat hanging open. They couldn't get out of the carriage like that, but they couldn't stay inside either. It was only pure good luck that Suzette hadn't yet seen the blanket-wrapped body.

"Where to, my lord?" his driver called out suddenly, apparently stirred awake by the violent movement of the carriage.

"Brilliant," Daniel muttered. The man apparently hadn't awakened to any of the earlier movements of the carriage, but chose now to rouse from his slumber. Exactly when Daniel would have preferred he remain asleep.

"Aren't you going to tell him?" Suzette asked, trying to raise her head.

"Tell him what?" Daniel asked, tightening his hold to keep her from being able to look around.

"To head for Gretna Green." Suzette's answer came muffled by his chest.

Daniel glanced down at her sharply, but the

hold he had on her allowed him to see only the top of her head.

"Is that not what you planned when you hustled me into the carriage?" she asked when he didn't immediately answer.

Daniel closed his eyes on a sigh as he recalled her happy, "There is nothing to be sorry for, my lord. I too am eager and can't wait," as she'd peppered his face with kisses. She'd thought he was rushing them off to Gretna, he realized and muttered another, "Brilliant."

"Daniel?" Suzette asked, trying to raise her head again and this time nearly managing it.

"My lord?" his driver asked at almost the same moment.

Growling under his breath, Daniel turned to the door. He risked removing the hand from her back and quickly worked the handle to open the door, he then pressed her head close to his chest again and leapt out of the carriage with her clinging to him like a monkey on a tree. By some grace of God he managed to get them out without banging either her head or legs on the way. Daniel then moved his hand from her head to her back to press her chest tightly against his to hide her bare breasts and started for the house at a quick clip.

Much to Daniel's relief the earlier carriage had passed and there didn't appear to be any others on the road. There was nothing he could do about the driver, however . . . except perhaps increase his wages to encourage him to keep his trap shut, he thought on a sigh.

"What are we doing?" Suzette asked uncertainly, lifting her head to peer around as he strode up the walk to the house.

Daniel didn't answer at once. He simply continued to walk, his jaw tight.

The door still stood open from when Suzette had come out after him earlier, and he strode inside with her and then continued on into the nearest room, a parlor. Pausing just outside the patch of light cast through the door from the candles in the hall, he set Suzette on her feet, and then quickly began to straighten her gown.

"Daniel?" she asked uncertainly, not helping him, merely standing still and peering at him with wide uncertain eyes as he slid her arms into her gown and pulled it up into place to cover her breasts.

"We aren't going to Gretna Green tonight," he said quietly.

"Why not? I thought—"

He interrupted her by asking abruptly, "What if we found another way to pay off your father's debts?"

Suzette blinked in surprise at the question and then shrugged. "Then I wouldn't marry and Tina and I would return to the country."

Daniel frowned. "Surely you wouldn't return to the country? You shall have to marry someday and should have your season. I thought all young women dream of their season."

Suzette sighed, but admitted, "I suppose I used to, but after seeing and hearing how Dicky treats Christiana, I'm not as eager to marry. If I didn't have to claim my dower to avoid this scandal, I think I'd just never marry."

"Not every man is like Dicky," Daniel argued at once.

"Even Dicky was not like Dicky before they married," she said dryly. "He seemed sweet and charming when he was wooing Chrissy. What is to say every man is not like that?"

"I would never treat a woman like Dicky has apparently treated Christiana," he assured her solemnly. "And many men wouldn't. I'm sure your father didn't treat you or your sisters and mother poorly."

"No, he was always a kind and loving man . . . except for his penchant for gambling us all into ruin every year or so this last while, he was wonderful," Suzette added dryly. "And while I am glad to hear you say you would never treat a woman as Dicky does, I'm quite sure Dicky would have said the same thing before he married Chrissy. How is a woman to know what a man is truly like before they wed?"

When Daniel merely frowned, at a loss as to how to answer that, she shook her head. "I do not understand why we are even discussing this. There is no other way to gain the money needed to pay off Father's debts. I need to marry. And you need to marry a woman with money. It doesn't seem to me we have much choice. You know that. It's why you came here tonight to tell me you had decided to accept my proposal. And I thought we were about to head for Gretna Green. Why are we now back in the house discussing these things?"

Daniel stared at her for a moment, the words on the tip of his tongue that he hadn't come tonight to say he'd decided to marry her. However, she was now eyeing him with narrow-eyed suspicion, and he had no explanation for why he *had* come here tonight other than the truth. He simply couldn't tell her that. Finally, he said, "We can't simply ride out in the middle of the night without telling anyone. We agreed that I would give you my answer tomorrow and I think we should stick to the original plan."

Daniel didn't wait to hear her arguments to that, and he was quite sure she *would* argue, so turned abruptly on his heel and hurried out of the room and straight out the front door at a quick clip. He pulled the door closed as he went, but wasn't terribly surprised to hear it open behind him before he'd got halfway down the sidewalk. However, he didn't even glance back at her call and picked up his pace, practically running the rest of the way to the carriage.

"Home," Daniel barked out to his driver as he jumped into the back of the contraption, then he pulled the door closed behind him and fell back on the empty bench seat as the carriage jerked forward. His gaze slid to the curtained windows at another shout from Suzette, but he resisted the urge to look and see if she'd stop and return to the house. He then glanced to the opposite bench seat and the blanketed bundle there. George. He still had to deal with the corpse and hadn't a clue what to do with him.

Scowling, Daniel shook his head. Even in death George was trouble. If not for him, Daniel would never have been in Suzette's room in the first place. He wouldn't have been caught there by her, dallied with the girl and then thoughtlessly left his cravat behind. She then wouldn't have chased him down to return it and certainly wouldn't have wound up nearly giving him her virginity in the back of a damned carriage.

It was all George's damned fault. It was also the dead man's fault that he was now sitting there frustrated and still hard as a dead hen. If not for his presence in the carriage, Daniel would right that moment be planted deep inside Suzette and taking them both to the heights of pleasure. But he wasn't, and was hard pressed not to give the dead man a good kick for it . . . Despite the fact that he should probably instead be thankful he had been stopped before he'd gone that irretrievable step.

Sighing at his own rather confused thoughts, Daniel leaned his head back and closed his eyes as he tried to bring some order to his mind.

He wanted Suzette. As a gentleman, he couldn't have her without marriage. And he didn't want her marrying someone else, like Garrison. But he wasn't sure he wanted to marry her himself. They'd only met that night for God's sake.

What he needed was more time to get to know her better, to see if there was more than lust between them, because while Daniel found he liked her and was charmed by her, they hadn't known each other long and the rest of his life was a long time to regret a decision. However, Daniel knew he wasn't likely to get that time. Suzette was only interested in marriage because she needed her dower to save herself and her sisters from scandal. If he or Richard paid off the father's debts and she no longer needed to marry, she would head back to the country and eschew marriage altogether thanks, *again*, to the dead man across the seat from him and his horrid treatment of Christiana.

Daniel opened his eyes to glower at George, and then sighed and shook his head. He still had to hide the body somewhere, and they had to sort out who could have killed George and why. All this on top of sorting out his rather sudden and extremely passionate feelings for Suzette Madison. Frankly, it seemed to him that in a matter of hours his life had become one big bloody, confusing mess.

Chapter Five

That is your emergency? You had my valet
roust me from a dead slumber to ask me *that*?"
Daniel asked with disbelief. His valet had awoken
him only moments ago with the news that the
Earl of Radnor was below, insisting he see him on
an urgent matter. With all that was going on, that
urgent matter could have been just about anything, most of it bad, so Daniel had thrown on his
clothes and hurried below in a panic only to find
out that the urgent matter was Richard's worry
over what he'd done with George's body. The realization was rather annoying since the man hadn't
seemed overly concerned the night before when
he'd been embracing Christiana in the master
bedroom window. Besides, after taking care of
George, Daniel had gone to bed, only to lay awake

most of the night fretting about what to do about Suzette. He'd only dropped off to sleep a couple of hours ago and was exhausted and cranky at being woken up so early.

"Well *you know who's* whereabouts is rather important to me," Richard said stiffly, and then pointed out, "And I wouldn't have had to wake you from a dead slumber to find out where he is if you hadn't left without me last night."

Daniel dropped into the nearest seat with disgust. *You know who* was George, of course. They had been calling him that since this conversation started just in case they were overheard by a servant. Scowling irritably at Richard now, he asked, "Well, what else was I to do? Sit about in my carriage while you gave *you know who's* wife a tumble."

Richard stiffened. "She is *my* wife, thank you very much."

Daniel snorted and said dryly, "My, we've changed our tune this morning, have we not? Last night you weren't at all sure you wanted to keep her."

"Yes, well, I hardly have a choice now. I've " He paused and scowled. "How the devil did you know I tumbled her?"

Daniel raised his eyebrows in disbelief. "Was it supposed to be a secret? If so, you shouldn't have done it in the front window for anyone on the street to see."

Richard's eyes widened in horrified realization and he simply stood for the longest time, until Daniel was irritated enough to prompt, "Well?"

Richard blinked as if awaking from a dream and asked, uncertainly, "Well, what?"

"Are you really planning to keep her?" Daniel asked with exasperation.

Richard sighed and moved to settle in a chair himself before confessing, "She was a virgin until last night."

Daniel blew out a silent whistle. "That was very remiss of *you know who.*"

Richard merely grunted. He looked pretty miserable, but Daniel wasn't feeling much sympathy at the moment. Aside from having had to deal with George's body on his own, he'd left the Radnor townhouse with aching balls and an erection that could have been mistaken for a pistol in his pocket. Richard on the other hand, had apparently had a jolly good time with his dead brother's not so legally married wife, or his own not quite wife depending on how you looked at it. A woman, Daniel recalled, who disliked her "husband" intensely and had been obviously soused and, according to Richard, had still been a virgin. Daniel didn't like to think that Richard had taken advantage of the woman; he wasn't the sort to do that. However, he was having trouble seeing how it had come to pass.

"So," Daniel said finally, "after a year of misery with *you know who,* whom she thought was you, she just forgave all and fell into your arms last night?"

Guilt immediately filled Richard's expression. He scrubbed at his face as if trying to wipe away the feeling, and then sighed and muttered with self-disgust. "I took advantage of an inebriated woman."

Daniel didn't know how to react to that. It just wasn't like Fairgrave to do something of the sort and he suspected there had been extenuating circumstances. Certainly, from what he'd seen, Christiana hadn't appeared to be trying to fight him off. In fact she'd been clinging to him like ivy, and if she was anything like Suzette . . . Daniel grimaced, the Madison women appeared to have strong passions. Even he had forgotten his better intentions and nearly taken Suzette . . . twice. And he didn't have any illusions on the matter. Had Lisa not interrupted them the first time, and Suzette not mentioned how cold his hand was and made him recall George's presence in the carriage the second time, Daniel *would* have taken Suzette's virginity last night, consequences be damned. He'd also probably be on the way to Gretna Green this morning.

Clearing his throat, he finally said, "Well, at least you are going to do the right thing and stand by the marriage."

"Which isn't even a legal one," Richard pointed out, and then his eyes widened. "What if she is with child from last night's tumblings? Technically, the child would be illegitimate."

Daniel grimaced at the thought, but tried to soothe him. "Well, one time isn't likely to bring about a child."

"True, but it wasn't one time," Richard muttered.

"Well even two . . ." Daniel began, but then noted his expression and instead asked, "Three?"

Richard stared back silently.

"Four?" he asked with disbelief.

Richard remained silent.

"Oh." Daniel sat back in his seat, somewhat impressed, but mostly envious as he imagined having Suzette five times or more, each time in different places and positions and . . . Giving his head a shake, he muttered, "Well, she must be very . . . er . . . inspiring. We must just hope she is not equally fertile." When Richard's shoulders slumped, he added, "Or you could marry her to ensure everything was legal."

"We are already supposed to be married. How the devil do I explain the need to marry again?" Richard asked with disgust.

Daniel opened his mouth to answer, but found he didn't have any suggestions to give. He was tired, and he hadn't even had breakfast or a cup of tea yet. How was he expected to come up with anything useful in this state? Considering sending a servant for at least some tea, he glanced to the door and noted that he'd left it open when he'd entered. Now Daniel stood and moved to it. Unfortunately, a glance out into the hall showed it empty of anyone he could send for the bracing beverage. Sighing, he closed the door and then moved back to his chair. Spotting Richard's distressed expression he realized that they really should have closed the door much earlier and grimaced.

The short walk had helped clear his thoughts somewhat though, and as Daniel reclaimed his seat he suggested, "Rather than present it as a need, perhaps you could suggest to Christiana that you *want* to do it again, as a sort of fresh start to the marriage to make up for this last very bad year. She will think you are the most romantic bugger alive, and you will be assured that any heirs are legal."

It was a rather good idea and Daniel was both surprised and pleased that he'd managed to come up with it in the state he was in. Still, that didn't prevent his being annoyed that his friend was apparently equally surprised when Richard commented, "That is actually a good idea."

"I *have* been known to have a good idea or two on occasion," he said with irritation.

When Richard merely grunted, he added blithely, "And then you could travel to Gretna Green with Suzette and I when we head off to do the deed."

"Yes, we could leave—" Richard began and then glanced at him sharply. "You and Suzette?"

Daniel concentrated on his fingernails for a moment, unwilling to meet his gaze. This was the grand plan he'd come up with while lying abed, tossing and turning last night. He wanted Suzette, but wasn't foolish enough just to take her and then possibly regret it. He needed time with her to get to know her better. If he didn't tell her today that he would marry her, Daniel had no doubt Suzette would not give him another second of her time. She'd simply return to her search for a husband and perhaps even run off to Gretna Green with Garrison or one of the other men she'd met last night.

Daniel was positive the only way to ensure he got at least some time with her was if he agreed to the marriage and then delayed it. She had two weeks, and he was hoping he could put her off for a couple of days and then head for Gretna Green at a desultory pace that would assure them several more days to get to know each other before he had to make up his mind. Of course, once at Gretna he'd have to decide for certain one way or the other. If he thought they would deal well together, his answer would be yes. If not, he would let her down easily and offer to pay the debt himself to prevent her marrying the first likely male she came across.

The only problem Daniel could see with this plan was that he would have to keep his hands to himself. From now on he would have to spend as much time with her as he could, but in the company of others to preserve his honor and her virginity. He didn't just want the woman, he already liked her, and had no desire to harm her person or reputation in any way. Daniel was not a debaucher of young innocents. Last night had been an aberration. For some reason the woman made all his better intentions fly out the window when she was close and he would have to watch out for that over the next couple of weeks.

Richard shifted impatiently in his seat and Daniel glanced to him. Realizing the man was still waiting for some sort of answer, he cleared his throat, and said, "Er . . . yes."

"You're marrying Suzette?" Richard asked slowly and carefully, apparently having trouble believing it.

"I haven't quite made up my mind," Daniel admitted, now picking imaginary lint off his trousers to avoid meeting his gaze, and then admitted on a sigh, "Though I am leaning that way."

When Richard's eyes narrowed suspiciously, Daniel knew exactly where his thoughts had gone. They'd headed directly where Richard's desires had led him last night. No doubt the man was thinking that he and Christiana had done the deed last night, so perhaps Daniel and Suzette had too. The suspicion annoyed him and he snapped, "I haven't tumbled her." To be fair, he followed up with the admission, "But it was damned close, and only *you know who's* presence prevented it in the end."

Richard appeared surprised at this revelation, not to mention a little confused, and pointed out, "*You know who* was in the carriage."

"Yes, well, so were Suzette and I at the end," Daniel admitted with disgust, recalling the moment he'd realized Suzette was clasping George's dead hand which she'd thought was his own.

"You had Suzette in the carriage with you and *you know who*?" Richard asked with dismay. "Did she know *you know who* was there?"

"Can we not think of another name for him?" Daniel asked with irritation. "This is getting annoying."

"Answer the damned question," Richard insisted.

"Well, of course she didn't know," he said finally. "Hell, I didn't know until I got in. In fact, it was my attempt to distract her from his presence that led to the 'damned close' bit." He sighed and added, "So it's ironic that it was also his presence that brought an end to it."

Richard ran an agitated hand through his hair and asked, "If you haven't bedded her, why consider marrying her? It's rather sudden, isn't it? You hardly know the chit."

Daniel stiffened at the perceived criticism, and snapped, "I know her as well as you know Christiana and you're marrying her."

"Christiana is a special woman and our situation is not a common one."

"Well, Suzette is just as special and our situation is not common either," he shot back, and then frowned as he realized what he'd said. Unfortunately, he couldn't dispute it. Suzette *was* special. Aside from the fact that he'd never encountered anyone who inspired quite the same depth of passion in him that she did, he found her unbelievably fascinating. Her tendency to just say what she felt was something not done by the majority of the ton, and after a childhood and early manhood spent living a lie to hide his family's poverty, Daniel found that blunt honesty refreshing. He also found her charming and amusing and spirited and . . .

Sighing, he explained, "She proposed to me at the ball, and then when she found me in her room, thought I had come to say yes to her proposal. Rather than explain my real purpose in being there I let her believe it because I couldn't come up with an alternate explanation for my presence. I am still trying to come up with one.

But I am also considering her proposal seriously in the meantime."

"Why the devil would she propose to you? She wants a husband in need of money who will agree to her terms," Richard pointed out.

Daniel grimaced. "Yes, well, I may have misled her as to my financial status."

Richard raised his eyebrows. "Why?"

"Because when she asked me about my income and such I assumed she was just another fortune-seeking debutante and lied. You can imagine my surprise when rather than scaring her off, my saying I had no money prompted a proposal." He shook his head and thought wryly that he had rather been hoisted with his own petard. But in his defense, it wasn't uncommon for fortune-seeking mamas and their daughters to chase him. In fact, the idea that Suzette had no interest in his hard-earned wealth made a nice change.

"So rather than just tell her that you have money—"

"I have no intention of telling her that, and you'd best not either," Daniel said grimly. "And don't even think about offering to pay off the father's gambling debts. I shall attend those myself whether I marry her or not."

Richard raised an eyebrow. "Why should I not offer to pay them off? It would remove the pressure the women are under."

Daniel felt his mouth tighten. "Suzette is not enthralled with the idea of marrying after all she's learned about Christiana's experiences this last year. She may very well bury herself in the countryside and eschew marriage altogether should she learn it isn't a necessity, and I can hardly get to know her better if she is at Madison Manor and I am at Woodrow."

"Ah," Richard murmured, and then cleared his throat and said, "Fine, I shall refrain from offering to pay . . . for now."

Daniel nearly slumped with relief. "Thank you."

Richard waved his gratitude away and changed the subject. "The good news is that since I've decided to uphold the marriage to Christiana, we can simply dispose of *you know who*. I was considering our options on the way here—"

Daniel shook his head and interrupted. "That might not be the best idea."

Richard paused and raised his eyebrows in surprise.

"I think perhaps it would be best not to dispose of him at all yet. At least not until we sort out this business of who killed him."

"Why?" Richard asked with apparent surprise, and then reasoned, "It is not as if he can be a witness in his own murder."

"No, but we cannot prove murder without a body," Daniel pointed out. "Whoever poisoned him will soon think they failed, if they don't already. They will try again."

Richard appeared upset at this suggestion, and said grimly, "Then I shall have to be careful about what I eat and drink. But I see no need to keep *you know who* around until we catch his killer. We can charge whoever it is with attempted murder when they try to kill me."

Daniel was silent for a moment. He was worried. They had enough problems without having to watch out for another murder attempt on Richard. He had been lucky in escaping the plans George had set out for him, but now there was a completely unknown person who had apparently wanted him, or George as him, dead and they had no idea who it was or why this individual wanted to kill him. It seemed to Daniel that it might be smarter to keep George around just in case they needed to prove the first murder attempt, or even the identity business. At this point they simply didn't know what was going on or what might happen. Finally, he just said, "It just seems to me to be smarter to keep you know who around until we have it all sorted out."

"Very well," Richard gave in. "Have you hidden him somewhere safe?"

Daniel grimaced at the question. "Er . . . well, actually no. I placed him in the pavilion in the back garden for the night."

"In the . . . ?" Richard stared at him blankly.

Daniel shrugged. "It was the only place I could think of. I needed somewhere cold, but covered and that was all I could come up with at the time." Besides, it had been late, he had been tired and cranky and really, where did one hide a dead man? The answer to that had been beyond him at the time. Now, he pointed out, "But he shall have to be moved before too much longer."

"Yes," Richard agreed grimly. "He definitely needs to be moved."

"I had an idea about that too."

"Do tell," Richard requested dryly.

Daniel ignored his sarcasm. "I thought it might be best to put him back in the master bedroom."

The suggestion had Richard's eyes bugging out. "*What*? You—"

"Now hear me out before you protest," Daniel insisted firmly. Really, he'd never known the man to be this excitable, but then they'd never before been in quite this position. "The girls have already seen that "Dicky" is gone and so believe you are you . . . which of course you are. They also know the bed is now in ruins thanks to the ice they packed around who they thought was you. So, we dump him back in the bed, you keep the windows open to cool the room, and then lock off the doors and keep the keys. Then you say you have ordered a bed to replace the ruined one and that no one should bother entering the room until it arrives and the chamber can be set to rights."

Daniel thought it a rather clever idea himself. Basically they would be hiding the body in plain sight. He sat back with a smile, finishing, "That way he is close at hand if we need him for proof of anything, and yet out of the way of being found."

"I suppose that could work," Richard said thoughtfully.

"It will," Daniel assured him, and then admitted, "The only real problem I see is getting him out of here and back to your townhouse in broad daylight."

Richard stiffened and lifted his head, eyebrows rising in question, so Daniel pointed out, "He has to be moved soon. One of the servants might decide to take a turn around the gardens and stumble upon him before the day is out."

"Damn," Richard breathed. He stared at him with horror for a moment and then lowered his head.

When Richard sat staring at his feet for a prolonged period, Daniel sat back to wait, sure the other man would come up with something. He himself wasn't up to the task at the moment. He was exhausted, his eyes gritty and a yawn threatening to force his jaws open. What Daniel really wanted to do was go back to bed. However now that he had recalled the problem with his choice of hiding spot for the body, he knew he wouldn't rest until it was moved. It had seemed a perfectly fine place to put the body at the time, but the moment he'd admitted where he'd put George he'd recognized the dangers in leaving it there. Daniel supposed he'd just been too tired and out of sorts last night to think of these problems.

"You don't happen to have an old rug you don't mind getting rid of?" Richard asked suddenly, and Daniel glanced his way to see that the horror that had been on his face had now been replaced with a smile. Richard obviously had an idea.

"Why, you're still abed."

Suzette shifted her eyes from the window she'd been staring at, the window Daniel had entered through the night before, and glanced to the door as Lisa entered and moved toward her.

"You're always up with the birds. Are you not feeling well this morning?" Lisa asked with concern.

Suzette grimaced and turned her gaze back to the window with a small shrug. She wasn't exactly sick, unless it was sick with worry. She had been lying here for quite a while now, simply allowing the events of the night before to replay in her head. The more she recalled them, the more concerned she was. When she'd found Daniel in her room, she'd been positive things would be all right. He had come to agree to her proposal. They'd marry, she'd pay off the gambling debts and all would be well.

The two passionate encounters they'd shared— first here in her room and then in the carriage— had only solidified her certainty in her mind. But the end of the night had left her in turmoil. Daniel had been so cold and curt at the end as he'd set her down, straightened her clothes and said they should leave things until today as agreed. After that he'd fled as if the hounds of hell were on his heels and she couldn't help fearing he'd had second thoughts, that perhaps she'd done something wrong and he'd reconsidered.

Perhaps she shouldn't have been so responsive to his kisses, Suzette thought with a frown. Perhaps he now feared she may be free with her favors. Or perhaps he was one of those men who expected women to dislike participating in such carnal delights and was disgusted by the pleasure she'd taken in his caresses and kisses. And she *had* taken pleasure in them. Suzette had never before experienced such raw and powerful need in her life. In fact, she'd never even come close. She'd never even been kissed before Daniel.

Suzette didn't know what she would do if he returned today with the news that he had decided
not to accept her proposal. She supposed she
would have to find another man to replace him,
but the problem was that she wasn't sure that was
possible. She couldn't imagine any of the other
men she'd met last night drawing such pleasure
and passion from her. The very idea of allowing
any of them to touch and caress her as Daniel had
done last night left her cold. It didn't bode well
for the future if she was married to a man who
couldn't stir her passion as Daniel had. Especially
now that she'd tasted that pleasure.

"Suzy?" Lisa asked uncertainly, settling on the
edge of her bed.

Sighing, she glanced to her and forced a smile.
"I am fine. I just felt lazy this morning."

"Oh." Lisa smiled with relief. "Well, I came to
tell you that Robert is here."

"Oh," Suzette murmured, not really caring that
Lord Langley was visiting. A family friend and
neighbor, Robert had spent a good deal of time at
Madison over the years. In truth, he had been at
Madison more than away from it and was like a
big brother to them all. An annoying big brother
who liked to tease and harass them like any true
brother did.

Shortly after Christiana had married Dicky and
moved to the Fairgrave townhouse in London
which Dicky apparently preferred to the family
seat, Robert himself had moved to town, aban-
doning them in the country for the lure of London
life. Apparently, he had kept track of Christiana

however, since it was his letters that had their father come to town where he'd wound up landing them in trouble again with his gambling.

"I thought perhaps you might want to ask him about Lord Woodrow," Lisa persisted. "I thought perhaps he could tell us if he is honorable and what he thought of him as a man."

That caught her attention and Suzette was suddenly sitting up. "That's a good idea," she announced, slipping her feet to the floor to rise. Perhaps she could learn enough to understand if she had erred horribly in her behavior last night, and how she might fix it if she had. Besides, she'd like to know more about Daniel, everything about him really. He was to be her husband after all. Well, at least she hoped he would be.

"I shall send Georgina up to you," Lisa announced, rising and heading for the door.

"Thank you," Suzette called, but didn't wait for the maid to arrive. Now eager to get below, she slipped from bed and began searching for clothes to wear. She had selected an outfit and was brushing her hair when Georgina arrived with a basin of water. Suzette smiled at the maid, and listened absently to her chatter as she quickly washed herself. She then dressed with the woman's help and stood patiently as Georgina again brushed her hair. The moment she was done, however, Suzette rushed out of the room and headed downstairs, eager to question Langley. She considered him a good judge of character and was curious to hear what he thought of Daniel.

The parlor door was closed when Suzette

stepped off the stairs. She almost stopped to look in, but then spotted Lisa in the breakfast room and headed there instead.

"Oh, that was fast." Lisa rose as Suzette entered, but then hesitated and asked reluctantly, "Did you want to break your fast before we join Christiana and Robert?"

Suzette glanced toward the food on the sideboard, but shook her head. "I shall eat something after we talk to Robert."

Lisa didn't hide her relief and Suzette wasn't surprised. While Suzette and Christiana had always looked on Robert as a brotherly figure, she suspected Lisa had developed something of a tender for the fellow the last couple of years. The girl had the tendency to watch him with calf eyes and trail him about like an adoring puppy. So far, Suzette didn't think Robert was really aware of her feelings, but then men could be incredibly obtuse at times.

"Shall we go join them in the parlor then?" Lisa hurried around the table toward her.

Suzette nodded and moved back into the hall, curious as to why the parlor door was closed. It really wasn't proper behavior for a married lady to be alone in a room with a man who was not her husband. But she knew nothing untoward would be going on in there. Now, had Lisa been alone in a closed room with Robert, Suzette might have worried the girl was attacking the man, but she didn't worry about that with Christiana. However, she wasn't terribly surprised when Lisa hurried to the door, opened it and strode right in declaring,

"There you are!" in a high trill, before finishing with a scowl. "Haversham said Langley was here. Why was the door closed?"

Suzette bit her lip with amusement as she followed Lisa inside and noted the startled expressions on Robert and Christiana's faces. It seemed obvious they'd been discussing something serious, but now appeared more surprised by Lisa's attack than anything.

It was Christiana who said soothingly, "I'm afraid I closed it without thinking when I entered." Managing a smile, their older sister added, "Come sit down. I was just about to ask Langley if there are any balls we should attend tonight."

"I thought we were attending the Hammonds' ball tonight," Suzette murmured as she and Lisa moved to take up seats on the settee with Robert. She noted the exchange of glances between Robert and Christiana and wondered what they'd been talking about before she and Lisa had arrived.

"Yes, of course," Robert said easily. "I think Christiana meant what other balls there are after it."

Suzette glanced to Christiana to see her nodding in agreement, but then turned her attention back to Robert as he began to list the coming events and balls over the next few days. Suzette waited patiently, listening with half an ear in case she needed to attend any of the events to find a replacement for Daniel, but finally interrupted him to ask, "Do you know Lord Woodrow?"

Robert paused, appearing surprised by the question. Obviously, Christiana had not revealed Suzette's plans or that she'd proposed to Daniel.

Finally, he said, "I—Well, yes, as a matter of fact I do. We were at school together. He is good friends with Richard Fairgrave."

Suzette shook her head at once. "No, he isn't. In fact he doesn't like Dicky at all."

"Really?" Robert asked with interest, and then glanced meaningfully to Christiana and said, "They used to be the best of chums in school."

Suzette hadn't a clue what the silent message was, but was too concerned with finding out what she could about Daniel to worry about it for now, and said, "What can you tell me about him?"

"His family is an old and respected one. He was the only child. His father was a second son, but Woodrow's uncle died about a year ago without issue and Daniel inherited the Woodrow estates and earldom."

"Oh Suzy, he's an earl!" Lisa squealed with excitement.

Suzette merely frowned, wondering why he hadn't mentioned as much, and what that might mean for her. Noting the way Robert was now glancing from her to Lisa curiously, she grimaced and gestured for him to continue.

Robert shrugged. "What else do you want to know?"

"What do you think of him?" she asked at once. Langley was usually a very good judge of character, though he'd rather fallen short on Dicky. But then his father had been ill at the time, and had in fact died shortly after Christiana and Dicky's wedding. Attending to his father, Robert hadn't spent much time at Madison when Dicky was courting Christiana, and when he *had* been there he'd been distracted and anxious over his father's health. Suzette suspected his father's death was the reason he had suddenly taken himself off to London. It seemed likely he'd been avoiding the family home full of such sad memories.

"What do I think of him," Robert murmured thoughtfully, his eyes slipping toward the ceiling briefly, before he glanced back and said with a small shrug, "I always liked him. He was smart, with a good sense of humor. He tended to stand up for the downtrodden, defending anyone some of the nastier fellows picked on. We do not move in the same crowds now, but I've never heard a bad word against him since that time either. He seems a fine fellow." He paused and raised his eyebrows. "Now why do you ask?"

"Because Suzette is going to marry him," Lisa announced with a grin.

Robert sat up straight, amazement on his face and Suzette scowled at Lisa and corrected, "We *may* marry. He will give me his answer today."

"*He* will give *his* answer?" Robert asked with amazement. "*You* asked *him*?"

Christiana definitely had not explained the predicament they were in then, Suzette thought and supposed she shouldn't be surprised. They had kept what their father had done quiet the first time as well. Robert was like family, and as such she didn't doubt he probably would have offered to help, but none of them would have felt comfortable with that. It would have changed the balance of their relationship, making them beholden to him, and none of them desired that. Besides, it was just plain humiliating to admit to such a horrible flaw in their father. And she had no intention of confessing it now, so said, "Why shouldn't a lady ask the man if she likes him?"

Robert appeared nonplussed by the question.

Not giving him a chance to recover, she asked, "Are his parents still alive?"

Robert hesitated, but then said, "His mother is, but his father died some years ago. That's why the title and estate went to Daniel rather than his father." He paused briefly to frown, and then added slowly, "I think I heard his mother was ill earlier this year, but I'm sure she recovered."

"Does he drink?" Suzette asked.

Robert seemed surprised, but thought briefly before saying, "I don't recall him drinking overly much when we were younger and I haven't heard that he has taken to drink since."

"What about gambling?" Suzette asked and noted the way Christiana and Lisa both stiffened and leaned forward a little. It was an important question considering what their father's gambling had got them into.

Robert shook his head with certainty. "I'm sure he doesn't. He always eschewed pastimes like that when we were younger. He said he thought anyone who threw money away on games was an idiot."

"Mistresses?" Suzette asked. It wasn't unusual for men to keep mistresses, either before or after marriage, but she found she didn't like the idea of sharing him with another woman.

"I am sure he has had them," Robert said with solemn honesty. "However, if he has, then he's been very discreet about it."

Suzette was about to ask another question when the sound of throat clearing made her pause and glance toward the parlor door. Haversham, the Fairgrave butler stood in the parlor doorway.

"Yes, Haversham?" Christiana asked at once.

"Lord Fairgrave asked that I relay the message that he has returned. He and Lord Woodrow shall be joining you here shortly, my lady."

"Daniel's here?" Suzette asked, sitting up and peering past the butler in hopes of spotting the man who had haunted her dreams last night.

"Yes, my lady. He is assisting his lordship in carrying something to the master bedroom."

"Oh." Suzette drooped a bit with disappointment, but her mind was now buzzing with worries and questions. Was he going to tell her his decision? He was supposed to. What was he helping Dicky carry upstairs? And would he take the opportunity to ask Dicky for her hand in marriage? She supposed, strictly speaking, that he should speak to her father, but Daniel was aware of the situation and probably thought it more appropriate to speak to Dicky.

"Thank you for relaying the message, Haversham."

Christiana's words distracted Suzette from her thoughts and she glanced up as Haversham said, "Of course, my lady."

"There!" Lisa said brightly as the butler turned to move away. "Dicky's going to join us. That will be nice, won't it?"

Suzette grimaced at Lisa's feigned good cheer. The young woman was peering at their older sister almost pleadingly and Suzette knew she was asking Christiana to give Dicky a chance. The young woman obviously believed his claims from the night before that he regretted his behavior and wished to make it up to Christiana. Suzette, however, was on the fence about Dicky. Despite Daniel's comments last night about a brush with death changing a man, she just had trouble believing he could change so much so quickly. Still, she supposed Chrissy was stuck with him as her husband and it would make life easier for her sister if he had experienced something of an epiphany and become a new man.

"Chrissy?" Lisa asked and Suzette glanced to Christiana as the other woman stood up.

"I should have asked Haversham to have a tea tray prepared and brought to us. I shall do it now," she announced as she hurried out of the room.

Suzette watched her go, and then simply sat there staring at the open door, waiting for Daniel to appear and put her out of her misery. Why had he suddenly announced last night that they should leave it until today as originally agreed? He'd followed her home and climbed in her bedroom window to tell her yes, for heaven's sake. At least, she'd thought he had. What if he'd really come to tell her no, but had been forestalled by her assumptions? Suzette hadn't really given him much of a chance to explain his presence, but had assumed that was why he was there and then had thrown herself at him like some loose woman.

Truly, she'd rather attacked the man when she

thought on it. She was the one who'd kissed him first in her room and then . . . well, things had got quite heated. Perhaps he hadn't wanted to tell her that he'd come to refuse her offer after indulging in such passionate moments. That would explain why he'd merely put her off in the end, Suzette realized with alarm and suddenly stood up.

"I need to change my slippers," she announced and then hurried from the room before anyone could question her. Really, it was a lame excuse, but was all she could come up with off the top of her head to escape. She simply couldn't wait any longer for Daniel's answer. The not knowing was driving her mad. Suzette intended to hunt down the man and make him tell her whether he was willing to marry her or not at once. There would be no more assumptions or delay. She simply had to know now.

Haversham had said Daniel was helping Richard carry something upstairs, so that was where she headed, hurrying up the stairs and then striding along the hall. She was just passing her room when a door up the hall opened and Daniel stepped out. Suzette paused at once, her heart suddenly racing. This time she was not going to run up and throw herself at the man. She would let him come to her and tell her what his decision was and that was that.

Chapter Six

Daniel closed the bedroom door behind him, but then paused, a little concerned about what might be taking place in the master bedroom. He and Richard had barely got the carpet-wrapped George in bed and covered him with the bed linens and blankets when Christiana had entered in search of her husband. She hadn't seemed to notice the lumpy presence in the bed destroyed by the melting ice, but she might if Richard did not get her out of there quickly, and if she saw George there would definitely be trouble. Everything would have to be explained to her and he wasn't at all sure how she would respond to finding out that Dicky really was dead, but hadn't really been Dicky at all. Not to mention the fact that Richard was the true Earl of Radnor and was a man she hadn't even met until the day before, just hours before he'd bedded her. She would probably be incredibly upset.

However, Richard had said he should leave and indicated he would handle things. Daniel supposed he would just have to hope for the best and go downstairs to wait and see what happened. There was very little else he could do at the moment. Shaking his head, he turned to start up the hall, but slowed as he spotted Suzette standing by her door in the hall facing him.

She looked beautiful to him in a gown of white muslin, her dark hair falling about her shoulders in soft waves. But her face was a little pale and there were dark smudges under her eyes that suggested she hadn't slept any better than he had last night. It made her look oddly vulnerable and delicate and as he came to a halt before her he couldn't resist reaching out to brush his fingers down her cheek.

"You look beautiful this morning," he said quietly, his gaze settling on her lips. They were slightly swollen and rosy at the moment as if she'd been biting them with worry and he had a strong urge to kiss them better, but made himself resist the urge.

"Thank you," Suzette murmured and managed a smile. She then blurted, "You look beautiful too. I mean handsome."

Daniel chuckled slightly, and let his hand slip back to his side before asking, "How did you sleep?"

"Horribly, I kept fretting," she admitted baldly,

verifying what he'd suspected, and then she just flat out asked, "Are you going to marry me?"

Daniel supposed he should be surprised at such a bold question, but he wasn't. He wouldn't expect any less from Suzette. Smiling wryly at his own thoughts, he nodded rather than actually speak the lie. The moment he did, a whoosh of air slid from Suzette. A smile crested her lips and she threw her arms around his neck and pressed those lips to his. Daniel stilled, fighting the urge to kiss her back. He wanted to, but knew where that would lead and it wouldn't lead to getting to know her better, unless one meant in the biblical sense. He was determined to get to know her in other ways, so reached up to catch her arms and withdrew them from around his neck so that he could urge her away.

"We need to talk," Daniel said gently, when Suzette stepped back to peer at him uncertainly.

"Oh," she breathed with relief. "Yes, of course."

She glanced around and then reached for the door next to them, opened it and started in.

"We need to discuss when to leave, and I should pack and—" Suzette's babbling died as she realized he wasn't following and she glanced back to where he still stood in the hall and said, "Come in, my lord. There is much to discuss."

Daniel grimaced, but shook his head. "I don't think it's a good idea for us to be alone for a bit. We seem to have difficulty behaving ourselves and—"

His words died as she moved back and caught his hand with a laugh to pull him into the room.

"I promise I shall not throw myself at you again, my lord. I realize I must have seemed very forward last night. I can only assure you I am not normally so bold with men. In fact, I have never been that bold before in my life with anyone else."

"I didn't think you had," Daniel assured her solemnly, taking several steps away to put a safe distance between them the moment she released his hand. Her lack of experience had been painfully obvious at first, though she'd learned quickly. He supposed he should be flattered that she'd responded so passionately to him, and it *was* nice to know that he wasn't the only one so affected by their closeness, however he was very aware that he was standing in her room, just feet from her bed and she was closing the damned door, leaving them alone and . . .

"I am glad you didn't assume I was free with myself," Suzette admitted, moving to a chest at the foot of the bed. "I did worry about that last night."

"No. I never assumed that," he murmured, watching as she knelt by the chest and opened it. She then leaned over to sift through the clothes inside, and Daniel found his gaze widening on her behind as it bobbed up and then waved gently about as she went through the items in the chest. Dear God, the style of today's gown was so thin that hers rode over her skin like a sheath leaving little to the imagination. She may as well have been naked, he thought as he noted the curve of her hips.

"How much should I pack, do you think?" she asked, lifting a gown out of the chest and sitting back on her haunches.

Without the view of her behind to distract him, Daniel glanced to the gown she'd lifted out of the chest and swallowed as he realized it was a night dress, a nearly diaphanous creation with little rosettes along the neckline. He could see right through it to the chest and bed and everything else on the other side of it and knew he would be able to see every inch of her skin through it were she to put it on. What the devil was an unmarried woman doing with a creation like that? he wondered with dismay.

"This was my mother's," she announced suddenly, turning to smile at him. "I have always loved it. Father had her clothes packed away and placed in the attic after she died, but I found this some years ago and took it to my room. I have never been brave enough to wear it. In fact, I'm not sure what moved me to pack it when we left for London, but I am now glad I did. I think I could find the courage to wear it with you."

Daniel swallowed, imagining her in the gown, and then out of the gown, and then on her back under him.

Suzette set the gown over the end of the bed with a pleased little sigh and then bent to search through the chest again, her behind once more bobbing before his eyes as she said, "I suppose I should take at least three or four dresses, don't you think?"

Daniel growled what might have been agreement as he watched her behind bobble about. Damn, the woman was driving him crazy.

"What is Woodrow like?" she asked suddenly, her voice coming muffled from inside the chest.

"I—It's nice, I guess. Lots of farm land and trees, a small pond for swimming. Of course the house still needs some repair," he answered, his voice and mind distracted by her behind.

"Will we live there or in the city, do you think?"

Daniel raised his eyebrows, the question actually garnering his full attention. Last night Suzette had said she wanted the right to live separate lives if she wished, but that question sounded as if she didn't wish to after all. That was encouraging, he supposed. Well, it would be if he'd decided to marry her. Clearing his throat, he said, "Woodrow mostly, though I shall have to travel to town on occasion for business."

"Oh, I'm so glad you said that!" Suzette smiled at him over her shoulder. "I grew up in the country and it's much nicer than town don't you think? The air is so sooty here, and it's so crowded and . . ." She shrugged and turned back to the chest. "I would just rather raise children in the country."

Daniel blinked slightly at the words as her behind bobbed into the air once more. Children? Of course were they to marry they would eventually have children, he realized and suddenly imagined a small Suzette with pigtails and sparkling eyes and a mischievous grin like her mother. The image was a charming one and Daniel found himself smiling.

"I should like to have a couple of boys as well as a daughter I think," Suzette said happily, speaking into the chest.

An image of two serious young boys rose in his mind, one standing protectively on each side of the mischievous girl and his gaze shifted back to Suzette as she added, "I suspect you were a handsome boy when young. I wish I could have seen you then."

Daniel tilted his head slightly, wondering if he'd imagined the wistful tone of her voice as she said that, but merely asked, "You won't mind missing town life?"

"What is there to miss?" she asked, rising up to glance over her shoulder again.

Daniel shrugged. "Balls, soirees, the theater."

Suzette laughed lightly and turned back to the chest. "I've never been to the theater, so surely won't miss that. Besides they have balls and soirees in the country, you know. Perhaps not as many as in London, and certainly not so grand, but—" She paused and glanced back to ask curiously, "Have you lived in town all your life?"

Daniel nodded which brought a frown to her face.

"Then you must be used to the rounds of social events. Will you find country life too rustic, do you think?"

"No," he said with certainty. Despite all the troubles he'd encountered with the reparations of Woodrow, Daniel had quite enjoyed his six months in the country earlier that year. He hadn't attended any local functions, but the peace and quiet and natural surroundings had been soothing after a lifetime spent in town. "Besides, we didn't attend many balls or soirees while I was growing up, and I haven't been to the theater much either."

"Why?" she asked with surprise.

"We were poor," he said simply. "My father was a second son. He inherited the townhouse in town, and held a position with the bank but had little else when he and my mother met. She, on the other hand, was the eldest daughter of very wealthy parents. They didn't think my father was good enough for her and were trying to force her into marriage with a baron whose wealth matched their own. However, she loved my father. She said she knew he was the man for her the first night they met."

"Oh, how lovely," Suzette murmured, giving up on the contents of her chest to turn and face him as he continued.

"Her parents didn't think so," Daniel said dryly. "When she went against their wishes and married my father, her family cut all contact with her."

"Oh no." Suzette frowned.

Daniel nodded, and then shrugged. "Still, Mother and Father were very happy together. Money was apparently tight but they were in love and didn't care. However, then my father fell ill and died and that is when things got really tough. Mother had to release the staff and started doing mending. She also sold furniture to augment our income. She couldn't afford clothes for balls and such, and the theater was out. We mostly stayed to ourselves to hide our lack of coin."

"But surely you visited others in town or . . ." Suzette let her voice trail away as he shook his head.

"We couldn't accept invitations out, because it

would mean extending return invitations, and no one was ever allowed in our home."

"Why?" she asked with a frown.

"Because most of the furniture was gone," he pointed out with a grin that suggested it hadn't bothered him. "It was sold off first to pay creditors and get us by. After that she sold her jewelry, one item at a time. Fortunately, most of it was quite good quality pieces she'd received from her parents while growing up, but there were a couple of lesser pieces my father had bought her as well and all of it went over the years . . . including her wedding ring and engagement ring from my father."

"No," Suzette cried with dismay.

"She sold those to pay for my schooling," Daniel admitted and couldn't keep the sadness from his voice. These last years as his return on investments had increased his wealth, Daniel had ensured his mother had anything she wanted. But the one thing he could not replace were the rings signifying his parents' love, and he knew those had been the hardest sacrifice she'd made. The engagement ring and wedding ring his father had given her had been irreplaceable. His mother had truly loved his father, and still did. His being dead these last twenty years had not made that love fade. Daniel knew without a doubt that parting with those rings had been one of the most heart-wrenching things she'd ever done.

"How sad," Suzette said softly. "It must have been hard."

"Yes, my mother had it very hard for a long

time there. She suffered horribly for her love of my father."

"It was a willing sacrifice," Suzette said quietly, and then added, "But I meant you. It must have been hard for you too."

Daniel's eyes widened, but he shook his head. "As a child I didn't understand that we were poor or lived any different than anyone else, and then I was away at school and that certainly wasn't hard. I had a warm bed, more plentiful meals than I'd ever before experienced and good friends. Richard was the best of them."

"I thought you said you were not friends with Richard," Suzette reminded him, her eyes growing narrow.

Daniel stiffened, hesitated, and then said carefully, "We were the best of friends as children. But I am certainly not friends with the man who has been the Earl of Radnor since the fire that burned down his townhouse."

Suzette relaxed a little and then sighed. "So the death of his twin really did affect him?"

Daniel hesitated again. He really didn't want to lie to Suzette about this, and had actually managed not to so far in this conversation by speaking very carefully. Finally, he said, "The fire in the townhouse and George's death both changed everything. However, now the Earl of Radnor is his old self and a man I am proud to call friend."

"Hmm," Suzette muttered, not looking fully convinced. She turned back to the chest and changed the subject, saying, "Your mother sounds an interesting woman."

"I suppose she is," he said thoughtfully. Daniel had never really considered it much, he'd just loved her as a son should love the woman who had sacrificed so much for him. But he acknowledged her traits, saying, "She's strong, smart, and charming. And she didn't allow her circumstances to make her bitter. While the loss of Father struck her hard, she said every day of sorrow since was worth those few precious years they had together."

Suzette released a little sigh into the chest. "She must have truly loved him."

"Hmm," Daniel murmured, but he was now wondering why he'd told her all that. Even Richard didn't know so much about him and his family.

"So your mother's family never forgave her?" Suzette asked suddenly, distracting him. "They didn't welcome her back on your father's death?"

"No." Daniel's mouth tightened, but he admitted, "My mother's mother apparently sent us food and money and such, whatever she could sneak out to us through her maid. However, she died while I was still in school and her husband, my grandfather," he added with disgust. "Apparently he is a bitter old bastard and has never relented."

"Perhaps he will someday," Suzette said quietly.

"I wouldn't care if he did. It's too late now," Daniel said firmly. While the man could have eased his daughter's troubles had he tried years ago, he hadn't, and now Daniel had. He didn't need or want anything from the coldhearted old fool.

Suzette heaved a sigh into the chest. "So much

sorrow and struggle. In comparison, I had an ideal childhood. While my mother died shortly after Lisa was born, I never went without, and grew up with lots of fresh air, lots of love and laughter and with my loving sisters and a doting father."

"Who has managed to work his way into a position where you are forced to marry to save your family from ruin," Daniel pointed out dryly. "For some, sorrow comes young and for others later. Life evens out in the end."

When she glanced over her shoulder in confusion, he pointed out, "I had my sorrow and struggles while young, while yours are happening now at the end of an idyllic childhood. Frankly, I'd rather have the young sorrow. I was a child, and didn't miss much. This must all be a terrible shock for you, however. I doubt you grew up imagining being forced to marry to save the family."

"No more than you probably did as a child," she said quietly.

Daniel remained silent. He wasn't being forced to marry for money, but couldn't say that. Besides, if not for Richard he would have been.

"Is it awful of me to admit I am glad?" she asked suddenly.

Daniel blinked in surprise and glanced to her. "Glad?"

"That you need an heiress and are willing to marry me," she said quietly. Suzette then turned to grimace and admitted, "I was worried you wouldn't and then I would have to find another prospective groom."

The thought didn't please Daniel and he

frowned as he recalled Garrison dancing with Suzette the night before. His mind then filled with a long line of bachelors who would have been happy to marry Suzette for her dower alone, and in his mind, each of them was leering happily at the thought of getting their hands on sweet, passionate Suzette.

"I didn't like the idea of that though," she continued on a sigh. "When you touch me, I feel . . . Well, I feel alive as I have never felt before," she admitted. "I didn't like the idea of any of the other men touching me that way."

Neither did he, Daniel thought grimly as she set a pale blue dress beside the nightgown, before digging through the chest once more. His mind was now full of those leering bachelors tossing Suzette to the bed and lunging on her one after the other. Bastards!

"And your kisses quite steal my breath," she informed him, her behind bobbing about again. "My lips tingle even now just at the thought of it." Suzette shook her head. "Although had you said no, I suppose I would have had to have let someone else kiss and touch me like that." She paused and said uncertainly, "Though perhaps I am wrong and it would have been fine. I mean, I hardly knew you when you kissed me and yet you stirred amazing passion in me. Perhaps a kiss is just a kiss and any one of the other men might have made me feel all hot and wanting too." Suzette glanced over her shoulder and asked, "Do you think that's possible?"

"No," Daniel growled deep in his throat, anger

and jealousy filling his thoughts as he imagined her with all of those men at once.

"Hmmm." She turned back to the chest. "Then I am not sure why you had such an effect on me. Perhaps it was the punch the Landons served. It was quite a bit stronger than I am used to. Perhaps it was really just that which affected me so."

Daniel stiffened, his eyes narrowing at the suggestion. She thought her response purely a result of drink? That it was the punch that had made her tingle all over? He'd see about that. She hadn't been drinking this morning, and he'd damned well make her tingle until she exploded. Suzette would never again think it was just the drink or that just any man might cause it, he determined and stood abruptly to stride toward her.

"I didn't think I'd had much of the punch, but perhaps I indulged more than I realized and—" Suzette's words ended on a gasp as she was suddenly caught by the waist and lifted off the floor. In the next moment, she was on her feet and being turned to face Daniel, and then his mouth was on hers, stirring up those tingles she'd mentioned and sending them shooting to every corner of her body.

Suzette responded at once, her hands slipping around his neck and her mouth opening eagerly. They still had much to discuss, but she was willing to wait to do so if it meant enjoying his kisses and touch again. Besides, she was beginning to find his kisses addictive, the first one making her immediately greedy for more. When Daniel sud-

denly picked her up again and carried her around
to the side of the bed, Suzette merely moaned as
his body moved against hers. He laid her on the
bed, and then started to straighten, and rather
than protest, she tightened her arms around his
neck, trying to keep him with her, but Daniel
easily freed himself and then stood upright.

Confused, Suzette watched silently at first, but
some of her confusion cleared when he quickly
shrugged out of his jacket and vest and removed
his cravat. She watched the movement and ripple
of his muscles as he set the items carefully on
a chair by the window, marveling at the sheer
beauty of his muscled chest, and then he moved
back to the side of the bed. Daniel crawled to kneel
next to her and urged her to sit up.

Suzette did so at once, glad when he kissed her
again, but it was a brief light kiss, pressed to the
corner of her mouth before his lips traveled to find
her ear. She tilted her head for him, her eyes drifting closed and then popping open again when
she felt his hands at her back. In the next moment
her gown dropped off her shoulders, and he was
urging her to remove her arms.

Once he had her upper body bared, Daniel
kissed her mouth again, this time a deeper,
more demanding kiss as he urged her back on
the bed once more. Suzette went willingly, her
arms around his neck at first and then she began
to move her hands curiously across the skin
stretched taut over his shoulders, and down his
back, before shifting them around between them
to explore his chest. He was hard and soft all at the

same time, his muscles moving under her curious fingers and she sighed into his mouth. Daniel allowed it for a moment, and then broke their kiss to allow his lips to trail down her throat, his chest moving away from her touch as he paused to nibble at her collarbone.

Suzette sighed and shifted restlessly on the bed, her fingers moving to clasp his head now that his chest was denied her. When he then moved on to worship her breasts, she moaned. An ache began between her thighs and her legs began to tremble. Suzette could only think it was a good thing she wasn't standing because she didn't think her legs would have held her up.

"Daniel," she groaned, tugging on his hair as he nipped and suckled at first one nipple and then the other. The sensations he was stirring were still too new for her to take for long and she wanted him to stop and kiss her again, but this time he ignored her silent demand and instead, his mouth continued its exploration, dropping to lick the underside of her breast before trailing kisses across her stomach.

"Oh," she gasped, giving up on his hair and grabbing for the blankets she lay on for fear she would hurt him by pulling too hard on his hair. When he reached the line of her gown where it rested at her waist, Daniel ran his tongue along the flesh just above it, setting her stomach muscles jumping. Suzette twisted her head to the side and back, clawing and tugging at the blankets. She sighed with relief when he gave up that torture and rose up. Suzette thought at first that he would return to kissing her and she desperately wanted that, but instead he shifted down by her legs and began to ease her skirts up her calves.

Suzette simply stared at him. Daniel, in turn, sat on his haunches, watching her as he skimmed the material upward. He moved it all the way to her knees and then suddenly stopped and clasped the ankle of her left leg to lift it off the bed. When he then pressed a kiss to the outside of her ankle, she swallowed and licked her suddenly dry lips, but then gasped in surprise when he suddenly lifted her ankle over his head to bring it down on the other side so that he could kiss and nibble the inside of her ankle. The action made her gown slide even further down her legs so that it now pooled high on her thighs, leaving the rest of her legs naked and barely covering her core, but Suzette bit her lip and didn't protest, merely tightening her fingers in the blankets as he began to nibble his way along her calf toward her knee.

When Daniel paused to lick the crease behind her knee, she jerked on the bed in surprise at the tingle that sent shooting through her. Suzette was almost relieved when he set that leg back on the bed, but he set it down to the side of him, leaving her laying with her legs splayed and he between them. In the next moment, he'd shifted to lie on his stomach and begun to nibble and lick at her other ankle and calf.

Suzette bit her lip harder and raised her head to peer down at him, feeling ridiculously vulnerable all of a sudden. That feeling didn't go away when this time his lips continued past her knee and burned a trail up one thigh.

"Daniel?" she breathed uncertainly.

"Shh," he breathed against her thigh and nipped lightly, before whispering, "Let me show you it wasn't the punch."

"I think I know it's not the punch alread— Oh!" Suzette cried out and clutched desperately at the blankets as he slid a hand up and pressed it against the core of her as he continued to nibble his way toward it. She didn't even notice that he was using his arm and face to urge her legs wider apart, until he suddenly withdrew his hand to press it against first one thigh as his other hand came up to press against the second. Suzette glanced down again then, startled to realize that her skirt now lay across her stomach with the bodice of the gown, leaving her completely bared to him, and then she watched in shock as he ducked his head between her spread thighs and began to do things she was sure the church wouldn't approve of.

Suzette lost the ability to speak then. Dropping back on the bed, she bucked her hips and writhed like a wild thing under the unbearable pleasure.

Daniel merely tightened his grip on her thighs, holding them firm as he licked and laved and sucked, drawing mewls and gasps, moans and groans. She began to make a high keening sound as the pleasure he was wringing from her mounted, and instinctively drew some blanket into her mouth and bit down to muffle the sound. But her hips instinctively rotated and bucked as she rode the waves he caused. When she next felt something pushing into her, Suzette spat out the blanket on a cry, her body arching and bowing on the bed as a rush of pleasure exploded through her that was so intense she felt sure she was dying.

As the shattering gave way to less extreme waves of pulsing pleasure, Daniel rose up and began to shift up beside her. Suzette hardly noticed until he bent over her and claimed her lips. She was still experiencing pulses of pleasure when his hand replaced his mouth and he continued to stroke her, his fingers dancing over her damp skin and then sliding inside her and withdrawing and then sliding into her again as he thrust his tongue into her mouth.

Suzette groaned, and clasped him tightly around the shoulders as a new pleasure began to build in her even as the old waves receded. As excited as she was, it was only moments before she was crying out and shuddering again as she was carried away on another explosion of pleasure. This time Daniel didn't continue to caress her, but slid his hand from between her legs and held her close as she rode out the waves riding over her.

It seemed a long time before the rush became a slow occasional pulse, and then Suzette opened her eyes and found him staring down at her silently, a curiously gentle expression on his face.

"It wasn't the punch," he said solemnly,

"No," she agreed.

"And you would not experience it with just any man," he assured her firmly.

Suzette smiled faintly at the combination of haughtiness and anger in his voice, and murmured, "Then I guess it is good you agreed to marry me. I should be very disappointed to spend a lifetime with a husband who did not make me burn as you do. You have ruined me for all others."

An expression she couldn't name flitted across

his face and then Daniel bent his head to kiss her again, this one sweet and slow rather than demanding and passionate. Suzette kissed him back, but that expression she'd caught now troubled her and she realized that while he had given her pleasure not once, but twice, he was still unsatisfied, his hardness pressing against her leg. It did seem unfair to her and she suddenly twisted on the bed. Daniel had laid one leg across her nearer thigh to keep her legs open as he caressed her, but now she threw her free leg over his and pressed her breasts against his chest even as she reached between them to find his hardness.

The moment she touched him, Daniel broke their kiss and growled, "No."

"But—"

"No," he said sternly. "This was for you. I'll not take your innocence."

"We are marrying. It is yours to take," Suzette pointed out, and then squeezed him insistently. "Besides, I want to feel you inside me. And I can feel that you want me."

Daniel remained completely still for a moment, and then suddenly released her and rolled away to get up.

"Daniel?"

Gritting his teeth, Daniel hurried to collect his vest and jacket and refused to turn and look at Suzette. He was holding on to his control by a very thin thread. If he turned and saw her there all tossled and sated, her gown twisted around her waist, he knew damned right well that con-

trol would snap. There would be no way to keep
from doing what his body was aching for and
bury himself deep in all that damp passion he'd
brought about.

He had been an idiot for starting this in the first
place, Daniel acknowledged as he quickly but-
toned his vest and then pulled on his jacket. It
was his damned pride that had made him decide
he had to show her it wasn't the punch, and that
not just any man could bring about this state. But
he should have known better. After all, did they
not say pride went before a fall? Like an idiot,
he'd gone through with the urge, never considering the strain it would put on him. Or maybe he
just hadn't wanted to. Maybe in his secret heart
of hearts Daniel had hoped something would
happen to break that control so he could finally
claim her and find his release. Fortunately, Suzette had brought up the bit about marrying her
and Daniel still had a sliver of conscience left. She
was his best friend's sister-in-law, or would be
once Christiana and Richard married. He was in
his best friend's home and she was a noblewoman,
not to be trifled with. Until he made up his mind
to marry her . . .

Daniel grimaced at the half-baked thought.
Who was he kidding? At this point, if it were
legally possible, he'd grab the first priest off the
street, drag him up here to marry them and then
be buried inside the woman before the door had
quite closed behind the man. Suzette was fire in
human form, her body hot and liquid in his arms,
her responses to him honest and unrestrained.

He'd had several mistresses over the years, a few of whom Daniel had thought wonderful lovers, and they *had* been. Practiced and technically impeccable, they'd milked him of passion with a skill that spoke of experience but, he now saw, little real passion.

Suzette was different, her responses were honest, her need real not feigned to jolly the exercise along, and that passion in her had called out to his own. Feeling her tremble with excitement had excited him, tasting her passion had made his own hunger stretch and roar, and just watching her find her release had nearly brought on his own. He wanted to possess that, and if it took marriage to do it, then dammit, Gretna Green here he came.

"Daniel."

He stiffened and felt his jaw drop as she suddenly stood before him, completely naked, apparently having shed the gown he'd all but removed himself. Daniel had been struggling with his cravat as he'd thought, but now she brushed his hands away and took the ends as if to manage the task for him. However, she paused and peered up at him solemnly instead.

"It is very chivalrous of you not to want to take my virginity, and I do understand and think it's honorable, but in one of the books I've read, they wrote of a way I could give you the same pleasure you gave me without you actually putting your maypole in me."

"What the devil have you been reading?" Daniel got out in a choked voice as his erection jumped eagerly in his trousers.

Suzette grinned at his expression, but then leaned up to kiss him, one hand drawing his cravat back off as she reached down with the other to caress him through his trousers. Groaning, he started to kiss her back, but then stilled as the sound of men's voices came muffled through the door. Breaking their kiss, he urged her away to a safe distance and held her there with his hands on her upper arms as he turned to peer toward the door with alarm. It sounded like Richard and Langley in the hall, headed in the direction of the master bedroom. He frowned briefly, wondering what the devil Richard was doing, and then shook his head as he wondered what the devil he himself was doing. Really he had to start thinking with something other than his manhood. Though he suspected that wasn't likely to happen until he'd sated the damned thing.

Grimacing, he turned back to Suzette and sighed with defeat. She was impossible to resist and he had been fooling himself to think that he could spend time getting to know her before satisfying his desire for her. Truly, she was like a house on fire in the midst of a hurricane, sucking him into her winds and burning him up all at once. All his good intentions and sensible decisions were nothing against the temptation she presented.

"Get dressed," he said firmly, turning her away and urging her toward the bed and the discarded dress lying there. "We will head to Gretna Green as soon as we can."

"But—" Suzette tried to turn back, her gaze on the bulge in his trousers, but he turned her firmly away again.

"I shall survive until we are wed," he assured her dryly, though that was debatable. The woman was driving him insane, Daniel acknowledged and then glanced down at himself with disgust and moved to the window. Opening it, he leaned out briefly to inhale several deep breaths meant to calm himself before joining the others, but truly a basin of cold water poured on his groin would have been more useful. Sighing, he closed the window and turned back to find Suzette back in her dress and struggling to do it up. Leaving the window, Daniel moved to help her, quickly doing up her stays.

"You'd best brush your hair," he murmured as he finished. "I shall be downstairs when you are presentable."

Leaving her then, Daniel turned and crossed the room. He slid out into the hall with more haste than thought and was pulling the door closed before checking to see if the corridor was empty. It wasn't. Richard was presently locking the master bedroom door, and while there was no sign of Christiana, Langley was with him. Daniel suspected this meant that both Christiana and Robert Langley now knew the particulars of what was going on. That was a relief of a sort. A secret like that was almost impossible to keep and they now had allies to aid in keeping it.

"I think perhaps you're right," Richard commented as he finished locking the door and straightened. "I will talk to Daniel and see if he can come up with any faults in the plan."

Straightening his shoulders, Daniel started toward them, asking, "Faults in what plan?"

Both men turned his way.

"Where did you come from, Woodrow?" Langley asked abruptly, his eyes narrowing suspiciously and moving to the door to Suzette's room.

"Oh . . . I . . . er . . ." Daniel waved back along the hall, but came to an abrupt halt as he heard a door open behind him.

"Daniel! Daniel, you forgot your cravat."

He turned sharply at that loud whisper to see Suzette hurrying for the stairs, apparently thinking he'd headed straight below.

Daniel rolled his eyes with a sigh, and then said sharply, "Suzette!"

She came to a shuddering halt, and glanced back, eyes widening as she spotted him, Richard and Langley in the hall.

"Oh." She turned slowly to face them and waved back toward the stairs, but then quickly jerked her hand behind her back as she noted the cravat waving about. "I was just going downstairs."

Richard made a sound that was half cough and half laugh behind him which drew an immediate scowl from Suzette. She then heaved an exasperated sigh, stomped the small distance to Daniel, shoved the cravat at him, and simply whirled away to march silently off up the hall.

Daniel quickly tied his cravat in its intricate knot around his neck, but his gaze was on Suzette as she went and a smile was trying to claim his lips. Any other woman would have been mortified at what had just happened. She however was annoyed and even exasperated. There was nothing usual about Suzette Madison. If nothing else, she would certainly keep him entertained the rest of his days, and not just in the bedchamber. Somewhat reassured by that thought, Daniel turned back to Richard and Langley as he finished with his cravat, and then grimaced when he saw Langley's glowering look.

"We are getting married," he announced at once to forestall any outraged accusations the man might be nurturing at that moment.

"You've decided for certain, have you?" Richard sounded amused.

"I am not sure that is the correct phrasing for it," Daniel admitted with a wry smile. "It would be more fitting to say I have bowed to the inevitable. The woman is a force of nature."

"That she is," Langley agreed, appearing to relax. "So, when is the trip to Gretna Green to occur? I should like to accompany you."

"The sooner the better," Daniel decided grimly. "If Suzette jumps out and drags me into one more room, I cannot guarantee she will reach Gretna as pure as she is now, and she is already less pure today than she was yesterday."

Chapter Seven

"hey're going to be very, very angry."

Daniel noted the way Richard grimaced at Robert's prediction, but held his own tongue. He was pretty sure Langley was right and the women would be angry at their defection, but then he wasn't too pleased about it himself at the moment.

It was nearly midnight the day after he'd encountered Langley and Richard in the hall. As he'd suspected, Christiana and Robert Langley now knew about George and all he'd done. Taking everything into account, the men had decided to head to Gretna Green at once and had immediately joined the women in the parlor to make the announcement. The suggestion had been met with horror and the assurance that "they couldn't possibly!" What the men hadn't considered was that the women would want to look nice for their weddings. They'd insisted they needed the rest of the day to pack and that they couldn't possibly go without their maids.

Rather than the swift journey in one carriage that the men had planned on, they had ended leaving the next morning, that morning in fact, with three carriages to carry the six of them, as well as the girls' maids and several chests. Three of the chests contained dresses, one held clothes for all three men, and one held George's body.

With such a large party, they had started the journey at a desultory pace, planning on stopping for meals and to take rooms at night to sleep. It would have ensured probably four days of travel to get to Gretna Green. Daniel hadn't minded that so much. While he'd basically decided to marry Suzette, he'd still welcomed the opportunity to get to know her a little better beforehand. However, he'd quickly learned he wouldn't get that opportunity. During this first morning of the journey, Christiana and Richard had ridden in the lead Radnor carriage while Daniel and Suzette had ridden in the Woodrow carriage behind it with Lisa and Langley as chaperones. Langley's carriage had followed at the rear of the small caravan, holding the maids.

However, Daniel's hopes of getting to know Suzette better hadn't come to fruition that morning. Langley had been decidedly quiet during that portion of the ride, giving grunts and one-syllable answers to Lisa's efforts to speak to him, so she'd turned to speak to Suzette instead, and

Daniel had been left mostly to listen to their chatter. He supposed he'd learned a little more about her through the conversation he'd witnessed, but it wasn't the same as actually talking to her himself as they'd done in her room. Daniel would have liked to have asked questions about her childhood and got her talking about it. He had revealed what he felt was a great deal of his own experiences growing up and now wanted to hear hers, but that hadn't happened. Instead, when they'd returned to the carriages after a stop for lunch at Stevanage, the girls had decided to ride with Christiana in the first carriage, leaving Richard to join the men in the second one.

The difference in the afternoon ride had been very notable. Where the carriage had been filled with a light and chatty atmosphere during the morning's ride with the girls, it had been much more solemn and grim with just the three men. They had mostly discussed George's murder and who might be behind it. Since they were coming to the situation mostly blind, having no idea who George had been dealing with or what he'd been doing this last year, they hadn't really got far on the subject and had finally fallen silent.

Daniel couldn't help thinking that Christiana might have been able to help more with the matter. Now that she knew everything, she seemed the best prospect for being able to tell them who he had chummed around with this last year and so on. However, she hadn't been there to question.

Daniel had been relieved to arrive at Radnor as evening fell. It had been a short-lived relief.

They'd disembarked to find the women all aflutter. It seemed during the second half of the journey Lisa had recalled a letter a street urchin had given her that morning to pass on to "The Earl." It had happened during all the fuss and bother of loading the carriages, and she'd unfortunately forgotten the letter until they were almost to Radnor, where they planned to leave George in the family vault. Christiana, suspecting it was for George and not Richard, had immediately opened the letter to find it actually was for Richard. Someone knew George was dead and suspected Richard had killed him to reclaim his name and title. The individual was demanding a rather large sum of money to keep their silence. Now, they not only had to find out who had murdered George, but also had to contend with a blackmailer. Things just seemed to be spiraling out of control.

The one good thing about the letter was that it had forced Christiana to explain all to her sisters and they would no longer be hampered by the need to hide facts or the presence of the dead body from Lisa and Suzette. However, that was somewhat tempered for Daniel by Suzette's annoyance with him. She was upset that he hadn't told her about it himself at some point. She felt sure husbands and wives shouldn't keep secrets like that from each other. Daniel hadn't pointed out that they weren't yet married, but had simply said it wasn't his secret to tell. Suzette hadn't seemed much mollified by the answer.

The discovery of the letter meant that the trip to Gretna Green had to be put off so that they could return to town at once to deal with the blackmailer. However, they had taken the time to set the chest holding George in the family vault first, and then had been held up when they were discovered by the Radnor minister. If not for the man's catching them in the vault, all three carriages would now be on the way back to town. However, that discovery had led to explanations and then the minister offering to marry Richard and Christiana at once. After all, the man had pointed out, the banns had been read and the license procured a year earlier. The only reason the marriage was invalid was because Richard hadn't attended the ceremony and signed the wedding register himself. Were the minister to marry them, and did Richard and Christiana sign the register before witnesses, the marriage would be legal and unbreakable. So they'd had the ceremony and then Richard had suggested the women go above stairs and refresh themselves while a quick wedding feast was prepared. They would dine with the minister and then return to town, he'd said as he sent the women off.

However, the moment the sisters were safely upstairs, Richard had taken the minister aside for a word and then begun hustling Daniel and Langley out of the house. He had decided they could travel faster without the women and would prefer to leave them safely here at Radnor rather than drag them back to town. The men could handle the blackmailer and then afterward return to collect the women and continue on to Gretna Green so that Daniel and Suzette could marry.

Daniel had not been pleased. He knew Suzette would be furious, but he was also rather annoyed himself. There was no way to get to know her better if they weren't even together. However, Richard had insisted on it. He'd argued that it was safer and he didn't wish the women involved with dealing with the blackmailer. He'd also pointed out that it was ridiculous to drag the maids and chests and all three carriages back to town when they would just be returning in a day or two to continue on to Gretna Green. Whether he liked it or not, Daniel had seen the sense in both arguments, so had finally capitulated. While the women were above stairs, the three men had snuck out of Radnor like thieves and ridden off in Daniel's carriage.

As annoyed as he was at having to leave Suzette behind, Daniel had to admit it was safer. They were also traveling much more swiftly with just the three of them and one carriage. They had stopped three times to change the horses, and it wasn't yet midnight, but he thought they were probably already about three quarters of the way back to London.

"They will get over their anger," he said now, hoping that was true.

"Trust me," Langley said dryly. "I have known the Madison sisters all my life. You will not get off easily for this. Either of you," he added, and then glanced to Richard and said, "I was glad to see . . ."

Daniel didn't hear the rest of what he said, his gaze had slid out the window to the moonlit sky as he wondered what Suzette was doing. He imagined she was still fuming over his defection. He supposed he would have some fence-mending to do when they returned to Radnor to collect the women. He would purchase a gift for her while in town, Daniel decided, and then brightened at the thought as he decided on an engagement ring and wedding band. He hadn't considered the need for either item before this and he was trying to decide if she would prefer something simple like a solitaire or a more elaborate multi-jeweled ring when his thoughts were interrupted by a loud crack and the carriage suddenly pitching to the side.

Daniel grabbed instinctively for something to hold on to as the night filled with sudden shouts and whinnies, but he was too slow and found himself tumbling about inside the carriage. He crashed into one wall, then another, all the while taking blows from the various body parts of his companions as the three of them banged about inside the vehicle. The carriage seemed to roll several times before it came to a stop, and then everything was suddenly still.

Silence was a heavy cloak inside the carriage until Daniel found the breath to groan. He had come to rest on his back on a relatively flat surface except for something that was poking him in the lower back. It was damned uncomfortable, but not nearly as discomfiting as the fact that he couldn't breathe. Something heavy had landed on top of him and was squeezing the breath right out of him. Probably one of the men, he thought a little faintly, or both of them, he corrected as the weight on top of him began to shift, stealing even more of his ability to breathe.

"Lord Woodrow?"

The darkness enveloping them suddenly gave way to blinding light as the carriage door opened above and his driver leaned in with a lit lantern to peer about. The light showed Daniel that it was indeed both Richard and Langley on top of him, but now Robert scrabbled to remove himself, making Richard grunt on top of Daniel as the other man sat up and then reached for the opening and pulled himself out.

"Damn, Richard, get off me, I can't breathe," Daniel gasped the moment he could get more air into his lungs, but Richard was already moving and muttering apologies as he inadvertently kneed and elbowed him during his efforts. Richard didn't immediately follow Robert out of the carriage, however, instead shifting his weight to the side to kneel beside Daniel as he asked, "Are you all right?"

"Battered and bruised, but otherwise fine I think," Daniel decided as he sat up. "You?"

"The same," Richard said and glanced up.

Daniel followed his gaze to the opening and the still waiting driver. Robert was now also peering back in at them, but Daniel's eyes sought out his driver.

"What happened?" he asked as he stood up.

"I'm not sure, my lord," the driver admitted, sounding unhappy. He and Robert both shifted back to get out of the way as Daniel began to pull himself out through the open carriage door, before he continued, "We were riding along fine and then I heard a crack, and the carriage pitched and began to roll. Fortunately, the carriage body snapped just behind the boot and the horses weren't dragged with it or they would have died for certain."

Moving out of the way on the side of the carriage as Richard began to follow him, Daniel glanced over his driver with concern and asked, "And you weren't hurt?"

"I was tossed, but landed on a bush. I'm all right," the man assured him, but then added with disgust, "But the coach is a wreck. I don't think it can even be fixed."

"As long as everyone is all right," Daniel said and glanced to Robert Langley in question.

"Fine," the other man assured him, easing to the edge of the carriage to leap down. "I got an elbow in the face during one of the rolls and will probably have a black eye, but otherwise seem fine."

Daniel grunted at this news and moved to inspect the two wheels on the upraised side of the carriage. Richard joined him as he inspected first the front and then back upraised wheel. Both appeared fine, so Daniel jumped to the ground and moved next to inspect the wheels presently lying flat on the ground. He frowned when he found the broken wheel and took note of the break of the spokes. Eyeing them suspiciously, he commented, "That's a rather straight break."

Richard was at his side at once. "You think they were cut?"

"Those three spokes certainly look like they

could have been," Daniel pointed out a trio of spokes next to each other where the breaks looked as straight as a cut. "The rest are more splintered and natural-looking breaks. They probably snapped under the pressure when those three gave way."

Richard frowned and glanced around as they both straightened. "I agree. The question is who did it and why? And when?"

"The why is easy," Daniel pointed out. "As far as George's killer knows, the poison didn't work. As for when . . ." He peered back at the broken wheel. "It couldn't have been done in town. There were four of us in the carriage this morning on the way to Radnor and the wheel would have given out then under that kind of weight had it been cut before we left London. Besides, you weren't even in my carriage on the way out of town."

"So it was done at Radnor or one of the three stops since we left," Richard reasoned.

Daniel nodded. Obviously George's killer thought he'd failed and was making renewed efforts to rid the world of the man. A bit callous of the fellow to make the attempt in such a way that he and Langley could have died with Richard, Daniel thought dryly. He glanced to Richard to note that he was peering about again as if expecting the culprit to leap out at them and couldn't blame him. If the spokes had been cut at Radnor or at one of the stops since then, it meant they'd been followed from town. The culprit may actually still be trailing them.

"Is that a carriage I hear?" Richard asked suddenly.

Daniel raised an eyebrow and listened for a moment, becoming aware of a faint sound that was definitely that of a distant but approaching carriage. "Yes, and it's moving quickly. We'd best get off the road."

Richard nodded and started to move. Daniel followed, calling out a warning to his driver as he went. The driver immediately urged the horses he'd been inspecting onto the grassy verge and then moved back to the edge of the road with his lantern and lifted it in the air to swing it back and forth to get the attention of the approaching vehicle.

"A coach and six," Langley said as a vehicle careened into view on the moonlit lane.

Daniel nodded, relieved when the oncoming coachmen spotted his driver and swerved to miss the man. The carriage didn't slow, however, but continued past at high speed.

"Wasn't that—?" Langley began.

Daniel heard Richard's grim, "Yes" to the unfinished question, but hadn't needed it. He too had recognized the three faces pressed to the window as the coach had sailed past. He shook his head as the Radnor carriage rode out of sight around the next bend. It had been Suzette, Christiana, and Lisa, all gaping out the window at them.

"I did tell you they would not take our leaving sitting down," Langley pointed out, sounding amused.

"You didn't say they would follow," Daniel said dryly.

Langley laughed and shrugged. "Why spoil the surprise?"

Daniel was shaking his head at the words when he became aware of the sound of another approaching carriage, this time coming from the direction the Radnor carriage had gone. It was no great surprise to see the Radnor coach now returning at a much more sedate pace.

"Time to face the music," Langley said dryly, heading for the door when it didn't immediately open to allow the women to spill out.

Daniel merely grunted. He suspected it wasn't a good sign that the women were staying quietly inside the carriage, and not coming out to see that they were all right. Sighing, he turned his attention to his driver and ordered him to tie the leads of their horses to the back of the Radnor carriage and then join the driver on the front. He supposed they'd have to stop at the next inn to leave the horses and his driver. The man would have to arrange for someone to collect the broken carriage and see if it could be fixed before following them back to town.

"Hello, ladies."

Daniel glanced back to the carriage at that cheerful greeting from Langley and was in time to see the other man disappear inside the vehicle to a chorus of polite hellos. Silence fell immediately after those were said, however, and Daniel watched as Richard now approached the open door. The man glanced in, sighed at whatever he saw, and offered a more subdued "Hello, ladies," as he entered as well.

One eyebrow rose on Daniel's forehead at the lack of response this time. Grimacing, he supposed he too would be met with less than pleasure at this point. No doubt Suzette and Christiana would hold him and Richard accountable for dumping them at Radnor. It appeared they weren't holding Robert accountable, however. Shrugging, Daniel decided to get it over with and offered a "hello, ladies" of his own as he reached the door. He wasn't terribly surprised to be met with silence, so merely took a moment to see that Robert, and Richard were on one bench seat with an angry-looking Christiana squeezed between them, leaving a sour-faced Lisa and Suzette on the other. He then got in to settle between the two women.

The carriage started off at once, jolting them about, and Daniel grunted as he got an uninten-tional elbow in the stomach from Suzette. She murmured an apology and he nodded, but then, noting that Richard had lifted a protesting Christi-ana onto his lap to make more room on the oppo-site bench, decided it was a good idea and caught Suzette by the waist to lift her onto his own lap. He had half expected Suzette to argue the move like her sister, so was pleasantly surprised when she settled comfortably there, simply shifting so that she sat sideways and could place one arm along his shoulders.

At least it was a pleasant surprise at first, until he found himself staring at her cleavage, which was right in front of his face now. It immedi-ately recalled him to the last occasion on which they'd been in this position and how he'd bared her breasts and made free with them, licking and suckling and—

A pinch on his earlobe recalled Daniel to where he was and the fact that his face had apparently been swooping toward Suzette's cleavage. At least, he suddenly found himself just inches from the sweet curves of the tops of her breasts. Made aware of it, Daniel straightened at once and glanced around to see if his near slip had been noticed, but everyone else appeared to have their attention on Christiana and Richard as she reprimanded him for leaving the women behind at Radnor . . . Everyone but Suzette, that was, Daniel realized, as he noted the completely evil smile on her face as she watched him and then gave her behind a little wiggle in his lap. It occurred to him then that this was the reason she had not fought his taking her on his lap. Suzette had realized how it would affect him and was using it as punishment for his own part in the defection.

"Little minx," he whispered.

Smile widening, Suzette shifted and wiggled about on top of him again, inadvertently leaning her breasts briefly closer to his face as she appeared to try to find a more comfortable position. He suspected the action was more to torture him than out of any true desire to get more comfortable and was proven correct when she murmured, "This reminds me of the first time we were alone in a carriage together, my lord."

Daniel closed his eyes against the view of her breasts not even an inch from his face as she twisted her upper body in his lap. Damn, she was so close that if he stuck his tongue out, he could run it across the top curves along the neckline of her gown, he thought. But then his eyes popped open again when she shifted once more and added in almost an undertone, "As I recall, we didn't reach our destination then either."

They hadn't been headed anywhere that night, though she hadn't realized it. But he still suspected Suzette was speaking of something other than Gretna Green when she said destination. At least, *he* was thinking of something else and was suddenly recalling kneeling between her legs, rubbing himself against her as he'd prepared to enter her before being recalled to George's presence in the carriage had brought an end to things.

Damn, the little witch was brutal, Daniel decided as he felt himself growing firm under her bottom. And the rest of the ride to town was going to be complete hell.

"What? George was poisoned?" Suzette asked suddenly, stiffening in his lap and withdrawing her arm from around his neck to cross both arms on her chest in an annoyed fashion that drew his attention to the conversation taking place around him.

Apparently they'd been discussing George and the blackmailer as well as the murder, Daniel realized as Christiana explained, "It seems George may have been poisoned. Daniel and Richard smelled bitter almonds by his mouth."

"Almonds aren't poisonous," Suzette said at once.

"Bitter almonds are used to make cyanide," Lisa explained. When everyone glanced her way, she shrugged and said, "I read a lot."

"She does," Suzette said dryly and then turned to Christiana. "What else don't we know?"

"You know everything I know now. And I only

found out about the poison after the wedding. I just hadn't had a chance to tell you," she added apologetically.

Suzette nodded and then turned a glare on Daniel. "What else?"

He sighed, aware that she was now annoyed with him again, thinking he'd kept more information from her, but he'd assumed Richard had told Christiana about the poison and that she in turn had told Suzette and Lisa when she'd explained everything else. However, he didn't say so, but merely assured her, "That's it."

"And why didn't you tell me yourself before this?" Suzette asked.

Daniel did consider explaining that he'd thought she'd known, but decided that was too much like pushing the blame on to Richard for not telling Christiana when he'd explained everything else, so simply said, "It wasn't my secret to tell."

Suzette didn't take it any better than he'd expected, asking in dry tones, "Where have I heard that before?" She then shifted on his lap to face forward again. On the bright side, it appeared Suzette was now annoyed with him to the point she couldn't even be bothered to torture him anymore. On the not so bright side, it appeared she was now annoyed with him to the point she couldn't even be bothered to torture him anymore . . . and he missed it. Who knew he had this masochistic streak?

"So we have a murderer as well as a blackmailer," Lisa said, drawing his attention away from what Suzette was no longer doing. He glanced to her as she asked, "Or do we think they are the same person?"

When Richard immediately glanced his way, Daniel shrugged helplessly. He was finding it difficult to think at the moment. While Suzette was no longer wiggling about on top of him, she was still on top of him, a firm weight on his semi-erection. On top of that, his hands were at her waist, just inches below her breasts, as well as inches above her bottom too. How was a man to think at a time like that?

"They don't know," Suzette said when neither man spoke.

"Well . . ." Lisa frowned. "Surely it wouldn't be easy for someone to get poison inside the townhouse without being discovered?"

Daniel did try to consider that, but Suzette chose that moment to shift sideways in his lap once more, apparently returning to her original torture. He once again found himself gritting his teeth against the feel of her wiggling about on top of him, and staring at the top curves of her lovely breasts where they rose out of her gown. The conversation going on around him was suddenly a very uninteresting buzz in his ears as he watched Suzette's breasts move with each inhalation of breath. At least it was until he heard his name again as Richard asked, "Do you have any idea, Daniel?"

His gaze shot to Richard, but he hadn't any idea what the man was asking until Suzette ducked her head and whispered, "Do you know who George trusted enough to admit to killing Richard and taking his place?"

Daniel shook his head at once, and then cleared his throat before saying, "I have been stuck at Woodrow since Uncle Henry died last year, trying to bring the estate back up to scratch. I only left just before receiving your letter from America. I didn't even know you—or George pretending to be you—had married. I have no idea what he's been up to this last year or with whom."

"It shouldn't be too difficult to find out," Langley put in. "There's nothing the ton loves more than a good gossip. A question here or there should tell us who George considered a trusted friend."

"So we need to question the staff, as well as nose out any gossip we can about what George was up to this last year and with whom . . . and I need to make arrangements for the money." Richard paused and glanced around at them all. "Can anyone think of anything else we might do to solve matters?"

When no one else spoke up, Daniel said, "I guess we shall have to start with that and hope we uncover some useful information."

When Richard nodded, Christiana suddenly leaned forward on his lap and retrieved a large basket from beneath the bench seat.

"What's that?" Langley asked curiously as she began to dig through its contents

"We had Cook pack some food for the journey while we waited for the carriage to be readied," Christiana answered.

"Food?" Richard asked hopefully.

"Yes." Christiana glanced over her shoulder at her husband. "Did you three not think to have a basket prepared before sneaking off like thieves?"

Watching the pair as he was Daniel was taken by surprise when Suzette suddenly shifted in his lap and leaned forward to reach for some thing under their own bench seat. He recovered quickly, however, and under the guise of keeping her from falling off his lap, caught her by the hips, and spread his legs a bit even as he shifted her so that she was on only one knee, riding it astride. An evil smile of his own curved his lips when he heard her gasp, and felt her grab at his calf to balance herself. As she worked to retrieve what turned out to be a second basket, he—again under the guise of preventing her falling—drew her backward along his upper leg, in a completely intentional caress.

Daniel was quite pleased with her breathless and flustered state when she straightened, and was satisfied that he'd just established that two could play at her torture game. Unfortunately, in the next moment that contentment gave way to shock when Suzette proved that she was better at it than he was, by using the basket as cover as she dropped one hand down, slid it beneath her bottom and squeezed him through his trousers.

It was then Daniel acknowledged that the wench was going to drive him mad until he got her wed . . . and probably for the rest of his life. But as she squeezed him again, he admitted that his ride to bedlam would be an enjoyable one.

Chapter Eight

J shall wait in the parlor."

Suzette glanced to Daniel as he said that in response to Richard's announcing he needed to change as they all left the breakfast room. They'd arrived back at the townhouse a little after four that morning and had all thought of little else but finding their beds for the night. Despite a short nap in the carriage, Suzette had been so exhausted on reaching her room, she'd barely responded to the light kiss Daniel had given her at her door before following Langley to the room the two men were to share. She hadn't even bothered to strip before falling on her bed and passing into sleep.

Her poor gown had shown the abuse and been a terrible mass of wrinkles when she'd woke this morning. That being the case, Suzette had been glad, if a little surprised, to find her maid Georgina there with her chest of clothes, ready to help her start the day. Apparently, the maids' carriage had made good time and reached the townhouse directly behind them. Georgina said the Radnor carriage was still in front of the house when theirs had arrived. Suzette supposed they'd managed to catch up because the Radnor carriage had been twice as heavy after taking on the men, so had been forced to travel more slowly. Aside from that they'd had to stop so Daniel could see to his driver and the horses as well as to arrange for his carriage to be collected and seen to.

Suzette watched Daniel turn into the parlor as Richard jogged up the stairs and then she moved up beside Christiana and touched her arm to get her attention.

"When do you want to start interviewing the staff?" she asked, watching Daniel settle on the settee in the parlor. They all had assignments for the day. She and Christiana were to question the staff and see what they could find out about who might have been bribed into poisoning George's whiskey. Lisa and Langley were going to make the social rounds in town and see what gossip they could dig up about George's habits the last year, while Daniel and Richard were supposed to be going to arrange for the money to pay the blackmailer. Richard was hoping to catch the blackmailer rather than pay him, but wanted to be prepared for any eventuality.

"We will wait until everyone leaves," Christiana decided. "Why do you not go keep Daniel company? I want a word with Richard about how he wishes us to proceed with the staff anyway."

Suzette smiled. It was exactly what she'd hoped to hear. She slipped into the parlor, pulling the door closed as she went.

The soft sound drew Daniel's attention at once and his eyes narrowed. "What are you up to?"

"Whatever do you mean, my lord?" she asked innocently as she crossed the room. "I merely thought to keep you company while you wait for Richard."

"Hmm. You don't need to close the door for that. In fact, you should know better than to close it at all," he pointed out, and stood to move past her to reopen it.

"Wait, I—" Suzette gave up on a sigh as the door opened, revealing Lisa in the hall, hand out as if she'd been reaching to open it herself. Muttering under her breath with irritation, Suzette dropped onto the settee and scowled at her sister and Robert as the trio came to join her. "I thought you two were going to make the social rounds?"

"Yes, but it seems rather early for that," Lisa said with a shrug. "So we thought we'd wait a bit. Besides, you two shouldn't be left unchaperoned in a closed room."

Suzette scowled at the gentle reprimand, and thought that sometimes having a younger sister was truly a pain in the behind. She listened silently as the other three started chatting about their plans for the day. None of them seemed to mind or even notice that she didn't join the conversation, but managed to keep up a steady stream of chatter without her contribution . . . until the sound of banging drew them to a halt and made everyone glance toward the ceiling. The sound appeared to be coming from upstairs, a steady *thump thump*.

"What on earth could that be?" Lisa asked, her expression mystified as she continued to peer at the ceiling.

"Er . . . perhaps someone is hammering something," Langley muttered, but the glance he exchanged with Daniel said something entirely different.

"Oh, that can't be hammering. It sounds like a piece of furniture hitting the wall." She frowned as the banging began to pick up in speed and stood up. "Perhaps I had best just go see what it is. If—"

"No, no. We have to go," Langley said, sounding panicked as he got to his feet and caught Lisa by the arm. "We really need to start on our inquiries."

"But—"

"Now," Langley insisted, hurrying her toward the parlor door.

Suzette watched them go and then turned to Daniel, who was avoiding her eyes to concentrate on picking imaginary lint off his trousers.

"Perhaps I should go check then," Suzette said, getting to her feet as the banging increased in speed.

Daniel glanced at her sharply, but something in her expression made him relax and shrug. "If you like."

Suzette grimaced. She'd rather hoped he'd try to prevent it and give her the opportunity to kiss him. She was sure that was all it would take before this prim attitude of his crumbled. She didn't understand the need for it anyway, they would marry soon. Besides, she would like their wedding night to be a pleasant memory in her mind, not the pain-wracked and blood-soaked event she'd read about. But for that to happen she had to ensure they got her maidenhead out of the way before they reached Gretna Green.

Of course, the parlor was no place for that, but Suzette had rather hoped to convince him to slip away from the room he shared with Langley and join her in hers that night to tend the matter. She'd only hoped to gain a kiss or two from him first to bolster her courage so she could make the suggestion. It appeared, however, Daniel was not going to indulge her. She would have to just blurt it out to him, Suzette realized, and almost did right then, but recalled that the door was still open. She quickly moved to close it and then returned to sit beside him, rolling her eyes when he immediately stiffened and shifted to put more space between them.

"Really, my lord, there is no need to act the frightened virgin. I am not going to attack you," she said with exasperation.

"Act the what?" he asked with amazement and then scowled. "I—"

"I should like our wedding night to be a pleasant one," Suzette interrupted before he could get too angry.

Daniel blinked, and then smiled faintly. "Well, so would I, and I promise I will do all I can to ensure it is pleasant for you."

"Good, then come to my room tonight and—"

"No," Daniel interrupted firmly.

"Please," Suzette begged. "I don't want my memory of our wedding night to be that of streams of blood and enough pain to make me faint."

"Streams of blood?" he asked with dismay. "Who told you there would be streams of blood and so much pain you would faint?"

"I read," she reminded him dryly. This time it didn't silence him, however.

"Yes, well I think it's high time you explain just what it is you are reading that you talk about maypoles and the breaching," he said grimly.

Suzette shifted with irritation. "I do not recall the name of the book. It was Lisa's."

"Sweet little Lisa?" Daniel asked with horror, and then muttered, "I definitely have to talk to Richard about the girl."

"Someone gave it to her," Suzette said with exasperation. "Actually, it was one of several books she got from someone passing through the village, but I have only read the one and it was about a young country girl who comes to London and through tragic circumstances is sort of tricked into becoming a prostitute. She tells all about her life during that time before she is reunited with her love, who was also her first lover." She frowned. "The first time for her was a wounding and she actually fainted and when she woke she was so sore she could not walk. Her name is—"

"Fanny," Daniel snapped.

"Oh, you've read it too," Suzette said with surprise.

"No, I haven't, I just recognize the description from someone else who did read it," he assured her firmly. "It is a banned book. How the devil did Lisa get her hands on it?"

"I told you, someone gave it to her," she said impatiently.

"Who?"

Suzette frowned. She had known it was a banned book, but that had just made her more curious to read it. Lisa had refused to say who gave it to her, probably because it was banned and she hadn't wished the person to get into trouble. Suzette suspected she knew who it was, but for the same reason was reluctant to reveal her suspicions to Daniel, so merely said, "She would not tell me."

When Daniel narrowed his eyes at her suspiciously, she scowled and said, "Stop looking at me like that, you are not my father."

"Too right, I'm not," he said at once.

"Then stop acting like you are and get back on topic, my lord. Will you or will you not visit my room tonight so we can get this blood and pain business out of the way so I am healed ere we get to Gretna Green?"

Daniel frowned and then took her hand and said softly, "I assure you, Suzette, it is not going to be like that. There might be a hint of blood, but certainly not streams, and I am sure there will be little pain."

Now her eyes narrowed. "Have you deflowered a virgin before, then?"

"Good Lord, no!" he said at once with an abhorrence that was more than convincing. It also made Suzette roll her eyes.

"Then you don't know, do you?" she asked dryly.

While Daniel frowned at the truth of that, Suzette crawled onto his lap and wrapped her arms around his shoulders. She didn't even try to kiss him, but merely laid her head next to his and whispered, "Please, Daniel. I don't wish every anniversary to be a reminder of a painful first experience when I know it could be one of pure pleasure if we just remove the barrier to it beforehand."

Sighing, he slid his arms around her. "It is so hard to think clearly with you close like this," he murmured, ducking his head to inhale deeply by her neck.

"Then don't think," Suzette whispered, and when he straightened, turned her head and caught his earlobe with her teeth before sucking it between her lips.

Daniel let his breath out on a hiss and turned sharply, catching her mouth with his own. Suzette smiled and responded to the demanding kiss he gave her, and then shifted to straddle his thighs on the settee. When her skirts hampered her, Daniel helped by pulling them up and out of the way. Suzette felt cool air touch her naked bottom, and then Daniel continued to hold the skirt up with one hand, but dropped the other to clasp and squeeze one round cheek. He then broke their kiss, used his hand at her bottom to urge her to rise up a bit and then closed his mouth over one nipple through her gown as soon as it rose into range.

Suzette groaned and clasped his head, then bit her lip as the hand on her bottom dipped between her legs, but stiffened as she heard a throat being cleared behind her.

Daniel released her breast and dropped her skirts at once. He then leaned to the side to look toward the door as Richard said, "Well, it appears I arrived just in time."

Suzette groaned and dropped to sit in Daniel's lap so that she could press her flushed face into his neck. She heard him sigh and felt him pat her back soothingly, but then he stood up, taking her with him, to set on her feet. Suzette felt him brush a kiss to her forehead and move away, but stayed where she was. She didn't embarrass easily, but really, Richard had just got an eyeful of her bare bottom and she would just rather not have to face him at the moment, so she remained where she was with her back to the door until she heard the parlor door close and the murmur of their voices moving away. The moment she heard the front door close, however, Suzette dropped onto the settee and buried her face in it, both embarrassed and frustrated.

"Well . . . that went well too," Daniel commented as they stepped out of the tailor's some hours later and started up the walk in the direction of the Radnor carriage. It was the second stop they'd made, and both had been very successful. He and Richard had only planned to make arrangements for the blackmail funds when they'd left the townhouse earlier and had managed the task with little trouble. However, Daniel had taken note of Richard's discomfort in his brother's clothes as they'd arranged the transaction, and upon leaving had suggested a quick stop at the tailor's before returning home. It hadn't taken much persuasion to convince Richard. The man had returned to England with little in the way of clothing befitting an earl and had been forced to choose from George's wardrobe. George had always had terrible taste, preferring bright colors more fitting on a peacock.

Fortunately, the tailor had been quick and efficient about his work, the task ending as successfully as the trip to the bank had gone. Noting the satisfaction on Richard's face, Daniel smiled and added an optimistic, "Perhaps we shall be lucky and arrive back at the townhouse to find that everyone has had such a successful day and the identities of the blackmailer and poisoner have been discovered so that we need only round them up."

"We should be so lucky," Richard said wryly.

"Was it not you who said just as we entered the tailor's that we were both lucky men?" Daniel reminded him with amusement. They had been discussing the women at the time.

Richard glanced around at his comment and opened his mouth as if to respond, but no words came out. He just stood there frozen for a heartbeat, and then in the next second grabbed Daniel by the arm and sent them both crashing to the side. It was so unexpected, Daniel didn't even have a chance to try to break his fall; he was just suddenly slamming into the ground amid a cacophony of screams and shouts as the people around them scrambled to get out of the way.

It was only when he heard the loud thunder of horses' hooves and the trundle of a carriage's wheels as they raced past that Daniel understood that Richard had been trying to get them out of the way of an oncoming vehicle. A faint breeze as the carriage passed told him how close they had come to being trampled and Daniel lay still and closed his eyes as he waited for his heart to stop racing.

"Are you all right, my lord?" someone asked the Radnor driver, Daniel thought, but didn't move until Richard said his name with concern. Releasing his breath on a groan then, Daniel pushed himself to a sitting position, muttering, "Yes. Thanks to you."

"It was a yellow bounder, my lord," the Radnor driver announced grimly and glared in the direction the post chaise had gone. "Probably rented. The postillion didn't even try to steer clear of ye. In fact, it looked almost like he was aiming for the two of ye."

Hearing Richard grunt a response, Daniel got to his feet and quickly brushed down his clothes even as Richard rose to do the same. Daniel finished and glanced to Richard as he straightened, frowning as he noted the line of blood trailing from the other man's forehead.

"You're bleeding," Daniel said with concern. "You must have knocked your head as we fell."

Richard raised a hand to his forehead, grimaced when he felt the scrape there, and then wiped the blood away with a sigh. When he then started toward the carriage, Daniel followed.

"Father has been punishing himself for what happened and my having to marry Dicky?"

Suzette blinked at Christiana's question, a little confused as to where it had come from. They had spent the morning having quite useless and unhelpful interviews with the staff in the hopes of learning something that might help determine who the blackmailer was and who had poisoned George. The task had been a complete waste of time so far and after the last interview with one of the upstairs maids, Suzette and Christiana had come down to the office and somehow got on the topic of the men, and then Lisa and the books she read.

Christiana had been scandalized that Suzette had read the banned book about the prostitute, Fanny, but had been positively horrified at the news that the book was actually young Lisa's and that she had read the book as well. Exasperated, Suzette had pointed out that Lisa was nearly twenty, no longer a child and should already have been settled with a husband and having children. Suzette really had no clue how that had led to Christiana's question about their father punishing himself.

"Yes," she said finally, her mouth tightening

with anger at just the thought of the man whose gambling had both landed Christiana in her miserable marriage with Dicky and was now forcing Suzette to marry as well. That anger showed in her voice as she snapped, "And so he should. I was actually feeling sorry for him, but then he went and did it again."

"That may not be true," Christiana said quietly. "He may not have gambled at all."

"What?" Suzette glanced at her sharply.

"Richard said there are rumors that Dicky had befriended a certain owner of a gaming hell reputed to drug its patrons and fleece them," Christiana said quietly. "He suspects it's possible that is what happened to Father."

The air slid out of Suzette's lungs in one sharp whoosh at these words and her mind was suddenly filled with memories of the morning she and Lisa had arrived in London. Biting her lip she said, "When we found him at the townhouse, Father kept saying he was sorry, and he didn't know how it had happened, that his memories were a jumble and he didn't even recall how he'd ended up at the gaming hell, just waking up there both times to learn he'd gambled us into ruin."

Christiana breathed out a little sigh and said, "He probably didn't gamble at all."

"Oh God." Suzette dropped weakly back in her chair. "I was so cruel to him the morning we arrived in London. I said some awful things."

"It is understandable under the circumstances," Christiana assured her. "How were you to know

Dicky may have drugged him to bring about his downfall?"

"Damn Dicky!" Suzette sat upright again, anger sizzling up her spine. "If he weren't already dead, I think I'd kill him myself."

"Hmm." Christiana was silent for a moment, but then said, "Although, if it weren't for Dicky and what he'd got up to, I wouldn't now be married to Richard and you might never have met and proposed to Daniel."

"That's true," Suzette realized with dismay. She probably never would have met Daniel without Dicky's actions bringing it about. Or perhaps she would have, but only in passing, never exchanging more than polite greetings and having no idea the passion that could burn between them. The idea was rather startling, almost scary really. She couldn't imagine never having experienced his kisses and caresses or anticipating everything else she was looking forward to in the future. Well, mostly looking forward to, Suzette supposed. She was still worried about the pain and blood. While Daniel had assured her it wasn't like that, he also had never bedded a virgin, so what did he know? On the other hand, Christiana had been a virgin until very recently with Richard. Eyeing her speculatively, she asked, "So you are content with Richard?"

"I think we might have a good marriage," Christiana answered carefully.

Suzette snorted at the prim words. "Oh, give over. A *good* marriage? I've heard the moaning and groaning coming from your room, both the night Dicky died and last night as well. *Oh Rich-ard, oh . . . oh . . . yes . . . ooooooh."* She rolled her eyes. "Then you scream like you're fit to die."

"You could hear us?" Christiana asked with horror.

"I'm sure the whole house can hear you," she said dryly. "He roars like a lion, and you squeal like a stuck pig." Suzette paused and then added, "Which I suppose is an apt description from what I read in Fanny's book." When Christiana didn't comment, she asked, "Did it hurt very much the first time he stuck his maypole in your tender parts?"

"His *maypole*?" Christiana gasped, her eyes gone wide.

"That's what Fanny called it. Well, one of the things," she added with a shrug and then repeated, "Did it hurt?"

Christiana groaned and covered her suddenly flushed face. She also didn't answer.

"Well?" Suzette asked persistently. Good Lord, what were big sisters for if not to help at times like this?

"A little perhaps," Christiana admitted finally. Her hands dropped from her face and she stiffened her spine as if headed to her own execution.

Suzette ignored that and said, "Hmm, Fanny fainted from the pain . . . And there was a great deal of blood, which suggests pain as well."

"Anyway, what happens in the bedroom is only a portion of marriage, Suzette," Christiana pointed out. "I must deal with him out of the bedroom as well and begin to think I may be able to."

Suzette recognized an effort to change the topic when she saw one, but let Christiana get away with it. She always had been the most squeamish of the three of them. Eyeing her sister, she said quietly, "He seems to treat you much more kindly than Dicky did. And he upheld the marriage to prevent us all from being cast into scandal." When Christiana nodded, Suzette admitted, "I thought at first that he avoided scandal as well, but Lisa is right, men do not suffer scandal like we women do and he probably did uphold it for your sake, which is really very chivalrous. Much more chivalrous than Daniel's marrying me for money."

When Christiana frowned, Suzette realized how bitter her words sounded and glanced away with a frown of her own. She *was* a little bitter about it, which was just silly when that was exactly what she'd been looking for, a man in straits dire enough that he would be willing to marry her for her dower and agree to leave her control of part of it, as well as allow her to lead her own life if she chose. Why did Daniel's agreeing to do just that suddenly bother her?

"Are you having second thoughts about marrying Daniel?" Christiana asked quietly.

Suzette swallowed and considered the question. Second thoughts? No. She wanted to marry him. She had come to like him and enjoy his company and . . . she just wished he really wanted to marry her in return.

"Perhaps Richard would be willing to cover Father's gambling debts. If we even need to cover them. If we prove he was drugged and didn't gamble at all—"

"Nay, 'tis fine. I doubt it would be that easy to prove and we have enough on our plate at the moment," Suzette said, the words tumbling quickly from her lips. Forcing a smile, she steered them firmly away from the uncomfortable subject and said, "Speaking of which, we should really get back to our task. Who have we not yet talked to?"

Chapter Nine

*D*o you know that fellow?"

Daniel leaned toward the carriage window to peer out at the man Richard was indicating. An older gentleman was pacing back and forth on the path in front of Richard's townhouse. He was well dressed, with gray hair, and had a hat and cane, but his noble appearance was belied by the fact that he appeared to be talking to himself as he paced.

"He looks vaguely familiar," Daniel said slowly, noting the man's facial features, but unable to place the fellow. "He seems a little troubled about something."

"Grand." Richard opened the carriage door to get out. "More trouble at my door."

"You do seem to attract it of late," Daniel commented on a dry laugh as he followed him.

When they reached the man, he was again paused before the townhouse door. He stood and stared at it briefly, and then muttering under his breath, the fellow suddenly turned. He just as suddenly paused and jumped back when he found Richard standing in his path.

Daniel peered at the man curiously as Richard asked, "Is there something I can assist you with, sir?"

For some reason the question made the man's eyes widen incredulously. "What?"

"I am Lord Radnor." He held out one hand. "Can I be of assistance?"

Daniel couldn't help noticing that the gentleman stared at the offered hand as if it were a viper. He then scowled and said grimly, "Surely you jest, my lord. After all you have cost me with your shady dealings, you think to act like you do not know me?"

Daniel raised his eyebrows at this response as Richard let his hand drop to his side. It seemed obvious to him that this man must have had dealings with Dicky this last year and—not unnaturally— was mistaking Richard for his brother.

"Why do we not go inside and discuss this?" Richard moved past the man.

The fellow turned to watch him open the door, then suddenly whirled back and started forward. Daniel thought the man was simply going to leave and took a moment to debate whether to stop him or not. After all, they may gain some information from him about George's doings as Dicky this last year, he thought. But before he could make up his mind, the older man jerked a black and ivory pistol from inside his jacket and instead of passing Daniel, stopped and pressed the weapon to his side. Glancing back toward Richard then, the man said, "Why do you not go in there and fetch the girls back to me while your friend and I wait out here instead."

Daniel was a bit startled by this unexpected turn of events, but not much alarmed for two reasons. First of all, they were standing on the street in plain view of anyone passing and no sane person would pull the trigger there. Of course, the fellow had been talking to himself, so perhaps he wasn't all that sane. But Daniel also wasn't that worried because the man was obviously a member of the nobility and he'd mentioned the girls who could only be the Madison sisters. Daniel was beginning to suspect he knew who the man was and why he'd looked familiar. And if he was right, he was pretty sure that the likelihood of being shot wasn't very high. Well, at least not on purpose, Daniel corrected himself wryly, as he noted the way the man's hand was trembling.

Richard turned back, and then paused as he took in the situation.

"Ha! Not so clever now are you, Dicky?" the armed man asked grimly. "Now give me my daughters. All of them. I'm not leaving a one of them here for you to abuse any longer."

"Your daughters?" Daniel asked with interest, his suspicions proven correct. The man was Cedrick Madison, Suzette's father. He looked familiar because he shared some of the same facial features as his lovely daughter, though they were much softer on her.

"Lord Madison?" Richard asked, sounding more amazed. Obviously, he didn't see the resemblance.

Madison appeared more interested in Richard than anything else, though he kept the gun pressed into Daniel's side as he sneered, "Save your games, my lord. You have managed to fool me one too many times already. I know you have mistreated my Chrissy. Robert told me everything after the Landons' ball the other night. He said the girls told him that you've treated her terribly and I've sorted it all out from there. You never loved my gel, it was all an act to get your hands on her dower, and now you've somehow swindled me again hoping to force my Suzette into the same position. Well I won't have it, and I am not leaving my Chrissy in your hands either, marriage or no marriage. I'll have it annulled. I'll take it to the King himself if I have to. Now fetch me all three girls before I lose my patience."

"Father?"

All three men glanced to the woman hurrying up the path toward them: Lisa Madison with Robert Langley on her heels.

"Father, what are you doing pointing that pistol at Suzette's fiancé? Put that away before you hurt someone."

"Nay," Lord Madison said firmly, grabbing her arm with his free hand and urging her to the side to keep her out of harm's way as he dug the pistol more firmly into Daniel's stomach. "I'll not let Suzette marry this blackguard. No doubt he's a friend of that devil's there, which means he'll be as bad as Dicky. Now, be a good girl and fetch your sisters, girl. We are leaving here and going back to Madison. I've sold the townhouse to pay the debts. There is no need for Suzette to marry anyone."

"You sold your townhouse?" Daniel asked with the first real alarm he'd felt since the man had whipped out his pistol.

"Aye." Lord Madison's smile was just plain mean as he glanced from Daniel to Richard. "The two of you didn't think I'd do that, did you? But I'd sell the estate itself before I let you rope another one of my girls into a miserable marriage." He stood a little straighter and added, "And I will see Chrissy out of her marriage as well."

"Oh Father," Lisa said with a sigh. "That wasn't necessary at all. Daniel agreed to let Suzette keep half her dower to pay off the debt and use the rest as she wished. He is not the devil Dicky was."

"And actually, Richard here is not the villain you think he is either," Langley added as he urged Lisa away to take her place at Madison's side. He then bent his head close and began to murmur. Daniel heard enough to know he was explaining the situation to the man and simply waited for him to finish. It took a bit of time, but eventually Madison lowered his gun and squawked, "What?"

Robert nodded solemnly. "Chrissy is very happy with the Earl of Radnor. *This* one," he added firmly. "And Daniel is a good and honorable man. He'll make Suzette a fine husband."

Daniel snorted at the words, his tone full of

disgust as he said, "Only if he doesn't tell her he sold the damned townhouse to make good on his debts. If she finds that out Suzette is just contrary enough that she may very well not marry me."

"I'm sure Lord Madison will keep that information to himself for now," Richard said, bringing a look of surprise to the older man's face.

"Why would I do that?" Madison asked with amazement. "If Suzette doesn't wish to marry him, I will not let her be forced into it."

Richard gave him a pained smile. "Under normal circumstances I would agree with you. However, after what I interrupted in the parlor between the two of them this morning, honor demands he marry her, and as her brother-in-law I feel it my duty to ensure he does."

"Eh?" Madison's eyes shot to Daniel just as he began to grin at the recollection of what Richard had walked in on that morning before they'd left. Suzette had just crawled onto his lap and he'd lifted her skirts to keep them from hampering her as she straddled his thighs, but he'd deliberately lifted it high enough to bare her bottom and had been pinching the tender flesh and considering doing much more when Richard had entered. Most scandalous. The girl was as good as ruined if it got out, and he'd damn well blab that tidbit all over town if necessary to get her to marry him. Suzette was not going to escape him now when he'd finally settled on marrying her.

Realizing that everyone was staring at him, he nodded easily. "I'd forgotten about that. Yes, she has to marry me to avoid ruin."

"You're sure he's a good and honorable man?" Lord Madison asked Robert doubtfully.

"Positive," Robert assured him, obviously fighting a grin. "Truly, just look how eager he is to do the right thing."

Daniel beamed at the old man when he looked his way again, appearing as pleased as he was at the idea of marrying Suzette and finally bedding the beautiful, passionate firebrand.

"Besides," Robert continued. "The fact that Suzie allowed him to take liberties with her proves she is not averse to the marriage. However, she can be contrary. It may be best to allow her to continue thinking for now that the marriage is necessary."

"Hmm." Madison grimaced. "Of the three of them she has always been the most stubborn and difficult." He glanced to Daniel. "Are you sure you know what you're getting yourself into? She won't make life easy."

"Perhaps not," Daniel said, and thought it an understatement. Suzette would never make life easy, but nothing easy was worth having and he added, "But life shall certainly never be boring with her either."

Madison relaxed and nodded solemnly. "There is much to be said for that. She is like her mother, and that woman had me hopping to keep up with her from the day we wed. Never regretted marrying her even for a moment."

"So you won't tell her that there is no need to marry?" Daniel asked hopefully.

Madison pursed his lips, his gaze moving first to Lisa, who nodded solemnly, then to each of the men before he heaved a sigh. "I shall talk to her, and if Suzie doesn't seem averse to marrying you, I will keep the sale of the townhouse to myself for now."

Daniel relaxed and nodded. "Thank you."

Madison turned to Richard then. Looking him over, he shook his head. "You look remarkably like Dicky."

"We *were* twins."

"Aye, well, there is a difference in the eyes. When you looked into his they were usually empty or calculating. Yours . . ." He shook his head, apparently unable to come up with a way to describe the difference.

"Perhaps we should move inside now," Richard suggested as a carriage passed by on the street.

"Aye. Let's go in," Madison agreed. "I could use a cup of tea nice and sweet. I got myself all wound up to come here and now feel quite worn out."

"Tea it is, then." Richard pushed the already open door wide and led the way inside.

Daniel gestured for Lord Madison, Lisa and Langley to precede him, and had just followed when a door opened along the hall. As he pulled the front door closed, Suzette stepped into sight from the office and glanced toward them with a smile. "I thought I heard voices out here."

Daniel grimaced and hoped none of the staff had been in the hallway during the conversation that had just taken place. With the door open for the entire duration they would have heard every word of what had just transpired.

Suzette had been glancing over the group, but

her eyes widened as she spotted her father. She started forward at once, asking, "Father, what are you doing here?"

"He came to rescue us," Lisa told her with a smile. "He even held Richard and Daniel at gunpoint until Robert and I explained the new situation to him."

"Oh, how sweet." Suzette paused before her father and hugged him, which seemed to leave the man a little startled. Apparently, he hadn't expected a warm greeting from her, and Daniel understood why when she said, "I am sorry I was so angry when we arrived in London, Father. You didn't deserve it." She pulled back and added, "Chrissy says the men think Dicky drugged you and just made you think you'd gambled the money away. It was all a trick to try to get our dowers."

Lord Madison glanced to Richard who nodded and said, "There are rumors that I, or Dicky really, has become quite chummy with the owner of a gaming hell famous for the trick."

"I had begun to suspect as much," Lord Madison admitted, sagging with relief. "I have no recollection of gambling at all, and what recollections I do have of the gaming hell are quite fuzzy flashes of being led through it, people talking and laughing, being told to sign something . . ." He grimaced and shook his head. "I have never cared for gambling and don't even know how to play the games of chance in those places. Yet there was the marker with my signature on it."

Suzette patted his back and hugged him again.

"Well, now that that is all straightened out, why do we not sit down and hear what everyone has learned?" Daniel suggested, eager to change the subject and move it away from anything to do with the markers and Suzette's need for marriage. He slipped to her side so that she now stood between him and her father. While he resisted the urge to take her arm possessively, Daniel wanted to. He wanted to be prepared to whisk her quickly away if Lord Madison should suddenly change his mind and blurt out that he'd sold his townhouse and could now pay the debt. The worry was enough to leave him tense and anxious and he wasn't happy to realize that he would probably remain in this state until he had Suzette wedded and bedded so that their marriage was final and irrevocable, which he couldn't do until they had this blackmail business of Richard's resolved. Fortunately, Richard was as eager to solve the matter as he.

"Yes, let's move into the parlor," his friend suggested, and then as everyone started to gravitate that way, asked, "Where is Christiana?"

"Oh." Suzette suddenly glanced along the hall with a frown. "I was just going in search of her. She was going to have Haversham fetch Freddy to us to interview, but has taken an awfully long time so I thought I'd best check on her."

"George's valet, Freddy?" Richard asked, apparently recognizing the name.

"Yes, George's valet," Suzette confirmed. "We realized that he might not have been fooled by the switch George made and if he somehow saw you the last day or two may realize you are not George. If so, he could be the blackmailer."

"Of course," Richard growled.

Daniel was just thinking they had probably sorted out at least one of their problems when the Radnor butler suddenly came hurrying out of the kitchens.

"Haversham, have you seen my wife?" Richard asked abruptly. "She apparently went looking for you to have you send Freddy to her."

"Actually, my lord, I was just coming to seek you out about that," the man said unhappily. "It appears Lady Radnor was unable to find me and went in search of your valet herself and has now found herself in something of a fix."

"What kind of a fix?" Richard asked with alarm.

"Well, I happened to be passing Freddy's room and overheard him saying that he intended to take her and force you to pay to get her back safely," he admitted grimly. "I believe he is planning to take her around to the office to try to find something first, however, so if we were to hide ourselves away in there and wait for him to approach we may be able to take him by surprise and relieve him of Lady Radnor without her coming to harm."

"That's actually a good plan," Daniel said, eyeing the butler with a new respect. He then glanced to Richard. "We should move quickly though, I don't recall a lot of places in the office to hide."

Richard nodded and turned away, pausing when Langley said, "I am coming too."

"And me," Lord Madison said firmly.

"Me too," Suzette announced.

Daniel frowned and was about to suggest she and the others wait in the parlor when Richard stopped and did it for him.

"There aren't enough hiding spaces for everyone. Robert and Daniel only will come. The rest of you need to get into the parlor and out of the hall so you don't scare Freddy off." His gaze slid to Lord Madison as the man opened his mouth to protest. "I trust you are the only person here who could keep Suzette and Lisa in that parlor."

Much to Daniel's relief, Lord Madison swallowed whatever protest he'd been about to speak and nodded with resignation.

"Do you think Christiana is all right?" Lisa asked, drawing Suzette's unhappy attention.

"Of course she isn't. Freddy has taken her by force and intends to hold her for ransom," Suzette pointed out with exasperation, and then frowned to herself, thinking that if she'd just gone with Christiana things may have turned out differently. That guilt was also making her wish she was out there now, helping to resolve the issue. Instead, she was stuck here in the parlor, being guarded by her father and Haversham.

Suzette scowled. Why was it that whenever there was trouble, the women were expected to sit about and wait, while the men charged in to the rescue?

"I believe I will go have Cook prepare a tea tray," Haversham announced suddenly, starting toward the door to the hall.

"Richard said we were to wait here," Lord Madison reminded him sharply, getting to his feet as if prepared to tackle the man did he not stop.

Suzette felt her eyebrows rise slightly at her father's aggressive stance. Whether he would have actually stopped the man or not, they would never know, because the butler paused at the door and turned back.

"Yes, he did, my lord," the man agreed politely. "However, it does occur to me that if we do not attempt to present at least a semblance of normalcy, it may spook Lady Christiana's kidnapper. And while it would seem perfectly natural for the three of you to be visiting in here together, my being here is far from natural."

Suzette glanced to her father to see him looking uncertain. "He is right, Father. It isn't normal, and that alone might spook Christiana's kidnapper and make him leave with her rather than risk going to the office. Surely, Haversham should just go about his duties?"

"I suppose," Cedrick Madison murmured reluctantly. Heaving a sigh, he nodded. "Very well, go ahead, but stay away from the office and don't do anything that might spook him."

"Very good, my lord."

Suzette watched enviously as Haversham slid from the room, and then stood and hurried to the door, murmuring, "I will just tell him to ask Cook for some pastries as well. Something sweet might settle my nerves."

"Suzette," her father said sharply.

"I won't be a moment," she assured him, speeding up to escape the room before he could protest further.

As she'd hoped, Haversham was already gone from the hall when she burst into it. Suzette turned to glance toward the office, debating going to listen at the door to see if anything was happening, but then turned sharply toward the kitchen instead when she heard her father's voice through the door, muffled but drawing closer. Hurrying up to the kitchen door as if she'd really intended to go that way all along, Suzette pushed into the room just as the parlor door opened behind her.

She heard her father hiss her name, but then the door closed behind her. Besides, Suzette wasn't paying attention anyway. Her eyes immediately searched the room for Haversham and widened when she found him. The butler was just heading out the back door with a rather large, wicked-looking butcher knife in hand.

"I suspect we shall be waiting a long time for that tea," she commented dryly.

Haversham froze and turned guiltily. He then stepped back inside and eased the door quickly closed before saying, "I was just . . . er . . ."

When he paused at a loss, Suzette smiled wryly and suggested, "Going to cut back bushes?"

Bewilderment covered his face until he noted she was eyeing the butcher knife in his hand. Grimacing, he lowered the weapon and said with great dignity, "I have already requested that Cook make up a tray."

"He did, m'lady, and the kettle's on," Cook assured her as she ran a rolling pin vigorously over a swath of pie dough on the counter. She then added, "Then he saw one of the boys slip past the window with a sack over his shoulder and started out of the kitchen after him."

"A sack?" The question came from behind Suzette and she glanced over her shoulder, not at all surprised to see her father there. Lisa stood behind him, wringing her hands worriedly.

"Well, I think it was a sack," the woman said, pausing in her rolling to move to the stove and stir a pot of something bubbling there. "But I didn't really catch more than a glimpse meself." She peered questioningly over her shoulder at Haversham, apparently expecting him to clarify the matter.

The butler grimaced, and said, "It was a certain sack that Lord Richard is awaiting in the office." He glanced to the cook and then back before continuing, "I just thought to follow and be sure he was headed to the office as expected."

Suzette frowned. It was possible the man holding Christiana had decided to go around to the office via the yard rather than risk carrying her through the house where he might be spotted by servants. However, if Chrissy was the sack over his shoulder, that wasn't a good sign. And the men were no doubt expecting him to come in through the hall door. They wouldn't be prepared for his arrival via the French doors. If he should approach the glass doors and spot something that spooked him, he might simply slip away with Christiana completely unnoticed.

"Good idea. I shall join you," Lord Madison said suddenly, selecting the largest of the knives remaining in a wooden block on the counter. "You girls return to the parlor. We shall be back as soon as it is over."

On that note, he moved to the door and followed Haversham out.

"Are we going back to the parlor?" Lisa asked.

"What do you think?" Suzette asked dryly, snatching up the rolling pin the cook had been using and moving toward the door.

"Wait for me," Lisa gasped.

Suzette glanced over her shoulder to see Lisa picking up and discarding several kitchen items before settling on a long, wicked-looking two-pronged cooking fork. Apparently satisfied that it would do, she hurried after her as Suzette pushed through the door.

Suzette crept along the back of the house, staying as close to the wall as she could. She didn't have to glance around to be sure Lisa was still behind her. Her younger sister had one hand on her back as they crept along several feet behind their father and Haversham.

The butler was in the lead, with her father on his heels, and beyond them Suzette could see their quarry. The man was standing outside the French doors to the office, peering in through the window panels. He had Christiana slung over his shoulder like a sack, holding her in place with an arm around her legs, and at first Suzette thought her sister was unconscious, but as her captor eased one of the office doors open and began to slip inside, she noticed that Christiana's eyes were open, and she was peering about to take in what she could see.

"She's alive," Lisa whispered with relief behind her.

Suzette nodded, but didn't say anything and continued forward, raising her rolling pin in case the fellow burst back out of the office and made it past Haversham and her father. She would feel no compunction at all about bashing him over the head with the item rather than let him escape with Christiana.

Haversham had reached the French doors now and Suzette saw him hesitate. Christiana's kidnapper had left the door open just a crack and the butler peered through the window briefly before easing the door open and slipping inside the room. A couple feet behind the butler, Lord Madison paused at the door as well to take in the situation, and then he too slipped inside.

Suzette began to move more swiftly then, rushing along on her tiptoes as she worried about what might be happening in the room. As she drew near she heard Richard say, "I won't let you leave here unless it's in chains," and knew they were confronting the kidnapper, but still moved as quietly as she could until she reached the door. She paused then on the threshold and took in the tableau, as much as she could around her father, who stood just inside the door. The butler stood in front of him, a bare step behind the apparently oblivious kidnapper, who still had Christiana over his shoulder. Suzette could see Richard approaching the desk from the opposite side of the room and Daniel was coming from around a settee, but she had no idea where Robert was.

"Where's Robert?" Lisa breathed behind her worriedly, and Suzette shook her head and raised a hand to shush her as the kidnapper cried, "Stay back or I'll cut her."

Suzette hadn't noticed the man holding a weapon in the brief glimpse she'd gotten earlier, but he must have one because Christiana suddenly squawked, "Ouch! That is my bottom."

"Put her down," Richard ordered.

"Go to hell!" the kidnapper snarled and whirled toward the door only to crash into Haversham.

From her position, Suzette saw the startled look on the man's face and then saw him turn a bewildered expression to Haversham. Even so she didn't realize what had happened until the kidnapper started to fall back and she caught a glimpse of the butcher knife protruding from his chest, blood blossoming around the wound. He'd skewered himself on the butler's weapon.

"Oh dear," Lisa said faintly behind her, and recalling her dislike of blood, Suzette turned quickly to see that the younger girl had gone terribly pale and was swaying on her feet.

"It is all right," Suzette said, quickly catching her arm and urging her a step away from the open door. "Take deep breaths."

Lisa inhaled several times and after a moment seemed to recover a bit, her color returning.

"All right?" Suzette asked with concern. Lisa had been known to faint at the sight of blood. But she appeared steady enough on her feet at the moment, perhaps because there hadn't been all that much blood, just a slow blossoming on the cloth of his livery. Whatever the case, she was recovering nicely and Lisa nodded, even managing a smile.

Suzette smiled back and then glanced toward the door as her father ushered a somewhat shaky Christiana out.

"I need a word with your sister," Lord Madison murmured as they approached.

Suzette nodded and watched them move toward the back of the garden and then turned back to Lisa. "We should go in now. Can you manage it?"

Lisa nodded. "I just won't look at him this time."

Suzette squeezed her arm, then led her to the door. Haversham was gone, but Robert had joined the other two men. All three of them were gathered around the body and pretty much blocking their entrance to the room, so Suzette and Lisa paused as Robert said, "Well, that is one problem taken care of anyway. The blackmail threat is over."

"Now we just need to figure out who poisoned George and is still trying to kill Richard," Daniel commented in dry tones.

"Well, I'm afraid Lisa and I didn't find out anything of use today," Robert said apologetically to Richard. "I think people were reluctant to gossip about you with Lisa there. She is your sister-in-law, after all. Perhaps Christiana and Suzette were more successful at discovering what servant may have administered the poison."

"We should ask them," Richard murmured and turned toward the doors. His eyebrows rose when he saw Suzette and Lisa there, but no sign of his wife. "Where—"

"Father wished to speak to Christiana. They

have stepped out into the garden," Suzette explained.

Richard glanced past them toward the yard, and then swung back to the room as the office door opened.

Suzette leaned to the side a bit to see that Haversham had returned. The butler entered stiffly, leading two men into the room. The red vests the men wore announced that they were Bow Street runners.

"Oh dear," Lisa said suddenly. "I don't think I can stay here."

Suzette glanced to her sister with surprise, but then realized it wasn't the arrival of the authorities that had so overset her, but despite her assurance that she just wouldn't look at the dead man on the floor, Lisa was now staring at him transfixed, her face paling by the minute.

"Come," Suzette said with a sigh. "We can wait in the parlor while the runners sort this out."

"Thank you," Lisa whispered gratefully, as Suzette ushered her quickly around the men and toward the door.

Chapter Ten

*Y*ou don't have to stay with me. I'll be fine by myself if you want to rejoin the others."

Suzette glanced to Lisa and shook her head. "No, it's fine. The Bow Street runners are probably asking a thousand stupid questions and doing . . . whatever they do," she said, waving a hand vaguely.

"Hopefully removing the body is one of those 'whatever they do's,'" Lisa said wryly.

"I'm sure it is," Suzette reassured her. "Or they'll bring in whoever does or tell Richard so he can. They certainly won't just leave the body lying about here forever."

Lisa grimaced at the very idea, and sighed. "I do wish I was not so squeamish about such things."

Suzette shrugged idly as she paced to the

window and glanced out. "Everyone has their flaws, and as they go, yours is not so bad. It isn't often you run into blood. Imagine if you fainted at the sight of pastries or something."

Lisa chuckled at the ridiculous idea as she'd intended, but then they both fell silent and glanced toward the door as it burst open and Daniel hurried in. Robert was on his heels, but Suzette's attention was on Daniel as he hurried across the room. The man was looking very pleased.

"It's done, they've gone," he announced as he paused before her and reached to pull her into his arms.

"That's good," Suzette said, peering up at him uncertainly. The man had seemed to be pushing her away and trying to make her behave since she'd met him, so she was a little surprised to find herself in his arms and to see his head lowering as if he meant to kiss her, right there in front of Robert and Lisa.

He didn't kiss her, however, not on the lips at least. Instead, his head moved to the side at the last moment and he pressed the kiss to the side of her neck below her ear and murmured, "The blackmail and murder are resolved and there's nothing more to keep us here. You know what that means."

"Gretna Green," she sighed, tilting her head a little to the side as he pressed butterfly kisses along the column of her throat. The gentle caresses were sending shivers down her back and raising desire to fog her mind, so it was a minute before his words sank in, and then she stiffened and said, "The murder is resolved too? Was Freddy the murderer as well as the blackmailer?"

"No," he murmured against the flesh covering her collarbone.

"Who was it then?" she asked with a frown.

Daniel straightened, a smile curving his lips when he saw her expression. "God, I love it when you get that annoyed look. It just makes me want to kiss you."

"Daniel," she growled, but his response was to kiss her, right there in front of Robert and Lisa . . . and her father, she realized as he cleared his throat in a very loud, intrusive manner to announce his presence.

Daniel released her to glance around and give the man a completely unrepentant grin. "Are you coming with us to Gretna Green?"

"Of course," he said, and while his voice was solemn, there was a twinkle in his eyes that suggested he was not displeased.

Daniel then turned his gaze to Lisa and Robert in question, who both nodded at once.

"Daniel," Suzette said, poking his chest to get his attention. "Who poisoned George?"

"I'll tell you on the way," he promised, catching her hand and heading for the door at almost a jog.

Suzette laughed a little breathlessly at his eagerness, but didn't protest or try to pull free as he led her into the hall. Once there, however, he released her hand and started toward Richard and Christiana, who were by the stairs.

"Richard, now that the blackmailer is caught and the identity of the murderer found, there is no reason to delay. We are heading for Gretna Green at once."

Richard groaned, but then straightened and said, "Certainly, we shall leave first thing in the morning."

"The morning?" Daniel asked, and Suzette wasn't surprised at the displeasure in his voice.

Richard nodded. "Well, the women will have to pack and—"

"The chests are still packed from this morning. At least mine is," Suzette interrupted and then glanced over her shoulder to Lisa as she, Robert and their father also stepped into the hall.

"Mine too," Lisa assured her.

Suzette glanced to Christiana next. While her older sister hesitated briefly, she did nod in the end and admit, "So is mine."

Richard immediately ducked his head to whisper something to her. Christiana whispered back, but the couple paused and turned their attention to Daniel again as he asked, "Richard, is your carriage still out front? I don't recall you sending your driver to the stables."

"I didn't," Richard admitted. "I wasn't sure we wouldn't need it again."

"Mine is still out front as well," Robert announced. "They just need to be loaded."

"Excellent." Daniel clapped his hands with satisfaction. "Then we merely need to have mine prepared and brought around, load them up and we can—damn," Daniel paused to mutter, "I forgot my carriage is presently out of commission. I will have to rent one for the maids."

Suzette bit her lip with frustration. There always seemed to be something to delay or interfere with their getting to Gretna Green. She was beginning to think someone had cursed them.

"We can use mine," Lord Madison announced. "It is out front."

Suzette beamed at her father. Everything was going to be all right. This time, surely, nothing would interfere with their traveling to Gretna Green and getting married.

After three days of travel, Suzette shouldn't have been so confused when she opened her eyes to find herself in yet another strange bed. However, it took a full moment before she recalled that she was in yet another inn room she was sharing with Lisa, and on the way to Gretna Green. The moment she did, however, Suzette was suddenly wide awake. It was the fourth and final day of their journey. They should arrive at the village of Gretna Green by dinnertime that day and moments later would be married. Afterward, they would have a celebratory meal with everyone, and then she and Daniel would finally consummate the marriage and be husband and wife.

The last thought took some shine off the smile that had been blossoming on her lips. It wasn't the finally being husband and wife part that dimmed her happiness, but the consummation itself. Suzette wasn't looking forward to it, and really wasn't pleased at the idea of her wedding night being spoiled by it being her first time. While Christiana had answered her question as to whether it hurt the first time or not with a weak, "A little perhaps," Suzette was not convinced. It had been obvious that Chrissy was distressed at discussing the subject, but had that been because it was such a personal matter, or because she didn't wish to scare Suzette by telling her the truth? Christiana had certainly changed the subject quickly at that point, and Suzette couldn't forget what she'd read about streams of blood and enough pain to make her faint.

She really wished she and Daniel had done the consummating part before now. Unfortunately, they hadn't been left alone since leaving London. Her father was taking his duty to guard her innocence until marriage very seriously during this journey and had enlisted her sisters as well as Robert and Richard to aid in the chore. Neither she nor Daniel was ever alone. Even when sleeping. They had taken three rooms at each of the inns they'd stopped at, one for Richard and Christiana, one for Lisa and Suzette and one for their father, Robert, and Daniel to share. Suzette didn't mind sharing with Lisa, but knew Daniel found staying with Robert and her father something of a trial. It seemed both men snored, and hogged the bed they shared.

Suzette smiled faintly at the idea of him crowded between the two men each night, an effort by her father to be sure he didn't slip out to meet her, she suspected. Tonight, Daniel would not have to share with them, however. He would be sharing with her . . . and there would be streams of blood and pain.

Sighing, Suzette shifted the blankets aside and slid out of bed to quickly dress. She had finished with the task and was brushing her hair when Lisa stirred awake and then sat up to glance around.

"What are you doing?" she asked around a yawn.

"Getting ready to go," Suzette said with a laugh. "You'd best get up and start dressing. Christiana will—"

"Dear God," Lisa muttered, dropping back in the bed. "We are not leaving early today, remember? We are leaving later, mid morning they said. We get to sleep late today."

Suzette paused in her brushing. "We do? Why aren't we leaving until mid morning?"

"I don't know," Lisa muttered, rolling on her side. "Father just said to go ahead and sleep late today, we wouldn't be leaving until mid morning." She glanced over her shoulder in question. "Did he not tell you?"

"No," she said with a frown.

"He must have forgot," Lisa sighed and turned away again. "Come back to bed and sleep."

Suzette stared at her silently, her frown growing. Why weren't they leaving until mid morning? They had left bright and early every day until now, and this was the last day of the journey. She would have thought out of all of them, this day would be the one where they set off with the rising sun.

Suzette set the brush on top of her chest with a sigh and considered undressing and getting back into bed, but knew she wouldn't be able to sleep.

However, she didn't wish to pace about the room until everyone else began to stir either. And she was thirsty. Grimacing, Suzette moved silently to the door and slid out onto the landing.

The soft murmur of voices from the great room below reached her ear as she eased the chamber door closed. Suzette moved to the rail to peer down over the empty tables. It wasn't until her gaze reached the door to the kitchens that she spotted the speakers. Daniel was there talking in low tones to the innkeeper.

Suzette smiled as her eyes slid over him, taking in his serious expression and slightly ruffled hair. It looked as if he'd just woken and hadn't yet even run a brush through his hair. There were also sleep creases on his cheek that made her smile widen. He was just so adorable and she found that the mere act of peering at him made her chest ache a bit. Unsure what that was but not ready to face it, she started along the landing toward the stairs, intending to join the two men, but she'd barely taken a step when the innkeeper nodded and slipped away into the kitchens. The moment he did, Daniel turned and strode through the room full of long empty tables and straight out the front door.

Eager to catch up to him, Suzette hurried down the stairs and outside, reaching the courtyard just in time to see Daniel enter the stables. She hurried after him, one part of her mind wondering what he was doing up so early when they weren't leaving until mid morning, and another part pointing out that they would finally have a moment alone together.

Suzette slowed as she reached the stables. She didn't see Daniel at first, but a slow scan of the building revealed him in one of the stalls near the back. He was saddling a horse, she saw, and moved forward at once.

"What are you doing?" she asked as she reached the stall where he was working. Her sudden question made Daniel jerk around with surprise. She'd obviously given him a start, but once he saw that it was her, a smile lifted the corners of his mouth.

"Good morning," he said, leaving the saddle sitting unfastened on the horse's back and moving to the stall rail to meet her.

"Good morning," Suzette said automatically. "Why are you saddling a horse?"

"Because I'm going to ride it," he said simply. "It will be faster than a carriage there, though we will have to return by carriage, I suppose. Mother enjoys riding on horseback, but she is getting older and was ill this last year. I don't wish to overtax her more than necessary."

"Mother?" Suzette echoed blankly.

Daniel chuckled at her expression and slipped out of the stall. Pausing in front of her, he slid his arms around her waist as he said, "Yes, Mother. I should like you two to meet, and I would like her at our wedding, so I am going to collect her. It's why we pressed on an extra hour last night. This inn is only an hour from Woodrow."

"Oh," Suzette breathed. Dear God, she was going to meet his mother! What if Lady Woodrow didn't like her? What if she hated her and refused to condone the marriage? What if—?

"What's going on inside your head?" Daniel

asked with a frown. "You look horrified. Don't you want my mother at the wedding?"

"I—yes, of course. I just—what if she hates me?" Suzette asked plaintively.

Daniel chuckled again and hugged her close. "She will not hate you. No one could hate you," he assured her and then pulled back and said, "Now, this is the first time we have been alone in days. Do you think I could have a good-morning kiss to see me off?"

Suzette blinked, her worries about his mother's liking or not liking her suddenly sliding away, if only temporarily, at the suggestion.

"Hmm?" he asked, lowering his head.

"Oh yes," she breathed and then his mouth was on hers.

It was not a good-morning kiss, Suzette decided as his tongue slid out to urge her lips open. At least it wasn't to her. Good-morning kisses, in her mind, were sweet pecks. This was more of a good-morning, good-afternoon and good-evening kiss all in one, she thought as his mouth devoured hers. Or perhaps it was more of an "I want to throw you in the straw, toss up your skirts and have my wicked way with you kind of kiss," she decided as his hands began to roam.

Damn, the man could kiss, Suzette thought faintly, slipping her arms around his neck and arching into him as his mouth slanted over hers. She then moaned as he slid one hand down to press against her bottom, urging her hips forward. When she felt his maypole press against her through their clothes in a "good morning" of its own, Suzette sighed and rubbed herself against him in a return greeting that made them both groan.

Tearing his mouth from hers, Daniel gasped, "I have to go," even as his hands found her breasts and he began to squeeze them through her gown.

"Yes," Suzette agreed, reaching down to cup his hardness through his trousers.

Daniel groaned, and kissed her hungrily again, his hands kneading the flesh of her breasts almost painfully in time to the rhythm of her hand along his hardness. Finally, he tore his mouth away again and muttered, "Damn, Suzette, if you don't stop that—"

He didn't finish whatever threat he'd intended, but sucked in a hissing breath through his teeth as she slid her other hand into the waistband of his trousers and found him without the hampering cloth in the way. Then he cursed and claimed her mouth again, backing her up as she continued to caress him.

Suzette felt something scratchy at her back and guessed it was a bale of hay, but between his kiss, the way he was now alternately kneading her breasts and lightly pinching her nipples, as well as her efforts to undo the buttons of his trousers with her free hand, she was just a bit too distracted to wonder about it.

She wasn't aware he'd undone the stays of her gown until she felt the cool morning air caress her back. He tried to tug the sleeves off her shoulders, but it would mean her giving up on his buttons as well as releasing him, and she wasn't willing to do that, so he gave it up and merely tugged the now loose neckline down below her breasts and broke their kiss to duck his head and latch onto one of them.

"Ah," Suzette moaned, and then added a "ha," as she managed to undo enough buttons that she could pull his maypole out and caress him more easily. Daniel stiffened and nipped at her breast, his hips thrusting into her touch as she clasped him, but his own hands had been busy, managing to tug up her skirts and burrow under to run up the backs of her legs.

Suzette gasped as his fingers urged her legs apart so that one hand could slide between them and touch her. She closed her eyes briefly at the explosion of pleasure it sent through her, but then began to squirm and released him to push at his shoulders and urge him away. Much more of his caressing and she wouldn't be able to think straight, and Suzette had been fascinated by a certain portion of Fanny's book describing a way to please a man with just your mouth, and wanted to try it.

Apparently thinking she wanted to bring an end to their interlude, Daniel released her at once. "I'm sorry, I shouldn't—"

The words ended on a hiss of surprise as Suzette suddenly dropped to her knees before him and took him into her mouth.

They both froze then. No doubt Daniel froze from shock, but Suzette paused because she wasn't sure what to do next. The book had been rather vague about the exact details of how to please him this way, drifting into strange, vague metaphors and nonsense. Giving a mental shrug, she just did what she felt like, tasting him with her tongue and measuring him with her mouth and then clasping his maypole in one hand so that she could remove it to kiss the tip.

Whether her attention pleased Daniel or not, Suzette couldn't say, but she was having a pleasant enough time exploring him thusly until he suddenly caught her by the arms and lifted her up, not just to her feet, but to sit on the bale of hay she'd earlier felt at her back.

"Did I—?" She'd wanted to ask if she'd been doing it right, however, Daniel ended the question by kissing her. Suzette gave in with a little sigh and slid her arms around his neck as he urged her legs apart so that he could move between them and get closer. His hands were on her breasts again at first, welcoming them back, but then one hand slipped away to find the hem of her skirt and slide under it.

His fingers rode along her thigh, pushing the material ahead of it and Suzette wiggled on the bale of hay under the caress, unconsciously moving her bottom closer to the edge. When he found her core, she froze and groaned, then broke their kiss to let her head fall back as his fingers moved against her excited flesh. Daniel immediately turned his mouth to other delights, nibbling her ear, her neck, her collarbone, and then dropping to claim one nipple again.

This time Suzette didn't try to break free, but gasped and arched into both caresses, her fingers knotting in his hair and holding on tight even as her legs wrapped around his hips, urging him closer. Daniel nipped lightly at her nipple, his fingers dancing over her swollen core, demanding a response that her body was eager to give. When she felt something pressing gently into her, Suzette thought it was his maypole and cried out, her legs tightening around his hips and dragging her bottom closer to the edge of the bale of hay as he continued to caress her, building the pressure inside her to almost unbearable levels.

"Daniel," she gasped, pleading for him to end this torture.

His response was to raise his head to claim her mouth and kiss her deeply as he continued his ministrations. Suzette clutched at his shoulders, her bottom sliding further forward into his caress as her legs tightened even further around his hips. When he suddenly withdrew from between her legs, Suzette could have wept with disappointment, but then she felt him brush against her hungry flesh again. She nipped at his lower lip and dropped her hands to his bottom, squeezing him tightly to urge him on. Even so she was completely unprepared when he obeyed the silent demand, clasped her hips and thrust himself into her. It seemed it hadn't been his maypole the first time, because what entered her now was much larger and drew a startled squeal of pain from Suzette, or would have, had his mouth not still been covering hers and caught the sound.

Daniel froze at once and broke their kiss to peer down at her with concern. "Are you all right?"

Flushing with embarrassment, she nodded. It really hadn't hurt enough to bring on the sound she'd issued, she'd just been startled by it. Though, Suzette supposed she shouldn't have been. It really hadn't been more than a pinch of pain, certainly not enough to make even the most faint-hearted faint. Maybe Fanny's lover had done it wrong, she pondered. Still it did feel odd to have him inside her, stretching her body and filling her up. It wasn't exactly comfortable at first, but then Daniel slid his hand between them again and began to caress her once more while still buried inside her.

Suzette moaned at her body's immediate response to his caress as all the heat and passion that had seemed to slip away just moments ago, suddenly came rushing back. She raised her mouth to his, relieved when Daniel immediately began to kiss her again. When she wrapped her legs more tightly around him, encouraging him, Daniel also began to withdraw and then slide himself back into her again while still caressing her, the action matching the thrust of his tongue into her mouth. He started at a slow pace, but as their passion built, he began to move more swiftly, and then he removed his hand so that he could clasp her hips and hold her in place as he pumped into her.

Suzette groaned and dug her nails into his shoulders, her body straining toward the pleasure she knew waited, and then she was suddenly, finally there. She cried out into his mouth, her nails and heels digging into him as the mounting pleasure suddenly exploded over her. Shaken by the strength of it, she held onto him desperately and merely rode the waves washing over her. Daniel continued to thrust once, twice, then three times more before he suddenly buried himself to the hilt, a deep groan ripping from his throat.

She knew exactly when the paroxysm finally ended for Daniel, because he immediately sagged against her as if all his strength had been drained.

"Damn," he breathed after a moment, and slowly straightened to peer down at her and say solemnly, "I'm sorry."

Suzette peered at him with surprise. "What for?"

"I shouldn't have— The stables are not exactly the best place for a lady to— Someone could have come in and— I never should have—"

Suzette silenced him with a kiss, and hugged him tightly as she whispered, "Can we do it again?"

Daniel's chest vibrated against hers with silent laughter, but then he gently eased back and said wryly, "As tempting as the idea is, I couldn't right now. Besides, I have to go." He pressed a kiss to the tip of her nose. "I'm sorry, but I really do have to go now."

Suzette sighed with disappointment and reluctantly released him when he pulled away. She watched him tuck himself away and do up his trousers before setting to work on straightening her own clothes.

When he started to move back toward the stall he'd been in when she'd arrived earlier, she slid off the bale of hay, grimacing as she became aware of a tenderness between her legs. Ignoring it for now, she followed Daniel to the stall, asking, "How long will you be?"

"It's about an hour from here by carriage and she will probably have to pack, but since I am riding there on horseback I don't imagine it will be more than two hours," he answered absently as he returned to saddling his horse.

"Can I accompany you?" she asked, reluctant to be parted from him so soon after what they'd done.

Daniel glanced her way with surprise, hesitated, but then shook his head and turned back to what he was doing. "No. It is better if I go alone."

"Why?" Suzette asked with a frown, and then, worry entering her gaze, she accused, "You're afraid your mother won't like me, aren't you?"

The question made him glance around at her again and he frowned at the suggestion, but said firmly, "No, of course not."

"Then why can't I come?" she asked, and then her eyes narrowed with suspicion as another thought struck her. "You *are* coming back?"

"Of course I am," he said with a laugh, not even bothering to look at her this time. He then caught the reins of the horse he'd saddled and led it out of the stall. Pausing before her, he gave her a quick kiss and then took her arm to turn her around, saying, "Now go on back inside."

Suzette tried to turn back, but he kept his hand on her arm and urged her forward, walking her to the stable doors and out into the courtyard, leading the horse by its reins as they went.

"Inside. Now," Daniel said firmly then and re-leased her arm to give her a gentle push in the direction of the inn.

Suzette sighed, but continued forward, walking to the inn door before stopping to turn back. Daniel was mounted by then. He gave her a smile and a salute and then urged his mount to move. Suddenly plagued by the superstitious thought that if she watched him out of sight it might be the last time she saw him, Suzette immediately turned and slipped inside the inn.

The main room was as silent and empty as it had been when she passed through it on the way out, and Suzette was grateful for that. Silly as it might sound, she was sure that anyone who looked at her would somehow know she was no longer a virgin, as if the experience had marked her somehow.

Shaking her head at the flight of fancy, Suzette started upstairs to return to the room she shared with Lisa. She thought she might be able to sleep now, and felt sure the rest would do her good. She really *was* tender at the moment. Perhaps a nap would give her body a chance to heal.

Daniel couldn't get the grin off his face for the first half hour of the journey to Woodrow. While his body automatically steered the horse along the path to reach his home, his mind was filled with memories of Suzette, her neckline down below her breasts, her skirts up around her waist, and her eyes burning with passion as he'd driven himself into her. It had felt like going home. Her arms, legs and entire body had hugged his with each thrust, and her sighs, gasps and mewls of pleasure had filled his ears. The woman was all that he'd hoped for and more. She was as uninhibited with her body as she was with her words. He had a lifetime to enjoy the pleasure of both and was truly looking forward to it.

His grin softened to a smile at that thought. Daniel had never been very keen on the idea of marriage. He'd resented the idea of a wife. He knew his mother was a rare creature among the ton, one who rolled up her sleeves and did what needed doing. From what he had seen of most women in the ton, this was indeed a rare and wonderful thing. Most of the women he'd met over the years had been spoiled creatures, as demanding as princesses, who insisted on scads of clothes because they couldn't possibly be seen in the same dress twice, chests full of jewelry to show off their status, and, he was sure, would have demanded his attention and company to attend every ball, every play at the theater and every entertainment available when he had work to attend to in order to ensure their continued comfort.

But Suzette wasn't like that. Daniel knew without a doubt that she too would roll up her own sleeves and do what was required if the need should arise. The very fact that she had been willing to sacrifice herself to avoid scandal for the rest of her family said as much. She had stepped forward to take up the chore herself rather than even considering that Lisa too could marry and claim her dower to aid in the endeavor.

Daniel was pretty sure he needn't fear her dragging him to every social event of the season either. Suzette had already told him she preferred the quiet and beauty of the countryside to the crowded, polluted city. As for fashion and jewels, while her clothes were well made and she always looked nice, they were not exactly the height of fashion in London society, but she didn't seem to care any more about that than she did for what people thought of her blunt speech. Oddly enough, the very fact that she didn't seem to care about the material things made him want to shower her with them.

Daniel smiled wryly at the thought and then glanced around with a start as a sharp crack sounded. It seemed to be coming from the woods on his right and he slowed his mount, his eyes searching the trees as he recognized that he was on the edge of his property. They'd had trouble with poachers, he'd been told, though there had been no sign of them during the six months he'd been here before setting sail for America. But now he wondered if that was what he was hearing: poachers going after the wildlife. He would have to mention it to—

The thought died in his head as another crack sounded and something slammed into his back on his right side. It felt as if someone had just kicked him. It knocked the breath right out of him and nearly sent him tumbling from his horse. Throwing himself forward, he lay flat on his mount and kicked his heels, urging it to speed up again until the beast was going at an all-out run. Another crack sounded, but Daniel didn't feel anything this time, and simply concentrated on holding on to the reins of his horse. His fingers seemed to be weakening and his breathing was labored. For one moment he feared a punctured lung, but a deep breath reassured him that wasn't the case. Shock, then, he decided.

And maybe blood loss. Daniel added the grim thought as he felt trails of warm liquid tickling their way down his side. It was damned good he was so close to home, or he might not have made it, he thought grimly, but wondered when the lightheadedness hit him a moment later if he would after all.

Chapter Eleven

Should we not wait for Daniel?" Suzette asked, as her father urged her to a table to join the others breaking their fast. Her gaze slid to the door, but she managed to resist rushing over to see if Daniel was riding into the courtyard. She had done so several times during the last half hour since the two hours she'd expected him to take had passed. Scowling as she allowed her father to urge her onto the bench next to Lisa, she muttered, "What is taking him so long?"

"Lady Woodrow would wish to pack a bag of clothes," Richard pointed out with unconcern, as he settled across from her next to Christiana.

"Oh, yes of course." She didn't tell him that Daniel had thought he'd be back within two hours even with the need to pack.

Breakfast was a cheerful affair with much chattering and laughter from the group, but Suzette found it difficult to pay attention as she kept glancing toward the door, impatient for Daniel's return. She was relieved when it was over and immediately hurried to the door, intending to go out and check the stables, but the innkeeper was returning from a trip to the stables himself when she opened the door and smiled at her sympathetically as he shook his head.

"No sign of him yet, miss. I'm sure he'll be along soon."

"Yes," Suzette murmured, and then managed a smile and added, "Thank you," as she stepped back for him to enter. She then turned to cross to the stairs, thinking she would go up and check once again to be sure she had packed everything and had not left a stocking lying under the bed or something. Suzette had already done so once, but a second look would not hurt. Besides, she had to do something. This waiting was driving her mad.

Rolling her eyes at her own lack of patience, she mounted the stairs and walked quickly to the room she and Lisa were sharing. She thrust the door open and started to enter, but paused as she spotted a letter on the floor just inside. Frowning, she bent to pick it up, eyebrows rising when she saw her name on the front in a neat scrawl.

Pushing the door closed, Suzette opened the letter and started to cross to the bed, but paused as she read the contents.

Dear Suzette,

I apologize for the inconvenience of my timing. However, I simply cannot marry you. Your behavior in the stables this morning was, frankly, nothing like what one would expect from a lady of the gentry. It was a base and sordid little incident. You behaved no better than a milkmaid by lifting your skirts for me there amongst the dung and stink of the stables. I find this has raised concerns in me regarding your ability to remain faithful as a wife. I worry that such violent passions combined with your unruly nature and apparent complete lack of control would leave me forever worrying over what lewd behavior you might be getting up to with any man who entered your sphere of influence. I would look at any issue we had and wonder if they truly were my prodigy or that of the footman's, or the stable lads, or any visiting male guests. I do not wish to live that way, so again, I apologize. However I will not be returning to the inn to continue the journey to Gretna Green. I wish you the best of luck for the future, but I shall not be a part of it.

Yours truly,

Daniel

Suzette was reading the letter for the second time when the door opened behind her. She barely heard Christiana's words as her sister said, "Oh, here you are, Suzette. Lisa and I thought to pass the time with a nice walk. The innkeeper has assured us that there is a lovely path leading to a water—Suzette?"

Christiana had reached her side and Suzette turned stunned and wounded eyes to her sister. Her voice was a bare whisper as she got out, "Daniel is not returning."

"What?" Christiana frowned and then glanced to the letter in her now trembling hands and tried to take it, but Suzette pressed it to her chest and moved away, too ashamed to let her read it.

"He doesn't want to marry me," she gasped, finding it suddenly hard to breathe. Her breath was coming in fast, hard pants, but little air seemed to be reaching her tortured lungs, and she wheezed, "My chest hurts."

"Here, sit down." Christiana was at her side at once, urging her to sit. Once Suzette had dropped to the bed, she rushed to the window to open the shutters and let in the breeze. Turning back, she ordered, "Breathe. Deep breaths."

Suzette sucked in air, trying to slow her breathing. After a moment it seemed to work, and her breathing became more regular.

"Let me see the letter, Suzette," her sister said quietly once she was almost back to normal.

"No," she said in a low voice, her hands pressing the paper even tighter to her chest.

"Well then, tell me what it says. I am sure you are just misunderstanding," Christiana said gently.

"Dear Suzette, I apologize for the inconvenience of my timing. However, I simply cannot marry you," she recited dully from memory. Even with only the two reads the words were burned into her brain.

"I suppose there is no misunderstanding that," Christiana said grimly. "Did he say why?"

"I am unruly, my passions too violent, with no self-control, and he fears my ability to be faithful after marriage," Suzette admitted and then burst into tears.

"Oh Suzie," Christiana murmured, hugging her close. She was simply holding and rocking her and allowing her to weep when a knock sounded at the door.

"Who is it?" Christiana asked, sounding displeased.

"Your husband," came Richard's answer in slightly amused tones.

Christiana hesitated and then snapped, "Come in."

Suzette immediately tried to stop crying and pulled away from her sister to mop at her face as the door opened.

"I just came to see—what's wrong?" Richard had merely poked his head in, but seeing his wife's angry face and Suzette's wet one, stepped into the room and pushed the door closed. He crossed the room asking with concern, "What has happened?"

"Daniel is not returning," Christiana announced, standing to move to his side. "He has decided he doesn't wish to marry Suzette, that she is too unruly, her passions violent and her self-control nonexistent."

Silence reigned briefly and Suzette glanced around to see Richard frowning thoughtfully while Christiana glared, awaiting a response. After another moment, her sister's expression became concerned. "Richard? Why are you not surprised? Surely this is a mistake or—?"

"I don't know," Richard admitted, and then hesitated before saying, "I know Daniel wasn't sure he wanted to marry her at first. But he knew if he said as much she wouldn't spend time with him, so he didn't tell her so that he could get to know her and decide." He frowned. "I was sure he'd decided to marry her though, so—"

"You mean he was lying?" Christiana asked with dismay. "He led Suzette to think he had honorable intentions, but he—"

"He didn't exactly lie," Richard said lamely, and then sighed. "When Suzette caught him in her room that first night she assumed that Daniel was there to tell her yes, and he just didn't correct her."

"What is the difference between that and lying, exactly?" Christiana asked sharply. "He allowed her to come to the wrong conclusions and didn't correct her."

Suzette frowned and asked, "If he wasn't there to tell me yes, what was he doing there?"

"We were there to get George's body," Richard answered quietly. "We had just collected George when you girls arrived home. We hid in your room not realizing it was occupied, and then I left him hiding in there with George while I took you and Lisa down to the office. I was trying to keep you busy long enough for him to get out with George, but then you were going to drink the whiskey, and I thought it was how George was poisoned and knocked it out of your hand and you stormed off."

"Oh." Suzette recalled how upset she'd been, thinking he was just trying to stop her drinking his whiskey that night. Richard had been trying to prevent her drinking what he thought was poisoned whiskey. She shook her head. That wasn't important now. Mouth tightening, she said, "Daniel was alone in my room when I entered. George wasn't with him."

"He'd thrown George out the window and was trying to follow when you entered," he explained, looking uncomfortable.

Suzette closed her eyes and turned her head away. "So he never wanted to marry me at all."

"That's not—I don't know," Richard said wearily. "You fascinated him, and he liked you and wanted to get to know you better."

"Well, he certainly did that," Christiana snapped. "I know he's been kissing her and more."

Suzette grimaced and asked, "But what about the dower? I thought he wanted the dower. Why give that up when he so desperately needed it?" The question had barely left her lips when she felt herself flush with shame. The answer was in the letter. Apparently even the chance to gain the dower and save his people was not enough to lure him to marry someone as base and lewd as she. Shaking her head she moaned, "My God, he is disgusted by me so much that he would rather give up the dower he so desperately needs than marry me."

"He doesn't need it," Richard admitted, and added apologetically, "That *was* a lie."

"And you *knew*?" Christiana asked with dismay.

"Of course he needs the dower," Suzette protested, recalling the stories Daniel had told her of his childhood. Surely those couldn't be lies too? Could they? Dear God, she'd believed every word. Mouth tight, she said, "He told me that his mother had sold all their furniture to survive, and even her jewelry and her wedding ring. He said they had no servants, and—"

"That is all true," Richard assured her, appearing relieved to be able to say so. "And when he came of age his mother *was* pushing him to marry for money. She had worked hard to try to hide their dire straits, convincing society she was just a horrible snob rather than admit she was poor. And everyone believed it. After all, her family is extremely wealthy. But her family turned their backs on her when she married Daniel's father, and she and Daniel were destitute after he died."

Suzette was relieved to hear him verify the story Daniel had told her, but frowned and pointed out, "But you just said he doesn't need my dower."

"He doesn't." Richard ran a hand wearily through his hair. "Daniel blurted the whole tale to me one night, about how poor they were and what his mother had sacrificed and that she now wanted him to marry a girl with money, and quickly." He shrugged. "Of course, I had suspected as much. We were best friends and I had seen hints here and there. I had just been waiting for him to come to me, and when he told me all that, I helped him with investments and—" Richard grimaced and then admitted, "He has almost as much money as I do now. He is rich. He does not need your dower."

"So he never really wanted or needed me," Suzette said miserably.

"He was just trifling with her," Christiana sounded furious, and moved to the bed. Dropping to sit on the side of it, she hugged Suzette tightly.

"I don't believe that," Richard said grimly. "Daniel is an honorable man. I wouldn't be friends with him if I thought otherwise. There must be some explanation."

"What?" Christiana asked grimly.

"I don't know," he admitted with frustration, and then held out his hand. "Let me see the letter."

"No!" Suzette crumpled it in her hand and held it close to her chest. There was no way she was going to let him read about what she'd done in the stables. It had seemed the most beautiful experience in the world at the time, but now seemed cheap and dirty somehow. She'd thrown up her skirts as lightly as a milkmaid and Daniel now loathed her for it. She was ashamed and didn't want everyone to know about her shame.

Richard and Christiana were silent for a moment, and then Richard asked to speak with his wife alone. When Christiana stood and moved to the door with him, the two began to whisper, but Suzette merely curled up in a fetal position on the bed and hugged the letter to her chest. She should burn it, or tear it up, but she just didn't have the energy.

Suzette heard the chamber door open and close and lay staring at the wall. She wasn't sure how long she'd been lying like that, empty and numb, when the door opened and closed again.

She didn't open her eyes, but simply listened to the soft pad of slippered feet on the hard boards. Someone settled on the side of the bed and began to rub her back soothingly. She didn't know it was Christiana until she whispered, "All will be well, Suzie. Richard and Robert are going to go after Daniel and see what's what."

Suzette stiffened. Richard and Robert would find out that Daniel had a disgust of her because of her loose behavior. All would know her shame. The thought made her turn sharply to Christiana. "You have to stop them."

Christiana raised her eyebrows. "Why?"

"Because," she hissed, sitting up. "You just have to. I don't want them talking to him."

"Why?" Christiana repeated insistently.

Suzette cursed impatiently and scrambled off the bed to go after Richard herself. She ran downstairs as quickly as she could and then burst out of the inn in time to see Robert and Richard riding out. Her shoulders sagged miserably. By the time she got to the stables and saddled up a horse to follow, they would be long gone and Suzette had no idea where Woodrow was or how to get there so would never catch up to them.

"Suzette, isn't it?"

She glanced around with disinterest, vaguely recognizing the man who paused beside her, but merely shook her head and turned to go back into the inn. Suzette heard him enter behind her and try to hail her again, but she simply ignored him and trudged back upstairs to her room.

When she slipped inside, Christiana was still there, seated on the side of the bed, reading a wrinkled piece of paper. For one moment, Suzette had no idea what it was, but then she recalled the crumpled letter and realized she'd left it behind. Closing the door, she leaned back against it wearily and waited.

Christiana lifted her head, her eyes filled with sorrow as she whispered, "Oh Suzie."

Suzette bowed her head, unable to meet her gaze as shame slid over her.

Daniel awoke to pain. It felt as if his chest were being ripped apart, and for one moment he thought he'd fallen off his horse and some predator was feasting on his wounded flesh. But then he opened his eyes and found himself staring up at a silver-haired woman who still showed signs of the beauty she'd once been. Catharine, Lady Woodrow.

"Mother?" he croaked with confusion, glancing around to see that he was in bed in the master bedroom at Woodrow. "How—?"

"Here." She urged him to sit up and held a cup of liquid to his mouth. As he drank, she said, "Mr. Lawrence was returning from inspecting one of the tenant farms when he came across your horse plodding along with you slumped on its back. He brought you home at once for me to tend."

Daniel nodded at the mention of his assistant and swallowed the liquid in his mouth as she took the cup away. John Lawrence was most competent and he hadn't had any qualms at all about leaving the care of the estate in the man's hands while he traveled to America.

"What happened?" she asked solemnly.

"I was shot."

"Yes, I had noticed," she said dryly. "In fact, I bandaged you up. But by whom were you shot?"

Daniel shook his head wearily. "I didn't see. I was coming home to collect you, and I cut through the woods." He frowned, thinking of the accident with the carriage when they'd thought the spokes cut halfway through, and then the carriage that had nearly run him and Richard down. They'd thought those to be attacks aimed at Richard by George's killer trying to finish the job. However, George's killer had claimed to know he'd succeeded in killing George and hadn't been interested in killing Richard at all, and Daniel believed him. It had made him suspect that perhaps those other two incidents had not been aimed at Richard at all. The fact that he'd now been shot seemed to verify his suspicions. He didn't say that, however. He had no desire to upset his mother, so muttered, "Perhaps a hunter mistook me for wild game through the trees and shot."

Lady Woodrow frowned at the suggestion, but let it go for now and asked, "Coming home to collect me for what?"

"Oh." Daniel blinked as he recalled exactly what he had been doing. If he didn't return, Suzette would worry herself silly and send a search party out for him. Hell, knowing Suzette, she'd probably come after him herself, and then she'd see Woodrow and know—

"What time is it? How long have I been here?"

he asked, sitting up and wincing at the pain it sent through his back and stomach.

"Lie down," his mother ordered sharply. "And answer my question. Collect me for what?"

"My wedding," he answered, but decided to lie back for just a little bit under her insistence. Just for a minute or two, but then he had to—

"Your wedding?" Lady Woodrow asked icily.

Daniel glanced at his mother warily. She only ever used that particular tone when very upset. And she did indeed appear upset now. Upset, shocked, horrified, bemused, perhaps even a hint relieved and happy, but mostly upset.

"Your wedding to whom? And how have you managed to plan a wedding without even mentioning it to me or my catching wind of it?" she asked grimly.

"Ah, well, it's not exactly planned as such," he said uncomfortably. "I mean it is, but it's not a big do. We are going to Gretna Green, and—"

"Gretna Green!" she squawked, and then pressing one hand to her chest, gasped, "She is with child."

"No, of course she's not," Daniel said with irritation.

"Then why the rush to Gretna Green?" Lady Woodrow asked at once.

Daniel shook his head helplessly. "It is complicated, Mother."

She eyed him narrowly. "Then perhaps you should take your time explaining it to me."

Daniel glanced away, and then said, "Her name is Suzette, and she—well, you will like her. She is much like you, strong and smart and sweet but with a temper. Suzette is nothing like the other women of the ton," he said with a smile. "She never bites her tongue for politeness's sake. She blurts out what she's feeling and you always know where you stand with her. She does not smile to your face and then gossip and criticize you behind her fan."

"I see," she said softly. "This Suzette sounds special."

"She is," he assured her solemnly. "And I hope the two of you grow to be very good friends. She grew up in the country with just her sisters and her father. Her mother died when she was quite young and she hasn't had a mother's guidance, so she may not be as well trained at some household things as most ladies, but that doesn't matter. It would be nice if you could like her for me."

"I'm sure we shall be grand friends," Lady Woodrow said soothingly.

Daniel nodded and then tried to sit up, but she pushed firmly on his shoulders to keep him down.

"Stay put, son. You have been shot," she said sternly.

Daniel shook his head. "I have to get back. They are all waiting for me at the inn."

"They?" she asked.

"Suzette, her sisters, their father, Richard and a fellow named Robert Langley. They are waiting for me to bring you back. They will be worried." He frowned and glanced around. "What time is it? I do not even know how long I have been gone. They may already be looking for me."

"Why ever did you not bring them all with you?" she asked, still trying to push him flat on the bed.

"Oh, er . . . well," Daniel sighed, and sank back on the bed to admit, "Suzette thinks I am marrying her for her dower."

Lady Woodrow blinked. "I beg your pardon?"

"I said—"

"I heard what you said," she snapped, interrupting him. "Now, please explain exactly why the poor young girl thinks you would marry her for her dower."

Daniel winced at her tone. Every word was razor sharp and precise. She was angry. Grimacing, he said, "Well, Suzette has a rather large dower, huge really, and she wanted a husband who needed money and—" He paused abruptly as he saw her expression becoming befuddled, and sighed. "It is a long story, Mother. Just suffice it to say I couldn't let her see how well set we are financially or she might not have agreed to marry me."

"That makes absolutely no sense at all, Daniel," Lady Woodrow said impatiently. "Women look for a good provider. They want a husband with wealth."

"You didn't," he pointed out with amusement.

"Yes, well I am not like most women of the ton," she said with a wry smile.

"Neither is Suzette," Daniel assured her solemnly.

"So you mentioned. Still I—lie down," she snapped when he tried to rise again. "You will lie there and rest and explain this to me."

"There is no time. I need to get—"

"You need to rest and recover. I will send word to the inn, and—"

"No," he cried, grabbing her hand when she stood up. "She will come here. You can't let her come here."

Catherine Woodrow raised her eyebrows, but sat back down. "Then you had best explain why. Or I will send for her and get to the bottom of this myself."

Groaning, Daniel closed his eyes briefly, but then opened them again and glanced to the door as a knock sounded.

"Come in," his mother called, and the Woodrow butler opened the door to look in.

"My lady, the Lords Fairgrave and Langley are demanding to see Lord Woodrow, and insist they will not wait any longer to do so." He grimaced and pointed out, "They *have* been waiting two hours. I fear I will not be able to keep them downstairs much longer."

"Why didn't you tell me they were here?" Daniel asked his mother with irritation and then glanced back to the door as the butler cleared his throat.

Once the man had his attention, the butler allowed the corners of his mouth to curve just the slightest bit before getting his face under control and back to the expressionless visage of a proper butler as he said, "It is good to see you awake and recovering, my lord. We have all been quite worried since Mr. Lawrence brought you home."

"Thank you, Watkins," Daniel murmured, and then cleared his throat and asked, "Are Richard and Langley alone?"

"Yes, my lord."

"Thank God," he muttered, sitting up again. This time his mother did not try to stop him and he said, "Please, send them up."

"Daniel. Please explain what you have been up to and why this young lady you are to marry thinks you are poor, when you have worked so hard these last ten years to ensure we are not. None of this is making sense."

He grimaced. "It's really a quite convoluted story, Mother."

"I don't care. I have time."

"Yes, but—" Fortunately, Daniel was saved from trying to put her off further by the arrival of Richard and Robert. The two men must have jogged up the stairs to arrive so quickly. They didn't bother to knock, but strode right into the room, both looking quite grim faced and even angry until they got a look at him.

"What the devil happened to you?" Richard asked with amazement as he led Robert to the bed.

"I was shot," Daniel said.

Richard frowned, but Robert snapped, "It was probably the Fates punishing you."

"Punishing me for what?" he asked with surprise.

"For breaking Suzette's heart," he growled. "She was crushed when she got your letter."

"What letter?" Daniel asked, glancing from one man to the other with confusion.

"The letter you left saying you had changed your mind," Robert answered, but was starting to sound a little less angry. His expression turning uncertain, he asked, "You did send a letter to the inn for Suzette saying you were breaking it off and wouldn't marry her?"

Daniel shook his head firmly. "I never sent any such letter."

When Robert and Richard just stared at him blankly, Daniel's mother said, "I can assure you he left no such letter. He has just told me he'd come to collect me to attend his wedding and has been trying to get up to return to the inn almost since he awoke. He appears quite eager to marry the young woman."

"Hmm," Richard muttered, his expression troubled as he glanced to Robert.

"I think someone had best start explaining things," Lady Woodrow said firmly. "I hardly think it was an accident that this young lady received a letter breaking the engagement and my son was shot, all at the same time. There must be some connection."

Chapter Twelve

$\mathcal{F}$or one blessed moment when she first woke, Suzette didn't recall anything, but then she became aware of her sore throat and gritty eyes, and recalled crying herself to sleep and why, and a small pitiful sigh slid from her lips as memory came crashing in. She was a fallen woman, abandoned on the morning of her wedding and left sullied and unmarriageable. At least, most men would think so.

"You're awake."

Suzette stilled and glanced to the girl who had apparently been seated by the fireplace. Lisa. She was standing now and moving toward her.

"How do you feel?"

Suzette shrugged and sat up, avoiding her gaze as she did, but then she asked, "I suppose you hate me too?"

"No, of course not, and neither does Christiana," Lisa said at once, hurrying the last few feet to sit on the bed next to her. "You ordered her from the room before she could say anything. She isn't angry with you. She understands. You love Daniel and wanted to express that physically. It's natural."

"I don't love him," Suzette muttered.

Lisa looked at her with patent disbelief. "Suzette, you have been following the man around like a puppy for days now. And if you do not love him, you are certainly doing a very good impression of heartbreak."

Frowning, Suzette lowered her head. She was sure she didn't love him. She couldn't. And yet the pain when she'd read the letter, the ache in her chest just at the thought of never seeing him again, the anguish as she'd wept . . .

"You love him," Lisa said quietly. "I know you. You have probably been telling yourself it was just convenience, and handy that the two of you had needs that fit each other, one needing a bride with a dower, the other needing a husband in need of a dower . . ." She shook her head. "But your eyes lit up every time he walked into the room and you hung on his every word. And the passion you felt and shared with him . . ." She shrugged. "That is love. You do love him."

"For all the good it does me," she muttered with disgust.

"Oh," Lisa hugged her tightly. "I felt sure he loved you too, Suzette. Maybe he is just afraid—or something. Maybe—"

"Maybe my loose behavior disgusted him," she

said dryly. "Maybe he fears I am like this with every man."

"Oh, I am sure that is not true," she said, her expression troubled. "He would have to know it was your first time. The streams of blood and horrible pain would have—"

"There were no streams of blood or horrible pain," Suzette said unhappily. "In fact, there was hardly any pain. A little pinch perhaps, and an uncomfortable stretching sensation and that is all. As for streams of blood . . ." She shook her head. In truth, she wasn't sure if there had been any blood at all. It had been dark in the stables. Certainly there hadn't been streams of it. That would have been noticeable.

"Oh." Lisa bit her lip. "It was your first time?"

Her head snapped up, eyes stabbing her sister.

"Of course it was," Lisa backtracked at once, and then said, "Well, Fanny must have been wrong then. Or perhaps it is different for everyone."

Suzette shook her head with disgust. "If you, who have known me all my life and *know* I have not been keeping company with men before this, doubts me, why would he not? He probably thinks I have been with half the royal navy."

"Why would he think that? We live nowhere near the coast," Lisa said with confusion.

Suzette glared at her and then shifted to get off the bed, crawling around her to do so.

"Where are going?" Lisa asked, standing up.

"For a walk."

"But I was going to read to you to cheer you up," Lisa protested.

"I don't want to be read to," Suzette said grimly as she slipped her shoes on.

"I could tell you a story," Lisa offered.

"No."

"I could sing, or—"

"I want to be alone," Suzette said impatiently, heading for the door. She just wanted out of there. She didn't want Lisa's pitying looks or attempts to cheer her. She wanted to be alone to consider what to do. If there was anything to do. Of course, there were things she *had* to do. She still had to marry to save them all from scandal. Here she was, just a day's travel away from Gretna Green, where she would need to wed, but with no prospective grooms around to marry. If Daniel hadn't wished to wed her, the least he could have done was say so days ago in London, where she could have found someone else. Now she was far away from the bachelors she had to choose from. What a bloody mess.

Daniel was an ass, and she was an idiot, and soon Richard and Robert would return and everyone would know just how much of an idiot she was, Suzette thought as she left the room and started down the stairs.

Although, she supposed, everyone probably did know by now. Christiana and Lisa did. No doubt by now Richard and Robert had caught up to Daniel and demanded an explanation, which he would probably give, and they would know. So that just left her father, and he would learn soon as well, she was sure. It was bad enough making such a mistake, but having everyone know just made it unbearable. Not that it mattered, Suzette supposed. Even losing their combined esteem did not hurt as much as losing Daniel's. She had thought . . . Well, it didn't matter what she'd thought. She'd obviously thought wrong. And now here she was, heartbroken, Suzette acknowledged, as she made her way through the main room and slipped out of the inn.

While she had instinctively denied it to Lisa, Suzette would acknowledge to herself that her feelings for Daniel had run very deep indeed. She had craved him like the very air she breathed, and still did. She'd wanted to touch every part of him, hear every moment of his life before their meeting and share every future moment there was. She'd sprung from her bed each morning since meeting him, eager to start the day and find him, not wanting to miss a moment with him. And he had seemed just as eager to spend time with her, which was why she was so crushed now to learn that he hadn't ever intended to marry her, had been leading her to believe he would just to "get to know her better."

Perhaps it had all been some plot to debauch her, Suzette thought. It wasn't a pleasant possibility to consider. It meant she'd completely misjudged the man and hadn't known him at all.

Avoiding even looking at the stables, the scene of her folly, Suzette walked around the inn and found a small path into the woods as she considered that perhaps Daniel was one of those bounders who went about deflowering unwary young debutantes naïve enough to—

Suzette shook her head. No. She couldn't believe that. Surely, she couldn't have loved such a bounder as that? In the end, she supposed it didn't matter. That was what had happened. She'd lain with him, he was refusing to marry her because of it, and she now had to face the consequences alone. Virginity was expected from a bride and she would never lie to a man and claim to still possess hers. And yet she had to marry, and probably sooner was better than later since there may be even more consequences to that morning's events in the stable.

Swallowing, Suzette placed a hand over her stomach, wondering if his seed had taken root. Was she carrying his child? Part of her hoped dearly that she was, that she would keep and have a reminder of their time together for the rest of their days in the guise of a Daniel Junior. Another part of her, though, was horrified at the thought, knowing that looking on that child would mean fresh pain every day as well.

Sighing, Suzette paused to lean against a tree and closed her eyes, wishing things had been different. Wishing he'd love her. Wishing she'd never met him. She could have happily gone an entire lifetime without knowing this pain . . . even if it meant forgoing the happy moments and pleasure that had preceded it.

"Oh, I'm sorry."

Suzette glanced around. A man stood, hesitating a few feet away, looking uncertain as to whether to continue on his way or stop. It was the fellow who had approached as she'd watched Richard and Robert ride off. The one who had asked, "Suzette, isn't it?" She had thought he looked vaguely familiar then. Suzette felt sure she should know him, but couldn't be bothered to work it out any more now than she had been then.

"You're crying," he said, concern filling his expression as he moved forward.

Suzette raised a hand to her face, surprised to find it wet. She hadn't realized she'd been crying again, but suspected she would do a lot more of it in the coming weeks as she grieved her loss. Realizing the man was coming to stand before her, she turned to move away, but he caught her arm.

"Please, what's wrong? Maybe I can help," he said softly, drawing her to a halt.

"Nothing," Suzette murmured, keeping her face turned away. "Please, don't trouble yourself. I am fine."

"Now what kind of gentleman would abandon a lady crying alone in the woods?" he chided, retrieving a handkerchief and turning her so that he could dab at her face and mop up the tears. "There, that's better."

"Thank you," Suzette murmured as he put the handkerchief away.

He nodded, and then glanced around before looking back and saying solemnly, "You really shouldn't be out here by yourself, you know. This close to the border between England and Scotland there is more crime than elsewhere and a young lady should never be unescorted in the area."

Suzette peered at the trees surrounding them. It looked peaceful enough. On the other hand, there could also be a dozen bandits and highwaymen hiding behind the surrounding trees and she would not know it until they leapt out at her.

"Come, I shall walk with you," he decided, taking her arm and urging her gently along the path. "There is a lovely little waterfall just a little further on. Perhaps we could sit there. I always find water soothing to my troubles, though I'm not sure why. But it has been that way since I was a small boy. Do you like water?"

Suzette mumbled a noncommittal reply. At that moment she wasn't sure what she liked or disliked, or if she liked much of anything at all. Mostly she just wanted to go back to her room at the inn and curl up in a ball on the bed and cry herself back to sleep. She didn't know why she hadn't just sent Lisa from the room and done that earlier, rather than coming outside.

"London is nice with its entertainments, but there is just nothing to compare to Mother Nature's artistry in the country, don't you think?" the man continued, chattering soothingly. "The fresh air, the birdsong, the rustle of the breeze through the trees . . . I always feel refreshed after a visit to the country. Ah, here we are. Isn't it lovely?"

Suzette saw that they'd moved off the path to the edge of a small pond with a waterfall pouring fresh water into it. It was quite pretty, she supposed with disinterest, and wondered if Daniel would have liked it.

"If I'd realized I was going to come across a beautiful young lady on my walk, I would have had the innkeeper's wife pack a picnic for us," her companion commented as he urged her to sit on a boulder next to the water. "However, I suppose we shall have to make do with what I did bring. You have your choice of a peach or a pear."

Suzette eyed the two items he'd retrieved from his pocket. She wasn't hungry, but took the peach to be polite and the fellow settled next to her on the boulder, leaving enough room that it could not be considered improper.

They were silent, watching the water cascade into the pond, and Suzette let her mind wander. Of course it returned to Daniel, to his smile, his kind eyes, his laughter, his kisses—

"Shall I dispose of the pit for you?"

Suzette glanced down with surprise to see that, hungry or not, she'd eaten the entire peach. And she hadn't tasted a bite. She held out the pit and watched silently as he tossed it into the pond.

"There." He relaxed on the boulder and then said, "It is none of my business, but you seem very melancholy, not at all the vivacious young woman I met at the Landons' ball."

Suzette stiffened and looked to him then, really looking this time. He definitely did look familiar, but she still wasn't placing him.

"I'm sorry," she said finally. "I danced with so many at the Landons' ball, and it feels like a lifetime ago. I'm afraid I don't recall—"

"I am the one man you *didn't* dance with," he said, smiling wryly, and then introduced himself. "I am Lord Danvers. Jeremy Danvers. I was on your card that night, but when I came to claim you for our dance, you seemed quite distressed and you rushed off."

"Oh," Suzette grimaced as the memory returned to her. He'd come to claim her just as she'd spotted Richard.

"Ah, I see the recollection on your face," Danvers said with amusement.

"I apologize, I am not usually so rude, but there was something of a family crisis," she said quietly, now recalling that Lisa had been alarmed at her not dancing with the man because he suited their needs and was not old or unpleasant. Suzette thought now that perhaps if Richard had arrived just a few minutes later, everything would be different. Perhaps she would have made her proposition to Danvers on the dance floor and never even given Daniel a second glance.

"There is no need to apologize," Danvers assured her, and then smiled wryly and said, "Although, I suppose I could hold you wholly responsible for my broken heart because of it."

Suzette blinked in surprise. "I'm sorry, I don't—"

Jeremy patted her hand soothingly, and shook his head. "Forgive me. That was just a moment's bitterness slipping out." He sighed and turned his gaze to the water, but then confessed, "When you rushed off so precipitously and left me without a partner, I asked a lovely young blonde if I might have the pleasure. We danced and chatted and laughed . . . I fear I was quite taken with her. I even fetched her punch and then asked for a second dance later in the night." He gave her a crooked smile and pointed out, "Very risky behavior, dancing twice in one night with the same lady."

"Yes," she murmured, turning her gaze to the water now.

"I met her again the next night at the Hammonds' ball and again danced with her twice and fetched her punch, and then she grew quite warm and we went out on the terrace and I snuck a kiss."

Suzette swallowed, recalling the kiss she and Daniel had shared at the Landons' ball.

"It was all quite intoxicating," Jeremy said quietly. "I fear I let myself get carried away and endeavored to "run into" her at several other places the last few days . . . She did not seem to mind and then, well, I fear I ended up asking her to marry me." He sighed. "I wanted to go to her father and ask for her hand, but she convinced me not to. She insisted we must run off to Gretna Green to marry, and at once."

Jeremy bent to pick up a stone he'd been worrying with the toe of his boot and tossed it in the pond before continuing. "Of course, the truth was her parents would never have approved. She is an heiress where I have only a barony, a small castle in northern England and little money to run it." He grimaced charmingly as he admitted that and shrugged. "I agreed and we set out."

Suzette's eyebrows rose. "Is she back at the inn?"

Jeremy shook his head. "It seemed she wasn't quite as taken as I. We rode night and day, got to Gretna Green and—" he shook his head with bewilderment. "She just changed her mind at the last minute. She burst into tears and fled. She would not even allow me to return her home, but insisted on renting a hack herself and returning on her own." He dug up another stone and bent to collect it as well. He weighed it in his hand briefly, and then tossed it into the pond before finishing, "So I am returning alone, still a bachelor rather than the newly married man I expected to be."

"I'm sorry," Suzette whispered, sympathizing with the man. His story was not that different from her own.

"The hell of it is, I have to marry relatively soon to fulfill my duty to my family," he continued unhappily. "I have been resisting marrying the first likely gel for money, and thought here I would manage a love match and still meet my family's needs, but—" He shook his head. "It seems I shall have to sell myself off to stud to the first likely hag with coin in her pocket to save the family estates from ruin."

Suzette stared at him blankly for a moment and then suddenly just burst into tears.

"Oh say," he cried at once. "I didn't mean to make you cry again. 'Tis all right, my heart is a little dented and wounded now, but I'll recover. I hope," he added unhappily, and then said, "Please don't cry."

"I'm sorry," Suzette muttered, dashing at her tears, and then, accepting the hanky he held out, she quickly mopped them up. "It is just that we are in much the same situation."

His eyebrows rose. "You need to marry for money?"

"No. Well, yes, but—oh," she sighed and quickly explained the situation and her need for a husband in need of money who would be willing to allow her to pay off the debt and live her own life.

"So you have a large dower and need a husband

in need of money, and I have a title and lands and need a bride with coin, and here we both sit brokenhearted and with no prospects," he said with a short laugh, and shook his head. "Fate has a nasty sense of humor, doesn't she?"

Suzette nodded solemnly and handed him back his hanky.

They were both silent for a moment and then he glanced at her and asked, "Would it be too bold of me to suggest we marry each other?"

Suzette hesitated and then glanced away. The thought had occurred to her, but it would mean telling him what she'd done.

"I wouldn't suggest it, only . . . well, I feel very comfortable with you," he admitted and then added wryly, "Believe me, I do not usually go about blurting my troubles to pretty ladies I've just met, and yet it seemed the most natural thing in the world to tell you." He smiled crookedly and added, "I even feel a little bit better for it."

Suzette managed a smile, but worried her lower lip between her teeth, wondering if she had the courage to tell him what she'd done. She did not feel uncomfortable with him either. He was pleasant enough, and rather charming in a non-threatening, not-at-all-arousing-like-Daniel way.

"And it does seem to me that if you cannot have a great passion, you should at least like and be comfortable with your mate," he added. "I think we could be good friends with time."

Suzette sighed and lowered her head. If she could not have Daniel, she supposed she could do worse than Jeremy. Of course, they'd just met, but he seemed decent enough, and at least, having suffered heartbreak himself, he would understand *her* heartbreak. And it would solve her problems and save her from the wearying business of searching for another possible husband. She just wished she didn't have to tell him what she'd done. But there was no help for that, she realized, and blurted, "I let my betrothed drive his machine up my strait."

Jeremy stared at her blankly, one sound slipping from his lips, a confused, "Eh?"

"He drove his nail up to the head," she explained, using another metaphor she'd learned in her reading.

"Er . . ." Jeremy got out, still looking bemused.

Suzette sighed with exasperation. "He buried his truncheon in my cloven field."

"Don't you mean clover field?" he asked scratching his head. "I've never heard of a cloven field. You must mean clover."

Suzette flushed with embarrassment. She couldn't recall anymore metaphors from her reading and it seemed something more to the point was needed here. "I gave him my innocence, my lord."

"Oh," the word left him on a long breath, and then he sighed, "I see . . . Well, that's . . . Oh dear."

Suzette lowered her head, awaiting his disgust and rejection, but after a moment he cleared his throat and said, "Well, I will admit I would not like another man's by-blow. However, I suppose we could resolve that matter by simply refraining from . . . er . . . nailing the clover until we know if you are carrying his child or not."

Suzette blinked and glanced to him in surprise. "You do not mind? I mean I—"

"You obviously love him," he said gently. "Your tears say as much, and I surely understand love. Though truly, I must tell you I don't think he deserves your love if he would take your innocence and then abandon you like this. Certainly, I never would have let my girl go had we gone so far."

Suzette felt misery slide through her and turned her head away with shame, but he patted her hand.

"It is surely not a flaw in you, but him," Jeremy said reassuringly. "And perhaps it is only because my heart is not engaged, but other than waiting to consummate the marriage until we are sure you are not with child, I see no reason for that to be an issue in our decision."

"And what if I am with child?" she asked on a whisper.

A moment of silence passed and then he suggested, "Why do we not deal with that if it happens? You probably are not with child, and we must hope for that, but if you are, well, there are many options to choose from. It might be a girl, who wouldn't inherit the title and estate anyway. Or the child might not make it to term." He shrugged. "Let us take this one problem at a time. We both need to marry and suit each other's needs in that manner. Let us leave the future to take care of itself."

Suzette let her breath out on a small sigh as she nodded, and actually felt a little better. Her heart still ached, and she suspected she would spend a lot of time weeping, and would no doubt weep at the wedding because it was Jeremy at her side and not Daniel, but at least the other issues were taken care of. Her family would be safe from scandal, the markers would be paid, and Jeremy did not appear to be horrified, scandalized or disgusted by what she'd done.

"Suzette?"

She peered over her shoulder as her father stepped out of the trees and into the small clearing.

Lord Madison frowned when he took note that she was not alone and said, "I have been looking for you for several minutes and was about to give up and go back to the inn when I heard your voices and followed them."

"Lord Madison," Jeremy said quietly, getting to his feet. "I realize it is not well done of me to keep your daughter company out here like this, but we came across each other on the path and I thought seeing the falls would lift her spirits."

"Do I know you?" Cedrick Madison asked, eyes narrowing on Jeremy.

"No. But I know of you. Actually, I hadn't realized you were here as well or I would have sought you out before this," he admitted with a wry smile.

"Why?" Lord Madison asked at once.

"Well, I thought we had some business," Jeremy admitted, but then quickly added, "but I think now we can forget that."

"What business?" her father asked sharply.

"It is nothing to be alarmed about, my lord. I—" Jeremy paused and frowned, his gaze sliding to Suzette and then he shook his head with a laugh. "I apologize, Miss Madison, I was about to suggest your father and I discuss this in private, but I've just recalled that you know all about it."

"About what?" she asked uncertainly.

"Your father's gambling," he said apologetically, and then turned to her father. "I happened to have a lucky streak at the tables the other night. Unfortunately, Cerberus did not have the cash on hand to pay my winnings and instead gave me your marker and suggested I collect from you. Of course, now that Suzette has agreed to marry me, I would feel an ass demanding the payment and—"

"Marry!" Lord Madison gasped, his eyes shooting to Suzette.

For her part, Suzette just glanced from one man to the other uncertainly. She felt as if the ground were shifting under her feet and wasn't certain what to think. Settling on Jeremy, she asked, "You gamble?"

"Not usually, no. But some friends convinced me to accompany them and as I say, I had a streak of luck." He shrugged, and then added apologetically, "I had no idea your father would have trouble paying until you explained why you needed to marry, else I surely would never have accepted the marker in lieu of payment from Cerberus. I understood your family was well off."

"There is no trouble paying," her father said grimly. "And there's no need for Suzette to marry. I have the money at the inn."

Suzette glanced at him with surprise. "You have the money? Where did you get—"

"I sold the townhouse," he admitted grimly.

"Oh Father," she said with dismay.

He shrugged. "We don't use it much anyway, and it is better than seeing another of my daughters forced into a bad marriage."

"Well," Jeremy said wryly. "All's well that ends well then."

"Yes," her father said grimly. "Come back to the inn with me and I shall pay you at once and finally be free of the damned thing."

When Jeremy nodded agreeably, Suzette's father took her arm and turned to lead her back to the path.

"I cannot tell you how relieved I am that it has all gone so well," Jeremy commented, falling into step behind them. "I will admit I was a bit concerned that you would balk at paying the marker and the interest."

Her father froze at once, his fingers digging into her arm.

Suzette glanced to him worriedly. "Father?"

Turning slowly, he narrowed his eyes on Jeremy. "Interest?"

"Yes." Lord Danvers appeared surprised at his reaction.

"What interest?" her father asked grimly.

"Well, let me see, when I won the marker two nights ago it was worth double what you originally signed for. I suppose it would be more than that now. However, I think I can dispense with the interest earned since then. It does seem ridiculously exorbitant for just a week's time. So just the amount I was to win would suit me fine. It shall keep the creditors at bay and give me plenty of time to find another bride."

"Double?" her father asked, sounding faint.

Jeremy's eyebrows beetled with concern. "Surely you aren't surprised? You did read the marker before you signed it?"

Lord Madison dropped her arm and Suzette peered at him with concern. It seemed obvious that her father hadn't read the marker, but then if he'd been drugged and basically robbed, she supposed he wouldn't have. Certainly, the amount had taken him by surprise and left him looking pale and old. He didn't have enough money from the sale of the townhouse to cover it, Suzette realized.

"It's all right, Father," she said quietly. "Jeremy said he would forgive the marker if we married and that is what we shall do."

"I am most amenable to that, my lord," Jeremy said quietly.

"No," her father said faintly, and then grabbing her arm again he said more strongly, "No. Come. We will talk to Richard first." He had only taken two steps before he paused abruptly and muttered, "They aren't here. They have gone to make Daniel—they should be back soon."

"They should have been back two hours ago," Suzette said grimly, silently finishing off the sentence in her head. They have gone to make Daniel *marry her*? Fulfill his promise? She had thought they had gone to ask him why he had rejected her, but instead she was suddenly sure they had gone to basically force him to wed her. What a choice. Life with a man who seemed nice enough, and whom she might grow to feel affection for eventually, or a man she loved with all her heart, who

was forced to marry her and would then resent her
for it all the days of their lives while her love died
a thousand deaths? Hard choice, Suzette thought
bitterly and raised her chin. "Obviously, Daniel is
not eager to be *made* to do anything. And frankly,
I wouldn't want him at this point anyway if he
was forced to marry me. I shall marry Jeremy. The
marker will be paid off through my dower and
never be brought up again."

"Suzette," her father said worriedly, but she
shook off his hand and turned to Jeremy.

"If you are still amenable, of course, my lord,"
she added more quietly.

"Of course," he said at once.

She nodded and turned to start onto the path.

"Please, Suzette," her father said, following.
"Don't do this. Just wait until Richard and Robert
return and see what they have to say."

"So that I can be told again that Daniel doesn't
want me?" she asked bitterly.

"You aren't thinking clearly," he insisted, taking
her arm and forcing her to a halt. "At least take the
time to consider things."

"Actually, Father, I am thinking clearly for the
first time since meeting Daniel," she admitted quietly. "He—I could not think at all when he was
near. I did things I know better than to do *before*
marriage." She flushed with shame as comprehen-
sion and sorrow entered his eyes and felt her throat
close up as tears filmed her own. She was forced
to whisper when she pointed out, "There might be
consequences. This takes care of everything. The
markers and those consequences if there are any."

"Oh Suzette," he said sadly.

She was frankly sick of hearing those two words together in that tone, and said with feigned unconcern, "I was an idiot. I wasn't foolish enough to think he loved me, but I thought at least he wanted to marry me for the dower."

"That's all Danvers wants," he pointed out quietly, glancing toward the other man who had paused several feet away to allow them privacy.

Suzette shrugged. "Then he can have it. I no longer care. And there are the consequences to think of. If I am with child . . ." She sighed. "It is best if the child has a name other than bastard."

"Does he know?" Lord Madison asked, glancing back toward Jeremy again.

"Yes," she said simply, and then shrugged. "It is essentially a business transaction, Father. Both of us gave our hearts to others and this is a marriage of convenience. It will be fine. He seems kind enough and I think it may work out all right in the end. I will marry him."

His shoulders slumped in defeat. "Then I shall come with you."

"You do not have to—"

"I am your father, and you are an unmarried woman; you need a chaperone. I will accompany you and stand beside you as you are married," he said firmly.

Suzette merely nodded. She was oddly numb now, empty. The decision had been made and her future was set and she felt nothing.

Chapter Thirteen

I never realized I had raised such a fool."

Daniel stiffened at his mother's words. "A fool?"

"Yes, a fool," Lady Woodrow said firmly, and then shook her head and muttered, "Letting the girl think you wanted her only for her money. What could you have been thinking?"

"It was what she wanted in a husband," he protested at once.

Lady Woodrow looked down her nose at him and assured him dryly, "No woman wishes the man she loves to want her only for her money."

Daniel blinked, a slow smile curving his lips as he asked, "You think she loves me?"

"Did I say fool?" she asked the ceiling and then

glanced down to him and snapped, "I meant idiot."

"Mother," he said with irritation.

"Of course she loves you, you dolt. Did you think she'd lie with every bounder after her dower?"

"Well, no, of course not, but—"

"Son, we women have it drummed into our heads from very early on that chastity is a must, that our virginity is the most valuable gift to give a husband. You men may run about rutting with every bitch in heat you come across, but we do not," she assured him acerbically.

Daniel's eyes widened incredulously. Bitch in heat? Was this his mother, the most proper Dowager Lady Woodrow? She never spoke like that, he thought and said, "But it is so soon. She can't possibly love me already."

"Lord love me," Lady Woodrow muttered, and then pointed out, "It is just as soon for you. Are you now going to try to tell me you don't love her? Because, my son, I know you well and I can tell you right now that would be a lie. Your eyes light up when you talk about her and your face goes soft. If you were thinking that you were just marrying her because you wanted to bed her, then you were deceiving yourself. You have done nothing these last ten years but cringe every time I have brought up the subject of marriage and producing grandbabies for me. You have not changed your mind and suddenly rushed this girl off to Gretna Green just because you want to bed her. Besides, from the explanations you three just gave, you've *already* bedded her!"

Daniel blinked and frowned.

She left him to puzzle through her words and his feelings and turned to Fairgrave, saying, "Now, Richard."

"Yes, Lady Woodrow?" He immediately stood up straighter.

"You and your friend here help my son to dress while I go have some clothing packed and a carriage prepared," she instructed. "We will leave as soon as all is ready."

"Yes, my lady," Richard said smartly and Lady Woodrow smiled and patted his cheek.

"You always were a good boy," she said affectionately and then left the room.

"Suzette's going to love her," Robert murmured as the door closed behind Lady Woodrow.

Daniel frowned. "Is that a sarcastic comment or do you really think they shall get along?"

"Oh, they'll get along like a house on fire," Robert assured him, moving to help Richard select clothes for him. "In fact, I suspect it will be the two of them against you in every argument, so you'd best start praying you and Suzette have all boys or you'll be woefully outnumbered."

Daniel smiled faintly at the advice, but just as quickly frowned as he thought of the letter and how callous it must have seemed after what they'd done in the stable. "How upset was Suzette?"

Richard grimaced and it was Robert who said solemnly, "I didn't talk to her, but I could hear her weeping from the hall. I have never heard such heart-wrenching sobs in my life. I would say your mother was right and Suzette loves you, for she truly seemed brokenhearted."

Daniel scowled at the thought and then asked,

"Do you think Mother is right and the shooting and letter are connected?"

"It does seem likely," Richard said. "It would be an odd coincidence if it weren't. After all, had you returned as planned, you would have simply told her the letter was a fake."

"Yes, but if whoever shot me thought me dead, why bother with the letter?"

"Perhaps they were not sure they succeeded with a mortal wound," Robert suggested.

"All right," Daniel conceded. "But then what purpose does the letter serve except to make her think the wedding is off, and why bother with that?"

Both Richard and Robert appeared as blank faced as he felt. It just didn't make sense, or at least he didn't see the sense of it just then. But it gave him a bad feeling.

"Come, give me those clothes. I think the sooner we get back to the inn and straighten this out the better. There is something afoot here that we aren't yet seeing."

"I do not see what the rush is. Why can we not stop at an inn and rest and continue on in the morning?" Suzette's father asked plaintively.

"My lord, we have barely been on the road more than an hour thanks to your delaying," Jeremy answered with what Suzette considered amazing patience. Certainly, with more patience than she had at the moment, but then she was very annoyed with her father.

After insisting on accompanying them, Cedrick

Madison had then dragged his feet as much as he could to delay the departure. He'd taken forever to pack when she suspected he hadn't really unpacked at all. They'd only stayed the one night at the inn and had planned to continue on today once Daniel returned with his mother. Surely, her father wouldn't have unpacked anything but a change of clothes. Yet he had been up in his room forever supposedly packing, and had come down only when Jeremy had finally gone upstairs and impatiently offered to help with the chore to speed things along.

Suzette had been rather impatient herself as she sat waiting in the main room. Christiana and Lisa had spent the entire time trying to convince her to wait for the men to return, something she simply hadn't wished to do. She'd suffered enough humiliation that day. So she'd sat waiting, starting in her seat each time the inn door opened, terrified it would be the men returned. Suzette had been greatly relieved when her father had finally come below.

However, even then, Lord Madison had further delayed them by insisting Suzette looked peaked and a meal should be eaten. Jeremy had tried to convince him that he would have a picnic basket prepared and they could eat in the carriage, but her father had been determined that they should eat a proper meal at the inn with Christiana and Lisa before departing. Unable to move him on the matter, they had given up and eaten, delaying their departure further.

Finally, they had left, but had not been on the

road for more than an hour and already her father wanted to stop.

"But look, it is growing dark," Cedrick Madison said now. "What if one of the horses steps in a hole, or twists a fetlock? Surely it would be safer to take a room and continue in the morning? It is not as if there is any great rush," her father said, sounding determined.

"My driver assured me he could deliver us safely despite the hour," Jeremy said firmly. "We shall take rooms when we reach Gretna Green."

Suzette glanced to Jeremy to offer him an apologetic smile for her father's behavior. However, he wasn't looking her way. He sat hands clasped in his lap and twiddling his thumbs as he stared out the window. He appeared deep in thought.

"How are you feeling?" Lady Woodrow asked.

Daniel forced a reassuring smile for his mother. She sat across from him beside Robert in the Woodrow carriage, while he shared a bench seat with Richard. "I am fine, Mother. The ride hasn't started my wound bleeding and it doesn't even hurt anymore."

Lady Woodrow nodded solemnly, and then said, "I don't believe you."

Daniel sighed. He really didn't feel that bad considering. His lower back ached and burned on the side where he'd taken the wound, and he didn't feel at full strength certainly, but he suspected nothing but the passage of time to allow it to heal would resolve the pain. At the same time, Daniel was sure a good meal and some ale would fix the other issue. As far as he was concerned, he had got off lucky. It could have been much worse. Though he'd lost a bit of blood, it seemed nothing vital had been struck. That was a good thing. And he was showing no signs of fever so, hopefully, his mother had done a thorough-enough job of cleaning the wound that he had bypassed infection.

"We are almost there. I can see the inn," he announced. His mother immediately leaned to peer out the window.

"I shall go ahead and ask the innkeeper to arrange for food while the two of you see him inside," his mother announced once the carriage had stopped and Richard and Robert had assisted Daniel out of the carriage. The truth was, while he was a little unsteady on his feet, he didn't need two of them, but hadn't refused the help, hoping the added assistance would mean less jostling about and therefore less aggravation to his wound. He suspected a dozen men could have been there to help and it still would have hurt like hell.

Grimacing, Daniel started forward at once to follow his mother into the inn. Much to his relief Richard and Robert merely walked beside him, there to lend support if needed, but neither man fussing unnecessarily.

His mother was standing in the door to the main room, surveying its inhabitants, when he caught up to her. Daniel immediately began searching for Suzette, but the room was empty except for the innkeeper and Christiana and Lisa. The two women were seated at one of the otherwise empty tables, their heads together and whispering worriedly to each other. However, they paused to glance around at the sound of the door closing.

The immediate change in both women was rather startling. They went from anxious worry to immediate outrage and fury in a heartbeat. Daniel couldn't help taking a surprised step back as they both suddenly rose and flew at him like a couple of harpies.

"You horrible, horrible man!" Lisa yelled.

"How could you even show your face here, you bounder?" Christiana snapped.

"You vile debaucher of innocents," Lisa added. "She loved you, you cad!"

"You've broken her heart! You should be shot for toying with her that way!" Christiana reached out to poke at him to emphasize the point, but Richard caught her before her finger quite touched him and pulled her back even as Robert hurried around Daniel to grab Lisa by the arm and stop any possibility of physical assault from her.

"Well!" Lady Woodrow's voice rang out, immediately startling both women into silence and garnering their attention as she moved to Daniel's side. Much to his amazement, she then smiled and said, "I am so glad to see you stand up for Suzette. It warms my heart to see such sisterly love. Alas, my own sisters did not turn out to be as loyal."

Christiana and Lisa stared at her blankly, and then Christiana turned to Richard and asked, "Who—?"

"My mother," Daniel interrupted quietly. "If you'll recall I went to collect her and bring her back to join the party to Gretna Green so she might also witness my marriage to Suzette."

"Yes, but you broke off the engagement," Lisa said angrily, and when he shook his head, said uncertainly, "You didn't break it off?"

"But the letter," Christiana said sharply. "I read it, my lord, there was no misunderstanding. You flat-out said you would not marry Suzette and as good as called her little better than a light skirt."

Daniel cursed under his breath, and then glanced to his mother as she took his arm to urge him past the women toward the tables.

"You need to eat," Lady Woodrow reminded him firmly. "You promised you would eat as soon as we arrived at the inn. It is the only reason I agreed to leave Woodrow without insisting you eat first and you shall keep that promise."

"But I need to speak to Suzette." Daniel glanced toward the stairs, sure she must be up in her room. Probably crying her heart out. Poor thing, he thought.

"You can speak to her while you eat. Now sit down and eat before you fall down."

"Why would he fall down?" Lisa asked, moving closer to get a better look. "He's so pale. What's wrong with him?"

"He was shot on his way to Woodrow," Richard answered. "And he didn't send the letter."

"What?" Christiana asked with horror.

Daniel started to turn around, intending to insist they tell him where Suzette was, but a shaft of pain as he twisted his upper body made him freeze and suck in a bit of air.

"Sit," his mother said firmly. Once she had him on the bench, she moved away saying, "Richard, go speak to the innkeeper and arrange for broth and a hearty meal."

Daniel, recalling what happened the last time he tried to turn, simply stood up and moved around the table to the opposite side so that he could see what was going on as Richard hurried over to the innkeeper and his mother turned her attention to Suzette's sisters.

"Now, you must be Christiana and Lisa," she greeted, taking each girl by one hand.

"Yes. How did you know?" Christiana asked.

Rather than point out that they had just been attacking Daniel on their sister's behalf and so were easily identifiable as relatives, she simply said, "Because I knew neither of you could be Suzette."

"Why not?" Daniel asked with a frown. He hadn't described her looks to his mother, just her personality and actions.

Lady Woodrow frowned when she saw that he'd moved, but merely shook her head and said calmly, "Because no doubt she is on the way to Gretna Green right now with what she thinks is merely some bachelor in need of coin who just happened to show up in her hour of need."

"What?" Daniel asked with disbelief and wondered where she could have come up with such a ridiculous idea. Suzette was upstairs, her heart broken and sobbing over the loss of him. At least that's what he'd thought, so was startled when Lisa nodded with wide eyes.

"Yes, Lord Danvers arrived and offered to

marry her in exchange for Father's markers and she accepted. How did you know?" Lisa asked with surprise.

Daniel was so stunned by this news that he almost didn't catch his mother's reply as she said, "Really, what else was the letter for but to ensure she thought there was no hope for her love for Daniel and would be willing to leave here promptly with another?"

"Damn, she's smart," Robert muttered to Daniel as he settled at the table next to him. "That hadn't occurred to me."

"Me neither," Daniel said grimly, getting to his feet. So much for her being upstairs nursing her supposedly broken heart.

"Sit, Daniel," Lady Woodrow said without even glancing around to see him on his feet.

The woman always had seemed to have eyes in the back of her head when it came to him, he thought grimly, and sat back down. He didn't know why he'd got up anyway. Suzette didn't love him. She'd cared so little she'd run off with the first man who offered for her. She hadn't even waited a full bloody day. He really had just been the first handy bloke to suit her needs and, apparently, any man would do. It was damned lowering after what they'd shared in the stables. If Suzette thought she would experience that kind of pleasure with just any man, she had a sorry disappointment coming . . . and it served her right, he decided.

"How long ago did they leave?" Robert asked as Richard rejoined them.

Despite his suddenly glum mood, Daniel found himself waiting tensely for the response.

"No more than an hour ago," Christiana murmured. "Father insisted on going with them and made them take the time to eat first. He also dallied as long as he could over packing though I'm sure he never unpacked here. I think he hoped you'd return with news before they left."

"Bless him," his mother said and then glanced to Richard in question, "How long until the food will be ready?"

"The innkeeper assured me it would be out right away. His wife has a stew on the hob and some left-over roast beef from last night. She's going to bring the juice of the stew and a roast-beef dinner for him right away."

"Good, good." Lady Woodrow ushered Christiana and Lisa to the table, and then suggested, "Perhaps we should all eat then."

When Richard hesitated and glanced uncertainly toward Daniel, Lady Woodrow waved her hand in a dismissing gesture and said, "Never mind him, he is sulking. His nose is out of joint because Suzette has run off to marry another. It's for the best anyway. This way we need not fight to get him to keep his promise to eat and he *does* need to eat."

"I am not sulking," Daniel said through gritted teeth as Richard moved off to let the innkeeper know they would all be eating. "And stop talking about me like that. I am sitting right here."

"I notice you don't deny your nose is out of joint," Lady Woodrow said easily as she settled on the bench next to him with Christiana and Lisa on her other side.

"My nose is not out of joint," he said now, and then raised his chin and added, "She has done me a favor. If she cares so little for me that she would run off with the first man who came along, then she has saved me future heartache."

"Oh but—" Lisa began, but was shushed by his mother.

"After he eats," she said gently, and explained, "Daniel can be terribly bullheaded when he wishes. It is better he eats before he rushes off to rescue her."

"Rescue who?" Daniel asked with a frown. "She went willingly, did she not?"

"I wonder why you cannot now even speak her name?" his mother said pensively, and then glanced around as Richard and the innkeeper and his wife approached, each carrying a platter. "Oh, here is the food. Wonderful."

Daniel scowled but kept his tongue. He wasn't saying *her* name because he didn't wish to, and he had no intention of rushing off to rescue her, he thought, as he grimly worked his way through the broth that had been set before him. She was getting married, not murdered. If he could be replaced that easily . . . He swallowed a spoonful of broth, and managed not to choke on either it or his anger. She had disappointed him, first by accepting without question that some letter he hadn't written could be from him, and second by accepting this other man's proposal. It was not at all like Suzette. He would have expected her to come hunt him down and demand answers. Especially after what they had shared in the stables.

At least she would have had she cared for him, Daniel thought as he pushed the empty bowl aside and pulled the plate with beef and rumbledethumps on it in front of himself. Rumbledethumps was a combination of potatoes, onion and cabbage that was common along the Scottish border. Daniel generally enjoyed them. He hardly tasted it this time though; his mind was on Suzette and her betrayal. Did she really think he could be so callous as to take her innocence and then break off their engagement?

"So, from what you boys told me at the house, there have been a couple of accidents this last week," his mother said suddenly into the silence as they ate.

Richard nodded. "It looked as if someone had cut three quarters of the way through three of the spokes of one wheel on the carriage we men were traveling in, and then Daniel and I were nearly trampled in town."

"You thought those accidents were not accidents at all, but murder attempts on you, Richard?" Lady Woodrow queried.

"Yes, but we decided they might be accidents after all when it turned out that wasn't the case," he said evasively.

She didn't press him to find out how he knew that, but merely said, "However, Daniel was also nearly a victim of both accidents?"

"Well, yes," Richard said slowly, obviously not following her.

"Considering his being shot today, I would guess

he was really the intended victim of the other two incidents, wouldn't you?" she asked gently.

Richard's eyes widened and he glanced toward Daniel with surprise, but got no reaction.

"And these attacks only started once Daniel agreed, or seemed to agree, to marry Suzette?" his mother asked next.

"It did occur to me that the friend of Dicky's who was supposed to marry her may be behind the accidents," Daniel admitted quietly.

"Why didn't you say something?" Richard asked with amazement.

Daniel shrugged. "It was just a suspicion. We didn't know the name of Dicky's friend who was supposed to marry Suzette, just that his nickname was Twiddly, and we were heading for Gretna Green right away. I assumed that once we were married the fellow would give up, so why worry about it? I felt sure that so long as we checked the carriages over thoroughly before leaving each morning, all should be well. And it was."

"Until you were shot," Robert pointed out dryly.

"That was unexpected," he admitted grimly. "I didn't expect such an open assault. Being shot would hardly be thought an accident."

"Did Suzette take the letter she received with her?" Lady Woodrow asked suddenly as he took another bite of food.

"No." Christiana leaned forward to peer past Lisa toward the woman. "I have it."

"May I see it?" she asked.

"Of course." Christiana pulled a crumpled piece of paper from her pocket and held it out.

Daniel's chewing slowed as he watched his

mother uncrumple the paper and try to flatten it out on the table. When she bent her head to read it, he leaned close to her side to read it as well, and sucked in a horrified breath as he read the cold words.

"How the devil did whoever wrote this know about the stables?" he asked with alarm.

"What about the stables?" Richard asked with confusion.

Daniel's mother ignored the question and murmured, "Hmm. Obviously whoever wrote this was watching you. If the two of you thought you were alone it's no wonder Suzette believed this letter could only be from you."

"Yes," he realized with dismay.

"And not only was this letter meant to break her heart, but her spirit too," his mother pointed out grimly. "The poor girl must have writhed with shame."

"Yes," Christiana said solemnly. "She thought we would all hate her now, even Lisa and I."

"What the devil does that letter say?" Robert asked, standing to come around the table.

Daniel snatched the letter and shoved it in his pocket. No one else would ever see it if he had anything to say about it. It was a cruel, nasty piece of work that made the beautiful interlude he and Suzette had shared seem like something lewd and sordid. A literary snake in the Eden he'd found in her arms.

Robert hesitated, but after a moment returned with resignation to his seat.

"And certainly she would believe no man would

want her to wife after reading those cruel insults,"
Lady Woodrow said now. "This fellow who suddenly appeared to claim her must have seemed
like a knight in shining armor in the dire straits
she is in, what with the need to marry to pay off
the markers and avoid scandal."

"His name is Jeremy Danvers," Lisa reminded
them. "He was on her dance card at the Landons' ball, but Richard's arrival at the ball made
her refuse the dance. She came and got me and
dragged me to Christiana instead of dancing with
him."

"Danvers?" Robert echoed. "Well he would certainly fill out Suzette's requirements. He has a
barony and land but no money to run it."

"It wasn't just that," Christiana said unhappily.
"And it wasn't just the shame or the fear that no
one else would marry her either. Father said Suzette is worried that there may be other . . . consequences of the event in the stable and she wished
to ensure all would be well on that end."

"What consequences?" Richard asked, and it
was a question Daniel was wondering himself.

When Lisa merely shook her head and flushed,
Daniel frowned. He almost repeated the question
himself to make her answer it, but then it suddenly hit him, as unexpectedly and sharply as
the bullet had struck him in the back. It took his
breath away just as effectively too. Suzette could
be with child.

Daniel was on his feet at once and heading for
the inn door. Whether it was the restorative power
of the food, or the bracing effect of the blood sud-

denly thundering in his veins, he didn't know, but his earlier weakness was gone now and his mind was as sharp as a knife blade and focused only on one thing. He had to get to Suzette. Daniel was so focused on this he barely heard the commotion behind him and was only aware that he was being followed when Robert spoke.

"Danvers," the man said with disgust as they stepped out of the inn. "I knew he needed coin but didn't think him the sort to sink this low."

"We will stop him," Richard said firmly, drawing Daniel's attention to his presence as well.

"We will," Lady Woodrow agreed, making them all stop and turn to see her leading Lisa and Christiana out of the inn. "According to the girls, Danvers's carriage only has two horses. We will travel in two carriages with four horses each and catch up to them in no time. The maids can follow more slowly."

Daniel scowled. "It would be faster if we men followed on horseback."

"Riding horseback might aggravate your wound. Besides, then you'd just have to wait for us anyway or return to collect us," Lady Woodrow pointed out sensibly, before adding, "And do you really think Suzette will listen to you after that letter supposedly from you?"

"Richard and Robert can explain—"

"She will listen more readily to a woman at this point," his mother said gently as she led the girls to where the men stood. "Besides, you are injured and the men may be busy with Danvers and his driver. The man has already proven himself willing to kill to gain her dower. He will not give her up easily." She shook her head. "It is better if we all go, then together we can tackle any situation that arises."

When Daniel hesitated, she reached up to caress his cheek. "We will catch them up, son. I promise. I would not risk your happiness and a possible grandbaby. You must know that?"

Daniel clucked with irritation at the delay, but knew it might be the smartest tack to take. With two carriages and four horses each they should catch up well before Gretna Green. And the women may become necessary if things got complicated. Certainly, Suzette would listen more readily to her sisters. On top of that, his mother was handy with wounds. She would come in most useful if anyone was injured or his gunshot wound reopened, which was a good possibility. Daniel had no intention of standing back and letting Richard and Robert fight his battle for him. He wanted to ring Danvers's neck himself.

"Very well," he said, finally, and then glanced to Richard and Robert. "If you two will see that the carriages are prepared, I'll pay our bill and have the chests brought down. Let's be quick. I should like to catch up to them before they marry and I am forced to make Suzette a widow."

Chapter Fourteen

I'm surprised, Danvers, that you didn't stop to speak to Richard before he and Langley left."

Suzette heard her father make the comment, but paid it little attention, her gaze staying trained blindly out the window as she tortured herself with memories of her time with Daniel. If only she'd done things differently, it would be him in the carriage with her instead of Jeremy, she thought and then grimaced at her own traitorous mind.

Her thoughts had been terribly uncooperative for the entirety of this journey so far. The fact that—despite her father's dallying—the men hadn't managed to return before they departed, told her that while Richard and Robert had obviously taken their time at trying to talk Daniel into going through with marrying her, he hadn't been convinced. And frankly, if he needed convincing, she didn't want him. He wasn't the man she'd thought he was if he would turn her away as he had.

At least that was what Suzette had told herself as they'd ridden away from the inn in Danvers's carriage. Of course she'd changed her mind back and forth several times since then. She loved him and would take him any way she could have him. She hated him for rejecting her and never wanted to suffer the humiliation of seeing him again. She hated herself for not behaving more decorously and for driving him away with her passion. And then she would return to loving him and taking him any way she could. It was exhausting and simply left her feeling lost and tired, because the reality was he didn't want her and she was going to marry Jeremy.

The very thought brought tears to her eyes and Suzette blinked rapidly to try to drive them off. Perhaps if she closed her eyes, she could pretend Jeremy was Daniel to help her get through the ceremony tomorrow, Suzette thought, and then frowned. At least she assumed it would have to wait until the next day. Surely, it would be too late when they arrived in Gretna Green, and they would have to take rooms at an inn and wait until the morrow to be married?

"Why would I speak to Richard?" Danvers said finally. While he'd tried to sound indifferent and unconcerned, something in his voice caught her ear and Suzette turned to glance his way, noting that the constant thumb twiddling that he'd been doing since they'd got into the carriage had stopped. His fingers were now clenched tightly together as he returned her father's stare.

"The two of you are friends, are you not?" Cedrick Madison asked as she turned her gaze out the window again. "I seem to recall you being there at the club and then the gaming hell this last time I lost so much."

"You remember that night?" There was definitely wariness in Danvers's voice now and Suzette wondered idly why that was, but didn't really care.

"Bits and pieces. Enough to recall that you and Dicky appeared quite chummy," Lord Madison said grimly, his hand massaging his cane handle. It was a sure sign that he was agitated, but then he'd been agitated since finding out she was going to marry Jeremy.

"We are friendly acquaintances only," Danvers muttered.

Suzette turned her gaze his way again, noting that his face was turned to the window and his thumbs twiddling around each other once more.

"How did you find out about my markers?" her father asked next.

"I told you, Cerberus gave it to me in lieu of payment," Jeremy answered shortly, his charming visage slipping.

"Aye, that's what you said," her father agreed grimly. "But I find it hard to believe that anyone would agree to an arrangement where they had to hunt down the payment themselves, or indeed that any respectable owner of a gaming establishment would even suggest it."

"Cerberus is hardly respectable," Jeremy muttered. His twiddling had picked up in speed so that the thumbs were whirling around and around each other very fast.

"Yes. So I've heard. I've been told he drugs and fleeces the unwary, like myself . . . which is why I find it so hard to believe that you won anything, let alone such a large sum."

Jeremy shifted impatiently and snapped, "Well, I did, which makes you most fortunate that I am willing to marry your daughter in lieu of payment, doesn't it? Can we change the subject now?"

Her father narrowed his eyes. "We have learned that Dicky led me to the gaming hell again and tricked me out of more money to ensure a friend of his could marry my Suzette as he had my Christiana," he said grimly. "And it's very odd that you happened to arrive to save the day just as my gel was getting her heart broken."

Suzette stared at her father, wondering when they had learned that. Obviously, it must have been discovered while she had been in the parlor with Lisa. What else had she missed? She frowned slightly and recalled that Daniel never had got around to telling her who had poisoned George. Not that she'd thought to ask him again. Cold as it was to admit, she was just glad the man was dead, doubly so now if he had planned to force her into an unwanted marriage too. Really, the only regret she had about Dicky's death was that she wished he'd suffered more.

"I have no idea what Dicky's motives were," Jeremy muttered. "And it was just happenstance that I arrived when I did. A happy coincidence that I ran into Suzette and heard her troubled tale."

He smiled at Suzette, but she didn't smile back. Her father's questions had drawn her far enough out of her self-pity so that her brain was starting to think again for the first time since receiving Daniel's letter.

"The only thing we know about this friend of Dicky's is that he is called 'Twiddly,'" her father announced, and stared meaningfully at Jeremy's hands, which had suddenly stilled mid twiddle. Mouth tightening, he accused, "You are the friend of Dicky's who planned to marry my Suzette. You were in on the scheme from the start, and the happy coincidence of your arriving just as the letter did tends to make me wonder if Daniel wrote it at all."

Suzette stiffened at the suggestion. He had her full attention now.

Cedrick Madison set his cane aside and turned to her to take her hands as he pointed out, "Daniel was damned eager to marry you, girl. He even asked me not to tell you about my selling the townhouse so that you wouldn't think you no longer had to marry."

"And you agreed to that?" she asked with amazement.

He shrugged. "You can be a stubborn girl, Suzette. And sometimes you are your own worst enemy. I had no trouble believing that you might avoid marrying him out of fear. But it was obvious to me that you both loved each other."

"You think he loved me?" she asked in a small voice, afraid to hope.

"I'm sure of it," he said solemnly, and then added, "No man would put up with your nonsense if he didn't love you."

Suzette frowned slightly at the backhanded compliment.

"But whether he did or not, Woodrow is too honorable to have his way with you and then take a runner," her father continued grimly. "Besides, he didn't seem to me to be a coward who would give such news in a cold letter. There is something wrong here. I think we should return to the inn and wait to hear about Daniel."

Suzette hesitated. Her heart was already broken, the worst that could come of their returning was more humiliation and while just moments ago she would have done almost anything to avoid that, her father's words had given her hope. If there was even the slightest possibility that Daniel hadn't written that letter . . . Surely it was a possibility? She'd never seen his handwriting before, and someone could have seen them in the stables and perhaps known about that.

Swallowing, she gave a small nod.

"That's my brave girl." Her father patted her hand and started to turn to Danvers. "Stop the—"

Suzette had been staring at her hands, but when his words died abruptly and Lord Madison suddenly slumped against her, she glanced to him with alarm.

"Father?" Suzette caught him as he started to slide toward the floor of the carriage and then

glanced to Danvers to see that he was holding her
father's cane by the bottom so that the iron handle
could be used as a club, which he had obviously
used on her father. At her glance, Jeremy smiled
coldly and shrugged, allowing it to slip through
his fingers until he was grasping the handle. He
set it on the bench seat beside him now and drew
a pistol.

"We will not be stopping," he said solemnly.
"And you *are* marrying me."

"Not bloody likely," Suzette snapped at once,
easing her father to rest in the corner of the carriage seat so that he slumped against the wall.

"You should have said something like, 'Over my
dead body,'" Jeremy said idly. "Then I could have
replied, 'No, over *his* dead body.' Because I *will* kill
your father if you don't."

Suzette stared at him, wondering where all
that gentle charm had come from and where it
had gone. It was like facing an entirely different man. Was it so easy to pull the wool over her
eyes? Apparently so, she thought unhappily and
opened her mouth; but before she could speak,
Jeremy forestalled her by saying, "Please don't
say anything as droll as, "You can't do this." He
grimaced and pointed out, "I already have. Now
use his cravat and tie him up," he ordered coldly.
"Tightly, mind. I should hate for him to get loose
and get himself shot before the wedding."

Daniel raised his eyebrows in question as Richard hurried back across the inn yard toward the
carriage. Rather than waste the time involved in

everyone getting out at each stop, one person did it. Richard and Robert had been taking turns at it to save Daniel from aggravating his injury.

"No sign of them?" he asked as Richard neared.

Radnor shook his head, his expression grim, and Daniel glanced to the carriage stopped behind their own in time to see his mother withdraw her head from the open door and close it. She had heard Richard's answer too and was now no doubt telling Lisa and Christiana the news.

After the first hour, their party had been stopping at each inn so that they could check to see if Danvers's carriage had perhaps been there and might be still. They had expected him to stop for meals or to allow everyone to stretch their legs and relieve themselves. Even if he had decided to drive straight through, the man would have to stop eventually, if only to change horses. However, it appeared he hadn't stopped so far.

"I begin to suspect he isn't going to stop at all and we are wasting time stopping at each inn we pass," Daniel admitted grimly as Richard climbed into the carriage.

"Hmm," Robert muttered with disgust. "If he shot you and wrote the letter Suzette received, then he'll no doubt be eager to get her to Gretna Green and get the deed done before anything can interfere."

Daniel sank back on the bench seat to peer at Robert and Richard across from him, then said, "Maybe we should stop checking each inn. We are wasting a lot of time, and even if they do stop and we pass them, it can only be to our benefit to arrive at Gretna before them. We could lie in wait then."

He waited for both men to nod their agreement before giving these instructions to his driver.

Suzette breathed out a little sigh of relief as she saw her father's eyes flutter. He had been unconscious for so long, she had begun to fret that Danvers had hit him so hard he might never wake again. But he was coming around . . . and now she could carry out the plan she'd come up with while waiting for him to regain consciousness.

Danvers had put his gun away the moment she'd finished tying up her father. Suzette supposed he didn't feel threatened by her enough to bother keeping it out. Whatever the case, he was twiddling his thumbs again and staring out the window into the darkness blanketing the countryside.

"We shall have to stop at the next inn," she announced coldly. "I need to use the facilities."

Danvers glanced at her with disinterest, and then turned back to the window. "No."

"I need to relieve myself," she insisted pointedly.

Jeremy merely shrugged. "Then you had best get used to a damp dress, because we are not stopping."

Suzette narrowed her eyes grimly. She had half expected this answer and come up with a contingency plan should it happen. She carried it through now and got up from her seat.

"What are you doing?" Danvers barked, glanc-

ing around with surprise when the rustle of
material warned him she was moving. She was
standing up when he looked and moving toward
him by the time he tugged his pistol out. Suzette
ignored it and turned her back to him, not terribly
concerned that he would shoot her. She was the
golden goose, after all. She was relatively safe—at
least she was until they were wed—so dropped to
sit on his lap.

"What the devil?" Jeremy gasped, sounding
alarmed now and trying to remove her by pushing on her back. "Get off me and sit in your seat."

Suzette braced her hands on the carriage walls
to prevent his shifting her. "If I am going to be
damp and uncomfortable because you are a rude
bounder, then so shall you be," she said calmly,
and then added, "Bear with me, my lord, this
should only take a minute."

She could hear the gasping sound of his sucking
in one horrified breath, and then he choked out,
"You can not mean to—"

"Yes, actually," she assured him calmly. "That
is, of course, unless you'd care to stop so I might
tend my needs in an alternate fashion . . . one that
leaves us both dry."

Suzette caught her father's open alarmed eyes
and winked. She then closed her eyes. Lord Madison got the message at once and closed his eyes
again, feigning unconsciousness. The moment
he did, she added, "Please make your decision
quickly, my lord. I fear I cannot hold it much
longer."

"All right, dammit!" Giving up on trying to

remove her, he banged on the carriage wall, yelling, "Stop the carriage, Thompson. Stop at once, I say."

The moment the carriage began to slow, Danvers said, "There, we are stopping. Now get off me, woman."

"With pleasure," Suzette said dryly and moved to settle herself demurely back in her seat. A glance Danvers's way showed him peering at her as if she were a madwoman or some unclean creature. She smiled sweetly in response. "I cannot wait until we are wed."

When Danvers's eyes dilated with a sort of horror, she chuckled softly, which brought a scowl to his face.

"Get out," he snapped, waving the pistol toward the door the moment the carriage stopped.

Suzette got out, and glanced back to see him eyeing her father grimly. Apparently deciding it was safe enough to leave the seemingly unconscious man, he muttered under his breath and followed her out, and then scowled when he saw her waiting for him. "Well, what are you waiting for? Get to it."

"Here in the middle of nowhere?" she asked with feigned surprise.

"Yes," he said firmly. "Get to it or we shall continue and you can wet yourself, alone. I shall ride on the top . . . where I can shoot your father if the two of you should try to jump out," he added dryly when she considered his words.

Grimacing, Suzette sighed and turned toward the trees, muttering, "Very well."

"Where are you going?" Jeremy asked

"Where do you think?" she asked sarcastically, continuing forward. "I am hardly going to tend matters here in front of you and your driver."

Much to Suzette's relief, he released a frustrated growl, but otherwise didn't protest. Not that it would have prevented her carrying her plan forward, but he could have made things difficult. She continued to walk for several feet until she found a nice wide stretch of bush for coverage. Suzettte considered it briefly and then glanced around to survey the area before hunkering down. Once assured she was out of sight, she called, "Sing or something."

"What?" Jeremy asked with amazement.

"Sing or recite a poem or something," Suzette ordered. "I cannot go if I know you are listening."

"Oh, for the love of—"

"It shall speed things along," she promised him.

Suzette heard him mutter a string of oaths and then Jeremy shouted, "You sing or speak then."

"I will not be able to concentrate on what I am doing if I am trying to sing or recite. Besides, I might grunt in the middle of it, and that would be as embarrassing as—"

"Oh, very well," Jeremy snapped, interrupting her. Apparently, he didn't have the stomach to want to hear exactly what she was claiming to be doing. In the next moment, Danvers began to recite the Lord's prayer, which was rather sacrilegious to her mind considering that she suspected he'd burst into flames if he dared enter a church, but she wasn't going to complain. Staying hunkered down, she moved to the side under the cover of the bushes until she reached a line of trees, then she raised to a half crouch and moved more quickly, weaving her way toward the lane, using the trees and bushes as cover. She continued forward until she was almost at the edge of the trees behind the carriage. Suzette then paused and glanced back, waiting for him to grow tired of reciting. She didn't have long to wait.

"Are you not done yet?" Jeremy bellowed impatiently after the third recitation.

She remained silent.

"Suzette?" he called, suspicion entering his voice. When silence was his answer, he cursed in a most impious way and started trudging forward into the woods. "Dammit! Where are you?"

She watched silently as he stomped up to where she had been and began to search the area, not surprised when he turned back toward the carriage and bellowed, "Thompson! Get over here and help me find the little bitch."

A slow smile spread Suzette's lips, the first she'd enjoyed since receiving the letter she'd thought was from Daniel. Jeremy was doing exactly as she'd expected. She watched the driver climb down from the carriage and tramp through the high grass until he reached the trees and then she caught up her skirts and sidled closer to the edge of the trees offering her cover. The moment the man had joined his employer, Suzette slid out of the woods, hurried around the carriage and climbed quickly up onto the driver's perch from the far side of the vehicle. She hadn't even settled on the seat before she had the reins in hand, then Suzette grabbed up the driver's whip and cracked it over the horses' heads.

The horses burst forward at once, nearly sending her flying backward off her perch. She managed to keep her seat, and slapped the reins now. The horses immediately began to pick up more speed. Suzette glanced around then, not surprised to see Jeremy and his driver running toward the road. Knowing they would never catch up, she wasn't concerned . . . until Jeremy suddenly stopped and aimed his pistol. She immediately ducked down, trying to make herself as small a target as she could.

At first, when Suzette heard the weapon's report and felt nothing, she thought Jeremy had missed, but then she saw the horse on the side closest to Jeremy stumble and slam into the horse on the left as he fell. In the next moment, both horses were going down and pulling the carriage to the side with them. Suzette didn't have time to think, she simply pushed herself up from the seat as the vehicle started to turn and threw herself away from it. She hit the ground with a bone-jarring crash and then, afraid she hadn't thrown herself far enough and the carriage would crash down on top of her, she instinctively rolled several times before stopping.

Suzette raised her head then to glance around. She couldn't see Jeremy and his driver, but the carriage had come to rest on its side several feet away. Ignoring the aches and pains assaulting her, she pushed herself to her feet and staggered back to

the carriage, her only concern for her father. Still
tied up, he would have been helpless to protect
himself as the vehicle had rolled. Worry eating at
her, she reached the carriage and—using the spare
fifth wheel, coachman's step and seat irons—
managed to climb up onto the upturned side of
the carriage. Once there she could see Jeremy and
his driver rushing toward her, but ignored them
and crawled to the carriage door to pull it up and
open.

It was nearly dark now, but was darker still in
the carriage, and at first she couldn't make out
much; but then Suzette began to be able to distin-
guish her father's form crumpled against the door
on the ground. Her breath caught in her throat as
she noted how still he was, and for one moment,
she feared he was dead.

"Father?" she breathed, not wanting to believe she'd killed him with her escape attempt.
Much to her relief his dark shape shifted as if he
were trying to turn and look at her and Suzette
breathed a heartfelt, "Thank God."

In the next moment she was grabbed from
behind and dragged away from the opening.
Danvers spoke, his breath brushing her cheek
as he snapped, "Get the old man out of there,
Thompson."

Suzette glanced back to see the driver moving
to kneel at the opening and survey the situation
inside the cab of the carriage, and then Danvers
was throwing her off the side of the overturned
carriage . . . literally. He tossed her to the ground
like she was a sack of waste. It wasn't a far fall,

perhaps six to eight feet, but even so it was painful. Suzette knew she no doubt had more new
bruises on her body, which was already carrying several from her first hard landing. She was
slower to rise this time and had to bite her tongue
to keep from groaning as she became aware of her
body's complaints over its recent rough handling.
It seemed to her it was worse now than the first
time she'd got up, but supposed her worry for her
father had raised her blood enough to keep her
from noticing then.

"Get up," Jeremy ordered grimly, but then
grabbed her arm to jerk her up without waiting
to see if she'd obey. He then gave her a shake with
his grip on her arm and roared, "I ought to kill
you right now."

"My lord?"

Jeremy glared at her for another moment, and
then turned to raise an eyebrow at his servant.
"What?"

"He's tied up," the man said uncertainly with a
nod toward the open carriage door.

Jeremy's jaw tightened and he asked sharply, "Is
that a problem?"

The man considered the question, and then
tilted his head and said cagily, "Not if you were
planning to give me a bonus or something . . . a
permanent raise, say."

Jeremy's eyes narrowed grimly. "Very well.
Now, get him out."

The driver nodded and then lowered himself
down through the open carriage door.

"Sit," Jeremy snapped.

Suzette hesitated, but then sat on the grass at the side of the carriage. It seemed the smartest move at that point. Jeremy looked angry enough to throttle her, and she couldn't run and just leave her father behind. Besides, her legs were a little shaky anyway. Sitting seemed like a good idea.

The moment she was down, Jeremy moved to the carriage and began poking around the driver's seat area. A moment later, he headed back toward her with a second weapon in hand. She thought it was a blunderbuss, and supposed she shouldn't be surprised the driver carried one. The roads were filled with highwaymen and bandits. No doubt the weapon came in handy.

Pausing beside her, Jeremy tucked the blunderbuss under his arm and proceeded to reload his pistol. The sight reminded Suzette of the horse he'd shot and she glanced toward the animals. The wounded one appeared to be dead, though she couldn't tell for sure; however, it wasn't moving. The other horse was still alive but tangled up in the reins and works and pinned to the ground by the dead horse. He was struggling to free himself, but wasn't getting anywhere.

Suzette frowned and turned to Jeremy. "One of the horses is still alive, but it's pinned. He can't get up."

Jeremy glanced toward the horses as he finished reloading, but then turned his attention to the carriage when the driver, Thompson, suddenly emerged from the cab. As they watched, he perched on the side of the carriage with his legs dangling into it through the opening. He then bent and pulled her father up and out to lie beside him, still bound. Within moments Thompson had both himself and her father on the ground.

Suzette eyed the older man with worry, glad to see that while he, like her, was a bit banged up, he seemed mostly fine.

"Good," Jeremy said as Thompson led her father to stand in front of him. "Sit him on the ground next to his daughter."

Thompson urged her father around to her side, and pushed on his shoulder to make him sit. He then glanced to Jeremy for further instruction.

"Now go see if the one horse can be saved." Jeremy waved his freshly reloaded pistol toward the struggling animal.

The driver glanced to the horses and frowned. In the short time since she'd first looked, the live horse's struggles were already growing weaker. She suspected the weight of the horse on top of him, along with his position, was smothering the poor creature, and guessed the driver had decided as much too when he said, "He won't last the amount of time it would take me to free him. Besides, two carriage wheels broke in the turn, we can't use the carriage anymore anyway."

"Just check the damned horse," Jeremy snapped.

Thompson scowled belligerently, but turned and stomped toward the horses. He hadn't taken three steps when Jeremy retrieved the blunderbuss from under his arm and shot the man in the back. The driver barely seemed to hit the ground before Jeremy tossed the empty blunderbuss aside and turned his newly reloaded pistol on Suzette and her father. "Up."

Suzette gaped at him and then turned to peer

at the unmoving driver and back. "You just shot him. In the back. For no reason."

"No one blackmails me," he said coldly. "Now get up."

She stared at him with disbelief, unable to believe anyone could be so cold. "But—"

"Shall I shoot your father too? Would that make you more agreeable?" he asked grimly.

"Hardly," she snapped, her shock giving way to anger. "You wouldn't be able to get me to do a damned thing if he was dead."

"I didn't say I'd kill him, I said shoot him," Jeremy pointed out calmly. "A warning shot in the arm, perhaps?"

Suzette got abruptly to her feet, and then turned to help her father up as well, when he was incapable of doing it on his own with his arms bound behind his back.

Once they were both upright, Jeremy caught her arm and jerked her so that her back was to him. "Hands behind your back."

Suzette hesitated, but supposed she didn't have a choice. She couldn't risk his shooting her father, so slid her hands behind her back, her mouth tightening when she felt him binding them with some sort of cloth. His cravat, she realized when he finished and moved up beside her.

"Now, start walking," he ordered, gesturing with his pistol.

Suzette hesitated, her eyes sliding to the horses. "What about the horse? He will suffocate to death if we just leave him."

"That's his problem," Jeremy said with unconcern. "Thanks to your foolish attempt to escape, he's useless to me now anyway. His death can be on your conscience."

Suzette didn't respond, but she scowled and thought *bastard* very loudly in her mind as she began to walk.

Chapter Fifteen

"Why are we slowing?" Daniel asked with a frown, leaning to the window to peer out. It was full night now, but with a new moon that cast the landscape in shades of gray. Still, he didn't at first see anything that would cause them to stop.

"It looks like there has been an accident," Richard said, peering out the opposite window.

Daniel slid along the bench seat to peer out the window Richard was looking out. Sure enough there was an overturned carriage on the side of the road ahead.

"You don't think it could be Danvers's carriage, do you?" Robert asked, slipping from the bench seat he and Richard were sharing to crouch on the floor and look out as well.

Daniel frowned at the suggestion and banged

on the wall of the carriage to signal his driver to stop. This time he did not leave Richard or Robert to get out while he waited in the carriage. Daniel had the door open and was climbing out the moment the carriage stopped. He even managed to do it without grunting in pain, though he would have liked to. Damn, his back hurt.

"All right?" Richard asked with concern as he followed him out.

Daniel ground his teeth together, but nodded and started toward the overturned carriage.

"What is it?"

Daniel heard his mother call that question from the carriage the women were riding in, but left Richard to answer. "An accident. We are checking it out."

The carriage lay on its side, two wheels broken. Daniel eyed the crest on the back as he approached, able to just make it out in the gray light cast by the moon, but he didn't recognize it and continued around to the front end. He spotted the body on the side of the lane as he neared the front wheels and immediately moved toward it with Robert and Richard following.

"The driver?" Richard suggested as the three men circled the body.

Daniel considered the man's livery and nodded grimly.

Robert knelt beside the body and examined him briefly, before announcing, "He's dead."

"He must have been thrown in the accident," Richard suggested.

Robert shook his head. He was still kneeling,

but was now examining his own hands, rubbing his thumb and forefingers together. "Blood," he announced and tugged up the back of the man's coat, revealing what even in that light looked a messy wound. The driver's back was a mass of small bloody holes.

"Looks like the work of a blunderbuss," Richard said with a grimace.

Robert let the coat drop back and straightened. "Highwaymen?"

"This is Danvers's carriage."

Daniel turned sharply toward the back of the carriage as Lisa made that announcement. The three women were gathered there examining the crest, and Christiana now nodded in agreement. "I recognize the crest too."

Cursing, Daniel turned and moved toward the front of the carriage, but Richard moved past him and quickly climbed up on top of the upraised carriage before he could do so himself.

"Empty," Richard announced a heartbeat later as he knelt to peer into the cab interior.

"Then where are Suzette and her father?" Lady Woodrow asked with a frown.

"They could be walking," Lisa suggested.

Daniel glanced to the dark form of the driver. It seemed doubtful to him that Danvers would shoot his own driver, which would suggest they had been attacked by outsiders, highwaymen or bandits. Swallowing the worry that thought instilled in him, Daniel said, "Spread out and search the area. If we don't find anything, we'll continue on and hope to find them walking further along the way."

Everyone spread out at once, searching the immediate area, and even widening the search to the edge of the woods on both sides of the lane. Much to Daniel's relief, other than a spent blunderbuss and the dead horses, they didn't come up with anything else.

"What now?" his mother asked as they congregated together after ending the search.

"Now we travel forward but more slowly," Daniel decided, when everyone peered to him for answers. "I want everyone watching out the windows in case they are walking through the trees rather than along the side of the road. If we don't come across them by the time we reach the next inn we'll regroup and decide what to do then."

"Off the road! Quickly, quickly!" Jeremy snapped, giving Suzette a push toward the trees that nearly knocked her down.

Managing to keep her feet under her, she followed her father off the road and across the grass into the trees. Lord Madison continued walking until he came to an area with thick brush that offered cover, and then dropped to his haunches to duck behind it without Jeremy's ordering him to. Suzette wasn't surprised. They'd already done this twice before when carriages had approached. At this rate it was going to take a very long time to get to Gretna Green. Not that she cared. She had no desire to go anywhere with the man.

Under normal circumstances, Jeremy would probably be waving down the carriages for a ride to the next inn where he could rent a hack to finish the journey. However, he could hardly do that when he was holding them at pistol point, which made her wonder how he planned to get them to Gretna Green and force her to marry him.

"Down," Jeremy snapped when she didn't follow her father's example and duck quickly enough. He also shoved down on her shoulder until she dropped to her haunches.

"Just how are you planning to get to Gretna Green like this, Danvers?" her father asked suddenly and Suzette glanced at him with a combination of surprise and relief. He hadn't spoken a word since regaining consciousness and she'd begun to worry he'd taken more injury than she'd realized. She was glad to hear him speak at all, but was also interested in the answer to the question and after giving her father a small smile, turned her head to peer through the darkness to Jeremy.

His face was pale in the darkness, seeming to reflect the moonlight, and she saw his jaw clench before he said, "We are going to walk until we reach an inn, and then I am going to leave you two tied up in the woods while I rent a hack to take us the rest of the way."

"Another driver to shoot?" she asked dryly.

"I will take the reins myself," he said shortly. "Now shut up."

Suzette scowled, but then turned her attention to the road as a carriage came into view on the lane. It was moving much slower than the last two that had passed. They had both been traveling at a gallop, obviously heading somewhere and eager to get there. But the driver of this carriage was keeping the horses moving at a slow trot, as if out for a ride through the park. There was also a second carriage traveling behind it at the same gait, Suzette noted, and narrowed her eyes on the vehicles as the hairs on the back of her neck began to stand up.

"It's the boys."

Suzette spotted Daniel and Richard through the open windows on the near side of the first carriage even as her father breathed those words beside her. The two men were leaning out of the windows, peering over the grassy verge and trees lining the road as if searching for something.

Them, she knew at once, and smiled as her father said, "There's Daniel. I told you he wanted to marry you."

"Shut up," Jeremy hissed as the second carriage drew close enough for them to see two women leaning out its windows much as the men were doing in the first. They too were scanning the surroundings they were passing through. Suzette recognized that one of the women was Lisa, but had no idea who the older woman was.

"Must be Daniel's mother," Cedrick Madison muttered.

"If either of you makes another sound, I will shoot Lord Madison," Jeremy warned in a grim whisper.

Suzette stared at the pistol that suddenly appeared before her face, pointing toward her father's head, and briefly considered chomping her teeth into Jeremy's hand and throwing herself forward, hopefully forcing the pistol away. But there was a chance it would go off before she got it pointed away from her father and she couldn't risk that, so she sat still and watched helplessly as the carriages continued past and then moved out of sight around the next bend.

Suzette started to rise then, but Jeremy caught her arm and jerked her back to a squat, barking, "Stay put."

"Why?" she asked with irritation. "They have gone."

"I want to be sure they continue and don't turn around," he said shortly. "Now shut up and just stay put."

Suzette grimaced, but did as she was told and remained squatting. However, it was becoming uncomfortable and she sighed impatiently several times as the seconds dragged past.

"Stop that," Jeremy hissed. "I am trying to listen."

"Oh, for heaven's sake," she said sharply. "They've continued on. Can we not move? I am hungry, cold and need to relieve myself for real now."

Jeremy glowered at her with displeasure and growled, "If it weren't for your rather handsome dower I'd be tempted to kill you right here and now."

"Instead you'll wait and kill us both after you have married her," Lord Madison said dryly.

Jeremy's expression closed, and then he said, "Don't be ridiculous. I have no desire to kill either of you. I just want to marry Suzette. Once that is done, I shall cut you free, my lord. I shall even allow Suzette to live with you if she prefers and keep the marriage in name only once it's consummated and cannot be annulled."

Suzette didn't believe him for a minute. He would have to kill them both. Consummated or not, the marriage could still be overturned if she went to the authorities and told them she'd been forced to it. Jeremy couldn't risk letting them live.

"Are you really so stupid you think we would believe that?" she asked dryly. "If so, you have even less sense than I first thought."

"You thought I had little sense, did you?" he asked, appearing more amused than offended. "And yet you agreed to marry me."

"My lord, I only agreed to marry you because I was desperate. No woman would agree otherwise," she assured him.

Jeremy ground his teeth and growled, "If Dicky weren't already dead, I think I'd kill him myself for saddling me with you."

Suzette wasn't terribly surprised he knew Dicky was dead. She merely shrugged and said, "You would have been standing in line, many wanted him dead." She then smiled and added, "I'm certain just as many would like to see you dead as well. I'm sure one of them will succeed eventually and you'll get your comeuppance."

Jeremy's eyes narrowed with dislike. "I'm starting to think even your sizable dowry isn't worth having to put up with your sharp tongue for any length of time."

"But then the plan has always been that you wouldn't have to put up with her long, wasn't it?" her father said sharply.

"I don't know what you're talking about," Jeremy muttered, his gaze turning back to the road.

"Although I suppose that wasn't exactly the original plan, was it?" her father corrected himself grimly. "Originally, it was supposed to be all three of my girls tricked into marriage through my supposed gaming. They were to be wedded, bedded and then dead. But I would have been left alive to mourn the loss while you, Dicky and some third man enjoyed their dowers."

"They were going to kill all three of us?" Suzette asked with a frown, wondering just how much she'd missed while she was in the parlor with Lisa. She'd already figured out Jeremy must be planning to kill her and her father once he'd forced her to marry him, but learning that Dicky's grand scheme had been to force all three girls into marriage and then kill them seemed so cold. He must have planned it out before even meeting them, and then had the patience to wait until each of the girls could be forced into marriage before seeing the end of it. It had already been a year since Christiana had married Dicky. How long would it have taken for them to get her father drugged and drag him to the gaming hell again? It could be another year or more if he followed the same pattern he had after the incident leading to Christiana's marriage. He'd spent most of the last year locked away in his office, hiding from his own shame and self-loathing for what he'd thought he'd done—gambling his daughter away. No doubt he would have done the same thing again after she was forced into marriage. Another year could easily have passed before they could trick him into thinking he'd gambled again, forcing Lisa to marry. The patience needed to carry out this plan was as frightening as the cold-bloodedness of it.

"All in one fell swoop," her father said in answer to her question. "The three of you were going to die in a tragic carriage accident."

"How do you know all that?" Jeremy asked with alarm.

"George's valet, Freddy, told all," Lord Madison announced, sounding pretty cold himself.

"Freddy," Jeremy spat the name furiously. "He was to find the markers and bring them to me. I would have claimed the money and given him some coin for his trouble." He scowled and asked, "How the devil did he get himself caught?"

"By being no brighter than you," Suzette snapped before her father could answer.

"God, you are a fishwife," Jeremy said with disgust and then muttered to himself, "It figures Dicky would marry sweet little mousy Christiana himself and stick me with the sister who was a harpy."

"Oh, boo hoo, poor you, having to put up with my sharp tongue to get all my money. You—" Suzette paused and blinked as what he'd said about Freddy sunk in. *He was to find the markers and bring them to me.* That had to be what he had been looking for in the office when he took Christiana there. He'd just died before he could find them. Turning an amazed look on Jeremy she accused, "You don't even have the markers."

"No, I don't," Jeremy acknowledged, and then

a cruel smile stretched his mouth. "Imagine, if either of you had just been bright enough to ask to see it, you wouldn't be in this mess. In fact, that was my one big worry when I approached you at the inn. I knew I could woo you around to the idea of marrying me." He chuckled and boasted, "Even without money I'm a catch. Wooing was the easy part, but I worried about being asked to present the marker. However, neither of you even thought to ask." He raised an eyebrow and said dryly, "Now who is the bright one?"

Suzette closed her eyes, mentally kicking herself several times for not thinking of that.

"I'm sorry, Suzie," Lord Madison said glumly. "I should have thought to ask to see it."

She blinked her eyes open and shook her head, her gaze searching out her father's face. Seeing the misery on his expression, she shook her head again. "No. I didn't think of it either. This is not your fault."

"Do you want to know what the best part of it all is?" Jeremy asked, practically crowing with glee. "After I've married you, claimed your dower, and you're both dead, I will ride back to London, search Dicky's office until I find the marker and then make the estate pay up as well. I'll get both the dower and the money from the marker."

Suzette watched silently as he laughed at his own cleverness, and waited until he stopped before asking, "So how are we to die?"

"Hmmm." He frowned. "I suppose another carriage accident would be a bit suspect when we just had one, and then I shot Thompson and will have to claim highwaymen did it, so that's out too." He considered for a moment and then shrugged. "I guess a fire would do. Dicky wanted to avoid that because his parents and brother died in fires. He thought it might look suspect. However, I don't have that problem. Besides, it will be slow and painful for the two of you and I like that idea."

"I really don't like you," Suzette said grimly.

Jeremy smiled. "Such a shame; fortunately, that isn't a prerequisite to marriage."

"Speaking of which, how do you intend to force me to marry you now that I know you plan to kill me anyway?" she asked dryly.

"Because you want to live and will do what I say, hoping to be able to save yourself later," he said with a shrug.

Suzette suspected that was true, but pointed out, "I'm only doing what you say now because you have threatened my father. But you cannot hold a pistol on him when we get to Gretna Green. No one will marry us if they see you wielding the pistol."

"I have considered that," Jeremy admitted, not looking terribly concerned and she understood why when he said, "I am going to hide your father somewhere bound and tied while we get married. You'll marry me if you want to see him again," he said with certainty.

Suzette stared at him with impotent fury. His plan would work. She would marry him to keep her father safe and in the hopes that they would find a way to save themselves afterward. And that was their only hope she realized. That Jeremy would make a mistake and they would somehow escape . . . or that Daniel and the others would be waiting at Gretna Green and save them.

"We've waited long enough," Jeremy said suddenly. "Start walking."

Suzette straightened at once, but Jeremy had to help her father rise as he had each of the other two times they'd stopped. The moment he was on his feet, though, her father was fine and started walking back toward the road.

"No. We will stick to the woods from here on out," Jeremy said.

Her father hesitated, but then turned back into the trees and continued forward. Suzette followed, aware that Jeremy was at her back.

"We must have missed them between here and the overturned carriage," Daniel said grimly as he led Robert and Richard back out of the stables.

While it appeared that Danvers's driver had been shot, probably by a highwayman, they had decided that the other three must have escaped uninjured, or at least well enough to be able to walk. It just wasn't likely that their robber would have dragged the three off. Highwaymen took money and jewels, not passengers. That meant Suzette, her father and Danvers should have been on foot and headed this way. However, when they hadn't passed them on the road, they'd assumed the trio had already reached this, the first inn since they'd found the overturned carriage. However, on questioning, the innkeeper had assured them that no one fitting their descriptions had arrived yet. Still, they'd checked with the inn's stable boy to be sure and had got the same answer.

"We could turn back and scour the road between the carriage and here again," Robert suggested.

Daniel shook his head. "We could miss them that way. They are obviously on foot. They must be traveling under the cover of the trees to avoid further trouble with bandits. They could arrive here while we are back at the carriage and be gone before we return."

"I wish we knew how long ago the accident happened," Richard murmured, glancing toward the lane. "It would tell us how near they might be."

Daniel grunted, his glance moving to the lane and then the trees surrounding the inn as he realized that Danvers, Suzette and Lord Madison could arrive at any time, and he wasn't sure what would happen if Danvers saw their party there. As far as he knew, Suzette and her father had no idea that Danvers might be the one who had sent the letter, or that the man may have shot him. He wasn't even sure of it, though he suspected that was the case. Suzette and her father's ignorance on the matter would keep them safe, but if Danvers saw Daniel and the others waiting here, he wouldn't want to approach. That would raise questions and probably protests, at least from Lord Madison, which might force the man's hand and make things much more dangerous for Suzette and her father.

"We will wait here," Daniel decided grimly.

"But we have to get the carriages and ourselves out of sight. Then we will lie in wait."

"Move faster," Jeremy snapped, poking Suzette in the back with his pistol.

Suzette ground her teeth at the irritating jab. He had been poking her in the back and harrying them to move faster for several minutes now and she was sick of it. Aside from that, she suspected her father couldn't move any faster. There was a reason he had a cane and it wasn't for affectation. The man had injured his leg in a riding accident years ago and it sometimes troubled him. All this walking was apparently aggravating the old injury, because she'd noticed him beginning to limp some distance back. She didn't say as much to Danvers, however. She already knew the man would have little sympathy, so she stopped walking altogether and simply said, "No."

"Move," Jeremy growled, giving her a shove.

Suzette turned and smiled at him sweetly, her eyelashes fluttering as she'd seen the females doing at the Landons' ball. The only thing missing was the fan as she breathed, "Oh, my lord, I am ever so tired and my feet are beggared, can we not stop to rest?"

"So," he said dryly. "You can *pretend* to be a lady when it suits you."

"As well as you can pretend to be a man when it suits you," Suzette shot back.

"God, you are such a trial," Jeremy growled.

"Yes, you've whined about that incessantly already," she said indifferently, and then suggested,

"So don't marry me. I'd rather marry Daniel anyway."

"Yes, I noticed," he sneered. "You acted no better than a bitch in heat with him when I saw you together in the stables."

"I acted like a woman in love," Suzette snapped, suddenly furious. The letter—his letter, she was sure though he hadn't yet admitted to it—had rained down all sorts of shame on her when she'd read it, but she was not going to feel that shame again. Giving a humorless laugh, she looked down her nose at him and added, "I'm not surprised you didn't recognize it was love you were witnessing. I don't imagine any woman could ever feel that fine an emotion for you. But take my word for it, what you saw was a woman in love giving herself to the man she loved and planned to marry."

"Love, was it?" Jeremy sneered with disbelief, and then added with cold amusement, "And yet look how quickly you agreed to marry me in his stead."

"You made me think he didn't want me," she said defensively.

"Yes, I did. And that was so easy it was almost pitiful. Was your faith in him so weak? Was your *love* so weak?" he asked with apparent disgust.

Suzette paled. Was her faith weak? Should she have dismissed the letter as a fake when she read it? While she and Daniel had never spoken words of love to each other, and in fact, she doubted he felt that for her, she was relatively certain he liked her at least. And now that her heart was no longer breaking she was quite certain that Daniel wouldn't treat any woman so callously. Had he wished to break off the engagement, his honor would have forced him to do it in person and as gently as possible. She half suspected he would have also endeavored to ensure she wouldn't have suffered for his decision, either by offering to loan her the money to pay the marker or by finding a replacement husband of good character willing to take his place and marry her. He was just that kind of man.

"How crushed you were to think he cared so little," Jeremy commented, and then tilted his head and said, "Or was it shame you were feeling for rolling about in the hay with him like a whore?"

"I am not a whore," Suzette said with dignity, but Jeremy merely looked her up and down as if she were unclean.

"No doubt you would have wanted to act in just as base a manner with me," he said almost accusingly. Danvers then shuddered, apparently repulsed by the very thought, and assured her, "You would have been disappointed."

"I'm sure I would have been," Suzette said dryly and was satisfied to see him flush with impotent fury.

"That's not what I meant!"

"Oh?" She batted her eyelashes innocently. "You mean you are not like Dicky, unable to function as a man with a woman? And here was I thinking perhaps you two suffered such an affliction because you had a strange man love for each other."

"Bitch!" he snapped, slapping her so hard that

her head turned on her neck without her being able to stop it.

"Say!" her father yelled.

Suzette saw him start back toward them, but turned slowly to look at Jeremy dispassionately and said, "I must have struck too close to the mark to cause such rage, Jeremy. *Did* you fancy Dicky, then?"

A roar of fury ripping from his throat, Jeremy lunged at her then.

Hands tied behind her back, all Suzette could do was try to back away. Before she'd taken two steps, Danvers's fingers were at her neck.

Chapter Sixteen

Something's wrong," Daniel muttered, staring out through the door of the stables and toward the trees.

"They *are* taking a long time," Richard said sounding grim.

"They are walking, and one of them may have been injured, making them walk slower," Robert suggested.

"If one of them was wounded, they would have hailed one of the carriages that passed rather than walk," Daniel said with certainty. The innkeeper had told them that two other carriages had stopped at the inn before them and reported the overturned carriage and dead driver on arrival. The first had been almost half an hour before they themselves had arrived at the inn. It shouldn't have taken much more than an hour to walk to the inn if they'd taken the road. Walking through the trees and underbrush may have slowed them down a little. It may even have added as much as another half hour if the land was very uneven, but he and the others had been waiting for nearly an hour now. Where were they?

"You don't think they bypassed this inn and continued on to the next?" Robert asked worriedly.

Daniel frowned at the suggestion. He doubted Suzette and her father would have willingly done that, but Danvers might have forced them to. It was a long walk to the next inn though. Cursing, he turned and strode to the first stall holding one of their horses.

"What are you doing?" Richard asked, following him.

"I am going to ride back through the woods and see if I can find them. If I can't we will travel on to the next inn and check there," Daniel announced grimly.

"You can't ride with your wound," Richard protested.

"It's a mere scratch. Doesn't bother me at all anymore," he lied blithely, grabbing a saddle off a sawhorse against the wall and moving into the stall to saddle the horse.

"I'll go," Richard offered, taking the saddle from him and lifting it onto the horse.

"Someone has to stay here in case I miss them and they arrive while I am gone," he said, scowling at Richard, but really grateful he'd taken over the task of handling the saddle. His wound had screamed with pain when he'd picked up the damned thing.

"You and Robert can stay here to watch for them while I go," Richard said calmly, cinching the saddle.

Daniel caught his arm. When Richard paused and glanced at him, he asked solemnly, "Would you stay here if it were Christiana out there instead of Suzette?"

Richard frowned and turned back to finish with the saddle. Once done, he sighed and shook his head. "Your mother is going to kill me for letting you go."

"She doesn't have to know," Daniel said firmly, and then smiled wryly and added, "In fact, I'd appreciate it if you didn't tell her. She'd come after me herself."

"You're damned right I would," Lady Woodrow announced.

Sighing, Daniel turned to watch her step into the stall. "I am going, Mother, and that is that."

"I wouldn't expect anything else," she admitted, not looking pleased. "But you are not going alone."

"Robert and Richard have to remain here in case they—"

"Then I am coming with you," she said simply and glanced to Richard to ask, "Would you saddle me a mount, please, Richard? Don't worry about it being a sidesaddle, I can ride astride."

"Yes, Lady Woodrow," Richard murmured and slid out of the stall to find a saddle and carry it to the next horse over.

"Mother, you are not—" Daniel began, but she interrupted him.

"Do you want to stand here and argue about it, or shall we go find your Suzette?" she asked abruptly. "Because if it's arguing you want, I will give it to you. But it will be a waste of time. I *am* going with you."

Suzette woke to pain. She seemed to hurt everywhere, her head, her throat, her side, her wrists, her ankle. Everything was either throbbing or burning. It was most unpleasant.

"Suzie?"

Recognizing her father's voice, she opened her eyes and peered around. It took a moment for her to realize the dark sentinels surrounding her were trees and that she was lying on the cold ground in a fetal position. She couldn't see her father though.

"Are you awake?" he asked, and Suzette realized his voice was coming from behind her. When she felt a warm hand clasp her own, she turned her head, biting back a groan as her throat protested the move.

"Father?" she asked, able to make out a dark shape behind her.

"Yes." He squeezed her hand. "How is your head?"

"It pains me," she admitted wearily.

"I am not surprised. You hit it when you fell. It bled badly," he added. "Is it still bleeding?"

"I don't know," Suzette said, wondering how she was to tell. It hurt, that was all she really knew, and then she frowned and asked, "When I fell?"

"When Danvers attacked you I rammed him

with my shoulders. It was all I could do," he said apologetically. "I was afraid he was going to choke you to death."

"He was very angry," Suzette said dryly.

"You have that effect on people," was his wry response.

Suzette gave a short laugh and then asked, "So ramming him was enough to stop him?"

"Well, that knocked you both down and got his attention. But I suspect reminding him he couldn't marry a corpse was the real reason he didn't simply go back to choking you," he admitted.

"Good thinking," she sighed.

"It worked," her father said, and then added apologetically, "Unfortunately you knocked your head on a boulder as you fell. So you have me to blame for your aching head."

"You saved my life," she pointed out, and tried to shift to a sitting position, but found she was anchored down somehow.

"He tied us together," Cedrick Madison explained. "He didn't have any rope, so he ripped strips off your gown and used those."

Startled, Suzette craned her head up and around to look at herself and saw that her dress was much shorter than when she'd set out that day. That explained why she was so cold, she supposed. "Where is he?"

"He was going to walk to the next inn to rent a hack and then come back for us. Hence the reason he tied us together. He figured that way if you regained consciousness before he returned, we wouldn't get far.

Suzette stilled and asked, "How long has he been gone?"

"Long enough that if we are planning to escape, we should get moving," her father said solemnly.

Suzette nodded, and immediately regretted it as pain shot through her skull. It felt like a squirrel was up there gnawing on her head above her right ear. She waited a moment for the worst of the pain to pass, and then said, "Count to three and on three we will both sit up."

Her father began counting.

"We must be halfway back to the overturned carriage by now."

Daniel didn't respond to that fretful comment from his mother.

"Surely they would have got farther than this by now?" she added, her gaze slipping over the woods on either side of them.

Daniel's mouth tightened, but he stayed stubbornly silent. He wasn't going to turn back until they'd reached the carriage, though he was sure his mother was going to suggest that next.

"Daniel, I think——" Lady Woodrow began, and then paused and reined in her horse. "What is that?"

He reined in as well and glanced to her to see her leaning forward on her mount, staring ahead and off to their right with bewilderment, and then a little alarm.

"What kind of creature is that?" she asked, her voice going higher in pitch with anxiety.

Daniel turned his head, following her line of vision and searching the dark woods ahead until he spotted movement. He leaned forward now himself, trying to make it out. It was still a good distance away, and large, as tall as a person but bigger around than one. Under the moonlight it was a patchwork of whites, grays and black . . . and he didn't have a damned clue what it was. It appeared to be leaping about, but was far too big to be a rabbit and its movements were clumsy, almost drunken as it weaved one way and then another in an awkward, hopping manner.

"I don't know," he finally admitted. Daniel watched it for a minute, and then said, "Stay here," and urged his mount forward. He kept the horse to a slow walk, his approach cautious because he wasn't sure what it was. But as he got nearer and heard the racket the creature was making, he realized it would never hear his own approach. The crackle of underbrush as it thumped about was loud enough to drown out any sound he was making. In fact, it was making so much racket that it took him a minute to realize it was speaking . . . English . . . in two different voices . . . one female and one male.

"Straight ahead, Father. You keep hopping to the right."

"I *am* going ahead, Suzie. *You* are the one who keeps going to the side."

"Not *your* ahead, *parallel to the road* ahead. Jump to your left instead of forward."

"Oh. Well why didn't you say so, girl?"

Suddenly Daniel knew exactly what he was looking at. Relief rushed through him, but was followed by a wave of laughter so strong that he had to bite his tongue and lower his head to keep

it from bursting out. He knew without a doubt
that his riding up, laughing his head off would
infuriate Suzette immensely.

"Is that her?"

Daniel glanced around to see that his mother
had ignored his order and ridden up beside him.
This close, she apparently had also recognized
that it was two people, bound back to back and
hopping through the woods in the most ungainly
fashion. Daniel nodded his head, not trusting
himself to speak without a laugh slipping out.

"Well." Lady Woodrow tilted her head as
she eyed the woman who was soon to be her
daughter-in-law. Finally, she said, "She must be
cold in that . . . er . . . whatever she is wearing."

Daniel turned his head back, blinking as he
took in what Suzette was—or wasn't—wearing.
He couldn't believe he had been so distracted by
everything else that he had missed that she wore
little more than a very short shift or shirt. At least
that's what it appeared to be at first, but then his
gaze slid to the torso of the outfit and he realized
it was a gown with a good deal of the bottom
missing. Her legs were naked almost all the way
up to her hips. Good Lord.

Digging his heels into his mount, Daniel urged
the horse forward, moving more swiftly now to
cross the remaining distance between them.

"Again," Suzette panted and they hopped again,
she to her right, her father at her back hopping
to his left so that they were moving, she hoped,
toward the next inn.

"Suzie?" her father asked, forestalling her repeating "again." He sounded as breathless as she was.

"Yes?" she puffed.

"Maybe we should be heading the opposite way," he wheezed. "After all, this is the way Danvers went and the way he'll come back."

"Yes," she acknowledged. "That's why we're going this way."

"It is?" he asked uncertainly. "Why?"

"Because he'll expect us to go the opposite way," she said simply. "We are only going this way for a little bit longer, and then we'll move deeper into the woods. He'll go right past us and when he finds us missing from where he left us, he'll continue on and search in the opposite direction, thinking we would head back toward the last inn rather than risk running into him at the next inn where he went."

She felt his deep chuckle vibrate along her back, and then her father said, "You always were a clever girl."

"Not clever enough," she said sadly. "If I'd only been smart enough to trust in Daniel—"

"Now, don't start berating yourself for that. Danvers obviously saw the two of you up to something in the stables that you thought no one else knew about. Of course you'd think it was him."

"You thought the letter might be a fake," she pointed out.

"Not at first. I only started to wonder because it just seemed a little suspicious that Danvers was there to rush you to wed after you got the letter. And then I remembered him being at the club with Dicky and me," he admitted. "So don't be blaming yourself for any of this. None of it was your fault. Danvers and Dicky had it planned at the start, and Danvers just carried on with the plan."

"Yes." She sighed and then glanced around. "Perhaps we should start hopping deeper into the woods now. Danvers could return any time and—" Her voice died as she noticed a dark shape approaching ahead. After a moment she recognized it as a man on horseback, and for one horrified moment, thought it was Danvers and they'd left it too late to get off the path. But then she realized the shoulders were too broad to be Danvers. In fact, the shape looked to her to be Daniel's. She had stared at the man and admired his form often enough to recognize it even in silhouette and she relaxed.

"It's Daniel," Suzette said out loud as she became aware that her father was almost vibrating with his anxiety.

"Are you sure?" he asked worriedly.

"Very," she assured him, but Cedrick Madison didn't relax until Daniel drew his mount to a halt and hailed them.

"Suzette, Lord Madison!" he said as he slid off his horse. He paused for the briefest moment once his feet hit the ground, not long really, but the way he held on to his saddle for that second made her frown, and then he was moving quickly to them, his face pale in the moonlight.

"Are you all right?" he asked, coming around in front of Suzette.

She nodded, hardly noticing the shaft of pain the movement sent through her head. Every hop they had made since she'd woken up had sent agony through her skull, so the small jolt of pain was easily ignored.

Daniel caught her face in his, and frowned as he saw the dried blood on her forehead. "You're hurt."

"I hit my head is all," Suzette said quietly, her eyes moving hungrily over his face. She'd thought she'd never see him again, and yet here he was.

Daniel didn't look reassured, but asked, "Danvers did this?"

She grimaced. "Yes."

"Where is he?" He glanced around.

"Father said he headed to the next inn to rent a hack," she answered.

Daniel relaxed a little, then met her gaze and said firmly, "I didn't write that letter."

Before Suzette could respond, a woman's voice drew her attention to the fact that Daniel hadn't come alone.

"For heaven's sake, Daniel," she admonished, as she dismounted. "Untie them. The poor girl is standing there in practically nothing. She must be freezing, and no doubt they are both hungry and exhausted. Explanations can wait until we get them safely to the inn and warm."

"Oh, yes," he muttered and quickly moved around to the side to examine how they were tied together. Suzette hadn't a clue how Danvers had done it, other than that he'd used her dress for rope, which left her nearly naked and cold, as the woman now approaching them had suggested. Suzette stared at her, noting that even tromping through the dark woods at night the lady had the air and grace of . . . well a true lady. Suzette knew she would have been tripping over unseen obstacles and twisting her ankle on uneven ground. Not this woman. She was steady and graceful and elegant even as she slipped a small knife from her sleeve and handed it to Daniel.

"Here, this will help," she said.

"Where the devil did you get that?" Daniel asked with surprise.

"I brought it with me from home. I brought a small pistol along on the journey as well," she informed him calmly, and then raised an eyebrow. "Did you not think I would pack weapons as well as clothes for this trip, what with everything that has happened?"

Daniel just shook his head and turned back to begin slicing through the makeshift rope. The moment he did, the woman turned her attention to Suzette and moved around in front of her.

"You must be Suzette. It's lovely to meet you, dear, I'm Daniel's mother, Catherine Woodrow," she said in greeting, sounding for all the world as if they were meeting over tea.

"Er . . . it's lovely to meet you too," she said uncertainly, feeling a little befuddled by the situation and what she should do. Normally she would have taken the lady's hand or . . . well, something, but she was standing there trussed up to her father, her hands bound behind her back, unable to do anything but smile crookedly.

"Daniel has told me a great deal about you," Lady Woodrow informed her with a smile as she undid and removed the cape she was wearing. "And I can't tell you how pleased I am that he has finally found a girl he is willing to marry. I was beginning to despair of that ever happening."

"Oh . . . er . . . I—" Suzette's vain attempt to respond sensibly died as the cloth binding her to her father suddenly went slack, taking all of its support with it. She hadn't realized how much she'd been leaning into her father's strength until those ties were gone, and she started to crumple toward the ground as her knees gave out.

"Here we are," Lady Woodrow said brightly, wrapping the cape around Suzette's back and catching her all at the same time. She kept one hand on her arm, but her other dropped to her waist, taking some of Suzette's weight for her as Daniel saw to her father, cutting his bound hands now so that he was completely free.

"Are you all right to walk to the horses, my lord?" Daniel asked, keeping a steadying hand on her father's arm for a moment.

"Fine, fine," Lord Madison said on a little sigh and then turned to Suzette and Lady Woodrow. He offered a small smile and nod to the Dowager Countess, and then glanced to Suzette with worry. "Suzie hit her head quite hard. She was unconscious for a long time and needs looking after."

"We will get you back to the inn and see to you both," Lady Woodrow said solemnly, shifting her hand from Suzette's waist to her shoulder so that Daniel could move the cape aside and slice through the rope binding her hands.

The moment he was done, Daniel handed his mother back her knife and then scooped Suzette up into his arms with a pained grin that made her frown. Before she could comment on it, Lady Woodrow spoke up, drawing her attention.

"I fear we didn't think to bring extra horses, Lord Madison," Lady Woodrow announced, slipping her knife back up her sleeve. She then slipped her arm through Cedrick Madison's and started him toward her horse as if she were strolling through the gardens, and added, "I fear you shall have to ride back with me."

"I'm sure it will be my pleasure, Lady Woodrow," her father said solemnly.

Suzette frowned as she noted that his limp was even more pronounced now than earlier. The hopping probably hadn't done it any good. He would need to rest it and perhaps apply a warm compress to ease the ache.

"I was telling the truth, Suzette," Daniel said quietly, drawing her attention to him as he started to carry her toward his own horse. "I promise you I didn't write that letter."

"I know," she said on a sigh. "I'm sorry I believed it, but he knew about the stables and—"

"You don't need to explain," he assured her as he reached his horse. Daniel then paused and admitted, "I was angry at first that you would believe I would break it off so coldly in a letter, but when I read what he'd written about the stables—" He shook his head. "Of course you would believe it was me. We thought we were alone."

She nodded, but didn't comment. Suzette really didn't want to discuss the fact that Danvers had been watching them in the stables. She just didn't want to think about it. Between that and the cruel comments in the letter, Danvers had managed to tarnish the experience for her somewhat.

Daniel kissed her on the top of her head, careful to avoid her injury, and then asked, "Can you stand for a moment while I mount?"

"Yes," she murmured.

"Hold on to the horse," he instructed as he set her down.

Suzette leaned against the beast and watched as he mounted. He then helped her climb on to the animal's back as well.

"Just relax," Daniel suggested as he settled her before him. "You are safe and we will have you back at the inn and comfortable in no time."

Suzette nestled against his chest, trying to keep her head still to stave off the worst of the pain as he urged his mount to a canter.

The ride back to the inn probably didn't take long, though it seemed interminable to Suzette. All the jostling about had her head aching so badly she felt sure that if she'd had anything in her stomach she probably would have tossed it up by the time they arrived at the inn. Fortunately, they hadn't eaten since first setting out with Danvers, and that was long gone.

As they broke out of the woods and entered the courtyard Robert and Richard came rushing from the stables.

"Did you get him?" Daniel asked, drawing his horse to a halt.

"Danvers?" Richard asked with surprise, moving to take Lady Woodrow's mount by the bit as she reined in beside them with Lord Madison in the saddle behind her. "No. Was he not with Suzette and Lord Madison?"

Daniel shook his head. "He left them tied in the woods and was supposed to be headed here in search of a hack to carry them on to Gretna Green."

"We've seen no sign of him," Robert assured him, moving up to take the bit of his horse.

Daniel scowled, but then said, "Here, take Suzette."

He passed her down like a child and Robert released the horse and caught her to his chest at once. He then frowned as he looked her over and noted her head wound. "What happened to your head, Suzie? Did Danvers do this?"

"No, I hit it on a rock," she said wearily.

"It's my fault," her father said with disgust as he dismounted. He turned to help Lady Woodrow down, explaining, "I meant to knock Danvers off her, but they both went down and there was a boulder behind her. A damned big one too. I should have taken a look about before I rammed the man."

"What was Danvers doing 'on' her?" Daniel asked, taking her from Robert.

Suzette glanced to him with surprise. He sounded strange, his voice cold, angry and afraid all at once.

"He was choking her," her father answered in oddly reassuring tones and Suzette couldn't help noticing that all the men were suddenly relaxing a bit as if this answer were more acceptable than whatever they'd been thinking. That's when she realized they had all immediately assumed the man had been trying to ravish her.

Still, Richard asked, "Why the devil would he try to choke you? He couldn't marry a corpse."

"He took offense to something I said," Suzette answered primly.

"Or perhaps several somethings," her father muttered.

Much to Suzette's relief, Daniel didn't ask what she'd said and turned toward the inn with her. Heading for the door, he said, "I'll see her settled in a room and then come back. Danvers should have been here by now. We will have to search the woods."

Unsure whether they were staying or not, they hadn't rented rooms at the inn and had to tend that now. Even so, they were soon upstairs in a room and Daniel was setting her on a bed.

"We need to speak when I get back," Daniel said quietly, pressing a kiss to her nose before straightening. "But I need to go search for Danvers now."

"You need to remove your coat and shirt and let me look at your back," his mother countered, leading Christiana, Lisa and Cedrick Madison into the room. Christiana and Lisa carried water and cloths and bandages, while her father just looked bewildered as to why he was there.

"My back is fine," Daniel said grimly, turning toward his mother.

"What is wrong with your back?" Suzette asked with a frown.

"He was shot. That is why he didn't return to the inn as expected," Lady Woodrow announced.

"Shot?" Suzette gasped, looking Daniel over more carefully. She couldn't see his wound through his clothes, but he did look a little pale, not so much she would have guessed he'd been wounded though. The fact that he'd been shot explained why he hadn't returned as expected, however, and Suzette immediately wondered if Danvers had done it. He *had* shot his driver in the back after all. Apparently, the man didn't like to face the people he tried to kill. Well, except her: they'd been face to face when he'd tried to choke her.

"You are not leaving this room until I see your back, Daniel," Lady Woodrow said grimly. "You have been riding about and lifting Suzette up and down and I am sure it has probably reopened. Now strip."

When Daniel scowled and looked as if he were debating ignoring the order, she threatened, "I will send for Richard and Robert and have them hold you down while I tend it if I must."

"Oh very well," he snapped and began to shrug quickly out of his jacket.

Satisfied, Lady Woodrow then turned to Suzette's father. "What about you, my lord?"

Cedrick Madison stood a little straighter. "Me?"

"Did you sustain any injuries that need tending?"

"Oh no, I'm fine," he assured her quickly, sidling toward the door.

"Then why did I notice dried blood in your hair

when you dismounted out front?" Lady Woodrow asked pointedly. "And why are you limping?"

"Oh, I just . . . the leg is an old injury. As for the head, well, I took a blow earlier," he admitted reluctantly, and quickly added, "But that was hours ago and I'm sure it's fine. I'll just—"

"Sit down and I shall take a look at it after I tend Daniel and Suzette," Lady Catherine ordered firmly.

Cedrick Madison sighed, his shoulders slumping, and then moved to sit in one of the chairs by the fire.

Suzette, Christiana and Lisa had been watching this all rather wide-eyed, but as Lady Woodrow moved to a now topless Daniel they all glanced at each other and suddenly burst out in grins. They had grown up pretty much without a mother, and really, Lady Catherine Woodrow was a revelation of sorts.

Chapter Seventeen

Suzette opened her eyes to a warm fire-lit room and glanced sleepily around, wondering where she was.

"Oh, you're awake."

The comment drew her gaze to a chair by the fireplace and the woman getting up from it. Daniel's mother. Lady Woodrow had tended Daniel's back and let him leave, with a firm admonishment to be careful, as he'd headed out to help Richard and Robert search the area for Danvers. She'd then tended Suzette's head wound, cleaning it but deciding it didn't need stitching, before giving her something absolutely vile to drink and telling her to sleep. Suzette had obediently lain down and closed her eyes as Lady Woodrow had moved on to tend to her father. She'd been sure she wouldn't sleep though. Her head had been pounding horribly. However, she had drifted off in the end, though she wasn't sure for how long.

"How are you feeling?" Lady Woodrow asked, pausing beside the bed and bending to press the back of her hand to Suzette's forehead. "You don't have a fever. Does your head hurt?"

Suzette shook her head slowly. "No. Thank you."

"Good." She nodded with satisfaction.

"Did they find Jeremy?" Suzette asked, glancing toward the door.

"You haven't been asleep very long. They are still looking," Lady Woodrow said and then grimaced. "I suspect they won't find him though. He must have spotted us at the inn and judging from that letter he sent supposedly from Daniel, he seems smart enough to go to ground like a fox in the hunt. I'm sure it's not the last we'll see of him though."

"The letter? You read it?" Suzette asked weakly, her stomach turning over when the woman nodded.

Lady Woodrow considered her expression, and then settled on the side of the bed and took one of her hands in her own. "That letter was meant to make you feel shame, but you shouldn't."

"Shouldn't I?" Suzette asked on a sigh. It hadn't exactly been proper behavior as the letter had pointed out.

"Well, if you should, then so should I," Lady Woodrow announced. "Because Daniel's father and I anticipated our vows as well, and also on our way to Gretna Green."

"Really?" Suzette asked with surprise. Lady Woodrow seemed so . . . well . . . so much a lady. It was hard to imagine her in the throes of passion.

"I was young once too, you know," she said with a grin. "And Daniel's father was the most wonderful man—charming, handsome, smart, funny. We were so much in love." She sighed sadly, and then glanced to Suzette. "Daniel is much like him, and if the two of you have only half the happiness his father and I shared, you will be very lucky indeed. But I think you will do better than that."

"I will try to make him happy," Suzette assured her quietly.

"I know you will, and he will do the same," she said with certainty, and then added, "He loves you, you know. I knew that within moments of his telling me he was marrying you. I have never seen him speak of anyone as he did you."

Suzette swallowed a sudden lump in her throat. That was the most wonderful thing she'd ever heard.

"And I think you love him too," she added.

"I do," she admitted on a whisper.

"So you will marry him even though he isn't poor?" Lady Woodrow asked with amusement.

Suzette scowled and then chuckled and shook her head. "Yes. Of course."

"Good." She patted her hand and stood. "I shall go see about getting you food. Now that your head is not hurting, you are probably hungry."

"Thank you," Suzette said and smiled faintly as she watched her go.

Once the door closed behind the woman, Suzette lay back in the bed with a little sigh, contemplating the possibility that Daniel might love her. It had been lovely and reassuring to hear from his mother, but would be even nicer coming from Daniel's lips.

Suzette smiled wryly at the turn her life had taken. She had started out thinking she couldn't possibly find love in the short time she had, so would have to settle for a husband who needed her dower enough that she could set the rules of their relationship and protect herself from an abusive marriage like Christiana had with Dicky. Instead, she'd found a man who didn't need her dower and who might actually love her. And who she definitely loved. On top of that she was gaining a mother-in-law whom she already liked a good deal, and thought she might come to have great affection for rather quickly. Lady Woodrow was definitely living up to her son's compliments and descriptions. She was a woman Suzette thought she might look up to. Certainly, she admired how she'd handled the men earlier. The woman was masterful and there was a lot she could learn from her.

Suzette wasn't sure how she'd got so lucky, but was grateful she had.

"There. You look perfect," Lady Woodrow pronounced, standing back to survey her handiwork.

Suzette beamed under the woman's approving expression and peered at herself in the mirror Daniel's mother had brought in. She wore her finest gown, a short-sleeved, empire-style dress that was so pale a pink as to be mistaken for white. On top of it she wore a sleeveless red pelisse with gold trim. Her maid, Georgina, had helped her to bathe and dress, but Lady Woodrow had then shooed the woman away and taken over helping with her hair. With it still wet from the bath, she'd worked carefully around the head wound in the hair above Suzette's ear, and arranged her long tresses in an array of pin curls on top of her head. The effect was quite lovely.

"You are beautiful," Lady Woodrow announced. "You and Daniel are going to give me beautiful grandbabies."

Blushing now, Suzette laughed, and turned to hug her. "Thank you, my lady."

"You are most welcome," Lady Woodrow assured her, hugging her back, but then complained, " 'My lady' sounds so stiff. You may call me Catherine if you wish, or—" She paused briefly and bit her lip, and then admitted, "I hope someday you will feel comfortable enough to call me Mother, but I would not pressure you to do so."

"Thank you. I should be pleased to call you Mother," Suzette whispered, moved by the offer. And it was true. She and Lady Woodrow had sat talking for hours the night before, after she'd returned with a meal for Suzette, only stopping when the men returned with the not unexpected news that Danvers could not be found. They had retired then, but had woken to continue their chatter as they dressed and went down to breakfast with the others and even during the carriage ride for the last leg of the journey to Gretna Green. It had taken three hours, but that time had passed in a trice for Suzette as she and Lady Woodrow chatted about books they'd read and things they liked to do, while her father and Daniel looked on smiling indulgently. Well, her father had smiled indulgently, Daniel had smiled, but his had been with a combination of indulgence and relief, and she knew it had been important to him that she and his mother like each other. Fortunately, they did. At least, she certainly liked and respected Lady Woodrow.

"Well." Daniel's mother gave her a slightly watery smile, and turned toward the door. "I shall go tell your father you are ready so he can come collect you."

Suzette watched her slip from the room and then peered down at herself with a little sigh of pleasure. The gown she was wearing was really more appropriate for a ball than a marriage in the courtyard of an inn presided over by a blacksmith, but Suzette didn't care. She wanted to look nice for her wedding. And she looked as nice as she ever had in her life, as good as she could, she thought, and hoped Daniel thought so too.

She smiled to herself at the thought of Daniel, and then her smile faded a bit and she released a little sigh. While Suzette had spoken a lot to Lady Woodrow since being rescued and brought to the inn, she and Daniel had never got to have that talk he'd mentioned. The men had been weary on returning from their search. They had apparently scoured the area on both sides of the inn, traveling as far as the overturned carriage on the one side and then just as far in the other direction, searching both the road and the woods for Danvers.

All of them had been both tired and disappointed not to have found the man, but Daniel was still recovering from a wound and had looked exhausted and pale, and Suzette had agreed when Lady Woodrow had insisted he find his bed and talk to Suzette in the morning. However, there hadn't been much chance to talk this morning either. Suzette had slept late, probably a result of the tincture Lady Woodrow had given her before they retired, and had rushed to dress and get below, arriving just as everyone sat down to break their fast. Once finished with their meal, everyone had been eager to get on with their journey and get this business done before something else could go wrong, so there hadn't been any chance to talk then either. And the moment they'd arrived in Gretna Green, Daniel had sent Suzette and the other women to ready themselves while he went to speak to the blacksmith.

Now it was time to get married and they hadn't had their talk. Suzette wasn't sure what he'd wished to discuss with her. He had already told her that he hadn't written the letter, which she'd pretty much figured out by then anyway. She thought perhaps he was going to tell her that he wasn't poor and in need of her dower, but she already knew that too.

In truth, Suzette was hoping he'd wanted to declare his feelings for her. Her father and his mother had both said that Daniel loved her. It would be nice to hear it from him though. But then she hadn't told him she loved him yet either, Suzette realized, and then glanced to the door when a soft knock sounded.

Crossing the room, she pulled the door open and smiled when she saw her father in the hall. He wore knee breeches and a frock coat and looked all ready to attend a ball. He also had his cane again and she supposed that Daniel and the men had collected it from the overturned carriage for him while searching for Jeremy Danvers.

"You look nice, Father," she complimented.

"And you've never looked so beautiful, Suzie," he said solemnly, and then added, "Your mother is probably weeping in heaven with pride and happiness for you."

"Oh." She waved a hand before her suddenly watery eyes and grimaced at him. "Don't say things like that, Papa. You will have me weeping at my own wedding."

"Sorry, child." He kissed her gently on the cheek and then urged her back into the room so he could enter.

"What are you doing?" she asked with surprise.

"I wish to speak to you before we go below," he said solemnly, pushing the door closed and urging her across the room to sit on the side of the bed. He settled himself next to her, took her hands in his and eyed her solemnly. "I just want to be sure you are positive this is what you wish to do."

Suzette frowned. "Was it not you who was trying to convince me to rethink marrying Jeremy and staying at the inn to wait for Daniel?"

"Yes," he agreed.

"And now you're trying to talk me out of marrying Daniel?" she asked with bemusement.

"No, no," he said at once, squeezing her hands. "No, Suzie, I'm not trying to talk you out of it at all. It is obvious to me that you two love each other and I think he is perfect for you."

"Well then what—?" She fell silent when he patted her hand.

Smiling wryly now, he shook his head. "I am not doing this right. It is just that you and Daniel have had such an unusual courtship. Well, really, you haven't had a courtship at all, and I just want you to be sure. I don't want you to feel you have to marry him because of anything that's transpired . . . and I want you to know that if you wish to take more time to get to know him now that there is no need or rush to marry, I will support you in that."

Suzette relaxed and leaned forward to hug him, whispering, "Thank you, Father. That means a great deal." Sitting back she added, "But I don't need more time. I want to marry Daniel."

"Well, good." He smiled, and then gave a little sigh and said, "I suppose it shall just be Lisa and I from now on then . . . and she will be off marrying her own husband soon enough too."

He shook his head. "It seems like just yesterday when you were all my little girls running around playing."

"We will always be your little girls, Papa." Suzette squeezed his hand. "You are always welcome to come visit Daniel and me at Woodrow. And now that you've sold the townhouse you will have to stay with Christiana and Richard when you go to town. You will see us. You are still our father and a part of our lives."

"Of course I will," he agreed, managing a smile that seemed weak at first, but then became more sincere as he said, "And you will all give me lovely grandbabies to spoil and watch drive you as mad as you all drove your mother and I."

A surprised laugh slipped from Suzette and she shook her head. "Both you and Lady Woodrow are on about grandbabies and we have not even married yet."

"Hmm." Her father stood and offered his arm. When Suzette stood as well and took it, he urged her toward the door saying, "Lady Woodrow seems a fine woman."

"Yes, she does," Suzette agreed with a smile as he led her out of the room. "I like her already."

"Well, it's mutual. She told me so herself." He paused to pull the door closed, and then urged her along the landing toward the stairs, asking, "Are you nerv—?"

When his question stopped mid-word and his steps faltered, bringing them to a halt, Suzette glanced to her father curiously and then followed his gaze to what had caught his attention. A man had just come out of one of the rooms further along the landing. He was a good distance away, even so, Suzette could see that he wore the coarse clothes of the working class and a short single-breasted jacket that was popular with stablemen. Assuming he worked in the stables here, Suzette was just wondering what on earth he was doing in a guest's bedchambers when he turned toward them and she saw his face. She was just registering that it was Jeremy Danvers when he spotted them and pulled his pistol from inside his jacket.

"I thought you said she was ready?" Daniel asked, glancing fretfully toward the inn. His mother had come down several minutes ago and sent Lord Madison up to collect Suzette. The group had then immediately moved out into the courtyard to wait . . . and wait.

"She was," Lady Woodrow murmured, glancing toward the inn as well. Sighing, she shrugged helplessly, and suggested, "Perhaps they are having a father/daughter talk."

"Hmm." Daniel tapped his fingers against his thigh, counting out the seconds as he waited, but his gaze was now trained on the inn door as he willed it to open. They should have been here by now and he was getting a bad feeling.

"You don't think she's had second thoughts because you aren't poor, do you?" Richard asked with a frown.

"I haven't told her that yet," Daniel said at once.

"Oh." Richard hesitated and then admitted, "I did."

"What?" Daniel turned on him with dismay and his friend grimaced apologetically.

"It was after she got that letter. I thought—"

Daniel didn't wait to hear what he'd thought. He was already headed back into the inn, his mind in an uproar. Leave it to him to fall in love with probably the only female in all of England who would refuse to marry him because he had wealth, he thought with disgust as he stomped inside.

Honestly, he did always seem to choose the hardest route to everything. So, of course, he would find himself in love with the most difficult woman he could probably find. But if Suzette thought she was going to back out of this wedding, she had another think coming, he told himself grimly as he mounted the stairs to the bedchambers. They had already consummated this marriage. She may be carrying his child even now. And he loved her, dammit! That had to count for something, he assured himself as he started along the landing. She was going to marry him if he had to—

Daniel stopped abruptly as he heard Suzette's voice coming from the door he was passing. It wasn't her door, but the door to the room he'd shared with her father and Robert last night. Frowning, he moved closer and pressed an ear to the wooden panel to listen. If she and her father were having a father/daughter talk, he would just slip back outside and force himself to wait patiently. If not though, and she was arguing with her father over marrying him, Daniel would—

That thought died as a male spoke next. He didn't recognize the voice, but it was not Lord

Madison, and since all the other males in their party were below, that left only one person he could think of. Jeremy Danvers. Daniel supposed that he should have known the man wasn't smart enough to stay in hiding.

Jaw clenching, he grasped the door handle and turned it as slowly and carefully as he could, then eased the door open enough to stick his head in and peer about. Daniel saw Lord Madison and Suzette first. Lord Madison was looking worried and grim, but Suzette just looked angry as she glared at the man holding a pistol on them and said with disgust, "You are an idiot if you think your stupid plan to marry me for my dower will work now. Even if you did force me to marry you, everyone knows what you are up to and it wouldn't stand."

"I have no intention of marrying a sharp-tongued little guttersnipe like you," the man he suspected was Danvers growled.

"Then what do you want?" Suzette asked sharply. "Why force us in here?"

"Because I need money, of course," he said dryly. "Thanks to you, I am going to have to go on the run now, and—"

"Oh, do not try to lay the blame for the mess you have made of your life at my door, my lord," Suzette interrupted, scowling at him. "You are the lackwit who knocked Father out rather than just let us out of the carriage, and you are the one who chose to shoot your own driver, and then tied us up. You probably shot Daniel too, didn't you?"

Daniel was looking at Suzette and didn't hear Danvers say anything, but he must have done something in deed or expression to suggest that was the case, because Suzette snorted with derision. "Fortunately, you made a mess of that as well and he still lives. And that fact is the only reason I will make this offer: if you leave now, Father and I won't say a word about this business today. Just go. We won't send the men after you."

"I am not going without what I came for," Danvers snapped. "I need money to buy passage to the Continent and to live off of and I know your father has the proceeds from the sale of his townhouse here somewhere." His gaze shifted to Lord Madison. "You said as much that first day when you found us by the waterfall. You said you had it at the inn and would fetch it at once. Instead, we left for Gretna Green. I thought you surely had it in the bag you packed and brought with you."

"I didn't trust you so I didn't take it with me," Madison said, and Daniel noticed he seemed pleased to be able to say so.

"I figured that out on my own," Danvers said bitterly. "I walked all the way to the inn only to see Woodrow and a woman riding out. I realized the entire party was probably there, so turned back. But, of course, he got to the two of you first," he ground out. "After he and the old woman headed back to the inn with the two of you, I decided my best bet was to find the proceeds from the sale of the townhouse and flee for the Continent, so I walked all the way back to the overturned carriage, but it wasn't in your bag."

"I left it in the chest in Robert's care," Madison said calmly.

"Then you can just get it now and give it to me if you and your daughter want to walk out of this room alive."

Daniel narrowed his eyes. He was unarmed and had been waiting to see what the plan was before deciding what to do. If the man was going to try to escape with Suzette, he would have slid to the next room along the landing, hid inside and leapt out to jump the man as they passed. However, that didn't appear to be the plan, and whether Danvers got the money or not, Daniel didn't believe he planned to let Lord Madison and Suzette leave this room, alive or otherwise. There was too much venom and fury in the man's voice. He hated Suzette and her father and blamed them for the failure of his plan and the situation he found himself in. He had also killed once already, that they knew of, and had tried to kill both him and Suzette on top of that, shooting him and choking her. Daniel suspected the man would shoot Lord Madison the moment he produced the money and then finish what he'd started last night and choke Suzette to death.

Judging by the expressions on Cedrick Madison's and Suzette's faces, they believed the same thing. Still, Madison nodded once and then turned away.

"What are you doing?" Danvers snapped, taking a step after him.

Daniel took that opportunity to slip into the room and ease the door closed. He then started to slide to the left, trying to get behind Danvers and out of his peripheral vision as Lord Madison calmly said, "I am getting the money for you. It *is* what you want, isn't it?"

"Fine. Just don't try anything funny," Danvers snapped, grabbing Suzette by the arm and dragging her close to his side.

Daniel continued to move left, aiming for the fireplace along the side wall and the poker leaning there.

"I wouldn't dream of it," Madison said dryly, opening a large chest against the wall and beginning to rifle through it.

Daniel sidled up to the poker and leaned to pick it up. Holding it firmly in hand, he then started forward, moving up behind Danvers.

"Hurry up, dammit," Danvers snarled impatiently.

"Robert put it in here, I—ah ha, there it is," he said suddenly.

Daniel didn't know what gave away his presence. He hadn't made a sound, was out of the man's vision range, and had nearly got close enough to hit him with the poker when Danvers suddenly stiffened and then whirled around. His eyes widened incredulously when he spotted Daniel there, and then he turned his pistol on him even as Daniel charged forward raising the poker overhead.

The blast of the pistol was incredibly loud in the room. Still, he heard Suzette scream as he jerked to a halt and peered down at himself, searching for a wound despite not having felt an impact. When there was no sudden blossom of blood or pain, he frowned and glanced to Danvers and Suzette in time to see Danvers fall, revealing Lord Madison still kneeling by his chest, but now holding a smoking pistol.

"Daniel!" Suzette cried and rushed to him, throwing her arms around his waist. "You could have been shot."

"But I wasn't," he murmured, dropping the poker to wrap his arms around her. "Besides, I was more concerned for you."

"There was nothing to worry about," she assured him, leaning back to eye him solemnly. "Father would never leave money in a chest in an inn room. Someone would steal it. He has had it on his person since leaving London. He just said it was in the chest so he could retrieve his pistol."

"Yes, I realize that now," he murmured, glancing to Lord Madison with a new respect as the man got to his feet and moved to turn Danvers onto his back.

"Father is a crack shot," she told him in a proud whisper. "He taught all us girls to shoot."

Daniel felt alarm claim him at just the thought of Suzette being allowed near a pistol, but managed a weak smile and then glanced to Lord Madison as he straightened.

"Dead," the man announced solemnly. "I shall ask the innkeeper to remove him while we have the wedding . . . if you still wish to marry," he added uncertainly. "Everyone will understand if this has made you wish to wait until tomorrow and—"

"No!" Suzette and Daniel said together.

Lord Madison smiled and nodded. "Then I shall just go have a word with the innkeeper about removing the body and join you in the courtyard. Do not start without me."

"I guess we should head outside," Daniel murmured, releasing Suzette as the door closed behind Lord Madison.

Suzette reluctantly removed her own arms from around him and allowed him to lead her to the door, but halted there and said, "I have something I need to tell you."

Daniel felt his heart drop several inches in his chest at her words and solemn tone of voice. Neither boded well, suggesting to him that she was about to make some grand confession and one he probably wouldn't like. Clearing his throat, he faced her and nodded. "Very well."

When Suzette breathed out a deep sigh, and stared at her feet briefly, his heart sank a little lower. He was sure that didn't bode well either. And then she lifted her head and blurted, "I love you."

Daniel blinked, waited a moment, still expecting some horrible confession, but then realized that this was the something she had needed to tell him. She loved him. His mother had said she thought as much, and while it had given him hope then, having her actually tell him so was just . . . well, it was wonderful.

"Thank you," he said finally, slipping his arms around her waist. "I love you too."

"Do you?" she asked uncertainly, and then

added, "Even though I'm not always a proper young lady?"

Daniel stiffened, recalling his words to her the first night they'd met when she'd protested his escorting her out onto the terrace because they hadn't even been properly introduced. His response had been, "Very true. However, I suspect you aren't a proper lady, so we should do well enough."

Noting the vulnerability and fear on her face, Daniel closed his eyes briefly with regret, thinking it was amazing how one careless comment could come back to bite a person. He had no doubt the memory of those words had helped little when she'd read the letter Danvers had left supposedly from him.

Opening his eyes, he caught her face in his hands and said solemnly, "You are a proper lady when it is required, and when you aren't, I love you even more for it. You are everything I could want in a wife, Suzette, and I love you just as you are; smart, funny, courageous and sassy. I do love you." He hugged her close, admitting, "I just wish I'd said it first."

Suzette shrugged in his arms. "You should have been faster then."

Daniel closed his eyes and burst out laughing. In the back of his mind he heard Lord Madison saying that Suzette was like her mother and that he had been kept hopping to try to keep up with her. Daniel didn't have a doubt in the world that it would be the same with Suzette . . . and he was looking forward to it.

Shaking his head, he tipped her face up and kissed her firmly. "Let's go out to the courtyard. I can't wait to make you my wife."

"All right," she murmured, pulling away and allowing him to lead her from the room before adding, "Though you aren't fooling me, my lord. I know why you are really so eager to marry."

"Why is that?" Daniel asked.

Suzette shrugged and teased, "You just don't want to have to sleep with my father and Robert on the return journey to London."

Daniel burst out laughing and hugged her close, thinking life would be a joy with this woman and he couldn't wait to start it.

HIGHLAND ROMANCE FROM
NEW YORK TIMES BESTSELLING AUTHOR

LYNSAY SANDS

Devil of the Highlands
978-0-06-134477-0

Cullen, Laird of Donnachaidh, must find a wife to
bear his sons to ensure the future of the clan. Evelinde
has agreed to marry him despite his reputation, for the
Devil of the Highlands inspires a heat within her
unlike anything she has ever known.

Taming the Highland Bride
978-0-06-134478-7

Alexander d'Aumesbery is desperate to convince the
beautiful and brazen Merry Stewart that he's a well-
mannered gentleman who's nothing like the members
of her roguish clan. But beneath it all beats a heart as
intense and uncontrollable as hers.

The Hellion and the Highlander
978-0-06-134479-4

When the flame-haired Lady Averill Mortagne braves
an unexpected danger at Highland warrior Kade
Stewart's side, she proves that her heart is as fiery
as her hair. And he realizes that submitting to their
scorching passion would be heaven indeed.